Arielle Immortal
Awakening

*The Immortal
Rapture Series
Volume 1*

Lilian Roberts

Cover Design by Shari Ryan
Edited by Jacy Mackin

Previously published as *Arielle Immortal Awakening*,
Self-published, 2012

This is a work of fiction. Names, characters, places, brands, media, and incidents are either the product of the author's imagination or are used fictitiously. Any resemblance to similarly named places or to persons living or deceased is unintentional

ISBN 978-1-945415-08-1

Library of Congress Control Number: 2014901473

FOR MY MOTHER

Thank you, Mom, for your unconditional love
and support of my dreams, and for telling me to
never judge my strength by comparison.

 *Chapter 1*

ARIELLE WOKE UP with a feeling of extreme delight and stretched in a leisurely way, knowing it was Saturday, and she had absolutely no plans at all.

It was still dark in the room, but looking at the clock on the nightstand, she could see it was almost noon. She sat up and swung her feet to the floor. Standing up, she approached the window and drew the curtains open, letting the sunlight fill the room with its brilliant glow.

She smiled happily as she stepped onto the balcony, and let her eyes wander along the beautiful landscape that stretched all the way to the ocean. The beach looked inviting, and the water was calm, with a light breeze moving across the waves, creating amazing shades of blue, green, and white. The sun was spreading a touch of glittery gold as far as her eyes could see.

A few sailboats were lingering in the water, but they didn't seem to be moving toward any specific destination. They seemed more like they belonged on a painter's canvas.

Arielle lived in Brighton, a small town on the southern coast of England. The house was located on Barrett Street, a stone's throw from the ocean. The weather was less than desirable during much of the year, so days like today had to be enjoyed as much as possible.

She got dressed slowly and walked down the hall and out into the garden. The air was fresh, and the scent of freesia was everywhere. It was quiet except for the soft whisper of the gentle breeze blowing through the trees. She wanted to enjoy the morning and fill her mind with life and energy before she made her plans for the day.

Her father, James Lloyd, was a man of outstanding character, great humor, and pleasant manners. He was a businessman and the owner of a large manufacturing company. He had a chosen group of friends with whom he enjoyed spending time golfing or discussing matters of common interest. Sometimes the discussions in his study got heated, but even many intense exchanges of thoughts and ideas, he and his friends always ended up all laughing, showing how content they were just being together and doing exactly what made them happy.

Arielle loved watching her father laugh. As a little girl, she used to hide behind the heavy curtains of his study and listen to his conversations with his friends. Often she fell asleep on the floor, and after everyone had gone home, her father, who was completely aware of her presence, would come to her hiding place, pick her up, and carry her to bed. Then, with a big hug and a kiss on her forehead, he'd whisper how much he loved her.

Her mother, Lady Danielle Lloyd, was a very beautiful woman who paid close attention to the way she looked. It was evident that she made every effort to look lovely at all times.

She was a woman of many talents and many passions. Her mother's piano passion was one of the many things that drew Arielle to begin piano lessons at a very young age. As a little girl she used to spend hours sitting on the piano bench next to her mother, watching her fingers glide effortlessly over the ebony and ivory keys in utter captivation. It didn't take long for playing the piano to become Arielle's private passion as well.

Mrs. Lloyd always kept busy by volunteering for organizations that needed the help and money. This type of work was in high demand in her circles. She often held small parties for the ladies who volunteered with her, serving them cake and tea and spending time playing cards and chatting. Although this kind of life seemed to be enough to keep her happy when Arielle's father was away on business, it was not the life Arielle wanted for herself.

Their home was comfortable, with large manicured gardens and plenty of rooms in which a young child could create her own fascinating world.

Arielle did plenty of that while she was growing up. She made up amazing, mythical friends and spent most of her time daydreaming and carried on imaginary conversations with the characters she created in her mind. She kept a journal in which she noted her innermost thoughts and the significant events in her life.

She knew that the house she lived in was not the only inspiration for her exceptional creativity. Ever since she was a little girl, she'd known there was something different going on in her mind.

Strange things were always happening around her, making her thoughts ricochet between confusion and fear. Some of the people she saw on the street, as well as some of the kids and teachers in school, had an unusual effect on her. The thing was, she was able to hear people's thoughts, and she could see their pain and feel their anxieties too.

At first, she thought it was fun, having a big secret that was totally her own, and she created a special place in her head for that group of people. But as time went by and she started to mature, she became more and more tired of the constant hubbub that occupied that part of her mind. There was nothing she could do to block any of the thoughts from coming in. She wanted to just cover her ears and run away.

It was a difficult burden, hearing other people's thoughts while walking down the street or being in class, and it was a very scary thing to feel like she could see right through people's souls. She learned to live with the nonstop talk in her head, but not without considerable difficulty.

Some nights, worrying about this would keep her awake, but she was afraid to talk to her parents about it.

She couldn't talk to her friends about it either; she was afraid they would think she was a freak. Many times she was unwilling to meet new people for fear that they would join that special group in her head and make her thoughts even more crowded.

She began to feel that what she had was some dreadful gift that would eventually drive her mad. Trying to drown out the information she was constantly receiving was difficult and exhausting.

In primary school, she met two very special girls, Eva Winters, and Gabrielle Taylor. These two girls were to become her lifelong friends. Gabrielle and Eva both belonged to the special group of people in Arielle's head, but with them, knowing their thoughts never felt like a burden. As they grew older she was happy to find out that they were friends she could trust with her life.

Arielle loved taking long walks in the garden with her father after breakfast. During those walks, she tried to remember how far back she had started hearing people's voices. She couldn't remember for sure, but it seemed to her it was around the time she turned six. She remembered saying something about her gift to her mother when she was nine years old, but her mum just smiled at her and told her that dreaming was a wonderful thing "for a child's imagination," but that she should be careful not to "take it too far."

She started to believe that if someone knew the truth about her they would think she was crazy, and that maybe nobody would ever see her as a normal human being. She desperately wanted to discover who she was and why this was happening to her. She wanted to search for peace and contentment in herself and find joy without interference from the outside thoughts that kept pouring into her head every day. After the day she mentioned it to her mother, she never brought the topic up with anyone else again for a very long time.

As they grew older Gabrielle, Eva, and Arielle were inseparable. Their parents also became best friends. The friendship between their parents made the girls' friendships, in turn, much stronger. They were more like sisters than friends.

Gabrielle was a happy, energetic girl of small stature. She was very slim with light brown hair and gorgeous green eyes. Arielle knew that "Gabby" loved her beyond any doubt and had never had any bad thoughts about their friendship. Gabby's thoughts were crystal clear, and Arielle never had a problem in knowing what was going on in her life.

Eva had long blond hair and blue eyes that glowed with a kind of inner joy. She never made a big deal about her looks, but she could take a person's breath away just by standing next to them.

Eva's thoughts were not as clear to read as Gabrielle's, and Arielle had no idea why. Some days she could see unmistakably what Eva was thinking or feeling, and other days her thoughts were very imprecise. This made Arielle feel that there was something unique about Eva. She seemed to have premonitions, often seemed to know what was going to happen before it did. This ability sometimes seemed almost freaky to Gabrielle and Arielle, but on the other hand, it was a pretty cool ability to possess.

Through the years Eva warned both of them to stay away from certain places or events, only to find out later that her advice had kept them out of danger. Arielle remembered one time when they had bought tickets months in advance to attend a concert at Hyde Park, but Eva had a premonition of something bad happening during the concert. She said she wasn't going to go, and begged Arielle and Gabby not to go either. They stayed away, disappointed, but also having complete faith in Eva's intuition. The next morning it was all over the news that three different gangs had attended the concert on the same night. Dreadful brawls had broken out, leaving a couple of innocent bystanders dead, and many more had to be transported to the hospital with gunshot wounds. The concert was canceled and there was complete chaos for several hours following the incident.

So when Eva warned them about something, they listened.

Eva believed that she was psychic, and always complained about having a hard time sleeping because of disturbing patterns in her head.

She believed that spirits were naturally attracted to her. Gabrielle was very intrigued by the whole spiritual world that Eva was experiencing, but Arielle wasn't sure that she was ready to accept the idea of ghosts. She felt like she had enough to deal with in her own dreadful gift.

When they were about thirteen, Eva had a terrible premonition that something horrible was going to change her life forever. Gabrielle and Arielle wanted to believe that she was wrong, but in the back of their minds they couldn't help but believe that something was about to happen, and, unfortunately, it did.

It was the year they all turned fourteen when Mr. Winters, Eva's father, was killed in a car accident. Eva was shattered and completely heartbroken; her father was her best friend, the man, who had supported every dream she ever had. He was a wonderful man and they had all loved him. During that time, Arielle remembered seeing confusion and anxiety in Eva's beautiful eyes, a perplexed look that never seemed to go away.

Of course, Arielle wanted to believe that Mr. Winters's death had nothing to do with Eva's premonition and that it was all just a weird coincidence. But she could see that Eva's thoughts were darker now. They invaded her mind spontaneously, and she never knew what to make of them.

A couple of months following her father's death Eva started to drift away in the middle of their conversations and decline invitations to go out. Arielle was worried about her, but she couldn't understand what was going on in her head since she couldn't see her thoughts very clearly. She noticed other peculiar changes in Eva's personality, too. Some of Eva's thoughts were dark and disturbing, though still hard to distinguish. Some of the apprehensive emotions coming from Eva made Arielle think that she was afraid of something or someone.

By now they were in secondary school, and Arielle thought they should be having a great time, but it wasn't happening. Gabrielle and Arielle tried hard to get Eva to spend time with them, to try to clear the air and get back to the happy threesome they had once been, but their pleading was to no avail.

The year they turned sixteen, to their surprise Eva suddenly accepted an invitation to spend the whole day with them at the beach. This would be the first time in a very long time that she had gone somewhere with them for the whole day. They went to the same beautiful spot ever since they were seven years old because it was private. A place where they could swim, play ball, and get a great tan with no intrusions.

It was now more than two years since Eva's father had passed away and she had become a complete mystery to her two best friends. There was something inexplicable in her actions, and sometimes Eva would disappear for hours at a time, and nobody knew where she was.

Arielle and Gabrielle loved her like a sister, and they were very concerned as they watched her become increasingly withdrawn. They decided to find out what was going on inside her. However, they never imagined that what they were about to find out would shock them to their very cores.

When they arrived at the beach, they spread their beach towels and lay down to enjoy the sunny day. Long minutes passed in silence before Arielle cleared her throat and released a long breath.

"Eva," she said urgently.

"What?" Eva's voice was hesitant.

"What's going on with you?"

"What do you mean?" Eva countered rapidly, feigning surprise. She knew exactly what Arielle was asking.

"We never see you anymore," Arielle continued. "Our outings have become fewer and fewer, and it seems like there is never a good time to talk anymore. What do you do with your time?" Arielle's voice hardened. "You don't even answer your mobile. So what's going on?"

Eva shrugged. "Oh, I've just been busy," she muttered, but her voice came out all quivery, giving away the lie in her casual answer. She could no more control the trembling in her hands than she could the nauseating feeling in the pit of her stomach. She remained quiet, but she could feel the weight of her friends' gazes on her.

"Come on, Eva, really," Gabrielle said in frustration. "We've been friends forever, and we've never kept any secrets from each other. Something is wrong; you're keeping us at arm's length. What's going on? Spit it out!" Gabrielle and Arielle were now sitting up on their beach towels. Silence fell between them as they both stared down at Eva and watched her face twist with grief and sadness.

"Eva, what is it?" Gabrielle asked again with great concern in her voice.

"Oh, God!" Eva shouted, and pushed herself upright. Her head dropped, and her body began to shake uncontrollably as she started to sob.

Her friends exchanged a worried glance as they both reached out, took her hands, and twined their fingers together. She looked at them in silence while they sat patiently, waiting for her to say something.

When she finally spoke, her voice was extremely shaky and barely audible. "Ever since my father passed away I discovered that I've some very strange – and very strong – powers, way beyond premonitions. They make me very nervous."

"What kind of powers?" Arielle asked. Suddenly she felt an uneasiness going through her body. She could see the whirling, the churning, and the obscurity that were taking over Eva as she spoke.

Gabby and Arielle became utterly enthralled as Eva started to speak.

"I'm afraid because I don't understand what is happening to me, but I can't stop it. I think I have special powers. I've tried to explore them, and they are beyond anything I understand. I've purchased many books, trying to find out why this is happening to me and why

I'm having all these visions. I've spent a lot of time researching, and what I've found out is that I have something like a sixth sense that I can use to communicate with spirits, and…and do other things that scare me to death. I can connect with spirits by using spells, but I can even do it at will. I can even dream walk and access the Twixt."

"The what?" Gabrielle interrupted anxiously.

"The Twixt."

"What the devil is that?" Gabrielle asked suppressing a frown.

"That's the place between the spirit world and the living world – and there I can talk with my father and other spirits."

"What in the world are you talking about?" Gabrielle's voice sounded almost like a squeak. "What spirits?" Her eyes were wide with interest.

"Just…spirits," Eva murmured. Her hands clasped Arielle's wrist to the point that Arielle felt pain.

"Do you mean the dead?" Gabrielle cried out, terror in her eyes.

Eva was silent for a short time. Arielle tried to close her mouth, which she suddenly realized was hanging open in astonishment. Eva gazed back at both of them anxiously and started to grind her teeth uneasily. All the blood had washed away from her face, turning it translucent and making her eyes look dark and distressed.

"How did that happen?" Arielle asked, trying to keep her voice steady.

When Eva answered, her voice was low, and she sounded scared. "When I lost my father I thought I had lost my whole world," she said. "He was my fountain of strength and self-confidence. I needed to talk with him. I needed to see him. That's when I bought all the spell books and decided to spend time learning how to use my powers and how to access the spirit world. I wanted to learn how to create a portal so I could bring him back. I made frequent visits to the cemetery. During one of those visits I fell on my knees beside his grave and closed my eyes as I wished him back using my will along with a spell, and he…well…*he came back*…" She spoke her last three words with extra emphasis as if to stress that this was a matter of fact.

Gabrielle and Arielle both gasped and looked completely stunned. They were trying to breathe normally, but they were having a hard time keeping their bodies from being taken over by fright.

"Stop it, Eva!" Gabrielle shrieked. She was short of breath and had a wild look in her eyes.

"Eva..." Arielle murmured, "what do you mean he came back?"

Eva closed her eyes and pressed her lips together as if it hurt her to explain. "He came back, and he was standing there in front of me. We talked, and he helped me understand that he is still here, just not easy for others to see. He told me that he will be here for me any time I need him, and he will always help me through difficult times. I know that every time I need him, I can bring him back."

This is wild...this is totally unbelievable, Arielle thought to herself, as she searched for the words with which to respond. Gabrielle was frozen in place, and Eva was sobbing again, asking them to try to understand.

"Eva, we're trying to understand, but you must admit this is a lot to absorb." Of course, Arielle was not completely surprised by Eva's confession since she had kept a secret of her own dreadful gift for many years. Her thoughts were drifting along when Eva's next statement hit her like a ton of bricks.

"That's not the scariest thing I have done, even though it's pretty unbelievable," she said slowly and carefully. She had their complete attention as they held her hands and gazed into her eyes, full of dismay. She was looking at them, a pleading expression on her face, her translucent skin strained. She wanted them to empathize with her, but she saw they were afraid.

"There's more?" Gabrielle practically screamed. Arielle put her hand over her arm, trying to keep her quiet, as Eva nodded.

"What else is there, Eva?" Arielle asked, trying to restrain her fear.

"I followed some of the spells in the books to see what I could do, mostly out of curiosity, and I got myself in way too deep." She sighed as she murmured the last words, her lips twisting in distress.

"How? What did you do?" Gabrielle asked again.

"Spirits appeared before my eyes each time I summoned them, but there's one in particular that has made her presence known to me more than I wanted her to. She showed up at the cemetery during one of the spells I did for my father, and she has appeared in my room a few times since then. It scares me to death." Eva looked at them again, and the fear in her eyes was clear.

"I don't mind telling you that I'm completely horrified," she continued. "I don't know how to get rid of her or what she wants from me. She just keeps looking at me, full of torment, breathless, suffering…and then at other times, she looks completely exultant. I keep asking her to go away and then she does, looking really sad; however, she keeps coming back. I know that I have to reverse the spell, but I'm too scared to try because I'm afraid I may create something even worse. I've tried to stay away from the books, but something keeps pulling me back. And I still have this girl showing up. I don't know what to do!"

"Oh my God," Gabrielle gasped.

Arielle's heart was beating fast, and she couldn't find a single word to say. This was simply unbelievable. She couldn't imagine how Eva's story could be true, but she believed her friend. She looked directly into Eva's eyes, forcing a smile. "We will try to help you, Eva," Arielle said. "Maybe you can try to get rid of your visitor by doing the spell while we're all together. I'm not saying I'm exactly excited about that, but we have to help each other. I also think that you need to stay away from those books and the spells."

Eva nodded in agreement and kept both of her friends wrapped in her arms.

"Let's start by spending more time together," Arielle said. "By having fun together like we used to do. We can't help you if we don't see you."

Eva finally smiled a real smile of gratitude and looked, for the first time in a very long time, truly happy.

They stayed at the beach for a few more hours and finally decided to head home. As they parted, they agreed to meet later on to go out and have fun. When they left Eva at her door, she was wearing a much brighter face than when they had picked her up, and that made them feel good.

The film they chose to see that evening was amusing, and they had a great time. For a while, it almost seemed like the good old days. Eva looked happy as if a weight had been lifted from her shoulders. She called Arielle when she got home to let her know how much she valued their friendship and how much she loved her and Gabrielle.

The phone rang again while Arielle was in bed, and this time, it was Gabrielle. Arielle was sure that Gabrielle was going to tell her she was freaked out with Eva's spells and summons, so she was a bit stunned to hear that Gabrielle was very intrigued with Eva's powers.

"You're crazy, Gabby," she said. "And I don't want to talk about any of this tonight." Before Gabby hung up, Arielle said jokingly, "Maybe we should have a *séance* one of these days."

She closed her eyes and thought about all the things Eva had told them. She had to admit that Gabby was right, there was something fascinating about Eva's powers. But then a light shiver spread through her body just before she drifted off to sleep.

They were now into the routine of the school year, and every day Arielle could see Eva feeling better and looking happier. Six weeks had passed. and life was getting back to normal. Eva was spending a lot of time with Jack Wallace, and they seemed to like each other. Gabrielle and Arielle felt it was likely to keep her away from becoming involved with weird spells and summons to the dead. Arielle could see Eva's thoughts, and these days they were pretty clear. Her relationship with Jack was not a serious one, but it was exactly what Eva needed right now. With Eva spending time with Jack, Gabrielle and Arielle spent a lot of time together. They didn't seriously care about any of the guys at school. The guy Arielle liked, Stefan Broderick, didn't seem to like her.

The year Arielle turned seventeen, one beautiful Sunday morning, she decided to talk to her father about her dreadful gift as they took their usual morning walk after breakfast. She told him that she wanted to attend the University of Brighton, and he thought that was a wonderful idea. What he liked the most was the fact that she would be staying close to home. His influence on her was profound, and he had always helped her understand the importance of the way she interacted with all the people she crossed paths with. He always made her feel important and always tried to discuss all her issues, complicated or not, and help her find good solutions.

After a short silence, she asked her father if they could talk about something that had been bothering her for years. He stopped and held her gaze with concern.

"Why did you wait so long to talk to me?" he asked gently.

"Well, I guess I was afraid that you would think I was crazy or something."

She was silent again, trying to put her thoughts together and find a way to discuss her dreadful gift with him. He stood there looking at her and waiting patiently.

Finally, he said, in a soft, understanding voice. "Well, go on..."

She started out by saying, "Daddy, I can hear other people's thoughts. I know all their secrets and troubles."

He didn't seem shocked at all. "Is it all people or just some?" he asked.

She stopped dead in her tracks, shocked to hear his question, struck dumb. Smiling, he motioned for her to continue, and she did.

"It's just some people. I'm not sure why some and not all. I'm not sure what the difference is. But that is what's happened to me. Do you think I'm crazy?"

Her father looked deep into her eyes as if he were trying to read her very essence. Then he smiled, with absolutely no surprise or wonder in his face.

"Is that all you wanted to tell me?" he asked.

She must have given him an odd look again because she couldn't understand why he was taking this information in so calmly as if they were discussing a book or a film.

"But...Daddy...I..." she was lost for words.

He smiled wide and chuckled. "You know, pumpkin, your grandmother had the same gift," he said softly. "The difference was that she could read *everyone's* thoughts, with no exceptions. Nobody could lie to her, and she sure knew who her true friends were." He smiled again, remembering. Then he continued. "Your great-grandmother was more like you. She could read some people's thoughts, but not everyone's."

Seeing Arielle's look of disbelief and consternation, he laughed out loud. "I sure hope your mother and I are not in that special group of people," he added.

"No, you're not!" she said emphatically. She could *not* read their thoughts, and that was an enormous relief to her.

He put his arms around her and said, "Arielle, I know that right now you probably feel that this is a curse, not a gift. But you can use it to your advantage in the future in a good way. Believe me, I know."

She was so relieved to talk with someone she loved so very much, and to have shared her secret.

She and her father continued to take private walks often, during which they talked about all kinds of things, including Arielle's dreams for the future. Often her parents would ask her to sit down and play the piano for them, and she was always happy to do that. Playing the piano powerfully influenced her emotions and gave her a deep sense of enthrallment and genuine pleasure.

It was on a Monday morning in mid-May, very close to the time of their commencement exercises, that Gabrielle and Eva suggested they should throw a graduation party. Arielle thought this was a great idea, so they went to talk to the Queen of Parties: Arielle's mother.

 *Chapter 2*

THE COMMENCEMENT PARTY was to take place at Arielle's house. Her mother loved giving parties, so the girls let her handle all the details. She filled the rooms with beautiful flowers; she had the ballroom floors polished, and decorated with impeccable taste.

Everyone that was invited showed up almost at the same time. It was pretty amusing to watch the variety of fashions and all the different hairdos. Gabrielle, Eva, and Arielle welcomed everyone and made small talk with each person who arrived before letting them go and mingle on their own.

After a while, people started to gather on the dance floor, and everyone seemed to have a grand time. Tall, lean, good-looking Jack Wallace, who had been Eva's favorite guy for two years now, walked up to where they were sitting. He had a warm smile on his face and to Eva's delight, he asked her to dance.

She seemed eager to be in his arms, and Arielle was pleased to see the old Eva back without the gloomy, troubled look in her eyes. When the music stopped, Jack kept Eva in his arms, whispering in her ear until the next song started. It was at the end of the second song that they watched them walk away holding hands and looking at each other in complete and utter bliss. Eva looked back and sent a quick, playful look to her best friends. Then she lifted her hand and waved at them just before Jack pulled her through the balcony doors.

Stony silence fell between Gabrielle and Arielle, trying to figure out what was happening out on the balcony. "What in bloody hell was that?" Gabby exclaimed, and abruptly they both exploded into laughter.

Gabrielle danced with Stefan Broderick, whom Arielle had always thought was the best-looking guy in school. If he had asked her out, she would have been delighted to accept, but she had a strong feeling that he didn't like her very much.

Stefan had come to their school during the beginning of secondary school, and he had smiled at Arielle every day when they crossed paths. She was sure that one of those days he would have asked her out, but then suddenly he started going out of his way to avoid her. She tried not to let it bother her, but the feeling was strange, and bitterness settled in the pit of her stomach. She didn't like to be rejected. However, Andrew Boyer was one of her dearest friends in school, so when he asked her to dance she was delighted. When the song was over, she thanked him and walked away to welcome some more friends who had just walked in.

"What a great party!" Arielle heard Stefan's voice close behind her, and to her surprise, he was talking to her. He was standing practically next to her, and as the next song started, he moved even closer without taking his eyes off of her. Just as he was about to speak, Andrew grabbed her hand and pulled her back onto the dance floor. She was completely startled.

"You promised this dance to me," he said, putting his arm around her waist and ignoring Stefan.

Arielle laughed because she liked Andrew so much as a friend. But she would have preferred to dance with Stefan and find out why he disliked her so much. She was deep in thought about this when she realized Andrew was talking again.

"I'm so happy to be here," he was saying. "This is a great party! I know that I can't dance very well, so if you want to sit down, I'll understand." They both laughed and embraced joyfully.

She was sad to hear that the University of Brighton had not been Andrew's choice and that he was going away to another university.

By the time the party was coming to an end, Arielle had danced with several boys and she was almost ready for the party to be over. She saw Gabrielle talking with James Drew, one of the guys she had gone out on a couple of dates with during their school year, but nothing earthshaking. The music had stopped, and people were leaving the party slowly, hugging, laughing, and showing what a great time they'd had. The party was a complete success, and Arielle had her wonderful mother to thank for that.

"Thank you, Arielle, I had a wonderful time," Andrew said, heading for the door. "Oh, Andrew, thanks for coming," she replied and waved.

As she was about to walk toward Gabrielle, she was startled to find Stefan standing right next to her again.

"Arielle...I was wondering if we can talk for a moment?" he said and gave her an alluring smile.

Ignoring the look of surprise on her face and not waiting for her answer, he took her hand and pulled her toward the balcony.

"I know that you'll never believe me if I told you that I wanted to ask you out the first moment I set eyes on you three years ago," he said.

Arielle blinked in surprise. "I do find that hard to believe. So why didn't you?"

"I lost my nerve. I thought you would turn me down."

"Well, you were wrong," Arielle said a bit petulantly.

"Well," he continued, ignoring the tone of her voice. "When I finally got the nerve to ask you, the guys at school changed my mind."

"What? How did they do that?" she asked.

"I became friends with them, and there was talk..."

Arielle was horrified, automatically thinking the worst. "What kind of talk?"

"The guys said that you had turned down every guy that asked you out, and they were waiting to see who the next loser was going to be."

"You're joking," she said. She was completely surprised, but thinking back she suddenly realized that what he was saying was correct. She *had* turned down several guys, but that was only because none of them were right for her.

Stefan's voice snapped her out of her thoughts again. "No, I'm not joking. I was not going to be the loser; I didn't want everyone to laugh at me."

Arielle frowned. "Stefan, it had nothing to do with any particular innuendos and rubbish talk. I just didn't want to go out with any of those guys, and so I turned them down."

"What about me? Did you like me?" he asked cautiously.

"Maybe then, but it's too late now," she said evenly.

"I wish I could go back and do it all over again," he murmured.

"I thought you didn't like me at all," she said in a low voice.

"What would ever give you that idea?" he asked, seemingly confused.

Arielle didn't try to mask her surprise. His question was utterly absurd. "Stefan, you wouldn't talk to me for three years, and you avoided being anywhere near me. I thought that was a pretty good indication of where I stood with you."

"Well, like I said, I was always afraid that you would turn me down, so I stayed away from you."

He reached out and tried to pull her closer, but she pulled away from him and smiled, letting him know that this was not a good idea. In spite of all the bad feelings she had about him and the anger she held inside for his rejection, she was happy about this turn of events. Unfortunately, she didn't hold the same feeling for him anymore.

Stefan winced at her reaction. "I'll be leaving for college in a couple of months, and I wanted to find out if maybe there could be something between us now that we are out of school," he said softly.

She smiled at him, but she didn't find it difficult to tell him that she wasn't interested in a relationship. He looked frustrated and hurt, but he too kept a smile on his face.

"I don't feel anything romantic for you, but I do like you," she said. Stefan was tall and stunningly handsome, even somewhat irresistible, but she felt sure that by the end of the summer she would probably have forgotten all about him.

As he started to walk away, she heard his voice, low but clear. "Maybe you'll change your mind over the summer."

Then he was gone, and she stood there staring into the night, thinking about what-ifs.

Gabby walked towards her, and Eva came back inside the house alone, all flustered, a wide smile on her face.

"What happened?" they both asked Eva.

Her smile got wider, and her eyes were sparkling. "Oh, nothing, I just had a great time with Jack. He's such a great kisser," she said, looking as if she might drift away. Then suddenly she broke into a soft chuckle. Gabby asked Arielle what had happened between her and Stefan.

"Oh, he wanted to ask me out," she said with a dry voice.

"Are you joking?" Eva and Gabby exclaimed simultaneously.

"No, not at all," she said thoughtfully.

"Would you have gone out with him?" Gabrielle asked.

"I think I *would* have liked to go out with him a long time ago, but not now. He's not the guy I'm waiting for."

"I hope you told him to get lost," Gabrielle said.

"I did, in a nice way," Arielle chuckled. "I don't think of him as someone I would fall in love with," she added. "He just doesn't fit the blueprint of the man I have in my head. Anyway, by the time we get back from our holidays he won't be here anymore. He's going away to another university."

They changed the subject, discussing the success of the party and all the gossip they had gathered during the night. They were staying overnight, so they went upstairs to get ready for bed. Arielle was happy about that. She was the first to brush her teeth and wash her face. When she walked out of the bathroom, she saw Gabrielle and Eva sitting on the bed whispering back and forth, pretty animated.

"What's going on?" she asked

"Eva and I are talking about witchcraft and her powers. I want to know what she can do and if she considers herself a witch," Gabrielle said.

Arielle walked over and sat on the bed with them. She looked at Eva. "Well, *do* you think of yourself as a witch? I'd like to know about that as well."

Eva was quiet for a short moment. She took a deep breath and appeared to be trying to find the right words to explain her powers. "I don't think that I'm a witch. All I know is what I've learned by reading the spell books I purchased," she said. "I'm trying to understand the powers I think I may have and try to use them to make contact with the Spirit World. Sometimes I'm in sync with some unpredictable and maybe dangerous spirits, and that scares me. I know now that there is this alternate plane that exists, parallel to our physical world. But I don't understand it."

"So... are you saying that spirits come to you even if you don't call on them?" Gabrielle asked.

"Yes, that's what makes me uncomfortable about this whole thing."

"What can they do to you?"

"I don't know, but I've read that some spirits are very manipulative, and they may seek to use me for their own ends."

"Oh my gosh..." Arielle muttered under her breath.

"I want Eva to do something with her powers," Gabrielle persisted, looking at Arielle as if for approval.

"Gabby, I thought we were going to help Eva *stop* doing spells and witchcraft. I'm sure that isn't a good idea," Arielle said.

"Come on, Arielle, aren't you even a little bit curious? I've been thinking about it ever since that day on the beach. We are together, so how bad could it be?"

Arielle had to admit that she was a bit curious, but she was also scared. She looked at Eva, who was looking down at her hands. "I don't want to do anything that might bring my visitor back. I'm a little scared of her, even though she has never done anything to hurt me," she murmured.

"How can you be scared when you are spending so much time at the cemetery alone and summoning dead people?" Gabrielle pressed.

"That's my father; I'm not scared of my father."

"Come on, Eva; we are all here together. Nothing is going to happen."

"I don't have any of my spell books, and I can't remember any of the spells."

"Well that's that, let's just talk about other things," Arielle said, standing up. She wanted to change the subject.

"Wait…" she heard Gabby saying as she jumped out of bed and sprinted to Arielle's closet. "I know you have the Ouija board we used when we were kids. Let's just use that. There are no spells involved, and it may not work at all."

"I'm not sure I like that idea either," Arielle said. "That board starts out pretty innocent, but soon it becomes addicting, and you can't stop. I remember talking to a lady in St Jean de Luz who told me that it's very dangerous to use this board as a portal to communicate with the dead. She said there were spirits out there that are prowling around, looking for innocent people, waiting to devour their minds. I don't want to do that. I'm scared."

Eva looked toward Arielle as Gabrielle rolled her eyes and moved to pull the board out of the closet. "That's absurd. Tons of people, and especially kids, use this board all the time. Come on, you guys, I'm bored to death," Gabby said. She was relentless.

Eva was now sitting on the floor. Arielle moved reluctantly and sat down next to her. Gabby set the board on the floor in front of them, lit a couple of candles that she took from the dresser, and set them on the floor. She turned the lights off and sat down across from them. They gazed at each other in silence, and Arielle could feel the tension building as she heard their thoughts, full of speculation.

"Why not try?" Gabrielle persisted in a low voice.

"Are you sure?" Eva said. She too was reluctant.

"Yes, I'm sure. Come on, Eva. Let's see what you can do!"

Arielle was filled with a kind of quiet dread. She didn't think any of this was a good idea.

"You guys have to stay quiet, plus there may be a considerable change of temperature in the room," Eva said. "Just try to stay calm and don't be surprised." She took a deep breath through her nose, exhaling slowly through her mouth several times.

"Concentrate on my visitor, and I'll call for her," she said.

They put their fingertips lightly on the heart-shaped planchette, closed their eyes, and tried to think hard about Eva's visitor. After a few moments of silence, Eva chanted a spell three times in a soft whisper.

"Guardians of the spirit realm, hear and guide my plea.
When the witching hour rings true,
Bring the girl that hunts me through."

There was deafening quiet in the room for a long time as the candles flickered, but nothing happened. They opened their eyes and looked at each other but stayed silent, waiting in the shadowy candlelight. Arielle was just about to get up and turn the light back on when suddenly the candles went out and then came back on again with bigger and brighter flames. Then they went completely out. All three girls gasped in disbelief as a cold breeze blew across their faces, and the curtains moved wildly in and out through the open window. Arielle stopped breathing, and she could hear Gabrielle and Eva panting hard.

They were in complete darkness but for the dim light slithering from the night's gibbous moon occupying the dark sky. Suddenly the wind ceased, and there was absolute stillness in the room. Arielle shivered, thinking it was about to turn dangerous. At the same time, she was curious to find out if Eva's spirit was present. She could read Gabrielle's and Eva's minds, and they were both scared to death, but also completely intrigued.

She picked up the lighter and lit the candles one more time. Then Eva asked, in a faint voice, "Are you here?"

Their fingertips barely touched the planchette as it glided slowly, but steadily, with the pointer stopping at the word "Yes." Arielle's body stiffened. She knew her friends felt just as frightened.

"What's your name?" Eva asked.

The pointer moved slowly to the letter J, then moved slowly around the board, gradually spelling the word "Juliet."

"Can you show yourself?" Eva asked in a quivery voice. There was a short lapse of time and the pointer moved again, this time to the word "No."

The tension in the room was thick, and they knew that Eva's visitor was in the room with them.

"Why not?" There was no answering movement on the board.

"How old are you?" Eva asked. The pointer moved to the numbers one and then eight.

"She's eighteen years old," Arielle whispered. "What does she want from you?"

"What do you want?" Eva asked reluctantly.

The planchette moved slowly this time, clearly forming the words "I'm waiting."

"What are you waiting for?"

The pointer moved again, forming the word "Jasper."

Arielle felt a cold chill run down her spine. Her veins felt fused, and her stomach was churning as if she might throw up. Looking at Eva and Gabrielle's faces didn't make her feel any better. They were all wondering who Jasper was and why Juliet was waiting for him.

"Show yourself," Eva demanded.

The pointer moved to the word "No."

"Juliet, show yourself!" Eva's voice demanded again, in a stern tone Arielle had never heard before. Their hands left the board, and they reached out toward each other, intertwining their fingers as stony silence fell in the room. Arielle heard Gabrielle draw in a deep breath as her own breath seized up in her throat, and her body started to tremble from fear and anticipation. She felt a cold shiver as if the temperature in the room had dropped to below zero in a blink of an eye.

Suddenly a light breeze blew through the open window, moving the curtains ever so slightly, but rapidly it grew stronger and stronger, and the curtains flapped wildly against the wall. There was a crashing sound that made them jump in fright, and their eyes widened as they watched the papers on Arielle's desk being swept up and whirled around the room. Small objects were violently thrown off of the end tables by the sofa and scattered all over the floor. The candles went completely out, letting darkness fall around them like a curtain of death. For a moment, there was silence, and they stopped breathing altogether.

Suddenly, there was a brilliant circle in the center of the room, glowing like a bright sun. A pale-faced young girl dressed in a beautiful white gown was standing in the center, wrapped in the glow. In place of her eyes were two dark holes; her long blonde hair was blowing in every direction as if the brilliant circle was a wind tunnel. Blood was dripping slowly out of her mouth, down her neck, and onto her white gown, turning the front of it completely red. Tears were pouring out of the holes where her eyes should have been, and her hands were stretched out toward the girls. One of her hands was clutching a chain with what looked like a Pentagon at the end of it, illuminated by the bright light of the circle. The girls gasped out loud, and Gabby let out a low scream. Arielle wanted to scream but she couldn't, and she couldn't move any part of her body. The girl was chanting words that had no meaning at all, but she looked distressed, suffering, clearly looking for Jasper.

"What do you want? I want to help you," Eva said softly. To Arielle, it sounded like Eva's voice was coming from miles away. The young girl looked startled by the words. Suddenly, her face, changed, the black holes filled with two beautiful blue eyes. Her tears had stopped flowing, and there was no blood anywhere to be seen. A beautiful smile covered her small white face and she looked peaceful and content. She opened her hand slowly, and the Pentagon fell on the floor with a soft thud as she and the bright circle disappeared into thin air.

 *Chapter 3*

THE CANDLES WERE BURNING again, the temperature in the room went back to normal, and the room looked as if nothing unusual had happened there, except for the papers that were spread all over the floor and the small items that had fallen off the table. Where a minute ago the girl had been standing, now only the chain and the Pentagon were left behind.

The girls sat in complete silence for several minutes. None of them made a move to pick up the Pentagon. Gabrielle and Arielle were trying to process this powerful experience. Eva had experienced it before, so she seemed to take it in stride. Arielle was trying to dispel the fear of insanity that had immediately come over her with the appearance of the girl. They had seen a ghost. She knew that it was an utter impossibility. It couldn't be real…but yet the experience she'd just had proved her wrong… *I must be going out of my mind,* she thought.

Eva was the first to move. She picked up the Pentagon, walked across the room, and turned the lights on. She examined the pentagon, twirling it between her fingers and bringing it close to the table lamp.

"There's writing on here," she said. "Juliet Garner 1982 – 2000." She turned the Pentagon over and read, in almost a whisper, "Juliet, wait for me. I love you, Jasper." Eva looked at them, her eyes tearing up.

"She's waiting for someone, and she can't move on. How can we find out who this Jasper guy is?"

"Maybe we can search the computer under the last name Garner and see if something comes up about her family and what happened to her. That would be a good place to start," Gabrielle said. But she also sounded sad.

"Guys, I think I've had enough for tonight. I do want to help, but I'm tired, and honestly, I'm a little scared about this whole thing," Arielle said. "I mean, messing around with the dead…" She was trembling like a leaf in a windstorm. Gabrielle and Eva nodded agreement. It was a bit scary, and they all knew it.

They also now knew that Eva's visitor was an eighteen-year-old girl named Juliet, who needed help finding the person she was waiting for – someone by the name of Jasper. Arielle pressed her lips together as she picked the board up, put it away in its box, and threw it into the very back of her closet.

"I was sure this board didn't work," she muttered.

"Well, you were wrong," Gabrielle said matter-of-factly.

"Now I know why she has been coming to me all this time. She needs help. But I'm not sure how I can help her," Eva mumbled.

"I truly feel bad about her, and I want us to help. We can start looking on the Internet tomorrow and see what we can find," said Gabrielle.

"How do we know what place to check in the search engine? What if she's not from Brighton?" Eva asked.

"Hmm, good point," said Arielle.

After a short pause, Eva suggested that they could first search for Garners in their town. Then, if that didn't work, they could check places around Brighton within a couple of hours drive since Juliet had to have lived somewhere in the surrounding area. That sounded like a logical plan, so they decided to go to bed and talk about it more in the morning. But Arielle sensed that Eva was still tense.

"What is it?" she asked, holding Eva's gaze. Eva soundlessly inhaled and smiled tensely.

"When I was doing all the spells I felt the heavy burden of all the problems I was receiving from different spirits," Eva said. "I want to help this girl, but after we find out who she is and what exactly she wants, I don't want to do this anymore." She was biting her lower lip, and Arielle could see that her thoughts were running a mile a minute.

"All right, we'll start on this tomorrow. And when we're done, we're not going to do this again. I'm going to throw that stupid board out tomorrow," Arielle said. She was pretty frustrated that this senseless idea had ruined the rest of the night for them. This Juliet girl was now invading all of their thoughts. She tossed and turned for a long time, and when she finally fell asleep, it was a restless, fitful sleep.

The first thing the next morning, even before breakfast, they sat in front of the computer. They searched the Internet by putting in Juliet's last name and her age. Then they moved from place to place, from family to family, checking the names under each household, and spent several hours without any results. They took a couple of breaks for lunch and dinner and continued their search until late Sunday night. They were tired and were planning to quit after pulling up Southampton, the last search for the night. In Southampton, there were only three households with the name "Garner." When they saw the name "Juliet" listed in one family group, they were startled and excited. The address was around fifty-five kilometers away from Arielle's house.

They agreed to drive there the next Saturday and try to find anything they could about the girl. She had been dead for more than nine years, so it might be hard to find out anything, but they were going to try. They talked with each other every day that week, laying a well thought out plan, and the next Saturday morning they headed to Southampton.

The drive was an easy one, and the more they talked about it, the more optimistic they were. However, as they got closer to their destination, Arielle could feel anxiety taking over, and she could see that Gabrielle and Eva felt the same way.

They parked in front of the address they had found on the computer. It was a huge house in a very beautiful neighborhood. They were completely startled to hear a young voice speaking, right next to the car. They looked over, and a young girl around fifteen or sixteen stood there with a wide smile on her face, books clutched in her arms, asking them if they were looking for someone in particular.

"Do you know who lives in this house?" Eva asked, pointing.

"Who are you looking for?" asked the young girl. Arielle was shocked to hear Eva's next statement, which didn't fit well at all with the very well thought out the plan they had laid out during the week.

"My sister has asked me to try and locate a couple of her best friends from secondary school. She moved to Germany to attend university a few years back and now she's getting married."

"Who are you looking for?" the girl asked again, a beautiful smile on her face.

"Juliet Garner." Eva's voice was a little shaky, but her nervousness wasn't too obvious.

The girl immediately lost her smile as a sad look took over her face. "She's not here any longer," she said, in a barely audible voice.

"Oh… Do you know where she is?" Eva persisted.

The girl's look of grief deepened. "She's dead. She died ten years ago." Her eyes welled up as she turned away from the car and started to walk toward the house.

"Wait! Wait!" Eva yelled. The girl stopped and waited without turning back to look at them.

"Who are you?" Eva asked. The girl slowly turned halfway toward them, and they could clearly see tears rolling down her face.

"I'm her sister, Rachel," she said, her voice breaking.

"Rachel, can we talk to you, please?" Eva pleaded.

"Come on in the house," Rachel said. "I'm sure my mum would love to see you."

They got out of the car and followed her inside, not knowing how far they planned or would be able to carry the lie Eva had created. Rachel called for her mother, and a short, attractive woman appeared at the door to the foyer.

"Mother, these girls are looking for Juliet."

The woman's jaw fell open, and her face showed clear emotional suffering at the sound of her daughter's name. Arielle could clearly read her mind, and she could feel the immediate change of the mother's emotions, like a roller coaster, full of highs and lows but mostly lows that were deep and long.

"Were you friends of Juliet?" she asked. Her voice was soft, filled with profound sadness.

"My name is Eva, and these are my friends Gabrielle and Arielle. We live in Brighton and my sister Briana, who was a friend of Juliet's, is getting married in Germany. She wanted me to locate a couple of her friends for her. That is what brought us here."

"Please come and sit down. I'm very happy for your sister," Juliet's mother said. There was sadness in her eyes as if she were thinking about how she had once wished the same for Juliet.

Arielle was consumed by guilty feelings over their lie, and she knew that Eva and Gabrielle felt the same way. But they couldn't change their story now. They had to move on and find out all they could about Juliet.

"Can we ask what happened to Juliet?" Eva asked. "I mean if you don't want to talk about it..."

"She was getting ready to go to university, and she was shot by accident during a party at a friend's house," Juliet's mother murmured, her eyes fixed somewhere in the distance.

Eva looked shocked, and then asked, "what happened?"

"It seems that the girl's younger brother, only six years old, got ahold of his father's gun – his father is a sergeant with the Southampton police department – and it went off. Juliet was shot in the mouth, and she died instantly." Tears rolled down the side of her face, making the girls' hearts break.

"Oh, Mrs. Garner, we are so sorry!" Arielle said. But the mother continued speaking with an empty look in her eyes as if she hadn't heard a word.

"We lost our beautiful daughter just a month before she was to be married to her sweetheart," the mother continued. She was weeping softly and had taken out a handkerchief from her pocket. "We buried her in her wedding gown because I knew how much she loved it and how she was looking forward to walking down the aisle to be with Jasper forever." Her voice broke, and she fell apart into a heartbreaking sob. Rachel put her arms around her mother and held her tight.

At the sound of Jasper's name Arielle felt a strong jolt go through her body and, looking at Gabrielle and Eva, she knew they felt the same way.

"I love you, mother," Rachel whispered as she looked at her mother lovingly and gave her a kiss on the cheek. Arielle had tears in her eyes, and her heart was breaking just listening to the mother, feeling her pain and sorrow. She looked over at Gabrielle and Eva, who were both looking down, clearly disturbed by the mother's words.

The fact that Juliet had been shot in the mouth reminded them that when they had seen her in Arielle's room that night, there had been blood coming out of her mouth and dripping onto her beautiful wedding gown.

"What happened to the boy she was going to marry?" Arielle asked.

"Oh… Jasper went through extreme mental agony and hurt. He seemed to do everything he could to move on and get back on his feet but he kept falling into deep depression, and nobody could help him. He committed suicide a year later, leaving behind a letter with just one line: *"She's waiting for me."*

Arielle stopped breathing as her mind went back to the Pentagon and the words they had seen on it: *"Wait for me. I love you, Jasper."*

The silence in the room felt like a cold blanket on her skin, and the air got so thick that it was suffocating. They were all looking down with broken hearts and eyes full of tears.

Mrs. Garner stood up and looked at them with a soft smile. "I wish Briana all the happiness in the world," she said.

They thanked her and left the house in complete bewilderment. They got into the car and sat without moving, without saying a single word. Then Arielle stepped on the gas while wiping the tears away from her eyes. She felt such a deep sadness, and she wanted to do something, but she had no idea what to do. She was so lost in her own thoughts that she was startled when Eva spoke again.

"So, what do we do with all that information?"

"I think you need to find a spell and try to reunite them," Gabby said authoritatively. Eva didn't seem to notice what Gabby had said; she was so deep in thought.

"Somehow she must have remained earthbound due to the emotional trauma she went through, and she hasn't been able to move on in her life-journey. She must be waiting for Jasper and refusing to head toward the light until he comes to her. She needs your help, Eva. They need to find each other and I think you can do it. And I think she knows you can do it; that's why she keeps coming to you." Gabrielle was out of breath from excitement. She wanted so badly to bring the two separated lovers together that Arielle could feel her eagerness and willingness to do her part to help.

Eva finally smiled and agreed that Gabrielle's plan was a good one, and they all decided to give Eva time to find the right spell, then get together and try to help Juliet before they went away on their holidays.

For the next week, they left Eva alone and waited for her to let them know when she was ready. Their thoughts were full of Juliet and the upcoming event. Arielle was sure it was going to be the biggest thing they had ever experienced in their lives thus far.

Finally on Thursday, Eva called them to say that they needed to get together and talk. They agreed to meet at Arielle's house that same evening at seven o'clock.

"Did you find the right spell?" Gabrielle asked.

"Yes," Eva said. "But there are several things that you both need to understand if we are going to do this the right way."

"What do we need to do?" Arielle asked, full of curiosity.

"First, we have to find a natural location free from outside disturbances such as noise, other people, phones, and any other outside interference. Preferably a place that is commonly used by spirits and that has a symbolic connection to our purpose. The perfect choice would be the house of the deceased person, but we can't do that. So the next best place, in my opinion, would be the cemetery."

"Oh, I don't like that at all," Gabrielle said, in a voice so low it was almost a whisper.

"Well, if we are going to do this we can't have any grasping and groping during the connection. We have to have our feelings in check, our hearts free of any other problems, and we have to stay neutral about what we are doing. If we can't do that, we can't do the spell."

There was quiet in the room, and nobody said a word for a long time. Finally, Arielle asked, "What else do we need to know?"

"During the summons, we have to bring a lot of love and support for the difficulties that surround Juliet to help her find Jasper. Love is the pulsation of contact in the spirit world, and that is what will also enable Jasper to find his way to Juliet's path. It's like giving him a soft push in her direction. Also, we need to bring candles. The cult books say that spirits are attracted to sources of heat and light."

"Is there anything else we need to bring?" Arielle asked.

"I'll bring vervain, saffron, and prepared incense to burn during the summons within the safety of a magic circle that we will draw, and that circle will also hold a symbolic item – the Pentagon that was handled by Jasper and Juliet. That will be the connection between them," Eva said. Then she looked at both of them very seriously and asked, "Do you think you can do it? If not, then let's not waste any more time on this, and let's just move on."

"No...we have to do this," Gabrielle said in a firm voice, and Arielle agreed.

"I think the best time to do it is on Saturday night midnight. Is that okay with you?"

"Yes," they both said. They were nervous about this decision, but also sure that it was the right thing to do.

"I'll pick you up first, Eva, and then Gabby," Arielle said. "And I'll bring the candles. What color do they have to be and how many?"

"There are different colored candles to be used for each day of the week. We need a black one because we are doing the summons on Saturday, and we also need three violet ones and three white ones."

They all agreed to be prepared and calm. They truly wanted to help Juliet move on to her final destination. Then they went home feeling full of the secret they had and wondering about how it would all unravel.

 *Chapter 4*

ON FRIDAY, Eva and Arielle decided to spend the afternoon together, going to the mall to do a little shopping. They needed to purchase all the items that Eva said they needed to gather for the cemetery.

Arielle spent a little time thinking of the upcoming holiday. Her parents loved the ocean just as much as she did, and they had purchased another home in a small town in France, St. Jean de Luz, that would satisfy their love for the water. Going there gave the family a chance to spend quality time together while away from home, school, work, and daily commitments. Eva and Gabrielle's families did the same, though in different places.

So as soon as school was out each year, the three of them went their separate ways for the summer months, looking to make new holiday friends, new memories – and some juicy secrets they could share with each other when they got back home.

Arielle would be leaving with her parents for France the following Wednesday. Eva and her mom were leaving on Monday for Alnmouth, in the northern part of England. Gabrielle and her parents would be flying to San Marco Island in Italy on Tuesday.

The friendship between Gabrielle, Eva, and Arielle was something very special. They shared all of their most intimate secrets, and they discussed every little thing with each other, whether it was important or not. Arielle knew Gabrielle's intimate thoughts and most of Eva's, and she told them most of her secrets, except for the secret of her dreadful gift. She knew she would tell them someday, but she was afraid they might not want to be her friend anymore if she told them. And she knew she couldn't live without them in her life.

They had plenty to talk about each time they got back home from their holidays, but so far there had been nothing earthshaking happening in any of their lives. But they wanted to believe that one of these days one of them would come back with something great to talk about.

Gabrielle loved horses and every time she returned from her holiday she would talk about how exuberant she felt each time she got on a horse and galloped through the beautiful green fields of San Marco. Arielle wanted to experience that feeling too, but she had just one problem: she was completely petrified of horses. She and Eva were more the beach or pool-relaxing type. She didn't like too much excitement. She was happiest just reading, listening to music, walking on the beach, and lying by the pool. She guessed that the most exciting thing she and Eva would ever like to be involved in was waterskiing.

Spending time in the sun was pretty important to all of them. They always wanted to come back with a dark brown healthy color showing they had been on holiday.

When it came to books, even though Arielle and Eva both loved reading, Eva's tastes had changed since her father's passing. Arielle loved to find new gothic romantic stories and classic books like *Pride and Prejudice*, *Rebecca*, or *Wuthering Heights*. Eva had once loved the same type of books, but now she was more interested in books about shadows, witchcraft, Celtic mysteries, and books of spells. It wasn't Arielle's thing at all. Still, she and Eva had the same taste in music, so they were able to share that.

Of the three of them, Gabrielle was the athlete, the horseback rider, the swimmer, the skater, the biker – the list went on and on. Just thinking about Gabrielle and what she would be doing on her holiday made Arielle tired.

That night she decided to read for a little while before she went to sleep. She stood up, picked up one of her favorite books, *Persuasion* by Jane Austen, and slipped in a leisurely way under the covers. She started to read and as usual, she got lost in the world of Anne Elliot and her love for the handsome and dashing Captain Frederick Wentworth.

This is the kind of love I'm looking for, she thought, *and why is it that I only seem to find it in Jane Austen's books? Especially in* Pride and Prejudice.

She sighed. She was glad they were leaving soon on holiday, and that she would have a little break from all these witchcraft and summons sessions; however she also knew that they had to get through this one last session on Saturday night.

Somewhere in the middle of reading her book she drifted off to sleep and the next thing she knew, her mother was calling her for breakfast. She gazed at the clock and saw it was already nine-thirty. She spent the day getting ready for her holiday, deciding which books to take, what music to listen to, and what clothes she would need. She laughed out loud thinking about how she had done this same activity over and over again, but somehow each time it seemed as if she had never gone on a holiday before in her life.

Around four o'clock the next afternoon, Gabrielle called her, full of excitement and enthusiasm.

"I can hardly wait for tonight!" she said. "I've been thinking about this for two days straight, and I haven't been able to sleep." She sighed a deep sigh.

"Just remember, you have to stay calm, with *no outbursts,*" Arielle reminded her, "if you want the summons to be successful." All Arielle wanted to do was to get it over with and move on with their lives. "We'll pick you up around eleven-thirty, okay?" she asked.

"Arielle, please let me come over to your house. I'm going out of my mind being alone. All I can do is think about tonight."

"Well, all right," Arielle said, chuckling at her friend's eagerness. "Come on over. Maybe you can help me pack."

"I'll be right there!" Gabrielle said, and the phone went dead. Just a few minutes later, she was startled to see Gabby walking through her bedroom door, all worked up, but smiling.

"Good Lord, did you fly here?"

"Arielle, I swear that if midnight doesn't come soon, I will just burst!"

Arielle had to laugh just looking at Gabby's face. She hugged her warmly, and they laughed together even though they knew what they were going to do that night was no laughing matter.

Finally, eleven o'clock came, and then eleven-thirty. As the hour approached Arielle grew even more nervous, and Gabrielle seemed to be a little bit less excited and a little more apprehensive herself.

Arielle called Eva just before they left the house. They picked her up and soon they were on their way to the cemetery. The iron gate was not locked, so they drove along the long winding lanes and covered pathways, blatant cues of the solemnity of death, and found their way to where Eva's father was buried.

The burial plots were small, but the spaces between the lots were large, with plantings and created landscapes unbroken by hedges. There were no stars in the sky, and the cloud-obscured moon made the night charcoal black. It was extremely quiet and very tranquil. Arielle knew that all three of them were contemplating the mystery of death.

Then Eva's voice broke her deep thoughts, asking her to bring out the candles. She watched as Eva moved between two lots and drew a large circle around her. She placed the candles a foot apart around the inside of the circle, and right in the middle she set the vervain, the saffron, the incense, and the Pentagon. Then Eva asked Arielle and Gabrielle to take a seat on the edge of the circle, close their eyes, breathe in deeply, and exhale several times.

"Meditate," she said. "Try to get rid of all unwanted thoughts and problems that may be occupying you. We all need to have a clear view of what we are here to do, and nothing else." They sat quietly for about twenty minutes, concentrating only on Juliet and Jasper, becoming more relaxed and more serene, wanting to see this matter through.

At the end of twenty minutes, Eva entered the circle and lit first the incense, then the vervain and saffron. Slowly she moved on to light the candles one at a time, starting with the black one and ending with the white.

"The light from the candles will illuminate the passageway between our worlds," Eva whispered. "Through these candles, there is truth in all communications that come to me." Then she sat between her two friends and asked them to hold her hands.

"Please concentrate very hard and try to merge Juliet and Jasper in your minds by repeating three words under your breath: "Juliet, Jasper, merge..."

They followed her instructions and began to quietly chant those three words together. Then Eva closed her eyes, and after a short pause, she started to chant slowly but with a firm voice.

"Guardians of the Spirit realm, hear and guide my plea.
When the witching hour rings true, bring my friends to me.
Other souls who hear my call are not welcome in this place.
Only the ones known as Juliet and Jasper may enter the sacred space."

Eva was quiet for a short time. Then she repeated the spell two more times. Nothing happened for a long while; it seemed like centuries to Arielle. But suddenly she was jolted by very evident changes in their surroundings.

They had been well prepared to stay calm and not make any gasping noises or show any fear. Their fingers were intertwined, and they grasped each other's hands tighter and stronger while, with their thoughts, they willed Juliet and Jasper together.

The wind picked up, and the swishing sound of tree leaves became a loud whistle, so loud that it made their eardrums hurt. Arielle closed her eyes tight and pressed her lips together, not sure of what was going to happen next. Suddenly she felt heat spreading across her skin, and she snapped her eyes open as her jaw dropped.

Right in the middle of the circle there was the familiar brilliant cocoon, its light surrounding Juliet. The sight was breathtaking; her hair was moving around her face to a light breeze, and her eyes were sparkling like two precious jewels. A mystical smile spread across her face as she looked intensely past their faces somewhere into the darkness, and her arms were extended as if they were waiting to embrace someone.

Their eyes were wide open, and their breath seized in their throats as they waited, still holding hands, still whispering the words "Juliet, Jasper, merge" over and over again. Not long after that, the whistling from the leaves of the trees stopped, and stony silence fell around them.

Arielle didn't think she could describe in words what happened next. A strong sound almost like thunder was heard, but there was no storm anywhere near. A soft white cloud moved around the outer part of the circle, pausing for a short time over each one of them. First Eva, then Gabrielle, and finally Arielle, who felt a soft touch as it passed over her and moved slowly towards the center of the circle. Juliet's eyes were on that cloud, and her smile was now even wider. But a second later, the cloud moved inside the brilliant cocoon and changed into a young man with open arms that encircled Juliet.

The brilliance of the circle was amazing, and the heat that it was producing was almost too hot to bear, but they didn't move an inch. Their embrace was a long one. There were tears in Juliet's eyes, and there was peace in Jasper's face. They both bent down and picked up the Pentagon, their eyes never leaving each other's faces.

Arielle was crying; she could not take her eyes away from the two souls that had found each other and could now take their final journey together.

As they moved away, Juliet looked back at Eva as if she was trying to say something, but they couldn't hear a sound. Eva smiled back at her with a look of complete gratification on her face, tears rolling down her face.

Arielle was still trying to get over the shock of the most amazing experience she'd ever had in her life. Nothing was left but the circle and the burning candles. Eva got up and extinguished the candles in the same order in which she had lit them. With the palm, of her right hand she moved the ashes of the vervain, saffron, and the incense around the outline of the circle, making it disappear. She picked up the candles, and they all moved towards the car without speaking.

They all cried, touched by the beauty of the experience and the positive outcome of their effort. Arielle's heart was calm, peaceful, and happy. She was thankful for her friends and thankful for her life.

When she was back safely in her room later that night, Arielle took her journal out of her desk drawer and climbed into bed. Her emotions were evident as the pen started to glide across the blank page.

May 29

Today I learned that there was no greater joy than that of true love. I saw two souls that searched desperately to find each other, even after they were dead. I saw the love, the passion, the devotion, and the need between Jasper and Juliet to be one. Their merging shattered my senses down to my very core. Apparently the definition of "love" is nothing like what I thought it would be, before to tonight's events. The turmoil in Juliet's face while looking for Jasper was astounding. I want so much to find that kind of love. I want the imprint of the man I fall in love with to reach the depths of my very soul. I want to fall in love and experience the warmth and the extreme sensation of exhilaration that Jasper and Juliet's faces displayed when they found each other.

I'm voraciously curious, and I've every intention to try and experience the same kind of love. However, I'm a bit terrified at the thought that I might not be able to find the guy that would fit the blueprint I hold so dearly in my heart and mind. What my future encompasses, I don't know, but love is a feeling I don't want to live without. After today, I can't possibly doubt the power of such an amazing feeling, such an astonishing commitment that exists between two souls in love.

Arielle had been awestruck by the power of the alluring concept of true love. She was lost in thoughts of pure fascination as she set the journal aside and lay back, stretching sluggishly, heart filled with wonder over such a powerful emotion. She hugged her pillow, closed her eyes, and let deep sleep claim her.

 *Chapter 5*

THE SUMMER HOLIDAYS were over again, and the time flew by, as always. Soon, Eva, Gabrielle, and Arielle were back at home, getting ready for school. They decided to rent a flat close to campus even though their homes were only about twenty-five kilometers away from the University. They were sure this was going to be a great place for them to have privacy but to also have the luxury of going home any time they wanted to do so. They realized that this was going to be a stressful time for them, meeting new people and settling into new routines.

They moved into their new flat the week before school started, and by the weekend, they were all settled in and pretty excited about the first day of school. Over the weekend, they sat down, as they always did, and talked about their experiences and all the exciting things they had done during the summer holidays.

Eva went first but by the disappointed look on her face they didn't expect to hear much. "Well, as you both know, I am a sun worshipper," she began. "So I spent most of my time on the beach reading or listening to music. And I did get a great tan, but there was no mystery and no adventure for me. I went to a few parties, and I met a very nice looking guy from Spain. At first, I thought it might turn out to be something interesting. I quickly found out that he didn't speak a word of English, and as hard as I tried I couldn't understand a word he said to me. I know he liked me, but how can you have anything romantic or exciting happen if you can't communicate at all? There were a few kisses, but nothing I would call earthshaking," she said with a sigh. "So, like I said, no adventure this year. I sure wish that one of these times I would meet someone special, someone, who would bring true romance into my life."

"Well, don't worry about it, Eva, my summer was pretty much like yours," Arielle said. "Except for two things. I didn't get a great tan like you did, and I didn't meet anyone special at all. I think at this point I would like to have met someone even if he didn't speak any English. At least I would have something to say about my holiday right now," she chuckled. Eva laughed and reached over to hug her.

Gabrielle seemed to be the only one with something exciting to talk about. "I went horseback riding with my holiday friends every day," she said with a twinkle in her eyes. "And this year I noticed a young man following us from a distance, but he never got close enough for me to see his face clearly. I could tell that he was tall with dark hair, and his horse was beautiful. His riding gear was extremely elegant, and he looked very mysterious. I asked one of the girls if she knew who he was, but she said she had no idea. However, she said she had seen him following them the previous year as well."

She looked at both of them to see their reactions and found them listening to her attentively. "Naturally, my curiosity about him was intense," she continued. "And what made it even more romantic was he followed us as we rode by abandoned castles and Roman ruins. I thought of him as the lord of one of those castles and how amazing it would have been if he was watching *me*." The faraway look in her eyes and the smile on her lips made Eva and Arielle think that she was somewhere back in Italy again, seeing her mysterious rider off in the distance.

"There were several girls in the group," Gabby said. "So I didn't know who he was there for, and I wasn't going to assume that he was there for me. But he sure made the summer more exciting," she said with a happy sigh. "Every day I looked forward to seeing if he was going to show up and he always did."

"Well, at least you have something exciting to think about this year, and something to look forward to next year," Arielle said. "I never even got a tan, and I spent *hours* lying on the beach." She sighed with disgust as Eva chuckled.

The first day of class was a bit stressful, and they were all a bit nervous. They were now completely independent, a new experience for them. The day might have been a complete disaster if they hadn't taken the time to buy their books and find their way around the campus beforehand.

Most students aren't sure of their major until they have a couple of years behind them, but all three girls were already pretty well set on their course. Arielle had signed up for her classes with a firm vision of becoming an engineer; Gabby was determined to become a surgeon just like her father and Eva wanted to follow in her father's footsteps too, and become an attorney. When her father was alive, he had owned a very successful law firm, which had been passed on to her uncle. He was running the firm for Eva until she was able to run it herself.

The second day of classes, they had chemistry class together. They sat next to each other and looked around at the faces that they would often be seeing for the next few months. Or maybe it would it even be years. Everything seemed so new, so different, and so exciting.

It was in chemistry class that they met Paul Wheatfield, a very pleasant and friendly young man. He looked at them as soon as they walked in, and smiled a big smile. He was beautiful with warm brown eyes, and it filled Arielle's heart with pleasure just to look at him.

After class, he walked up to them and introduced himself. Talking almost in unison, all three girls started to introduce themselves, telling him they were pleased to meet him.

"So what's the deal, you come in threes?" he said, laughing as they stopped and started again, trying not to interrupt each other in their eagerness to talk to this incredibly handsome young man. They laughed too. Almost instantly, they struck up an easy friendship, and when one of the girls needed a lab partner, Paul was there to help. Usually, Arielle worked with Paul, and Eva and Gabrielle worked together.

By the second month, they had settled into a routine that was neither too difficult nor unpleasant. They loved the classes they were taking and sometimes they would study together so they could help each other with the more challenging problems.

Paul became a close friend, and fortunately, he didn't belong to that special group of people in Arielle's head whose thoughts she could hear. He was very reserved, dressed with extremely good taste, and preferred to protect his privacy. Arielle had a strong feeling that he liked her, but he had never come out and actually asked her for a date. She didn't think about it too much because she wasn't interested in him in that way. He was beautiful, but she knew he wasn't the man she was waiting for. She liked him as a friend and figured that was as far as she would ever take it.

The girls came to learn that Paul's father was a producer and his mother a director in the movie industry. They were both very successful and very well known. The three girls had an open invitation every time Paul's parents visited the school and took Paul to lunch or dinner. Though they were careful not to intrude too much, they enjoyed several fine meals with Paul and his parents.

Paul also had three close friends that he introduced to the girls, Alex Durand, Robert Gibson, and Damien Sanders. They were interesting guys and the more they hung out together, the more the girls liked them.

Robert was of average height with hair that looked almost black against his white skin. He had dark blue eyes, and though he was very handsome, there was a restlessness in his eyes that made it clear he was burdened by something. His girlfriend, Rachel, was a little strange and hardly ever talked to them when they were together.

Alex was a little different. His moods were unpredictable. Sometimes he was full of high spirits and other times he fell into near melancholy, a character trait that intrigued the girls.

Damien had a great sense of humor and beautiful, friendly, warm, honey-colored eyes. His girlfriend was Danielle, and she was just as nice as he was.

Time rolled by, and they met many people with different tastes and ideas. The variety was wonderful since it created a nice mix of personalities. Some of their classmates became temporary, casual kinds of friends, and some became truly good friends.

When they didn't have a class or didn't have to study, they would spend time at the local pub on campus having a beer, coffee, or tea.

The girls thought they had absolute control in setting the pace of moving forward with their chosen, very challenging vocational fields. They kept up with their school routine, their socializing, and each summer went on holiday with their families. Two years into their university studies they were startled to find out that their lives were going by too fast. At the end of the second year of their studies, they finally realized they had to take careful control over their lives and slow down enough to enjoy each and every day.

Coming back from their most recent summer holiday they found themselves back in their apartment, glasses of wine in hand, discussing their summer activities, hoping that this time one of them would have an exciting, magical, fairytale-like story to share. But once again the news was pretty much the same as in previous years. They had nearly given up on the notion of meeting their white knights in shining armor, the true loves that would sweep them off their feet. They all were so anxious to meet that one special man and fall deeply and completely in love with him. But that was beginning to seem an impossible dream. They were now in their third year at the university and, except for that one missing element; they seemed perfectly content with the mixture of attentiveness to their studies, their general routines, and pleasure that consumed their lives.

Arielle knew that trust had always been the foundation of the friendship between the three of them. She was now at a point in her life that she had thoughts and desires that she could no longer share with her parents. She loved them dearly, but she felt some things had to be kept secret, which she either held for herself or shared with Gabrielle and Eva. So they became the sharers and keepers of all her secrets, and she became the keeper of theirs. She was sure that she could trust Gabrielle and Eva with her life, and that they would never violate that trust.

Around the middle of the first semester of their third year, Gabby told them that she had met a guy named Marcus in one of her classes and that she liked him a lot. She had gone out on a few dates with him, and now she wanted Eva and Arielle to meet him. She seemed to be quite taken with him and his charming ways.

So a couple of weeks later they agreed to go out together, along with Paul and Damien. They arranged to all meet at the girls' flat first.

When Marcus walked in the door, Arielle's lungs seized as their eyes engaged for a split second. Marcus was amazingly good looking; very tall, with perfect features and a great build. He was dressed all in black, making him look very mysterious. His hair was very dark, almost black, and so were his eyes. As he entered the flat, he smiled at Gabrielle, took her in his arms and kissed her passionately. After enjoying the kiss, Gabrielle introduced him to the guys first, and then she brought him over to meet Eva and Arielle.

"Arielle, Eva, this is Marcus," she said. Though she tried, she couldn't hide the excitement in her voice.

"Hello," he said, holding out his hand for a shake. His voice was soft. "I've been looking forward to tonight. Gabrielle talks about you all the time. I'm so glad to meet you."

His smile was captivating, but there was something a little bit eerie about him. He didn't belong to that special group of people in Arielle's head, so that she couldn't hear his thoughts. However, when his hand touched hers, an uneasy feeling ran through her body, making her shiver and cringe. His gaze was intense and short, but in that fragment of time, his eyes reflected only emptiness as if she were looking into a hollow space. When Arielle gazed back at him, she felt like she was being drawn into a black hole. *How strange*, she thought.

He didn't pay attention to her reaction as he moved over to shake Eva's hand with a wide smile on his beautiful face. Arielle turned to watch Eva's reaction, and as his hand touched hers a troubled look stretched across Eva's face, too, and her eyes narrowed, showing nervousness. He clearly noticed

Eva's reaction, and as he pulled his hand away he winced at her startled look. For a short time he seemed to be searching for the proper thing to say, but soon he gave up and walked away with an edgy smile on his face. He moved to where the guys were standing and got into a conversation with Damien.

"So? What do you think?" Gabrielle asked.

Eva and Arielle exchanged a look. Then, forcing enthusiasm, they told Gabby that he was very nice looking. She seemed pleased with their remarks. She walked over to stand next to Marcus and slipped her hand in his.

"There's something very peculiar about that guy," Arielle whispered to Eva. "What is it? I can't say exactly what bothers me, but I just don't feel good about him."

Eva looked relieved that Arielle was expressing the same fear and hesitation that she felt. "I know just what you mean," she said.

"But we can't let Gabrielle know," Arielle said. "At least not unless we can figure out what it is that's bothering us."

Despite this rather unsettling beginning, the night was fun, and the film was great. Paul suggested that they stop at the pub for a while, and that is where Marcus met some of his friends. They were all dressed similarly, in dark clothing, and they all talked in low voices. He didn't bother to introduce his friends to Gabrielle's friends. That was a bit odd, but they didn't think too much about it.

They had been there about an hour when Gabrielle approached to say that she was leaving with Marcus. While she was talking to Paul and Damien, Arielle noticed that Marcus had fixed his eyes on Eva, and she could swear that his expression was sarcastic. Eva and Arielle were a bit shocked by his apparently hostile attitude toward her, but they didn't say anything for fear of upsetting Gabrielle.

The evening didn't seem so much fun anymore, so Arielle asked if Paul and Damien could take her and Eva home. They dropped the girls off at their flat, but not before mentioning how strange they had felt talking to Marcus.

"He seems to be very weird," Damien said, shaking his head with a troubled look, and Paul nodded in agreement. Arielle and Eva thanked them both for a nice time and walked inside, completely perplexed about Marcus.

Although they still couldn't pinpoint the reason for their concern, they were both overwhelmed with a dreadful turmoil and confusion over the darkness that seemed to surround their friend's new boyfriend.

"There is a frightening, unnatural stillness about his eyes," Eva said. "I don't think I've ever seen that on any person I have ever met."

"I know," Arielle said. "It's like looking into infinity. There's no emotion, no life. How strange is that?"

"I don't know what to make of him," Eva said. "It's like he's living in an empty body as if his soul is dead." Eva's voice was barely audible, and her last words made Arielle's heart race and a cold chill run from her head to her toes.

"Do you see anything at all? Please try," she said, appealing to her friend's ability to perceive things others could not.

"Arielle, everything I see surrounding Gabrielle is dark and scary.

There is something very bizarre going on. I can see her face one moment and then the next it's as she vanishes into thin air. I don't like the images I'm getting at all."

By this time, they were both pretty worked up, even a little frantic, and they wanted to do something without knowing quite what.

"He seems to have some twisted control over her," Eva said. "I think we need to find out something about him. But how?"

A stony silence fell between them as they sat, buried in overwhelming thoughts, searching for resolutions.

"Arielle, I don't mind telling you that this guy fits the profile of the characters in all those Celtic Otherworld books I've read. And right now I'm pretty scared."

Suddenly Arielle had an idea. "Eva, listen," she said. "Robert is in journalism, and he has access to a lot of information. Why don't we ask him to look into cults and alternative groups and their activities? I remember there was some stuff going on in Brighton a couple of years ago. Some of it was pretty scary."

"Well, why not?" Eva said.

Arielle picked up her mobile and pressed Robert's number on the keypad. He lived only a couple of doors away from their flat, and he was happy to come right over.

When he arrived, they explained their suspicions and fears about Marcus and told him how worried they were about Gabby. They asked him not to tell anyone about their concerns, not even Paul and the rest of their friends.

They were completely taken aback when Robert told them that he didn't like Marcus either, and he also thought there was something peculiar about him. He said he would be happy to look into the situation because he had a feeling that Marcus was involved in some cult. Arielle told him that her gut feeling was that Gabrielle already knew what Marcus was doing to her, but maybe he had made it impossible for her to get away from him. "Robert, I know Gabrielle has always been intrigued by this kind of stuff, but she was also pretty scared to cross that line," Arielle remarked, adding, "Frankly, I'm really worried about her."

"All right, then, I'll start on this tomorrow," Robert said.

Both girls hugged Robert gratefully at the door and thanked him for his willingness to help.

 *Chapter 6*

THE NEXT DAY, immediately after Arielle's first class she went looking for Gabrielle, who was in the library with Marcus. They were sitting at a table, just looking at each other as if they were talking, but without saying anything. *Pretty crazy,* she thought as she approached them. Completely ignoring Marcus, she asked Gabrielle if she could stop by the flat that afternoon.

"Why?" Gabrielle asked.

"It's my mother's birthday. I'm making some preparations, and I need your help," Arielle said with a firm voice. She saw Gabrielle looking at Marcus as if for his approval, and that made Arielle cringe. Once again Arielle noticed that there was absolutely no expression on his face and no emotional reflection in his eyes.

Arielle clenched her fists angrily but decided not to say anything. She made a point of staring meaningfully at Gabrielle and waiting for her reply. She wasn't going to take no for an answer, and Gabrielle must have understood that clearly because suddenly she agreed that she would come over later.

Arielle walked away, furious with Marcus and wishing that his thoughts were not sealed off from her head. It would have been much easier to get to the bottom of this if she could read his mind.

This whole affair had begun to feel a bit like déjà vu for Arielle. The way Gabrielle was behaving reminded her of Eva and what she had been like when she had been all wrapped up with the spells and the magic books, right after her father had passed away. It was clear that Gabrielle was spending a lot of time with Marcus, and that school was not her priority anymore.

It seemed to Arielle that Gabrielle's control over her life was unraveling and dissolving. She and Eva began to feel that they didn't even really know her anymore.

They were sitting in the living room in complete silence, waiting for Gabrielle to arrive and thinking of all the things they needed to discuss.

"Arielle, I think he is deeply involved with dark witchcraft," Eva said. "He fits the profile that I have read about in the spell books. And if I'm right about this, Gabrielle is in danger." She pressed her lips together, feeling a tremor course through her body. She reached over and took Arielle's hand in hers, and their gazes locked. "Thank you for being there when I needed you," Eva murmured. For a moment they simply sat, looking at each other. "And now we have to save Gabby," she added. Arielle smiled warmly and nodded, squeezing Eva's hand.

Not too surprisingly, Gabrielle was late, but she did show up before they began to worry about her. She looked startled at the serious tone of Eva's voice when she asked her to sit down.

"What's wrong?" Gabrielle asked. She sounded only slightly worried, but she also sounded like she was trying to hide her true feelings.

"Gabby, there is something bad going on with Marcus, and you are getting sucked into a very unsafe and very treacherous life," Arielle said. "You aren't going anywhere until we get some answers from you. You know that Eva can see the future, and she sees that Marcus's thoughts are dark, and his eyes are colder than anything we have ever felt. I don't know what death feels like, but if I had to compare it to something, that would be Marcus."

Gabrielle pursed her lips and looked away from them; she didn't seem to want to say anything. But Arielle could hear her thoughts, and they were very cloudy. She could see that Gabrielle was scared, but something was pushing her to continue with whatever it was she was doing.

"I'm not sure I can talk about this," she murmured.

"Gabby, please. We're trying to help you."

Gabrielle's face was pinched and set in a tense expression. Arielle couldn't believe how dark her thoughts had turned in such a short time. What in bloody hell was going on in her head?

"I see this going to a very bad place," she heard Eva say. "He seems like the devil to me," she added.

At those words, Gabrielle sprang from her seat. "No!" she exclaimed. She looked frantic, her eyes darting about as if she were trapped and wanted to escape. "You are wrong!" she said. "He is a very nice guy, he's just... just..." Then she stopped talking again and started looking around the room as if she were afraid of someone or something.

"He's just what, Gabby? Come out with it, he's just what? And what are you looking for? There is no one here but the three of us," Arielle said. She reached out toward Gabby and made her sit back down.

But Gabby just stared at the floor, refusing to utter a single word. Eva and Arielle knew they weren't going to let Gabrielle go anywhere that night, not until they knew what was going on between her and Marcus.

Then Gabrielle's phone rang, and she reached for it, but Arielle took it right out of her hands. She saw Marcus's name on the screen, and she let it ring until it stopped. Gabrielle gazed at her, totally dismayed. As her eyes welled up with tears, she took a few deep breaths.

"Gabby, I'm going to call your father right now," Arielle said. She took a deep breath and then added. "I think we should have him come over and see if he can get something out of you. As we have said before, we see this thing going to a very bad place for you. We're scared, Gabby."

"No, please don't get my dad involved," Gabrielle said. "I don't want my family mixed up in this."

"You don't want them mixed up in...what...Gabby? What is going on?"

Gabrielle glared at both of them with a wild look in her eyes. She made hard fists and began pounding on the sofa and mumbling something.

"We can't understand you, Gabby, what are you saying?" Eva asked.

Suddenly she stopped pounding on the sofa. She sat up straight, looked at them defiantly, and said, "Marcus is a warlock." She annunciated her words very distinctly as if Arielle and Eva were small children incapable of understanding.

Arielle gasped in horror and stood up, feeling sick to her stomach, and clenching her fists by her side. Eva, clearly overtaken with shock, let out a soft cry. Then all three sat there in stunned silence.

She wasn't sure how long they stayed that way, but after a while Arielle realized that she was pressing her lips together, trying to stop herself from screaming. Eva was gasping for air and murmuring over and over again, "I knew it…I knew it…"

"I'm scared," Gabrielle murmured. "I don't know how to tell him that I don't want to be involved in witchcraft." She started crying softly.

"What are you doing when you spend time with him?"

Gabrielle wiped her tears, took a deep breath, and then told her story.

"Ever since we played with the Ouija board that night I got curious about this kind of thing," she said. "I told Marcus about playing with the Ouija board, and about Eva, and about that night, we went to the cemetery. He didn't seem at all surprised. In fact, he said that he would like to expose me to bigger and better things. So I went to a few séances with him and his friends, and watched him contact the other side." She sighed deeply, shook her head as if experiencing everything all over again. Then she continued, "He told me that these spirits are good – not demonic or possessive. They just try to use him as a port to communicate with loved ones who are still here."

Arielle was biting her lower lip so hard that she was sure she had bitten through the first layer because it became painful.

"What else has he told you?" she asked with a quivering voice.

"He said that he has to sacrifice animals to his master to make sure he keeps his powers."

At this revelation, they gasped in shock. In fact, they were beyond shocked, they were scared to death. How had Gabby gotten involved with someone like Marcus?

"What else did he say, and what else has he done?" Eva asked.

"He told me that he has been crowned a master. One night while he was in a trance he took all six of us to the cemetery, where he brought back several spirits and they talked. I couldn't understand what they were saying – it was all noises and mingled voices full of anguish and cries of despair. Pretty eerie, but intriguing." She got that scary, faraway look in her eyes again. Then she said, "I want to stop. It's overwhelming me. But I do feel a strange pull toward Marcus and his world that I can't seem to resist."

"Do you love him?" Arielle asked her. Gabrielle didn't reply, she just sobbed. "Come on, Gabby. Do you love him?" she pressed.

Gabby looked as if she was pondering the question in her mind for a short time. Then, blinded by tears, she replied. "No, I really don't believe that I love him," she said. "I think he is fascinating. But no, I don't love him."

"Then you need to stay away from him. He is definitely the wrong person for you," Eva said.

"She's right, Gabby," Arielle said as she saw Gabrielle hesitate. "And he will control you as long as you let your curiosity take over your spirit." She picked up Gabrielle's phone and handed it to her. "Please call Marcus and tell him you've changed your mind, and you're not going out tonight."

Gabrielle nodded assent, and reached for her phone. Eva and Arielle walked to the other end of the room so she could make her call with some privacy, but they remained close enough to make sure that she didn't change her mind. It seemed that he tried to talk her into going out with him, but she held her ground, and insisted that she was going to stay home.

"He will use his power to make her go back to him," Eva whispered.

"We need to help her break away from him," Arielle said in a low voice. "Let's see what Robert finds out, and in the meantime, we've got to keep a close eye on her."

Gabrielle got off the phone and went to take a shower. They were quiet until they heard the water running. "I wonder what Marcus's obsession with Gabrielle is all about. What if he is using her for some journey into the otherworld?" Eva murmured.

Arielle's mind was trying to grasp what Eva might mean by or about the otherworld. "What do you think he wants her for?" she asked.

"Well, if he is a master warlock he must be devoted to a God, who is most likely terrifying to a normal person like you and me. But to him, it is his source of power, and he uses that power for dark and mysterious practices." Eva paused, trying to remember everything she knew about warlocks. "I read that they are usually after the soul," she said. "Which of course has everything a person could ever need. If you lose your soul, you lose yourself. He has to give his god a gift to appease him to receive his superhuman powers," she continued.

"What kind of a gift?"

"All the books say that sacrifices are the only gifts that please these gods. They could be human, they could be animals."

Arielle's heart was hammering in her chest as fear paralyzed every part of her body. Eva kept talking, as if she were in a trance, and as she talked she continued flipping through the pages of a horror book.

"Eva, stop!" Arielle begged at last. "You're freaking me out, I'm not going to be able to sleep tonight. Let's see what Robert finds out about Marcus before we make this a much bigger deal than it really is."

Eva looked at her in surprise, wondering what could be so scary.

"I've got to go to bed," Arielle said. "I can't stand to think about this anymore tonight."

Around two o'clock in the morning, she heard a knock at the front door. She jumped out of bed and ran into the living room, where she found Eva. Gabrielle's room was in the back of the flat. Apparently she hadn't heard anything.

"Did you hear that?" Arielle whispered.

"Yes, I did. There's someone at the door," Eva said in a murmur.

Holding hands, they walked toward the door and didn't turn the light on.

"Who is it?" she asked softly.

"It's me, Marcus," a voice said from outside. Instinctively, they pulled themselves closer together.

"What do you want?" Eva said. She made her voice sound as stern as she could while trying not to wake Gabrielle.

"I need to talk to Gabrielle."

"She's not here," Arielle lied. "She's spending the night at her parents' house."

"Okay, thanks," he replied. His voice was soft with not a hint of anger. They heard a car door slam, a car pulling away, then complete quiet.

"What in bloody hell did he want at this hour?"

"I don't know, but I'm glad you said that," Eva said. "Now we have to tell Gabby in the morning to make sure we're not caught in the lie."

They went back to bed but it took a long time for Arielle to get back to sleep, and when she slept it was restless.

In the morning Gabby was still there, and seeming a bit more like her old self. They told her what had happened the night before. She agreed to cover their lie, and promised to stay away from Marcus for a couple of days, telling him that her parents needed her at home.

To their relief, Marcus seemed to believe her story and didn't make any trouble for Gabrielle. They ran into him a few times, and he was very polite when he saw them. But every time they saw him they felt that same clutch of cold fear and that same uneasiness about his character.

Three days later, when Robert called them, he said he had some information to share with them, and asked them to meet him at his place that afternoon.

Gabrielle's car was still at her parents' house from the previous day, so they dropped her off there and told her they would call her a little bit later. "Please, Gabby, *do not* go out with Marcus until we talk to you again," Eva said. "Give us at least until this evening. After that, we will leave you alone, and you can do whatever you want to do."

Gabrielle agreed to their request. They left her at the door and could see how happy her mother was to see her as she waved to them and they drove away. When they arrived at Robert's flat, he met them at the door, and they were hardly inside before he started talking. "You are not going to believe this at all," he said. His face was flustered, and his voice was very disturbed.

"What is it, Robert?" Arielle said.

"Well, I found a few stories about things happening in the area about four years ago, and Marcus is in the middle of all of them. He was a junior in secondary school when all of this took place."

They took the newspaper articles he was holding out toward them and started to read aloud. As Eva read, Arielle sank onto the sofa in utter dismay.

> *"The Sussex authorities have discovered the body of the missing secondary school student, Alice Norwell, buried in a shallow grave in Preston Park. They fear it is the work of a cult group called Dark Shadows. They believe the girl was used as a human sacrifice as her heart was missing. Four teenagers have been arrested and charged with murder. Charges were filed*

this morning against the leader of the cult, Marcus Fairchild."

Both girls jumped with fright and began to gasp for air as they read Marcus's name. The names of the other three cult members were also printed in bold letters, but they didn't recognize any of those names.

Eva picked up another article and began to read.

"This morning the district attorney announced that the cult group Dark Shadows is believed to be responsible for three other murders of young women in the past four years. Their leader, Marcus Fairchild, is being held without bond in the city jail."

Arielle was now barely breathing as overwhelming thoughts were invading her head. Her whole body felt sick inside, and she suddenly didn't know whether she was going to pass out or vomit. Suddenly she stood up and ran to the bathroom.

When she came back out, Eva was talking quietly with Robert. They both seemed to be very disturbed. They turned towards her as she stood there completely lost for words.

"Arielle, you really need to see this one as well," Robert said. He handed her another article. She sat down again, dry mouthed. She could feel her heart hammering within, pulverizing her chest. Eva sat next to her, trembling, they both looked at the article. This time, they read silently.

"The prosecutor did not have any witnesses and could not hold the charges against Marcus Fairchild. The other three cult members were interrogated separately; they all accused each other in an attempt to receive lighter sentences. They were questioned about their leader, but they never accused Marcus of any wrongdoing. The authorities and the prosecutor believe beyond any doubt that Marcus Fairchild is the person that ordered the sacrifices, they had to release him due to lack of evidence against him. They have advised young ladies in the area to be very careful in their associations with cult members."

The last line of the article stated that cult members never accuse their masters of wrongdoing, as they are afraid of repercussions by devotees of these satanic beliefs.

Arielle and Eva were both completely stunned. They leaned as far back as the sofa would allow as if they had been pinned to the back of it by the weight of what they had just learned.

"I truly believe this guy is guilty of those crimes," Robert said. "But his followers have protected him. I would suggest that you keep Gabrielle away from him by telling her the complete truth." His voice was very calm and soothing. Seeing how upset they both were, he came over and sat between them, putting his arms around them.

"Robert, can we ask her to come here to talk, in case of Marcus comes over to our flat again before we have a chance to talk with her?" Eva asked.

"Sure, go ahead," Robert said. "Let's do it now and get this over with."

Rising to her feet Eva faced both of them for a couple of minutes, then started to pace back and forth. Finally, she leaned against the doorframe, and they heard her shaking voice, eager and anxious.

"This man has broken the most fundamental human law by taking a life," she said. "It's terrifying to think that Gabrielle could have been his next victim."

As Eva spoke, Arielle squeezed Robert's hand, feeling fear and a pang in her gut. Robert's blue eyes were meeting hers, and he tightened his hold on her.

"It'll all workout, Arielle, trust me," he said. "Call Gabrielle and I'll be here with you both when she reads these articles." His mouth was slightly lifted in a soft, assuring smile.

Feeling a bit nervous, Arielle picked up her phone and called Gabrielle, who answered on the first ring.

"Hi Gabby, can you come over to Robert's place?" she said, trying to keep her voice from shaking. "It's very important," she added.

"I'll be there shortly," Gabrielle said. "Is everything all right?"

"Yes, we're fine," Arielle said, not exactly answering her friend's question. "But we really need to show you something."

"See you in a few," she said, and the phone went dead.

Twenty minutes later she walked through Robert's door with a wide smile on her face, looking just as beautiful as ever. There was nothing about her to show either stress or anxiety as if everything in the world was in its perfect place.

"Hey there, what's up?" she said, greeting Robert as she came in, and looking over at Eva and Arielle, who were sitting on the sofa. "Why the long faces?"

"Gabrielle," Robert said, "We wanted to show you something and maybe talk about it for a little while. You should probably sit down."

Gabrielle sat down in the chair across the table from them, her face full of anticipation. Robert handed her the first article, and she started to read quietly. It was a short article, but it seemed to take a long time for her to look up or say anything. Arielle was sure she had finished reading.

Next Robert handed her the other two articles. She took them from him with shaking hands and without looking up. She read each one of them slowly and shuffled them back and forth as if she wanted to read them over and over again. They were watching her carefully and suddenly it happened.

Her head fell forward, and her hands fell to her sides, the articles spilling to the floor. She had blacked out. They ran to her, laid her on the sofa while Robert brought a wet towel to wipe her face.

"Gabby…Gabby…" Arielle whispered close to her ear as she shook her slightly.

Gabby opened her eyes and looked around, completely disoriented. Arielle helped her sit up, and Gabrielle moved her gaze between the three of them as if she were trying to remember what had happened, and finally her eyes stopped at the newspaper articles spread across the floor. Her body went rigid as she started to hyperventilate and her eyes looked pinched as if she were in physical pain.

Eva moved first and sat down next to Gabrielle, putting her arm around her shoulders, looking helplessly frustrated. Robert and Arielle sat down across from Gabrielle, who remained perfectly still for a few long moments.

"Oh my God," she murmured. She seemed to be in absolute shock, but clearly was beginning to get a grasp of the information contained in the documents. Suddenly her shoulders began to shake as she started sobbing and gasping violently. They all remained silent, letting her cry the stress out of her system. Eva took her hand and held it, stroking her comfortingly on her back.

Finally, Gabrielle looked up and glanced at the three of them quickly. Obviously, she was wondering what to do next.

"Gabby, are you all right?" Arielle asked.

Gabby took another deep breath and tried to smile, but it turned out to be a poor attempt.

"Well, I'm sickened by what I've read," she said. She stopped for a second or two before continuing in a shaky voice. "And I can't believe I used such poor judgment when it came to Marcus. I guess I was mesmerized by his looks. When I think that something like that could have happened to me…" Her voice trailed off, and she broke once again into soft sobbing. Then suddenly, as if she had just thought of it, she looked at them with panic in her eyes. "How am I going break up with him without letting him know that I found out about his past history?" she asked.

"Just tell him the truth," Arielle said. "You'll soon be leaving on holiday, and you aren't sure when you'll be coming back," she said. "Have you made any commitments to him at all?"

"No," Gabrielle said quickly. "We have just been dating but nothing serious. And sometimes we kiss, but nothing more." She took another deep breath and seemed to be calming down a bit. "There may be something of an issue with him since he has exposed me to his otherworld. But thank God I've not seen anything really bad."

"Just tell him you're not interested in those activities any longer," Eva advised.

To their relief, it seemed that the shock of what she'd learned had brought Gabrielle back to her normal self. She had been informed about the truth, and she was going to do the right thing. They told her they would be there to support her when she informed Marcus of her decision. Robert offered to be there as well in case she needed his help.

They knew now they couldn't trust Marcus and his friends. So the plan was to let him know that if he didn't go away quietly and leave Gabrielle alone, they would expose him to the authorities.

 *Chapter 7*

AN FEW DAYS LATER on a Friday, early in the afternoon after class, Gabrielle approached Marcus in front of the library. Eva, Arielle, and Robert stayed hidden behind a building, watching as he reached to embrace her and she pulled away. He looked shocked, and they couldn't hear the conversation that ensued, but it lasted quite a long time. At one point they could see that Gabby tried to move away from him, and he locked his arm around her wrist, but she twisted away and told him something that made him step back and agree to whatever she was saying.

Even from a distance they could clearly see that his face looked cold as a statue, but it appeared that Gabrielle was holding firm, and they were so proud of her. Arielle reached over and squeezed Eva's hand, and they shared an excited smile. Then Gabrielle turned around and walked away as Marcus stood watching her until he couldn't see her any longer. She walked around the corner of the building where they were all waiting, smiling, looking happy and relieved.

"So, what happened? Tell us!" Arielle practically squeaked.

"I just told him I didn't want to be around him and his friends any longer, that they scared me. First, he said he loved me, and he didn't want me to leave him, but when I told him I didn't love him, that's when he got nasty. He started threatening me, telling me I'd be sorry, in a very scary way. So then I told him that I knew about his past and that I had spoken to my father about it. And that my father would be willing to reopen his case and expose him if anything ever happened to me. He looked shocked and upset, but he backed off immediately and said that he wouldn't want to keep me if I didn't want to be with him."

Gabrielle turned to look at Robert. She held his gaze for a short moment and then, reaching out, she put her arms around him and gave him a warm hug.

"Thank you so much, Robert," she whispered. "I'll never forget what you did for me."

In reply he just smiled, squeezed her warmly, and gave her a peck on the cheek. "What are friends for?" he asked, putting on his most charming smile.

"Well, I think if you don't need me any longer, I'll just leave you girls here," he said.

"Thanks again, Robert," Arielle and Eva said simultaneously. "We owe you big time!"

"I'll see you later," he called out, grinning happily as he walked away.

Arielle needed to check out a book from the library for next week's test, so Gabrielle and Eva waited for her as she went inside.

"Gabby, Marcus is a liar," Eva said in a low voice. "He doesn't love you, he doesn't know how to love. You were just a simple conquest. His eyes are impassive, and his heart is cold. He doesn't have the ability to love anyone but his Satan god." Gabrielle winced at the sound of Eva's unyielding voice.

"He is a murderer," Eva added. "He'll find someone else to take your place, and we need to stop him." She gave Gabby a meaningful look as she added, "You must take this to your father and the authorities."

Gabrielle looked like she was considering Eva's request. She looked down at her feet, her fingers moving idly back and forth on the cover of a book in her arms. Finally, she looked up into Eva's eyes. "I'm afraid to tell my father about this," she said, and her expression grew worried.

"You need to forget about your fears, Gabby, you *must* do the right thing," Eva said. "Gabby, people like Marcus never rest until they accomplish what they are after."

Gabrielle exhaled several times in sheer frustration. Then she finally nodded, forcing a smile.

"All right, I'll do it, but I want you to be with me when I tell him."

"Gabby, you are not the bad person here – Marcus is," Eva reminded her in a voice that was soft and loving.

Arielle came back with her book tucked under her arm. Immediately she noticed Gabrielle's tense expression. "What's going on?" she asked.

"We're going to see Gabrielle's father," Eva said firmly.

"Great!" Arielle said, pleased to hear the news. Eva handed Gabrielle her phone before she had a chance to change her mind.

"Call your father and find out if we can go to his office right now," she urged. Gabrielle took the phone and thoughtfully keyed her father's number.

The receptionist answered. "Dr. Taylor's office."

"Hi Stephanie, this is Gabrielle. Can I speak to my father please?"

"Hello, Gabrielle," Stephanie said pleasantly. "Your father is with a patient right now. Is this important?"

"Yes, please tell him that I need to see him as soon as possible. It's urgent!"

"Hold for a moment," Stephanie said. Gabrielle waited nervously, biting her nails and glancing between Eva and Arielle. Then Stephanie was back on the phone.

"Your father will see you as soon as you can get here."

"Thank you, I'm on my way." Gabrielle pressed the end button and handed it back to Eva.

"Okay, let's go before I lose my nerve," she said.

They went down the steps in a hurry, and got into the car before she could finish her sentence.

"Gosh," they heard her murmur.

"What is it, Gabby?" Eva asked.

"My father will be bloody livid!" she said with a nervous chuckle.

"Rubbish," Arielle said. "It'll be alright. What you're about to do is the right thing.

"I know that I'm doing the right thing, but I'm still scared about telling my father the details," she said with a trembling voice. "He'll be awfully disappointed in me." She swallowed hard.

Arielle reached over and took her hand. "We're going to be by your side," she said.

"Sometimes it's not easy to do the right thing, but it still needs to be done, for your sake and others," Eva encouraged her.

Arielle couldn't stop thinking about the girls that had been Marcus's victims in the past.

When they arrived at Dr. Taylor's office, Gabrielle had a hard time getting out of the car. She was fearful of her father's wrath for attending those rituals and involving herself knowingly with a warlock. Dr. Taylor welcomed the girls in his office with a wide smile on his kind face and asked them to sit down.

"What a wonderful surprise!" he said. "How was school today?"

"Fine," they all answered in unison.

"So what brings you this way?" he asked.

"I needed to talk to you, Daddy," Gabrielle said in a quivering voice.

He was now watching her carefully. He stood up and walked around his desk and stood in front of Gabrielle. "What's the matter, pumpkin? Don't you feel well?"

"I'm fine, Daddy, but I have something dreadful to tell you, and I'm scared." His face grew concerned.

"What is it, Gabby? You know I'm always here for you. You don't have to be scared of me," he said nervously. He paused for a long moment and then slowly he asked, "Is it about a boy?"

"Yes, sir," she replied, very close to bursting into tears.

His face turned pale and his eyes narrowed watching Gabrielle intently. He tried to keep his voice low and calm and asked, carefully annunciating each word, "*Are you pregnant*?"

"No!" she exclaimed in utter shock, her cheeks suddenly flushing red.

His face showed visible relief, but he was still concerned. "Well then, it can't be that bad, can it?" he said. Gabrielle gulped and then, taking a deep breath, she went into the ugly details of her experiences with Marcus. Arielle watched Dr. Taylor's face change as Gabby spoke. He looked like he might go into utter shock.

He remained silent, listening to Gabrielle without interrupting. He seemed to be lost in thought as Gabrielle went on to explain what Robert had found in the old newspapers about Marcus. As he listened, he frowned, rubbed his temples, and shook his head. The thought that his beloved daughter had been engaged in something so bizarre and frightening was difficult for him to absorb.

After she finished speaking Gabrielle bowed her head for a moment.

Then she looked up at her father apprehensively, jaw set and lips tight.

Finally, he coughed and cleared his throat. "Well, we have to go to the authorities," he finally said, standing up, and added, "You did the right thing coming to me. You have no idea the horrible memories you've brought back into my mind. I have a vivid memory about this incident. I remember the distraught faces of the unfortunate parents of the girls that were missing. I remember your mother and I feeling extreme anguish for those poor girls and their families, and…" He didn't finish his sentence. Turning towards Gabrielle, he stared at her in sheer horror. "Good God, child! You could have been his next victim!"

He reached for Gabrielle, and she fell into his arms, breaking into tears. He held her tightly and ran his hand up and down her hair, caressing his only daughter with love and understanding. "You girls are going with me to the police station right now. You'll have to provide the police officers with all the information that you have so far." They nodded in agreement as he walked back to his desk and pressed the intercom. "Stephanie, please cancel my last appointment. I've got an emergency I have to deal with." Then he picked up his coat, and they were on their way.

The police station was buzzing with people. Dr. Taylor walked to the front desk with the girls on his heels. To the officer at the desk, he explained the purpose of their visit, and they saw the constable's surprised look. He immediately picked up the phone, said something inaudible, and in a very short time, a man in plainclothes appeared at a side door. He looked at the constable, who pointed in Dr. Taylor's direction with a very serious look on his face.

The man approached Dr. Taylor with a brief smile, extended his hand, and introduced himself as Inspector Thornton. "Are you here about the Marcus Fairchild case?" he asked, and Dr. Taylor nodded. The inspector looked at the three girls, nodded at them with a soft smile, and then asked them to follow him to the back. They walked through a couple of long hallways and reached a door that displayed the sign "Chief Inspector."

The inspector stopped and knocked firmly. "Come in," said a

strong, deep voice. The detective pushed the door open and stepped aside to let them in.

As they crossed the doorway, they saw an older man with silver hair and a kind face sitting behind a desk filled with piles of papers. He lifted his head as they entered and stood up. He reached out to shake Dr. Taylor's hand, introducing himself as Chief Inspector Conway. He invited them to sit down, pointing at the chairs in front of his desk as Thornton walked over and stood by the chief's desk. When they were seated, he gazed at the three girls with clear interest, and finally, his eyes rested on Dr. Taylor.

"How can we help you?" he asked in a gentle voice.

Eva's father handed him the newspaper clippings and told Gabrielle's story in detail. The more he talked, the more Conway seemed to be absorbed. When he was finished, there was a deafening silence for a short period as the officers exchanged meaningful glances.

Finally, Conway spoke. "You have no idea, young lady, how very lucky you are," he said, looking at Gabrielle, who was visibly nervous.

"The information you see here," he said, shifting the clippings between his hands, "is a couple of years old. However, there have been four more similar disappearances of young ladies your age that we have tried to keep quiet to avoid panic from spreading across campus." His eyes were narrowed to slits, but he was now smiling in pure satisfaction. "I've been after that bloody son of a bitch for five years, and I haven't been able to get one little thing on him, but now I've got him!" He pounded his fist on the desk in a clear sign of gratification.

"I'll need you to show me the places they hold those meetings and the places he and his friends frequent. We'll set up surveillance, and we'll catch them in the act. We'll finally round up the whole dirty bunch; this time, he isn't going anywhere. I am determined to give justice to all those poor parents that had to bury their young daughters," he said, adding a curse under his breath. "Thank you so much for bringing this to our attention," he finished, and stood up, extending his hand toward Dr. Taylor and shaking it with clear pleasure. "And you... thank you, young lady, for having the courage to tell your father," he said, turning toward Gabrielle.

Gabrielle turned to smile at her best friends.

They left the police department pleased. Marcus was a murderer, and he was going to pay for his crimes. Chief Conway now had all the information he needed to follow the activities of Marcus and his followers, bring them to justice and put them away where they couldn't hurt another soul.

"I just can't believe I got caught up in his world," Gabrielle murmured as they left the police station. "I never thought of what the consequences might be. Thank you so much," she whispered, embracing Arielle and Eva one at a time.

Dr. Taylor embraced his daughter warmly and planted a huge kiss on her forehead. "I'll be home for dinner tomorrow night, Daddy," Gabrielle said as he dropped them off at their car back in his parking lot.

"Come and visit soon," he said, extending his gaze to Eva and Arielle. "Mrs. Taylor will love to see you."

"Thank you," Eva and Arielle replied in unison, and Dr. Taylor went back into his office.

"Well, now we can go back to our normal lives," Eva said as they reached out and hugged each other one more time before piling into the car.

"I'm sure that it'll take some time to feel really normal again, but for a start, why don't we go out with our friends and have some fun?" Arielle said. She was overwhelmed with relief that Gabrielle was out of Marcus's reach.

Later in the evening, they went back to their flat, poured three glasses of wine and sat around the front room together. They laughed and talked, just as they used to do in the days before Marcus. To them, it seemed a perfect ending to a perfect day.

The next day Paul called and asked Arielle if he could come over. Gabrielle and Eva had decided to go out, and since Arielle had a little studying to do, she had stayed behind.

About half an hour later, Paul showed up at their door. He looked excited and anxious to talk. *What could it be?* She wondered. Paul was studying archeology and she always enjoyed sitting with him and listening to the wonderful stories he had to tell about the exciting, far-away places that he was going to visit when he completed his studies. But this time something in his manner made her think it wasn't archeology he wanted to talk about.

"Can we talk?" he asked in a low voice as he came into the flat.

"Sure," she said smiling. "Come on in." She waved toward the sofa. "Is there something wrong?" she asked.

"No, there is nothing wrong," he said, "but I'd like to talk to you about something that is pretty important to me. Are you alone?"

"Yes," she replied, a bit confused.

He stopped and looked away from her as if he were wondering whether to continue with what he had to say. Finally, he took a deep breath, and then said, "Arielle, it's very difficult for me to convey to you how I feel. So I hope that you will just listen to me and not take lightly anything I'm going to say."

Now she was worried. She thought maybe something terrible had happened. Still, she told him with a smile that she was listening.

He took her hands in his and pressed them softly. When he spoke again his voice sounded worried. "I've tried so hard to hide my feelings," he said. "I was afraid that I might destroy our friendship. I've desperately fought the desire to talk to you about what I'm about to say, and I've lost the battle."

He put his arm around her and drew her close. "I'm desperately and utterly in love with you," he said quickly, afraid that he might lose his nerve.

Arielle was speechless. She tried to say something, but she couldn't think of a single thing to say.

Then Paul kissed her, and she felt a sudden desire sweep over her. But it was gone just as quickly as it had come. She could see the sincerity in his eyes and she knew that he genuinely meant what he had said.

"Paul, I love you to death," she said, finally. "But not in the same way. I don't want to hurt you, and I don't want to lose you as a friend. I love you. But I'm not in love with you."

She watched his face change as he pulled away and looked back at her, hurt in his eyes. She started to say something, but he stopped her.

"You're not going to lose me," he said in a soft, husky voice that she could barely hear. "I'll always be here for you, Arielle. I love you unconditionally, and I don't expect anything in return." His voice barely a whisper, he added, "I thought you might have the same feeling for me, so I decided to talk to you about it."

"Paul, please forgive me," she said. "I didn't know. I had no idea!"

"There is nothing to forgive," he said with a soft smile, and as he said it he touched her cheek tenderly. "You will always be my number one girl."

"Thanks Paul," she said, daring to chuckle. "You know, you'll always be my number one guy as well."

And what she said was true. She couldn't imagine being any fonder of anyone. They looked at each other and laughed softly.

"You're an incredible girl," he said.

"You know, Paul," she said, "though I can't return the same kind of love to you, I want you to know how important you are to me." Then she hugged him warmly.

He stayed for a little while longer but soon decided that it was probably time for him to be going home. "I hope this doesn't make it awkward between the two of us," he said. "I mean, you know. I hope it doesn't damage our friendship."

"Don't worry about that," she said. "I don't think there's anything you could do to make me not want to be your friend. We're going to be okay," she said. She knew that seeing him around would only intensify the pain for him, but she just couldn't cut him out of her life.

Arielle had been looking for the kind of love she had been reading about in her favorite books: *Pride and Prejudice, Romeo and Juliet, Wuthering Heights.* And she had always wondered if she would ever find her Mr. Darcy or her Heathcliff. Paul was wonderful as a friend, but he just didn't fit the blueprint of a soul mate.

It was coming to feel like a more and more remote possibility. But she knew that what she wanted was to find someone who would make her feel the way Liz Bennet felt for Mr. Darcy. She knew it was a dream, but for right now she knew she had to hang on to that dream.

Chapter 8

> *I am so happy to be back in St. Jean de Luz. There is something magical about this place. It may be just the sheer beauty of it all; then again it may be the incredible warmth that surrounds our family when we are here. Everything around us is so serene and so comforting: amazing white-sand beaches, crystal-clear ocean, and wonderful weather. My parents enjoy taking long walks through the beautiful gardens, admiring the splendor of it all. There are days that the three of us take drives down to the beach to admire the beautiful sunsets, and on the way, we take pleasure from the wonderful lush greenery and cascading waterfalls. I am trying to enjoy as much time as I can with my parents because I know my life will be changing once I am out of school.*

That was what Arielle wrote in her journal in the first few days of her summer holiday back in the South of France. She was so happy to be there again!

This time, she visited several bookstores in town and purchased some compelling new novels to get lost in while sitting by the pool or the ocean. Her iPod was loaded with music by her favorite bands. Each and every morning she headed to the beach or the pool with her beach bag.

Almost two months later, she was still totally unsuccessful in getting the perfect tan, but she wasn't giving up. She was going to forgo the pool and head to the beach with the sole purpose of achieving her goal, a nice dark tan.

What she loved most about being in the South of France was that when they were there, she spent most of her time alone. It was wonderful to have peace and quiet with no thoughts and no worries that belonged to other people.

This was the year she was turning twenty-one, and little did she know it would also be one of those summer holidays in which her life would take an unexpected turn into the unknown.

One Monday morning, about two weeks before their holiday was to end, she woke up feeling exceptionally well rested. She decided to enjoy staying in bed just a little while longer. She closed her eyes again and tried to plan her day. Maybe she would lie on the beach, maybe she would do a little shopping, and maybe she would call Margaret, one of her summertime friends, to have lunch at one of those little sidewalk cafés on the boardwalk.

When she opened her eyes again, the sun was shining through the slats in the blinds. She got out of bed and pulled the blinds up, flooding the room with sunlight. She put on her little blue bathing suit, grabbed her beach towel, and headed outside to find that it was a glorious, sunny day.

The sun kissed her skin, and she felt the kind of warmth that automatically makes you feel happy. She smiled to herself as she got into the car and drove to the beach.

Several people had already placed their beach chairs, blankets, and beach towels, and had claimed spots as close to the water as they could. Children were running, laughing, and splashing in the ocean without a care in the world. There were several guys sitting on their surfboards, waiting to catch a wave. The place was just dripping with charm.

She decided to take a walk along the beach. Digging her toes into the warm white sand, she looked for a familiar spot, away from all these people whose thoughts she could hear. She was desperate to get away from them.

As she walked by one lady, she could hear her thinking, *I wish I could be on a cruise ship with a gorgeous looking man and a cool martini in my hand, rather than being here running after these darned kids.* She put her head down as she walked past so the lady couldn't see the smile she was suppressing.

She walked for a while longer and finally came to a lovely, quiet cove. No one else was there. It was perfect. She spread her beach towel on the soft sand and took her iPod out of her bag. She plugged her headphones in and, turning the music on, she lay down and closed her eyes, hoping to spend a couple of peaceful hours there listening to her favorite music.

She had only been there for a few minutes when she had a strong feeling that she was being watched. She sat up and took a careful look all around, but she couldn't see anyone nearby, or anyone looking at her. The feeling that she was being watched was unbelievably intense. She lay back down and closed her eyes. She was hoping that today she might *finally* get a tan.

The next time she opened her eyes she realized that she had fallen asleep. Integral by Pet Shop Boys was playing through the headphones. Arielle sat up slowly, reached for her iPod, and shut it off. She looked around and noticed that the beach was completely empty. The sun was going down, and the water had lost its bright blue color. Now it looked dark and uninviting. She pulled the headphones out of her ears and threw them into her beach bag along with her iPod and the unused tanning lotion. She rose to her feet, took another look around, and decided that it was time to head home. She bent over, picked up her beach bag, and threw it over her shoulder. With the other hand, she picked up the corner of the beach towel and turned around to shake the sand off.

She was panicked when her eyes fell on a young man standing about ten feet away from her with a soft smile on his face. She felt a strong sudden jolt course through her body and fear overcame her. She couldn't imagine where he had come from or how she could have missed seeing him standing so close.

He was shockingly beautiful as if he had jumped out of the pages of a fashion magazine. He was tall and thin with broad shoulders, a muscular body, light, sandy hair, and the most captivating, intense green eyes she had ever seen. His features were flawless. His lips were sensuous, beautifully curved into a soft smile, showing a set of perfectly white teeth. He was wearing a pair of jeans and a light blue shirt open in the front, revealing his muscular chest. She felt an unusual shiver slide across her muscles. She stared at him and quickly swallowed. She wondered how long she had been standing there watching him, completely mesmerized, when his voice made her jump.

"*Bonjour!*" he said, his lips curved slightly.

Her throat suddenly felt swollen. She realized she was completely alone on the beach with a stranger. Not a good situation.

As she started to speak their eyes met, and immediately her mind went blank. She felt a jolt that made her body quiver, and extreme heat surged through her veins. She was in a complete fog with absolutely no clear thoughts at all. Time stopped as their gazes locked, and a strange sensation coursed across every muscle, intensifying the heat that was already enveloping her. She had absolutely no idea how long she stood there gazing into his eyes. When she finally decided to move, she felt off-balance, frozen in place. What a strange feeling! She didn't remember ever having had such a reaction to any other human being. The man was so beautiful that she didn't have the strength to take her eyes off of his face.

She tried to collect her thoughts and act normal, but she didn't seem to be able to do that as long as their eyes were engaged. It took every ounce of strength she possessed to finally drag her gaze away. She inhaled deeply and tried to act as if the sight of him was not absolutely turning her body and mind upside down.

Strangely, after the initial shock of seeing him, she didn't feel fear, though in an abstract way she was aware that she was in a dangerous situation. It was a very odd feeling. She still felt a bit guarded, not knowing what he could possibly want from her, or how long he had been standing there looking at her. There was something about his eyes that dazzled her so that she had to look away from his face until his soft, beautiful voice filled her ears and made her look at him again.

"I'm sorry," he said, still in French. "It looks as if I have startled you and that was not my intention. I live here a great part of the year and I have never seen you on this beach."

He was startled with the sudden passion that surged through every muscle in his body as his gaze examined Arielle's undeniable appeal. She was absolutely gorgeous. Tall and lean with beautiful long legs, an intoxicating body in that barely-there, little blue bikini, and that amazing face. She was the absolute definition of *his* perfect woman. Her lips were alluring, sensual, luscious, and the sight of them was dangerously arousing to him. He drew a deep breath and locked his gaze on hers.

Arielle blinked, swallowed hard, and forced herself to look away, averting her gaze down to her feet, unable to speak. What in the world was happening to her? She was acting like a complete moron! And then she realized she hadn't been able to make out a single word he had said after the words "I'm sorry…"

As she started to regain her composure she looked up to make sure that he was still there. It only took a second as their eyes engaged one more time; then she lost control of herself again. She felt like she was suffocating and she couldn't utter a single word. In a flash, she realized that he had some power in his eyes that was affecting her in a very strange way.

She drew a deep breath and with a great force of determination, yanked her eyes away from his mouth-watering body and his gorgeous face. She was sure that every time she looked into his emerald eyes she wouldn't be able to act like a normal human being.

Then she heard his beautiful voice again. And she thought she also heard a faint chuckle. "Did you just move here or are you here on holiday?" he asked. He was still speaking in French, but Arielle was fluent in the language, so she completely understood every word he was saying. She was sure he would notice how nervous she was, but she didn't care at this point.

"My parents have a summer home not far from this beach. We have spent our summer holidays here ever since I was born," she said in English.

"You're English!" he said, in perfect English, excitement in his voice. She nodded quietly.

"You said you have been coming here ever since you were born, how long is that?" he asked with amusement in his voice.

"Twenty years," she said with a soft smile.

"I wonder how I never noticed you before," he said. "You are very beautiful!" Then his lips curved appreciatively.

She wanted to tell him that she had never thought of herself as very beautiful, but she just smiled shyly and said, "I come to the beach quite often."

He didn't seem to be one of the people who belonged to that special place in her head as she had no idea what he was thinking or what he wanted from her.

"What's your name?" he asked in his soft, velvety voice.

"Arielle," she replied. She knew her voice was breaking, and she was sure he noticed, since he smiled, never taking his eyes off of her.

"Well, I really must be going," she said, as she began to move away from him so that she could shake the beach towel in the opposite direction. That is when she lost her balance and started to fall. She never saw him move toward her, but suddenly his arms were wrapped tightly around her, and their bodies softly collided against each other as he caught her. How could he have moved so fast?

But she dismissed the question as soon as she felt his warm, perfect body against hers. Her heartbeat accelerated, and her pulse hammered in her veins as her mind focused on the closeness of his body to hers. It was an emotion unlike any she had ever experienced before in her whole life. She closed her eyes for a moment, and she suddenly felt she wanted to stay like that, in his arms forever. He didn't seem in a hurry to let her go, and she didn't make a move to leave his arms.

When she opened her eyes again, his beautiful face was only inches away from hers. She began to fall apart again as their eyes were locked, and she would have dropped to the sand if he weren't holding her tight. Every bit of her existence wanted to stay in his arms for the rest of her life. His face was magical. His lips were partly open with that fantastic smile, and all she wanted to do was lean into his embrace and sink into a passionate kiss.

"Are you okay?" he asked.

She nodded, smiling, and whispered softly, "Thank you, I'm fine." She made sure that she had her balance back before pulling away from him and started to walk back down the beach toward her car.

"Can I walk with you?" he asked.

"Sure," she said quietly. Was any of this really happening?

Later she couldn't remember at all what they had talked about, and soon they had reached her car.

"Do you come to the beach often?" he asked, as he reached out and held the car door open for her. His voice was so soft, so gentle, and so seductive.

"Yes, I try to come here every day," she said.

"Well, maybe I'll see you again, then," he said. His voice was mesmerizing and had the effect of setting off waves of passion in her every time he spoke.

"Maybe..." she said, thinking, *What in the world is wrong with me? Why can't I just tell him that I'm dying to see him again?*" But she didn't.

How she wished that he had asked her to stay! But he just stood there and watched her get into her car and drive away. She looked in her rearview mirror, thinking that this had to be a dream. No real person could be as beautiful as he was, but he was still standing there, watching her until she couldn't see him any longer.

"Oh my God!" she said aloud, suddenly. She had forgotten to ask his name! She was pretty disappointed about that. All she knew was the vision of his beautiful existence, but she had no name to call him by.

Arielle had the strong feeling that she had found the man of her dreams. She wanted him so much, she felt she would give anything to keep him for the rest of her life. He was her magical private vision, her desire like none other, the man she had been waiting for! How could someone so beautiful, so unbelievably gorgeous, exist in real life? She tried to control her thoughts, and felt that she was not really herself any longer, but someone living in a dream.

She went to bed that night barely able to sleep and kept looking at the clock, waiting for morning to arrive so that she could run down to the beach and hopefully see him again. Finally, she fell asleep, but her dreams were nothing like she thought they should have been. She dreamed about him, but instead of dreaming about the desire to be with him in her dreams, she was afraid – in fact, nearly petrified – by his existence. She was trying to run away from him. She wasn't able to move while he was gaining on her, and she was terrified.

She woke up trembling, her heart was racing, and her camisole was drenched in sweat. She sat up in bed and tried to remember the details of her dream, but she couldn't. She felt fear and shivered all over while a cold feeling ran through her body. How strange it all was!

She shook her head as she lay back down and stared at the ceiling. "How strange," she mumbled again. Why in the world would she have such a dreadful dream following the magical time she had had with the most beautiful person she had ever seen? Eventually, she drifted back to sleep, and when she opened her eyes her room was full of sunlight.

 *Chapter 9*

NOW THAT SHE WAS AWAKE all she wanted to do was to be close to him. She picked up a croissant on her way out the door and drove to the same spot where she had parked the day before. She was praying that he would be there. Sure enough, when she opened the door of her car, there he stood, waiting for her, lips curved into a mesmerizing smile. Could this be real?

He looked glorious! He looked so beautiful she wanted to touch him to make sure he was not a mirage. She smiled and remembered her reaction from the previous day, she avoided looking directly into his eyes. His beautiful lips were once again curved into that magnificent smile of his. Heat surged through her veins, and it was as if, for Arielle, the whole rest of the world disappeared.

"Good morning," he said in that soft, mind-blowing voice. "Did you sleep well?"

"Yes," she lied. "I slept quite well, thank you. And what about you?"

"No, not so well," he replied.

They walked together down to the same cove where they had first met. This time, he sat next to her on her beach towel.

"I thought about you all night," he said. Then he added, "I can't believe that after all these years and after all the time I've spent on this beach and in this town, this is the first time I've laid eyes on you. What a waste of time!"

She smiled, pleased, and thought of how embarrassing it would be to tell him how she had felt in the short time she had spent with him the day before.

They fell to talking easily. But she had to find out his name before she forgot to ask again. Just at the moment she was thinking this, she was completely startled to hear him say, "My name is Sebastian, Sebastian Gaulle."

It sounded precisely as if he were answering the question in her mind; but how would he know what her question even was? *Sebastian! What a beautiful name*, she thought to herself.

By now she was wondering if there was anything about Sebastian that she wouldn't like. She wanted to find out a few things about him, and she had to do it before the day was over. She didn't want to leave him again without knowing anything more about him.

"I think you said you are here a large part of the year," she said. "Is this your holiday place as well?"

"I live here most of the time, but not always," he replied.

"How old are you?"

"Twenty-seven," he said with a muffled chuckle, "And no, I'm not married," he added.

She looked startled.

"I sensed this would have been your next question, am I right?" He was smiling again, his smile lighting up his beautiful face.

"No, I don't think I was going to..." she started to say. Then suddenly she realized that he was right. That *was* going to be her very next question. All of a sudden her heart began to race. Was he able to read her mind? *No, that can't be possible*, she thought to herself. She smiled, thinking it had to be just a lucky guess on his part.

"So, you are twenty years old?" he asked in his mesmerizing voice.

"Yes," she replied. "But I'm going to be twenty-one in a couple of months."

"Are you in school?"

"Yes, I attend the University of Brighton. I've one semester left of my junior year, and I'm really looking forward to next year."

"Try to enjoy your time in the university," he said thoughtfully. "I think life becomes a little more complicated once you're out of school."

"Well, I've one more year to go before I'm out of school," she laughed happily.

He laughed along with her and added, "I'm sure you'll be excited when you get to the end of the road."

"Well, I guess I'm anxious to find out what the future holds for me once I'm out of school," she said. "But right now all I can think of is getting back and finishing the last semester of this year."

Sebastian seemed to be enjoying the conversation. He kept smiling and nodding, wanting her to go on and on.

"Is Brighton home, or is it just the location of your school?" he asked.

"We live in Brighton."

He was quiet for a few minutes and then he said, "I'll not be happy to see you go. Now that I've found you I'd really like to get to know you better." He sighed, a rueful grin on his gorgeous face.

It was getting late, and she had to get back home. She didn't want the day to end, but she tried to look calm and cool as she stood up, picked up her beach towel, and started to walk towards her car. He walked with her as he had the day before.

"Will you be here tomorrow?" he asked as he held her car door open for her.

"Yes," she answered as she slipped into the driver's seat.

"I'll see you then," he said. His voice was warm.

"Okay," she replied, trying to keep a jubilant smile from taking over her face. What pleasure, to know that this beautiful man wanted to see her again! She looked in her rearview mirror again as she drove off and he had not moved an inch. As before, he stood there watching her until she couldn't see him anymore.

Back at home, she couldn't stop thinking of him, not even for a moment. Sebastian was simply the most amazing person she had ever met. She couldn't wait for the next morning to come so she could run down to the beach and see him again. That night she drifted off to sleep in utter bliss.

The next morning she woke up early and ran downstairs to have breakfast with her parents. She told them she would be spending the day at the beach with friends, and that she might be a little late coming home. She jumped into her car, unable to stand the excitement of what this day would hold for her.

As she arrived at the beach, she could see that he was there waiting for her, looking like the most beautiful human being she had ever seen. Once again they walked together to her favorite cove and shared her beach towel.

Their conversation drifted to various subjects, but there was only one thing she wanted to know, and she couldn't stop thinking about it. She wanted to ask him if he had anyone special in his life. She was a little embarrassed to ask, so she kept silent, thinking that it would probably come up sooner or later.

Finally, he reached over, put his finger under her chin and lifted her head up to face him. His touch was warm and inviting. He stared into her eyes, and it happened all over again. Her body grew hot, her breath halted in her throat, her heart raced, and she stopped breathing. She wondered if she would ever get used to this type of reaction. His lips curved up into a wonderful smile that filled her body with a strange desire.

"So, what were you going to ask me?" he said. "You look like you want to ask me something."

She was trying to catch her breath. Finally, she just came out with it. "You told me that you aren't married, but I was wondering if you have someone special in your life," she murmured shyly.

"No, I don't have anyone special in my life," he said. "And that has been entirely my choice."

"What do you mean, entirely your choice?"

He gazed deep into her eyes without dazzling her this time, and he took a deep breath before he answered.

"I've been looking for that special someone for a very long time," he said. Then he added, "I want to feel just as Darcy did when he found his special someone in Liz Bennet."

Arielle was thunderstruck. She couldn't believe she had heard him right. She pursed her lips and repressed a shocked sound that was ready to burst out of her mouth as she looked back at him, stunned. This was just too coincidental, and it was the second such incident in two days' time.

She started to get very nervous. If he could read her mind, then he already knew that she was crazy about him. He knew that she thought it was love at first sight. *Oh God*, she thought to herself, *please don't let it be true. If he can see inside my head, he will know that right now I feel so embarrassed that I would rather die than have him know my thoughts.* Her face must have appeared exactly as she felt because she heard him take a deep breath again and she saw a slight smile on his lips.

Her eyes narrowed, her jaw clenched, and she prepared herself to manage his dazzling gaze before she peered deep into his eyes warily.

His brows slowly rose, inquiringly. "What?" he said, the smile never leaving his face.

"How...why..." she stammered, thoroughly confused.

"How...why...what?" he repeated, that smile now permanently fixed on his magnificent face.

Her eyes narrowed as she gazed at him again. She was still in doubt, but she was almost sure that he could read her mind.

"What made you refer to Darcy and Liz Bennet just now?"

"Why do you ask?" he replied.

Her voice came out firmly now. "Sebastian, I want to know why it is that you brought up Liz Bennet."

"Well that's pretty simple to explain," he said. "It's because *Pride and Prejudice* is one of my favorite love stories. Someone like Liz Bennet would be the perfect partner for me."

She stared at him with her eyes stretched wide open, utterly stunned as he continued.

"I want to feel exactly like Darcy did about the girl that I will spend the rest of my life with. Are you familiar with the story?" he asked.

"Am I familiar!" she exclaimed, clapping her hand over her mouth, still in shock. "Sebastian! That is my most favorite story. I've read it over and over again. I want to feel the same way Elizabeth did about Darcy. I have turned down numerous requests for dates because I've always been looking for Darcy. I know that's a bit crazy, but, well, that's just me." She laughed, not sure why she was saying all those things to him.

"Fascinating," he whispered. "Well, it seems that we have something in common," he murmured.

They sat there together silently for a long time. She hoped that he would say something first, and finally he did. "I guess I don't need to ask you if you have someone special in your life," he said, "since you have just told me that you are still looking for your Darcy."

She looked up at him, and he was smiling. *I just found him!* She thought, but she said, "Oh, I guess I've been pretty busy at school, and I haven't spent too much time looking for him." She laughed quietly, thinking of Paul and his unsuccessful attempt to date her.

"How much longer will you be here?" he asked, suddenly serious.

"We're going home in a few days."

"Oh," he said, obvious disappointment in his voice and her heart skipped a beat.

She kept her eyes on him, wondering if she would ever get used to his amazing looks. She would have loved to tell him that all she wanted to do was stay with him forever. She knew that in a few days she would have to leave him and go back home. School was starting in three weeks.

"Can I phone you?" he asked.

"Sure," she said. "I'd like that very much." She gave him her number and smiled blissfully.

"Will I see you again tomorrow?" he whispered.

"Yes," she murmured, lost in thought.

"Same place, same time?" he asked, chuckling.

"Yes, yes," she said, and this time, she watched him walk away. His walk was so graceful and seamless, his body so perfect. When he looked back at her and smiled, she wanted to run after him and have him hold her in his arms again, but all she could do was watch him walk away.

When he was out of sight, she folded up her towel and walked slowly back to her car. Her mind was full of him, going over every word he had said to her. She could hear his voice in her head and feel the warmth of his eyes.

When she got home, her mum told her that she had a message from Eva.

"Her mum was in an accident, darling," she said. "She's going to be all right, but Eva sounds pretty upset."

"Oh! What happened?" Arielle asked, but didn't wait for an answer. She ran up the stairs, shouting back over her shoulder. "I'll call her!" Then she went into her room and closed the door behind her.

Eva picked up the phone on the first ring, her voice distressed and agitated.

"Eva, I heard about your mum. I'm really sorry, what happened?"

"Thanks for calling, Arielle," Eva said. "We are still in Alnmouth, and she's going to be okay. But what really upset me is the fact that I had a vision of the accident, and I was not able to get her on the phone before it happened."

"What do you mean?"

"I tried to call her, but she had left her mobile at home. I could have prevented it, but I couldn't reach her," she said, and started to cry.

"Oh Eva, I'm so sorry to hear that," Arielle said, "but it's not your fault, and it sounds like your mum will be fine."

"Oh, Arielle, you're right," Eva said with a sigh, and she stopped sobbing. "I've been blaming myself. The doctor said Mummy will be in the hospital for the next two weeks, but when she goes home, she'll be perfectly fine. I feel so bad that she has to go through all this."

"Stay strong, Eva," Arielle said. "I know that she's in the right place to become healthy again. Is there anything you want me to do?"

"No, not really," Eva said, sniffing and blowing her nose discreetly. "I was just lonely, and I needed to talk to you. Thank you so much for being there."

"Eva, you know you can call me any time," Arielle said. "I love you, and I'll be praying for your mum."

"I love you too, Arielle. I'll see you soon."

After Arielle had taken a shower, she went down to take a walk in the garden to try to clear her mind before dinner. It was a warm, clear night, and the sky was full of bright stars. Arielle loved looking up at the constellations, it gave her such a sense of wonder at the size of the universe. The sight of the sky full of stars created a magical sensation for her because she knew that what she was seeing was an original experience of her very own, nothing like what any other person might be seeing, even if they were looking at the same sky. A light breeze blew across her face making her smile.

Well, she thought to herself. *Tomorrow is going to be the fourth day I'll see Sebastian, and I can't wait.* She was wondering where he lived and if he lived alone. What type of work did he do? Did he have family or friends he spent time with? What did he enjoy doing with his free time? All these questions flooded her mind, and she had no answers for any of them. She realized that after all the hours they had spent talking, she knew very little about him. She knew that he was someone who awakened feelings in her she never knew she had. He was her Darcy! This thought filled her body with exhilaration. She hugged herself in excitement and shivered. When she lay in bed that night, she closed her eyes and thought about the next day, smiling.

In the morning, the closer she got to the beach, the more eager she felt. She parked her car in the place she had the previous days, but Sebastian wasn't waiting for her this time. At first, she tried to tell herself that maybe she was just a little bit early and that surely he would be there soon. But as ten minutes turned to twenty and then thirty, she had to admit that it didn't look as if he was going to come.

She was so disappointed. She took her beach towel and walked over toward the cove where they had been the day before and sat down. By then it was midday, and he was still not there. She started to get worried and by the afternoon, she was totally consumed with dreadful thoughts. Maybe Sebastian *did* have a serious girlfriend. Maybe he was *not* interested in her at all. Maybe the last three days had just been a short, beautiful, but foolish dream. Tears filled her eyes, and her heart felt an empty ache, a physical churning as if it would break. How could she have been such a fool? To think that he would feel the same way she had in the three short days that they had known each other. How could someone like him fall for someone like her?

She sat there, unable to move, and tried to reason with herself. She reminded herself that she really didn't know him at all. Finally, she decided it was time to get up and make her way home. As she began to move, she felt the weight of sadness overwhelming her.

"Hello there!" a familiar voice said. All the bad thoughts that had been flooding her head disappeared the moment she heard his voice. She spun around, and it took all the strength she had to keep from running to him and throwing her arms around his beautiful body.

She smiled a wide smile that made it completely clear that his presence was the only thing she had been waiting for that whole day.

"I'm so sorry for being late," he said. "Something came up, and I couldn't get away." He sighed as his gaze was fixed on her. "Did you miss me?" he whispered.

Yes! She wanted to scream at the top of her lungs, but she just nodded.

He walked right up to her with that amazing smile, wrapped his arm around her waist, and pulled her close. The hot sensation that rippled through Sebastian stirred him painfully, and he pulled her even closer. Arielle stopped breathing.

He tried desperately to suppress his eager desire, but that was difficult; he was utterly captivated by her very existence. "I couldn't wait to see you again," he murmured eagerly.

He placed his finger under her chin and lifted her face toward his, his eyes piercing straight through her eyes, and there it was again. She could feel her heart hammering, pulverizing her chest, so loudly that she was sure he could hear it.

Before she could move, his lips brushed against the side of her face, down her neck and across her collarbone, leaving a hot sensation in its path. Her head fell back, her eyes closed, and as he stopped at the hollow of her throat she stopped breathing, and she heard him moan softly. His hand pulled her head toward him, and his lips moved against hers with a desire that was more powerful than anything she had ever known. She returned his kiss with the same passion, and she felt completely and utterly happy.

"I know that the time I have spent with you is very short and not enough to come to any conclusions," he said. "However, I'm pretty sure that I've been looking for you all my life." He lowered his voice and stared into her eyes without dazzling her, and she was thankful for that. She still couldn't help thinking that he was a figment of her imagination. He couldn't possibly be real. *Could he?* He certainly didn't look real. Nobody she had ever seen before was even half as handsome as he was. *Please don't go away,* she thought to herself, her pulse still pounding her veins.

"I'm not going anywhere, Arielle," he murmured.

She pressed her lips together, feeling extremely stressed and embarrassed. She didn't realize that she had said those words out loud again. He was watching her carefully.

"What's wrong?" he asked.

"Nothing," she said in a low voice, barely audible. How could she ever make this work? The following week they were leaving for Brighton, and in three weeks school would start. But she knew she had to see him again.

"Sebastian," she said. "My parents are having an *adieu* party this Sunday for all their friends, and I would like to invite you to be my date…if that's something you would like to do." His arms pulled her tighter against his body. He bent down and covered her lips softly one more time and accepted her invitation without moving his lips away from hers.

It was late at night when he finally walked her to her car. He opened the door for her, but he didn't let her get in. Instead, he leaned against the car and pulled her close. She was happy to fall into his arms again, and his kiss made her weak, and she stopped breathing. He kissed her deeply, and her mind lost all connection to reality. *I should really have more restraint*, she thought, and chuckled thinking about it, but it was too late. He already knew she couldn't stand being away from him.

She didn't want to let go of him, and she didn't want the magical moment to end, but she also knew that if she didn't get home sometime soon her father would come looking for her.

"Arielle," she heard him saying, "I have to take care of some personal business, and I'll not be here for the next two days. But I'll be back in time for your party."

Her face fell, her lips pressed together, and a cold feeling came over her. She didn't like the idea of not seeing him for two whole days. It seemed that the whole purpose of her being there now was so that she could be close to him. What would she ever do while he was gone? *This is crazy*, she thought. She had only known him for four days! Why should his absence be so upsetting to her?

He noticed the change in her and whispered, "I'll be back before you know it."

His lips brushed softly against her ear, and she shivered. He moved his lips slowly, softly, and when he reached her lips, the kiss turned hot and fervent. Her knees buckled, and if not for his tight embrace she would have dropped to the ground. He chuckled as he steadied her within his arms. He seemed reluctant to let her go, but eventually he did.

"Please think of me, and try to miss me."

Try to miss him? What a silly statement, she thought. She missed him already, and he wasn't even gone yet.

She drove away with a heavy heart. She wasn't happy about not being able to see him for the next two days, but he was coming back. And he was coming to their party! These thoughts made her smile with a sense of contentment deeper and more perfect than any she had ever known.

When she got home, she found her parents sitting at the dinner table, engaged in a pleasant conversation. As she entered the room, they both looked up and smiled.

"Hi, pumpkin," her father said happily.

"Hi, Daddy," Arielle replied, walking over to him and planting a kiss on his forehead.

"Did you have a nice time?" he asked.

"Yes, thank you, Daddy, it was great!"

Her mother straightened in her chair and asked, "Are you going to eat dinner with us?"

"No thank you, Mummy, I'm not very hungry." She walked around the table and gave her mother a hug.

"Good night!" she said softly, smiling at both of them. She felt an urge to run upstairs, but she calmly walked to the fridge, picked up a cold bottle of water and climbed the stairs slowly.

After she had taken a shower and gotten ready for bed, she realized that she had been unable to wipe the smile of blissfulness off her face. Heat coursed through her veins as she remembered his lips moving against hers with hunger and passion. She walked across the room, took her journal out of the dresser, and climbed into bed. She held the pen in her hand and closed her eyes, wanting to bring back into her mind every vivid moment, to feel his embrace and feel the warmth of his lips on hers. She took a deep breath and sighed. Warmth enveloped her as the pen started to glide across the empty page.

August 2

I must admit that I never expected tonight to reveal emotions that have become so palpable in the last three days. I can hardly comprehend the excitement and the sensation that Sebastian has unleashed in my life. I'm very sure that I have found the man that fits the imprint in my mind. He's perfect, he's beautiful and unbelievably sexy. I've found my Darcy, and I'm falling in love. I can still sense his sensuous lips on mine, and I can feel the warmth of his embrace.

I was afraid that I might never experience such a feeling, but when he comes near me, my whole body quivers with excitement. I never had emotions that could rock me to my very core. His touch makes my heart pound in my chest, and his emerald eyes make me breathless. I feel a million butterflies invade my stomach when he talks to me. I'm so happy to be alive, and I can't imagine even one moment of my life without him. I know he is "the one," I can feel it in my bones. I want to be with him every moment of the day, and I feel empty and miserable every time we separate. My heart will never be the same again. I want to share my life with him with a need that tears at me. I have leaped into this amazing feeling with both feet, and now I must find out what lies beyond.

Arielle put down the pen and closed her journal. She slipped it under her pillow and lay down. Sebastian's touch had roused a seductive desire in her that was so profound she nearly shuddered. Then sleep claimed her in the midst of her wild thoughts.

 *Chapter 10*

AS SEBASTIAN STOOD and watched Arielle drive away, loneliness consumed him. He didn't move at all until her car was completely out of sight. His head was spinning, and he was totally overwhelmed with excitement.

Her body was so magnificent, and he could still taste her sensuous lips. He didn't want to tell her that he had been watching her lying on that beach for two months before he finally found the strength to approach her. He didn't want to tell her that he was completely mesmerized by her very existence.

Just the thought of holding her in his arms filled him with a feeling of complete exhilaration. His body burned with anticipation just looking into her eyes. Obsession.

He chuckled at the thought of the confusion that had spread across her beautiful face when he had released on her all of his dazzling power. Arielle was a completely open book in his eyes. He could read every thought she had, and he was elated to find out that she wanted him. In fact, she was crazy about him, and his body ached for her.

For centuries he had walked the earth looking for the girl of his dreams. He had waited for so long that he was starting to believe that it would never happen for him, and now it had. She was the girl he wanted to be with for eternity. He felt a warm feeling taking him over as he turned and walked to his car.

It was getting dark, and the streets were empty. The weather was damp, and he could feel a light mist. He pressed on the gas pedal and before long the lights of the town disappeared in his rearview mirror. As he pulled into the garage, he knew that this was going to be a long night.

He had an early flight for London the next morning, but that was not his biggest concern. In his mind, he was trying to resolve a couple of important issues that he was facing. He knew he had to tell Arielle who he was – and what he was. This seemed to be an impossible task. What if she didn't accept the truth and just walked away?

The other issue was Annabel. She was his major nightmare for as far back as he could remember. He had married her in 1577, but it was an arranged marriage, and it was a disaster from the start. The annulment was final in 1579, but Annabel had never accepted the separation. She was furious about Sebastian's rejection of her and had vowed revenge.

She never interfered in the short, unimportant affairs he had been involved in through the years. And there had been quite a few of those. There were a couple of women he had dated centuries ago for longer periods of time – Savanna for three years and Julia for almost five years – but to Sebastian they were just affairs, nothing more. To Savanna and Julia, it was more serious. They had been in love with Sebastian. When he moved on, they were both bitter and in the mood for revenge.

As the years passed, the importance of getting Annabel completely out of his life was never on the top of his list. But the picture had changed a couple of months ago, when he had noticed Arielle lying on the beach.

At first he thought she was just another beautiful girl, but every day he found himself being drawn to the same spot on the beach, only to watch her from a distance. A strange awareness began to take over his whole existence, and he was completely unfamiliar with this new sensation. She was like a magnet that kept pulling him toward her, and he had no power to resist. He spent nights lying awake, trying to understand what was happening to him. He remembered the day she hadn't shown up and the sharp pain that swept through his bones when he thought she might not return again. He was completely confused by this, not being able to accept the simple fact that he was anxious because he didn't know where she was, and he had an unbelievably strong urge to see her.

On the second day that she didn't show up, the stress became so intense that he could hardly function. Nothing seemed important other than the fact that he needed her to breathe. If he had a heart, it would be breaking, and that is when he realized that he was in love. He loved this girl, and at the time, he didn't even know her name. This is what he had been missing all his life on this miserable planet. He had been going from one girl to another looking for something but never finding it. He knew he had to meet Arielle, and he was determined to use every gift he possessed to make her love him.

It took all the strength he had in him to walk up to her and introduce himself. Her voice caressed his soul. Her eyes were like two sparkling sapphires, her limbs long and graceful. Her face was like alabaster, and her lips were sensuous, stirring feelings in him like no other woman had ever done before. He knew he was looking at the girl that was going to be his partner for eternity. He was looking at his future, all he had ever lived for.

Her eyes had captivated him from the very first moment he saw her. He had the undeniable sensation that he had gazed into those amazing sapphire eyes before. He had lain awake for three nights following their actual meeting on the beach, trying to recall and explain the shocked feeling that burned through his body whenever their eyes met. Her deep blue eyes seemed to be etched in his mind from somewhere far in the past, but he could neither recall the time nor shake away the sensation. There was nothing in the world that could change that feeling. But how could that be possible when he had never met her before? By the fourth day he had set that feeling aside because he couldn't find an answer and it was driving him crazy.

One thing was for sure, from this moment on the issue he had with Annabel was now at the top of his list. He never understood how Annabel always knew which girls he was dating and whether the relationships were serious or not. If she found out that he was truly in love, he knew she would try to hurt Arielle, and he couldn't allow that.

The trip to London was both for business, and for attending the annual ball at his adopted parents' home, the Dillon estate. He also wanted to talk with Olivia Dillon, the woman who had been his mentor and his mother through his immortal life. She would be the one he would turn to for the advice he needed to make sure Arielle was safe.

Arielle's image filled his thoughts as extreme excitement and warmth took over his body and made him smile with complete bliss. He had fallen in love with her unconditionally, and he didn't want to live without her. What a wonderful, overwhelming emotion of delight! He wanted to marry this girl and embrace her for all eternity.

During the flight to London he thought back over the two miserable years he had spent with Annabel, and how he had become what he was.

When Sebastian was growing up, everyone was aware of the existence of immortals. However, they were not aware that many young people had become immortals for the sole purpose of living an endless existence. It was said that immortals could bestow immortality on mortals who were at the edge of death. Immortals could walk into water without getting wet and enter fire without being burned.

For centuries the authorities went after immortals. They were considered evil, even demonic, and the punishment was cruel. It was known that they were incredibly strong and fast, so when they were captured they were locked into cells and starved. Then they were beheaded in the middle of the town square in front of all the townspeople so they could witness what became of immortals. Sebastian winced at the thought.

Annabel was the daughter of Sebastian's father's best friend, and she was someone Sebastian had disliked from a very young age. He was twenty-two years old when he married Annabel, and he had hated every moment of his life with her from that day on.

It was an arranged marriage, and both Sebastian and his real parents were completely unaware that Annabel was one of the young people that had joined the immortal world. He was in utter and complete shock to find this out on their wedding day. He had never loved her, had never wanted the marriage, and had never consummated it. He learned to hate Annabel during the time they spent together with deep-rooted feeling. He knew she could destroy him, that his mortal existence was no match for her immortal powers. Two years after the marriage he filed for an annulment, and when it came through Annabel was furious.

She looked at him with fire in her eyes. "I can kill you," she hissed at him, "but I would rather make the rest of your miserable, mortal life dismal. I will destroy any relationship you try to have in the future. I will never let another woman be part of your life. I will watch you die alone and miserable." Oh how he hated her!

In 1580, a global pandemic of severe influenza occurred, and Sebastian lost his whole family – both real parents and both of his brothers. That was the most horrible time in his life, and he suffered the worst pain he had ever suffered. The loss shattered his spirit and broke his heart. He'd loved his family so much, and then he was completely alone. Totally inexperienced, he was left with all the responsibility for the family business; he had no idea what to do with the huge family wealth and various liabilities. But he had to pull himself together and make things happen, and he rose to the occasion.

Sebastian's mind went back to the time when his life had changed so unexpectedly and so drastically. The day of his twenty-seventh birthday he was out with his friends celebrating. A fight broke out, and he was in the middle of it. He was hit hard in the back of his head. He remembered the incredible pain he felt and the blood that covered his face. He remembered moving in and out of consciousness. Finally, he passed out.

When he came to, he was alone in his room in bed. He had no idea who had brought him there, how he had gotten there, or when, but he had been unconscious for nearly three days. At first, he thought that maybe the whole thing had been just a dream, but the state of his clothing told him otherwise. There was blood on his shirt, his pants, his hands, and face, so he knew that the fight he remembered had been real. But he couldn't feel any pain, and he was shocked to find out that he was perfectly fine; there were no cuts on his head, his face, or any other part of his body. He remembered thinking that he must have lost his mind. He checked himself again and found that there was nothing wrong with him at all. He clearly remembered being repeatedly hit, remembered the pain he had felt on the back of his head, and the blood that had blinded him just before he passed out. He just couldn't understand what had happened to him at all.

He got out of bed, and while he was cleaning up, he noticed a beautiful silver ring on his right hand with some strange designs on it. He had never seen this ring before, and when he tried to take it off, he was unable to do so. The ring was tightly placed on his finger, and it would not budge. This was extremely peculiar, and as he kept looking at the ring, he felt a sudden, strong jolt. His mind traveled back to the day Annabel had told him about her immortality. She wore a ring almost like this one, and she had told him that it had something to do with providing protection for her from the sun. He felt a growing anxiety and fear. What had happened to him? What was going on? He resolved to find some of his friends and try to solve this puzzle, or at least get some answers as to what had happened.

Several of the friends he had been with that night showed signs of having been in a bad fight, and they were all totally shocked to see that Sebastian had not a single bruise or cut. They clearly remembered him being in the middle of the fight and on the floor bleeding. But they couldn't remember seeing him leave the place, and they couldn't understand how he could have gotten up and left in the condition he had been in. They had all thought he might even be dead, so they were astonished to see him totally unscathed.

Not getting any answers from them, Sebastian gave up trying to figure what had happened, and just moved on with his life, until he gradually realized that there was something very strange and different about him. He started to notice many things that he hadn't seen in any other human being except Annabel. For example, he never got sick anymore, and every time he hurt himself he healed within minutes without any assistance from a doctor or any medicine. He could read the mind of every person he crossed paths with, he was extremely strong, and he could move with incredible speed. He also noticed that he never had any dreams at night, he couldn't cry, and he couldn't feel his heartbeat anymore.

He was sure that immortality was the explanation for the changes in his life, but how and why had this happened to him? There was only one person he knew of who might have done it, and her only motive would have been to punish him for centuries to come instead of for a short and limited mortal life.

Sebastian shivered again, remembering the fear and loneliness that had consumed his life for years following the discovery of his immortality, and the way his hatred for Annabel had grown stronger with every single day that passed.

It has taken me centuries to feel secure about who I am and what I want. This was Sebastian's last thought as he heard the flight attendant announce their preparation for landing at Heathrow.

It was raining in London when they landed. Sebastian drove to meet his friend Nathan, as planned. Nathan was also immortal, and was the head of foreign affairs in Sebastian's company. After a brief meeting, Sebastian went to his hotel suite to rest and refresh for the annual ball at the Dillon estate.

The Dillon ball was a grand annual affair that Sebastian had attended every year with Nathan. It seemed that this would be the last year he and Nathan would be going to the ball alone. Nathan had met the girl of his dreams and they were making wedding plans.

When they arrived at the ball, Loren Dillon, the Dillons' only daughter, met them at the door. She had met Sebastian five centuries ago. They had become close friends and she had brought him home to meet her family. The Dillons fell in love with Sebastian and he with the Dillons. Sebastian had been alone, scared, and had great difficulty in understanding how to handle his new life as an immortal. The Dillons helped him with his struggles and answered his questions, and he in turn found love in the Dillons, and the warm sanctuary that he needed more than anything else in his life. The Dillons claimed him as their own son, and he was more than happy to claim them as his immortal parents. He adored Loren as a sister, and throughout the centuries he had become quite the protective brother.

Loren was a tall, gorgeous girl with long black hair and beautiful blue eyes. When she saw him walk in, she ran toward him and fell into his arms. "I am so happy to see you both!" she squealed. "Mother said you were coming, and I just couldn't wait, I have missed you so much!"

Sebastian held her tight in his arms and planted a big kiss on her cheek. "You are still just as beautiful as ever," he said.

Loren hugged Nathan, and told him how happy she was to see

him again. Then she took them both by the hand and pulled them across the room.

The ballroom was full of people drinking and socializing. Nathan and Sebastian knew most of them, so they walked through the crowd smiling, shaking hands, and waving until they got to the place where Sebastian's mother was sitting with some of her friends. She stood up when she saw them approaching, and stretched her arms out to embrace them.

"Welcome! I've missed you both so much! I wish you would come and visit more often," she said.

Sebastian returned the hug and smiled at her warmly. "Don't worry, Mum, I will try to come more often in the future."

She turned to Nathan. With a smile showing at the corner of her mouth, in a soft but mock-stern voice, she said, "And you – you live here! So you have no excuse for not visiting more often."

She gave him a look as if daring him to disagree with her, but of course he didn't. He just chuckled and said, "I'm sorry too, Mrs. Dillon, but Sebastian keeps me awfully busy." He cast a look at Sebastian and they both laughed out loud.

Olivia Dillon was a very beautiful woman. Sebastian loved her like his real mother, and she had always given him good advice and great guidance. As soon as Loren took Nathan to the dance floor, she motioned for him to come closer and made him sit right next to her. When she fixed her eyes on him, she knew right away that something was wrong.

"Well, what is it?" she asked him. Her voice was tender and caring.

"I have to talk with you, mother," he said. "It's really very important."

"Oh! Can it wait until tomorrow? Let's say around eleven-thirty? If not, we can go upstairs and talk about it now."

"No, it can wait," he said. "I'll be here a couple of days. And I had planned to come back tomorrow for this specific reason."

"All right then, tomorrow around eleven-thirty. Now, let's enjoy the party, what do you say?"

"Yes, I would love that," he said.

Loren came back toward them, pulling Nathan, who was following her like a puppy. "All right, it's your turn to dance," she called to Sebastian as she took his hand and pulled him to the dance floor. He let the music fill his mind and closed his eyes. How he wished he could be holding Arielle in his arms and kissing her warm, sensuous lips!

"Sebastian!" Startled, he realized Loren was calling his name.

He opened his eyes and looked at her with a warm smile. "I am so sorry, Loren. My mind is preoccupied, and I just got carried away."

"Is she pretty?"

"Yes," he said, chuckling, "she's gorgeous." He gave her a big squeeze, making her giggle. When the music stopped he kissed her, and walked over to the other guests to make small talk.

He returned to the hotel late that night, anxious about the next day. He wanted to fall asleep and dream of Arielle, but of course as an immortal he couldn't dream. He closed his eyes and was startled by the vision that filled his mind: he saw Arielle standing there, with tears in her eyes. Why was she crying? She looked as if she were trying to tell him something, but he couldn't hear her voice. His eyes snapped wide open and he felt shaken by the strong vision. What did it all mean?

Chapter 11

IT WAS 11:20 when he arrived at the Dillon estate the next morning. Everything looked quiet compared to the night before. He used his key, let himself into the foyer, and called out for his mother. Edwin, the faithful butler, appeared and motioned Sebastian to follow him through the huge halls, through the study, and into the garden.

Olivia Dillon was sitting in her chair reading a book. She looked up and smiled wide when she saw him approach. "Good morning, dear! Did you sleep well?"

"Yes, thank you, mother," he said.

"Come take a seat next to me and let's discuss what's bothering you so much. Nothing is entirely fixed in life, you know that " she said. "Disaster may come, but we can always find ways to circumvent it."

Sebastian had first met Olivia Dillon in 1643 while visiting Württemberg, in the southwestern part of Germany, east of the Upper Rhine. Württemberg was a beautiful Alpine town with lovely painted houses, exquisite cafés, and great nightlife. It was very well known among the immortals.

The Dillons were a very influential immortal family with great ties in high places. Olivia Dillon had extraordinary powers and had been happy to make Sebastian a new addition to their family. She gave him advice and guided him to the right people and the right places. He looked up to her and loved her like his real mother. She was the person he had turned to every time he needed help or advice. This was one of those times, and he knew she would know what to do.

"What is it? Let's talk about it," Olivia said. Her voice was full of concern.

"Mother, I'm in love for the first time in nearly five centuries. I've found the perfect girl for me. I want to marry her and make her my wife. Her name is Arielle."

"Sebastian! It's about time," Olivia exclaimed joyfully. "I've been waiting to hear those words for centuries. Then what's making you so unhappy and so worried?"

"Well, I have a couple of issues that I would like to talk to you about. The first and most important is Annabel. She's not willing to let me go, and I'm afraid for Arielle's safety." He paused and then continued. "She hasn't been much of a problem for me up to now, but she vowed to destroy my life if I ever fell in love with another woman. I've no idea how she finds out who I'm dating and how important my relationships are, but she seems to be very well informed and it complicates my life."

"I always thought she would become a big problem someday," Olivia murmured. "And what is the other issue?"

"My other issue is the fact that Arielle has no idea of who I am – and more important, what I am. What if she doesn't accept me when she finds out? I love her so much! A rejection, would crush me completely."

"Why would she ever reject you? I don't understand." Olivia's gaze had grown inquisitive.

"Mother, Arielle is a human."

"Oh…indeed!" she said. Then she sat quietly for a long time. Finally, she got up and asked Sebastian to follow her. They entered the house and went straight upstairs to the master bedroom. She walked up to the dresser, opened the bottom drawer, and pulled out a black leather box. She placed it on the top of the dresser and, taking a small key from a hidden place on the back of the mirror, she unlocked it and took out of it a small leather book and a little black velvet pouch.

"This will have to be the answer for now," she said quietly.

Then she asked him to sit with her on the huge sofa by the window. Out of the little pouch she pulled a shiny gold pendant with a gorgeous blue stone in the very center. As he looked closely, he could see an amazing carving of a strange looking beetle in the middle of the stone.

"This is a real scarabaeus that belonged to the Egyptian Pharaoh Djoser of the third dynasty," Olivia said. "This beetle is the guardian of the holder. The Quintessence – the four elemental forces in the universe: Earth, Fire, Air, and Water – created it. The scarab was placed in the very center of the pendant, representing the heart that holds the mind and the soul of the individual who wears it. The owner is protected from all evil and anything bad that could harm them as long as it's on their body."

She handed him the book. "Open it," she said.

A large pentagram took up the whole first page.

"This is the book of elements. It holds some very powerful spells. If Arielle ever decides to use the book she will have to study the contents very carefully as it can bring disastrous results if not used correctly. The pentagram represents the five elements of the spiritual and physical self: Spirit, Water, Earth, Air, and Fire. Magic could be very dangerous, coming into physical contact with spirits. When the spell is cast it will destroy the enemy; in this case, Annabel." She sat quietly for a short time, letting him absorb her words.

"Make sure that Arielle does not part with this necklace until we have a permanent solution for Annabel. It has to be on her body at all times." She paused and then added, "One other very important thing is that Arielle must know the truth about you before you give her the necklace, and especially the book. The stone is very powerful and will keep her safe. And the book is priceless." She paused again and added, "I'll try to think of some other ways we can help you without having Arielle use the spells in the book, but it will take me some time to think about this." She didn't say so, but deep inside she knew just as Sebastian did that the ultimate solution would have to be Annabel's complete annihilation.

"I wish you had come to me a long time ago, Sebastian. If you had, I know that by now I would have had a good solution to this problem."

"Mother, I assure you that I would have come to you if I had ever experienced an emotion anything like this before," he said. "I've lived without it for five centuries, so it's a very extraordinary and special feeling. I feel that it completes my very existence. I love her."

"So what's your next step?" Olivia asked.

"Well, I guess first I will have to make sure that Arielle knows the truth about me, and that she still wants to be with me after she knows who I really am. One thing I know for sure is that she loves me, so that gives me hope."

"I'd love to meet her," Olivia said with a pleasant smile.

"Oh, I'm counting on that," he said, smiling back at her.

Olivia had the extraordinary power of looking into the future. As she looked at Sebastian, she debated whether she should bring up what she could clearly see going on in his head. Finally, she sighed and grinned. Her face displayed a brilliant smile, and he could see that she was thoroughly enjoying the moment.

"Are you going to actually do what I see in your head?"

"Well, I figure what's another year of college? Maybe three? After all, I've already waited for hundreds of years." And they both broke into hearty laughter.

"I think it's a great idea," Olivia said. "And since you are going to be in England for the next year or so, I hope you will make yourself more visible in this home. Maybe you can persuade Loren to attend university too. It would give her something to do."

"There is no question that you will be seeing more of me," Sebastian said. "I want you to meet Arielle, and I'm going to look for a place to live before long. I feel a lot better now that I know Arielle will be safe, thanks to you. I also know that if I don't have to worry about Annabel hurting Arielle, I can handle anything she throws my way."

"Make sure you stay very close to Arielle," Olivia said. "And remember, there are other ways to hurt her besides just physical ones. You will have to protect her in every way you can." For a short moment she said nothing and Sebastian waited patiently. "I wonder why Annabel wants to hold on to something that has been dead for centuries now," she mused, adding, "I always thought that your father made a big mistake choosing her for you."

Sebastian was so overwhelmed with happiness and gratitude that he reached out and embraced his second mother.

"Can you stay for a nice drink of salve?" she asked.

"Yes, of course," Sebastian replied.

"And now tell me about Arielle," she urged as she poured their drinks.

"She is one of the loveliest creatures on this earth. She is absolutely the most beautiful girl I have ever laid eyes on, and graceful in everything she does," he said, smiling happily and sighing.

"Well, she sounds just perfect!" Olivia said, handing him a glass. "You sound so happy, and I can see that you really love her."

"I don't think I was really alive in the last five centuries," he said, chuckling. "I think I was just roaming this earth looking for someone who would make me happy. But I never experienced anything like what I've found in Arielle."

"What will you do if she can't accept you for who you are?"

Sebastian didn't answer for a moment. "I don't think I would be able to find any reason or any purpose to exist," he finally said. "I feel like I can't breathe when she is not with me, and it has only been four days since I've met her. I don't feel *anything* without her. She has given purpose to my life. She is the woman I want to be with for as long as I live."

"Remember, she is a human," Olivia said gently. "She will get older. She might get sick, and eventually, she will die."

"If anything ever happens to Arielle, it will be the end of me. I couldn't possibly exist without her," Sebastian said.

"I want you to think hard about what it will be like when she starts having difficulty with *you* remaining young while she is getting old," Olivia said thoughtfully. "It will be hard for her to accept, no matter how hard you try to make her understand that you still want to be with her."

"I know... I have thought about that as well, but I don't have a solution. And I don't mind telling you that I am scared when I think about all these things," he sighed.

"Well, for now, try just to be happy and face the issues as they come. It is a lot easier if you don't have everything mapped out way in advance."

They sat in the garden for a while longer. It was a perfect day, and Sebastian enjoyed just being there in the calming presence of his mother.

He left the house early in the afternoon feeling much better. He knew he now had something in his possession that would keep Arielle safe from Annabel's wrath, and that brought him huge relief from the worry he had been suffering. That left only one main concern – that

Arielle would feel the same way about him after she found out about his immortality.

He went back to the hotel and got ready for the meeting he had scheduled for that afternoon. There would be another round of meetings tomorrow, and then he would be on his way back to Arielle. He couldn't wait!

The meetings were important because Sebastian was the owner and CEO for IIRL, the family business that had started centuries ago to acquire land all over the world, but had now evolved into manufacturing new products for various businesses around the globe. They had buildings and laboratories in many countries, and they were quite well known. Sebastian's business associates didn't know anything about the immortal friends that he had put in key positions to run the company. All they knew about him was that he was a good businessman and a great boss even though he was very young.

When he had finally finished all he had to do in London, he happily headed back to France. When the plane landed in St. Jean de Luz it was two o'clock in the afternoon. He didn't want to waste any time: he wanted to get home in time to get ready for Arielle's party. He could hardly stop smiling as he drove home from the airport, thinking of nothing but her.

He went straight to his room, took a shower, and lay down for a few minutes, wanting to unwind until it was time to go. After his time in London he felt sure that he had found at least a temporary solution for the worst nightmare of his life.

Around seven-thirty he got out of bed and got ready for the party. He was standing in front of the mirror, whistling a joyful tune when Annabel suddenly appeared.

He knew this encounter was not going to be pleasant, but he kept his cool and pretended that her presence didn't affect him at all. He was frustrated at not being able to prevent her from showing up any time she wanted to and invading his privacy. He considered Annabel's ability to move effortlessly from one place to another a curse. Unfortunately this is exactly what she chose to do that night. She had been waiting for Sebastian at his house, and chose this moment to confront him.

Annabel was a very striking woman, though her looks held no charm for Sebastian. "Where are you going tonight?" she asked him, sounding arrogant.

"That is absolutely none of your business," he said in a matter-of-fact tone.

"Oh, but it is," she said. Her eyes, filled with fury, were scrutinizing him, trying to discover his plans for the night.

A sudden thought made Sebastian quiver. Did she already know about Arielle? And if she did know, what was she prepared to do? He pursed his lips in frustration but tried to keep his cool.

"Annabel, I am losing patience with you," he said. "I hate being close to you, and I can't tolerate the sight of you. Do me a favor and leave me alone. Go and find someone else to be with for the rest of your miserable life. I don't want you coming into this house anymore."

"But how can I do that?" she asked in a falsely sweet tone. "Haven't I promised you a life of misery?" Her cruel, uncompromising promise burned like a fire in her eyes. "I thought your mortal life would be short, but somewhere along the way, someone changed the rules." She chuckled with a miserable, insinuating laugh, and he understood exactly what she meant. She was the one that had changed the rules to make them suit her. "Now I've all of eternity to make you miserable, and that is a very long time," she said. "There's no woman that will dare to defy me. I'm sure something is going on with you these last two months, and I'm determined to find out what it is. Remember, Sebastian, I'm not joking." She glared at him with true loathing.

"You know that you'll have to get through me first," he said. "And we both know you are no match for me now. I'm not a mortal any longer and I'm much stronger and faster than you'll ever be. So watch your step."

"I'll follow you anywhere you go, and I'll make sure your plans are ruined. Just try me," she replied with a hiss and walked into the other room.

Sebastian knew that Annabel was going to be a problem. Arielle had no idea who she was, and he couldn't allow Annabel to create a scene in front of Arielle's parents. He decided reluctantly that the best thing to do was to stay away from the party and hope that he could explain to Arielle later the reason he hadn't shown up, and hope that she would forgive him.

Suddenly the terrifying thought that he might not see her again rippled through his soul. He couldn't stomach the thought of not being close to her.

He decided to call her, and looked for the piece of paper with her phone number on it, but he couldn't find it anywhere. He began looking frantically, going out of his mind with anxiety. The vision he'd had in London flashed before his eyes. Her beautiful face, her tears, and something that she was trying to tell him. Oh! He felt shattered, helpless! Even though he possessed all the powers in the world, he still couldn't fix this dreadful moment. He knew Arielle would be hurt and that he would be the cause of it. How could he expect her to forgive him when he couldn't forgive himself?

He got into his car, knowing that Annabel would follow him, so he drove with no particular destination in mind. How would he ever explain to Arielle his not showing up? He knew it wouldn't be hard to find her again, but that trying to regain her trust was going to be a challenge. He was falling into deep despair, knowing that he couldn't keep his promise to her, and that she would be going home in a few short days.

He drove by her house – that was the closest he could get to her tonight. He saw the lights, the happy faces of the people, and heard the wonderful music. "Oh, how I wish that I could see her beautiful face and stand by her side, holding her hand," he thought. If he could have cried, he would have wept bitterly. But as an immortal, there was no such relief for his pain.

It was morning by the time he drove back home and found Annabel waiting for him, a disgusting smile on the face he detested so much. He knew that he would have to stay away from Arielle to keep her safe as long as Annabel was around even though the pain of staying away from her was unbearable.

Still, he had never been happier in his life, and he knew he couldn't allow Annabel to create any major issues between Arielle and himself. He just had to find somehow a chance to explain to Arielle about Annabel. He had to!

The next week he had meetings scheduled in Germany and Spain. He hoped that Annabel would leave soon and that the whole thing would blow over. As soon as she was gone, locating Arielle would become his next quest. He was sure about the depth of her feelings for him. What he didn't know was if she would be able to forgive him.

Chapter 12

AFTER SEBASTIAN LEFT, Arielle stayed home for the next two days. She lay by the pool, read her book, and listened to her music. She didn't go to the beach; she didn't want to be there without Sebastian. She knew deep in her soul that she was desperately in love with him even though they had only known each other for four days. She had only one desire, and that was to be in his arms and listen to his magical voice. Sebastian was her Darcy – she felt this and knew this with her whole heart and soul. It was a wonderful feeling.

The day of the party, the whole house was buzzing with caterers, florists, and tons of other people coming in and out of the house, getting everything ready for the party, down to the last detail. Her mother's best friend, Myranda, and her daughter Jane had flown in from London for the party and were going to stay on for a few days afterward before they all flew back home together.

Jane was like a little sister to Arielle, and Arielle was glad she would be there to help keep her busy until Sebastian got back. She was so looking forward to introducing her beautiful and enchanting dream to her family! She wanted everyone to meet the man who had captured her heart forever. She was boiling over with love, and she could hardly wait to be in his arms again.

"What do you say we drive to town, do a little shopping?" she asked Jane. Jane was sixteen, a wonderful, beautiful, bubbly girl, and they always had fun together.

Arielle was planning on getting back to the house around five o'clock with plenty of time to get ready for the party. The party didn't start until eight o'clock, so there would be ample time for Jane and her to shop, walk around, and get back in time to take a shower before it started.

The street cafés were buzzing, and Arielle could hear people's happy thoughts as they enjoyed the day. She and Jane both got caught up in the wonderful holiday atmosphere, they talked nonstop and laughed about every little thing.

As they turned down a quiet narrow street, they noticed a small quaint bookstore. They both loved reading, so they walked inside to take a look and see if there was anything interesting to purchase. As they walked around the bookstore, Arielle's eye caught the title of a large hardcover book. The first line read "The Gaulle Fortune," and right below that it said "Sixteenth Century."

Seeing Sebastian's last name, she pulled the book from the shelf and ran her fingers over it. She walked up to the woman behind the counter and asked if she could tell her anything about the Gaulle family. The woman looked up from her papers, and seeing the book in Arielle's hands, she said, "Sure, what is it that you would like to know?"

"Anything at all will be more than I know now," Arielle replied, chuckling.

"The Gaulle family is one of the oldest and most famous families around here," the woman said. "Their home or I should say their castle, is located up the hill behind the thick forest, which starts at the end of town on the west side and extends for quite a while, to the point where the next town begins. The house was built in the middle of the sixteenth century when the first Gaulle gentleman arrived.

"He spent a lot of money in those days: he brought tons and tons of stone from the Abbey and used it to build one of the most beautiful homes in this part of the world. It is a magnificent site, well worth visiting. The house is fabulous, and it looks quite mysterious and inviting to anyone who is interested in exquisite architecture."

"Have you seen it?" Arielle asked.

"Everyone who lives here has visited the location at one time or another, but no one has ever been allowed inside. It has a fascination for all who see it, though. Don't all things as old as that?" she asked with a soft laugh.

"I suppose that's true," Arielle replied.

"Imagine: the house was built in the sixteenth century, but the material used in it goes as far back as the eleventh century."

"Do you think we should see it?" Arielle asked.

"You should most certainly be sure that you both see it."

Arielle knew that she had to see the house. She thought she would go ahead and ask the next question even though she already knew the answer.

"Does anyone live there?"

"I'm not sure if anyone is there right now. However, I know that there is a young gentleman who lives there a large part of the year. He loves to read, and he is here quite often. His name is Sebastian, and he's one of the nicest young men around. He's unbelievably handsome, to the point that I find it hard to stop staring at him. If I were a little younger..." she sighed, and her voice trailed off. She laughed again softly, and the girls joined in. Arielle knew exactly what she meant. Sebastian was the most beautiful human being she had ever seen as well.

"I have heard that a young lady has also been seen there at different times through the years," the bookseller added. At these words, Arielle's mind jolted to attention.

Who could that be? She tried not to jump to any conclusions, but she had a sinking feeling. Could the young lady be Sebastian's sister or a cousin? She hoped there was an innocent explanation, and she recalled that Sebastian had assured her there was no one special in his life.

As she put the book back on the shelf, she heard the bookseller's voice saying, "There is a lady there, Mrs. Wilson. She and her family are hired to do the cleaning and take care of the grounds. She's the person to ask for if you decide to visit the house. She is very familiar with the history of the Gaulle estate. She's been there for several years."

Arielle thanked the woman and walked out of the store. *Why did I have to ask?* She thought. *Why did I have to get all these bad thoughts in my head?* And in spite of her resolve not to jump to any conclusions, she was finding it hard to feel at ease.

She knew that she would have to ask Sebastian about this tonight, but how could she do that without making him wonder why she had been asking questions about his family? But as she and Jane walked quietly to her car, she knew she wouldn't feel reassured again until she had all the answers to her questions.

They arrived home at quarter to five, and they both headed to their rooms to take showers and get ready for the party. As she prepared, Arielle's thoughts were in the house behind the hill and the young lady that she had heard about. Who could she be? She wanted to be the one that he thought of, the *only* one who was special to him.

She lay down on her bed, trying to stop thinking about this and relax. But all she could do was think about the mystery girl and the more she thought about it, the more upset she became. Finally, she got up and got into the shower. She stood there for about thirty minutes with her eyes closed, letting the hot water run over her body without moving, as if she could wash the worried thoughts from her mind. But it was hard to chase them away even then.

Suddenly her mother's voice came from the other side of the door startling her. "Arielle! Please be ready on time. The guests will be arriving at eight o'clock sharp!"

Arielle didn't answer. Her mind was still up the hill on the other side of town.

"Arielle! Are you getting ready?"

"I'm trying, mother!" Arielle replied a bit irritated.

"Please try not to be late," her mother called out as she made her way down the hall.

Arielle sighed, got out of the shower, and began to prepare herself for the party. Tonight she wanted to look amazingly sexy, completely irresistible. She wanted to bewitch Sebastian, to make him fall completely in love with her. She chose a black cocktail dress with spaghetti straps that fit her body snugly in all the right places and enhanced her looks. She chose a pair of high heels that made her legs look incredibly long and absolutely beautiful. She picked out a pair of shoulder duster silver earrings, and a large, beautiful bracelet to accent her simple little black dress. She wanted to dazzle him as much as he had dazzled her. She took one last look in the mirror and smiled. She liked the girl that looked back at her!

At eight o'clock she went downstairs as the guests began to arrive. The house was absolutely beautiful down to the last detail, and the guests were greeting each other by embracing, kissing, and all looking extremely happy.

Arielle glowed with pride when she saw her mother. She walked over to her and gave her a big hug as she whispered in her ear, "Mummy, you look fantastic!" Arielle's mother smiled softly in reply and gave her a little squeeze.

Just then Isabella Roux, one of her mother's social acquaintances, walked up to them. Isabella was very sophisticated, and tonight she looked exceptionally beautiful in her classy clothing.

Perhaps because Isabella's stepfather was in the parliament, she seemed to think she was better than everyone else. Arielle and her mother made small talk with her, both suppressing the urge to smile at Isabella's airs. They shared a quiet chuckle as she swept away, off to impress the next person.

Everyone they had invited was there. The Chevalier family had brought their son, Richard, whom Arielle detested. They had spent a lot of time together during their summer holidays when they were very young, and they really did have a lot of fun in those days. Arielle had always been nice to Richard, but as they started to get older, he began to get on her nerves. He thought that they should be more than friends, and though she had made it clear she was not interested in him that way, he continued to pester her. She had finally gotten to the point where she truly detested him. Now he came hurrying toward her as she quickly moved away.

"Arielle!" he called out, "are you not pleased to see me?"

Without looking at him, she muttered, "Not really."

"What's wrong, Arielle?"

"Richard, please leave me alone," she said. She smiled to soften her words, but it was a thin, unhappy smile.

"You know that we are meant to be together," he continued in his obnoxious voice.

"Richard, please," she said. "You ruin every occasion for me as soon as you show up." There was extreme frustration in her voice, half from his irritating manner and a half from her impatience as she waited for Sebastian.

"But..." he started to say, and she interrupted him in a firm voice.

"Richard, please. Grow up and just stay away from me! I don't like you at all!" She had run out of patience and out of polite ways to reject him.

His face was filled with anger and resentment as he turned around and walked out the front door. He was too vain to just leave the party, and she was sure he would be back to hit on another girl before the night was over. Richard was the last person in the world she wanted to have a conversation with tonight. "How can someone so handsome be such a jerk?" she thought with irritation.

Jane walked up to her and took her hand. "Tristan is here, and he looks amazing!" she said.

Tristan was the son of Andre and Isabella Roux. He was a great guy who was much more like his easygoing father than like his vain mother. Arielle followed Jane into the other room, and her eyes met his. "My gosh," she murmured. Jane was right!

Tristan was absolutely beautiful. He wore a pair of black pants with a light blue shirt that hugged his extraordinary muscular body. His face was warm, tan, and surrounded by rich sandy hair. His eyes were hazel, and his lips were sensuous and beautiful. As they drew close, he smiled, showing perfect white teeth.

Arielle didn't remember ever having seen Tristan the way she saw him tonight. She could now remember her mother saying that he was around thirty years old, that he had graduated at the top of his class from medical school and was a surgeon at a big hospital in Paris. He walked up to her and embraced her warmly.

"Arielle!" he exclaimed. "You have grown up to be a gorgeous young lady. I hardly recognized you! I can't believe the change in you since the last time I saw you," he said in French.

"Well, it has been over eight years since the last time you saw me," she said, laughing.

"Yes, you're right about that," he said and laughed along with her as he drew her closer to him and kissed her on both cheeks.

Happy to see him, she smiled back. "It's wonderful to see you, Tristan," she said.

"It's nice to see you again, also, Jane," he said, smiling at the girl as he put his arm around Arielle's waist and moved her to the dance floor. As they moved to the music, for a few moments, Arielle forgot all about Sebastian and the fact that he had not shown up yet.

When the music stopped, Tristan walked back with her to where

Jane was standing. "My parents will be visiting Brighton next month to celebrate your twenty-first birthday, Arielle," he said. "And I'm planning to come too. I have some meetings scheduled around the same time, so that it will work out beautifully." Arielle smiled, pleased.

"Your French is very good," he added with a smile.

"I have been practicing quite a bit," she said. "After all, we're here every year, and I can't expect everyone to speak English." They both laughed, and Arielle felt so happy that all her efforts at learning French were being appreciated.

After Tristan had moved away, she walked towards the big window, hoping to see the man of her dreams walking up to the front door, but she didn't. She tried to walk around and socialize with Jane, but her mind was filled with excitement and eagerness; she just couldn't wait to see Sebastian again.

But as the time passed, she started to get a horrible feeling he wasn't going to show up. How could he make a promise that he wasn't planning to keep? He could have refused her invitation, but he hadn't done that. He had said he would be there. Her heart began to sink as she remembered the words of the woman in the bookstore. Maybe it was all a lie. Maybe she had imagined all the words she heard him say on the beach.

When midnight had come and gone, it was clear that he wasn't coming. With a heavy heart, Arielle walked around the room, saying goodnight to all the guests, making sure that she pleased her parents. Then she went up to her room, sick at heart.

Well, here was the end of a beautiful dream. How could she have been so stupid? She burst into tears of outrage and frustration. How could she have allowed herself to be hurt so badly by a man she didn't even know?

Two days went by, and Arielle saw no sign of Sebastian. He never even tried to call her, and she knew that he had her phone number. She woke up each morning with a cloud of depression settling over her and went through the day in a mood of black despair. She was certain that Sebastian was the man she wanted to be with for the rest of her life, and her heart was broken.

The day before they were scheduled to leave for Brighton she asked Jane to go with her to visit the house that they had talked about with the bookseller in town. "That would be wonderful! " Jane said, eyes sparkling with excitement.

This was going to be Arielle's last, desperate attempt to see him again. She didn't have to tell him that she had gone there to see *him;* she could just say that the bookseller in town had suggested she should see the house before leaving for England. That sounded like a good excuse, and it was more or less true.

They drove out to the edge of town and took a small two-lane road towards the house. At the end of the road, there was a fork. To the right she could see a small gravel road leading to a parking area right below the house. To the left, the road went straight up to the front gate. They chose to park below and take a small path leading to the house, up a steep rise between beautiful trees and flowering shrubs.

She could smell the fragrance of blooming jasmine and sandalwood. It was in the middle of a scorching summer, and the heat was unbearable. The air felt heavy, making it hard to breathe. When they finally reached the top of the hill, they let out a cry of exhilaration, not believing their eyes. The house was magnificent! Jane and Arielle looked at each other unable to speak, their mouths open in amazement.

Arielle had a strange, muddy taste in her mouth. She was pretty excited even though she was also a little bit scared, wondering how they would be able to gain access into the house. She was sure she would have to lie unless Sebastian answered the door, and she started trying to think about what she would say if she encountered someone other than him. She looked over at Jane; she could see that Jane was just as excited and scared as she was, though putting on a brave front.

What would it be like to be the lady of this magnificent house, married to Sebastian? Arielle wondered to herself, looking up. She remembered reading in the book she had seen in the bookstore that the house was of Tudor origin but that it had been restored a couple of times in the last four centuries. It was really beautiful. Next to the house stood a tall, mysterious tower. It must have been wonderful in its day, but today it looked like a gray phantom, enclosed by empty stonewalls. It was amazing yet forbidding.

The walls were built with massive, flat gray stones – imported from the Abbey, the bookseller had said – and every six feet a set of incredible carved stones created a very mysterious, fascinating pattern.

The huge windows reached from floor to ceiling and were made of beautiful beveled glass reflecting a variety of colors. The panels on the side of each window were carved with striking designs. The small pieces of glass were diamond-shaped, with painted images arranged to form various patterns and shapes. Some of the patterns were displayed after the emblem on heraldic armor while others replicated beautiful landscapes, flora, and fauna. In the center of each and every window was an elaborate letter G. Arielle was sure it referred to the Gaulle family.

As they both stood there, mesmerized, they could not help thinking of how powerful the house looked. It felt like a huge magnet that was pulling both of them towards it and filling them with the desire to explore every inch of it.

There was something about the stones that surrounded the house that made Arielle feel as if she had been transported to another era. The front door was massive and made out of beautifully carved oak. The two handles in the middle were made out of heavy intricately wrought iron.

They climbed the stairs and stood in front of the magnificent door. Just as Arielle raised her hand to grab the handle, the door opened, and a small, very attractive middle-aged woman stood in the doorway. Arielle and Jane were both taken aback since they hadn't even had the chance to knock. "*Bonjour!* I saw you coming up the hill," the woman said. Her voice was soft and kind. "Can I help you?" she added with an inquisitive look.

"I'm Arielle Lloyd, and this is my friend Jane," Arielle said. "I'm a friend of Sebastian's, and I was wondering if he's here. He told me that he would show me the house before I left for England," she lied. "We're leaving tomorrow, and this will be the last chance we have to see it," she added. She was a bit surprised at how easy it was to lie once she had gotten started.

She was driven by her compulsion to see part of the world in which the man of her dreams lived if there was any way possible to do so.

"I'm sorry, but Mr. Gaulle is out of the country. Please come in," she said, smiling. "If you're friends of Mr. Gaulle I'm sure he would have no objections to my showing you the house."

She was smiling, and she had a very friendly air about her. It seemed as though she was happy to see them as if she were eager to have company.

Arielle and Jane stepped into the great hall and followed Mrs. Wilson into a huge room decorated with gorgeous antique furniture and huge tapestries hanging from the high ceilings. They were both shocked by the incredible beauty of the place.

Arielle's heart was beating fast, and she could feel the air thickening around her. She wasn't sure if it was fear of the unknown or the fact that she was standing among very old and very incredible things that were part of Sebastian's world. Suddenly Jane touched her arm, and it made her jump.

"I'm cold," she whispered, and Arielle suddenly felt a chill come over her as well. She started to think of Sebastian's ancestors and the ladies who had lived there, who had purchased all these beautiful things and were responsible for decorating the room so exquisitely.

There was no doubt in her mind that a great deal of love and caring had gone into choosing each and every item in the house. She thought of all the great balls that must have been given in these huge rooms, as well as the sadness that must have taken place throughout the centuries.

"It's so exciting to be here!" she heard Jane whisper.

She nodded and walked further in. There was an absolutely beautiful, very wide staircase that led to the upper level. *To the bedrooms,* Arielle thought.

In the dimming light, the room was full of shadows. Suddenly she had the weirdest feeling that all the people who had lived in this place were now looking at her and Jane, wondering what they were doing in their home and what they wanted.

"Do you know when Sebastian will be back?" Arielle asked. She tried to keep her voice bright and casual, not at all the way she felt.

"No, I never know how long he will be gone when he leaves," Mrs. Wilson said. "Would you like me to show you around?"

As she gave them a tour of the house, Arielle moved through the rooms in a state of bewilderment, completely mesmerized. There were so many hallways and so many rooms, and they all looked dark and scary with heavy satin curtains hanging in all the windows. The rooms seemed to be about twenty to twenty-five feet high and the beveled glass windows with the amazing designs reached from the floors all the way up to the ceilings, which were decorated with remarkable murals. Someone had gone to great pains to make sure everything was done with exquisite taste, down to the last detail. The amazing stained glass windows allowed sunlight to pour through and bathe the furniture and all the woodwork in a lush late afternoon glow.

In the background, servants moved about silently. Pictures of Sebastian's ancestors, those who had lived there, hung on the walls in the hallways and the rooms. Arielle was sure that famous painters had painted many of them. *What a mysterious world!* She thought as she looked at portraits of men in armor and beautiful women wearing gorgeous gowns. She thought of them laughing and crying in the very place that she and Jane were standing right at that moment. It was almost as if she could still feel their presence in the room.

They went back down through the main staircase and were getting ready to thank Mrs. Wilson for her kindness and hospitality. Jane was smiling and sheer enthusiasm covered her face. "I have never been to any place like *this* before!" she said, her face glowing with excitement.

Just then she heard Mrs. Wilson say, "Miss Annabel!" She sounded startled as she added, "I didn't hear you coming."

Jane and Arielle froze in place. Arielle hadn't heard footsteps either, but as they both turned around, they could see a woman standing on the top of the landing.

Annabel was of medium build with gorgeous blond, silky hair. The coldness of her gaze sent chills down Arielle's spine. Her face was absolutely flawless. She was dressed in a soft blue pantsuit that made her look very striking. Arielle had never seen a more beautiful woman.

There was a complete and uncomfortable silence in the room. Not knowing what to say, Arielle and Jane just stood there waiting for someone to speak. They looked at each other and instinctively moved closer together, reaching out to touch hands.

Annabel moved with elegance as she descended the staircase. Then she looked directly at them and held their attention. It was as if they were transfixed and couldn't move.

Arielle felt lightheaded and weak. She suddenly felt she couldn't breathe as if there were no oxygen in the room. Her nostrils were filled with the strange smell of death, and all she could think was that she needed to get away from this place as quickly as possible. She told herself that her imagination was running wild, but her thoughts ran in a panic. *What is her relationship with Sebastian? Does she know how I feel about him? Does she know all the wonderful things he has whispered to me?* These questions raced through her head as she fought the feeling of dread that was sweeping through her body.

As that feeling became stronger, she wanted to run away. She wondered what would happen if she fainted right then and there. Finally, Annabel spoke. When she did, it was in a very cold voice that struck terror in both Arielle and Jane.

"What are you doing here?" she asked.

Suddenly Arielle knew she had made a big mistake in going there. There was no way she could explain why she was there, why she wanted to see the house. But she collected her thoughts as well as she could and replied as calmly as she could, trying to keep her voice from shaking. "Hello," she said. "My name is Arielle, and this is my friend Jane. We visited a bookstore in town, and we saw a book that had some very interesting history about this house. The bookseller advised us that it would be a wonderful thing to visit the house and experience its greatness up close. We are sorry for the intrusion, and very much appreciate the time Mrs. Wilson has taken to show us around."

She knew that she had told Mrs. Wilson an entirely different story, but she was terrified to use the same lie with Annabel. All she could do was pray that Mrs. Wilson wouldn't say anything about her lie.

"How do you know my husband?" Annabel continued frigidly.

The question hit Arielle as if someone had just punched her in the stomach. She didn't care anymore about being caught in a lie; all she cared about right now was what she had just been asked. What did she mean by her "husband"? She couldn't be referring to Sebastian. She was sure that was not a possibility at all.

"I'm not sure that I know your husband," she said.

"I thought I heard you tell Mrs. Wilson that you were a friend of Sebastian's?"

Arielle swallowed the lump in her throat. "Oh yes," she mumbled as her heart crashed to the floor. She knew she had to say something and get out of there as quickly as possible before she fell apart completely.

"We.... We met a couple of days ago in town," she stammered. "He also told me about your beautiful home, and I wanted to see it."

Annabel smiled at Arielle with a look that was full of smug satisfaction, and something else too, something strange that Arielle couldn't fully grasp.

"Thank you so much, Mrs. Wilson," Arielle managed to say. Then she took Jane's hand, and they walked, nearly running, for the door. Once outside they broke into a run and didn't stop running until they were out of sight of the house. They both tried to catch their breath as thousands of questions filled Arielle's mind.

She had started to feel sick to her stomach, and she wanted nothing more but to be back in her room, alone, where she could gather the pieces of her broken heart.

She was sure now that all the things Sebastian had told her were lies. And she had believed all those lies, just like a sixteen-year-old schoolgirl. She vacillated between anger and confusion, still not able to believe that she had been fooled.

They got home as the sun was going down. Arielle went straight to her room without talking to anyone and closed the door. She wanted to be alone, and she wanted to think. She wanted to cry…oh, what a fool she had been!

So it had been just a summer dream, nothing more. Tomorrow they were leaving, and she was sure this would be the last time she would ever come to St. Jean de Luz. It would take a long time to forget someone like Sebastian. She never wanted to come back to a place that would remind her of the feelings she had held for him and the love that she now knew only existed in books.

Her eyes were full of tears as she thought about how easy it had been for him to make her fall in love with him, make her feel that he was her Darcy. She was sure he must have had a good laugh about the whole thing. Now she was angry, so angry that she was trembling.

She had been just a joke to him. *Oh, what a fool I've been!* She thought over and over again. That night, she recorded a short note in her journal.

August 12

I waited for this astonishing feeling for as long as I can remember. I'm shattered at the thought that I grasped it only to lose it again in a short moment. The profound awareness of my heart being shattered into a million pieces is unbearable. I don't have the strength to gather the fragments, and I still don't want to give up Sebastian.

Today has to be one of the worst days in my life. I've lost the man I fell deeply and irrevocably in love with. A million words can't describe this awful pain. I lost the man who moved into my very essence and imprinted his name in my very soul. I let him in without any reservations. Oh, God! What am I going to do? I'm madly in love with him. He lied about me being his Lizzy, he didn't show up as he promised, and his rejection is shearing my body apart layer by layer. The pain is unbearable, the tears unstoppable, and the void huge. I'm frustrated and so profoundly disappointed in myself, believing his lies like a reckless schoolgirl.

Then she closed her journal, and, hugging her pillow, cried and cried until sleep claimed her.

That night she slept badly. She dreamed of Sebastian, and he looked so sad. In her dreams, he kept calling her name and reaching out for her, but she couldn't get close to him. Every time she fell back to sleep she had the same dream, and it would make her wake up in a cold sweat, looking around the room, expecting him to materialize in front of her. It was a very bizarre dream, yet it seemed real enough to keep her awake all night long.

Finally, it was morning, and she had to get up and start preparing for the trip home. She was already packed. Her parents had told her they would leave around eleven o'clock to be sure to have enough time to catch their flight. Then she heard a knock on the door and heard Jane's voice, asking if she could come in.

"Yes, come on in, darling!"

Jane looked upset as she walked through the door. Without even saying good morning, she said, "Arielle, I had the strangest dream about the lady we met yesterday at the Gaulle estate."

Arielle stopped combing her hair and looked at her. "What was it, Jane?" she asked.

"She was telling me to warn you to stay away from Sebastian," Jane said, giggling nervously.

"Oh, I can believe that," Arielle said, laughing too. "She scared me, too," she added, faking a smile. "Don't worry about that. Just go and get ready. We should be leaving shortly."

Jane came over to her and gave her a big hug. "I love you, Arielle! You are just like a sister to me!"

"I love you too, Jane," Arielle replied and hugged her back, patting her comfortingly.

The day was very warm, and they left for the airport shortly after ten-thirty. As they got further away from their summer home, it occurred to Arielle that she had ceased to believe that there was anything for her in St. Jean de Luz.

Sebastian now seemed like a dream that would never come true. She could not erase her feelings for him, and she didn't think that she would ever feel the same way for another man. Her heart was broken, and the emptiness that she had felt before she met him was back again.

 *Chapter 13*

THEY HAD BEEN BACK HOME in Brighton for less than a couple of hours when the phone rang. Gabby's voice was exactly what Arielle needed to hear. Gabby talked nonstop for the longest time until she realized that she had not given Arielle a chance to say a word even.

"I'm sorry, Arielle, I'm just so happy you're home. I have so much I want to share with you that I haven't given you a chance to talk," she finally said. "Have you been home long?"

"Only for a couple of hours."

"Can I come over?" Eagerness was evident in Gabby's voice.

"I wish you would," Arielle said with a chuckle, knowing that she needed to talk to Gabby about her own news. But it sounded like Gabby had something exciting she couldn't wait to share, and Arielle didn't want to ruin her friend's exciting news if that were the case.

"Are you all right? You sound a bit down," Gabby said.

"Um…I need a friend right now," Arielle allowed.

"Oh! Is something wrong?"

"I'd rather talk when you get here," Arielle said, adding, "There is a lot to tell you."

"I'll be right over," Gabby promised.

It seemed as if Arielle had just put the phone down when she saw Gabby walking through her bedroom door. They ran into each other's arms, and immediately Arielle's eyes welled up. Gabby looked at her in shock.

"Arielle! You look terrible! Your eyes look like you've been crying for days. Are you okay?"

Arielle drew in a deep breath and tried to hold back her tears. "I'm alright," she said. "I'd rather listen to your good news first, though. What happened? You look radiant, you look absolutely great!"

"Oh, I'm so happy I can hardly talk," Gabrielle gushed.

"Did something exciting happen to you on holiday?"

"Well not exactly on holiday," Gabrielle said. "As it turned out we spent only about five weeks in Italy. Then we had to come back because something unexpected came up with Daddy's practice. So I spent the rest of the summer here. I thought it was going to be a complete bore, but as it turned out, it has to be the best summer of my entire life."

Her voice was so excited that Arielle couldn't wait to hear the details. She felt like she needed some good news.

"Two weeks ago Stephanie had a party, and she invited many of our friends from school. I really didn't want to go, but I had nothing else to do. But Arielle, this party changed my life." She looked radiant. Arielle had really never seen Gabrielle look so happy before.

"So what happened?"

"There is a new guy on campus. His name is Troy Vasser and oh, Arielle, I'm in love!" she squealed, squeezing her eyes shut as if trying to bring up his image in her mind. Then she squeezed Arielle's hands.

"Details, please!" Arielle said, squeezing Gabby's hands back excitedly.

"He is unbelievably gorgeous, and I'm not exaggerating. You'll see for yourself. He looks like he isn't even a real human being. He's so beautiful! He is tall; he's got brown hair and hazel eyes. I saw him walk in, and he took my breath away. His eyes locked with mine instantly, as if he were looking for me. I was so mesmerized I thought I was going to die." She stopped, as if remembering, then giggled.

"He walked right up to me and introduced himself. We talked for a long time, just enjoying each other's company. We danced practically the whole night, and he took me home when the party was over." She had a beautiful smile on her face, and her eyes were shining.

"I hope he's not like Marcus," Arielle said. Something about the way Gabby was describing her new love made her a little uneasy.

"No...Not at all, you'll see."

"Then what happened, tell me more!" Arielle giggled. She was so happy for her friend, she momentarily forgot her own misery.

"Well, the next day he came over to borrow a book that we had talked about the night before. And he asked me if I wanted to go to the cinema. That was our first date."

"Did you have a good time?"

"He is Italian, and he's gorgeous!" Gabby said, completely ignoring the question she had been asked as another brilliant smile spread across her face.

"He hasn't been here for very long, but he's so nice, he has already made a lot of friends. We seem to have a lot in common, and we love being together. I have seen him almost every day now since the party. He is intelligent, passionate, and an amazing kisser." She chuckled again softly.

"I have put every effort into finding something that I don't like about him and truly, Arielle, he is perfect in every way. I'm crazy about him! I'm completely and utterly in love with him. I have never felt this way before. I can't wait to see him each and every day. If I don't see him, I feel empty and unhappy, as if he somehow makes the whole world magical. I lose every thought I ever had when I'm in his arms. He is so freaking perfect!" She smiled softly, and Arielle knew exactly how she felt. She hugged her friend with excitement.

"I'm so happy for you, Gabby, and I can't wait to meet him."

"Well, now tell me what happened with you," Gabby said, breaking away from their embrace and looking at Arielle curiously. "You seem sad."

"Well unlike yours, I think this was the worst summer of my life," Arielle said. "My heart is broken, and I don't know how I will ever find a way to repair the damage."

"What's wrong? Who broke your heart?"

"I fell in love this summer with the most beautiful man on this earth. And he was in love with me too, or at least he said he was…" She blurted out the words, hesitantly at first, and then in a sort of rush. "And now my heart is shattered into a million pieces," she concluded, breaking into tears and sobbing uncontrollably.

"Arielle! You never called me? I never knew you were in love," Gabrielle said. She was looking at her friend in amazement, the joy is now gone from her face, replaced with concern.

"Gabby, this is the man I've dreamed about my whole life. The man I have been waiting for, the one who completes the blueprint of my existence! I feel like I've been struggling for years trying to find him."

"Is he French or English?"

"He's French, and his name is Sebastian. He walked up to me at the beach last week and for the next four days, he turned my world upside down. He made me feel like I had never felt before. He made me think that we had been looking for each other all of our lives. He made me feel just the way you have been describing when you are with Troy."

"He sounds wonderful! So why are you so sad? And why is your heart broken?"

"He had to go away on business, but he promised to come to my parents' party the weekend before we left. But then he never showed up," she said. She stopped, fighting back the tears that were threatening to start all over again, but it was in vain. As she succumbed to hot tears of hurt and frustration once again, Gabrielle reached over and squeezed her hand, her beautiful face now clouded over with concern for her friend. "I tried to see him again in the next couple of days, but he never came back to the beach. Then I decided to take Jane Wainwright with me to visit his family estate, thinking that he might be there and that I would get a reasonable explanation. He wasn't there when I went, but I found out that he's married to one of the most beautiful women I have ever seen..." Another torrent of tears made it difficult for her to continue. "I'm devastated," she concluded. "I wish that I had never met him."

"You didn't see him or talk to him before you left?"

"I didn't. And now I feel like the pieces of my heart are scattered all over St. Jean de Luz. How am I ever going to get over him? I am so hurt and so angry I could scream."

Gabrielle just looked at her friend, her eyes full of love and understanding. Arielle saw how bad Gabby felt for her, but there was nothing she or anyone could say to make her feel better. She was glad Gabby was there, though, because she knew she needed to get this heartache off her chest. So she kept talking.

"He was romantic, beautiful, attentive. He said everything I was longing to hear, everything that made me fall in love with him. He said he was looking for the special girl that would make him happy for the rest of his life." With these words, she began once again to sob softly.

"How can I go on, Gabby? How can I concentrate in school? Why did this have to happen to me?" Tears were rolling down her face, and she couldn't stop.

Gabrielle put her arms around Arielle and was silent. They stayed holding each other as she cried for a long time. Finally, Gabby pushed her friend back softly and handed her a tissue.

"Pull yourself together and let's think about this, Arielle," she said. "What do you know about him?"

"Not much at all. I found a book about his family, but I didn't purchase it."

"Okay then, let's start with that," Gabrielle said in a very matter-of-fact tone of voice.

"What do you mean?"

"Let's go to a bookstore tomorrow and try to find the same book again."

"But how would that give us any clue about Sebastian?"

"Sometimes family secrets say a lot about the family members," Gabby said, looking at her significantly.

"Okay, let's do it," Arielle agreed. Then she continued with her story, telling Gabby all the details of her meetings with Sebastian, and the words that had been exchanged between them. She cried again as she remembered how wonderful it had been to be with him. Once again she could feel her emotions taking over her.

"Oh, Gabby!" she moaned through her hands as she covered her mouth, trying to suppress the sound of her sobbing, "I'll never be the same person again!"

"Arielle, you need to pull yourself together," Gabrielle said, handing her a tissue. "There may be a very good explanation for why he didn't show up. Please don't cry any more."

Then she held Arielle's hand while she calmed down, waiting for her to stop feeling sorry for herself. Arielle reached over and embraced her. How lucky she was to have a friend like Gabby!

It was late by the time Gabby finally left, promising Arielle to be there bright and early in the morning so they could go together to the bookstore. After Gabby had left, Arielle went right to bed, and to her surprise that night for the first time since her parents' party, she slept soundly.

The next morning Gabrielle and Arielle drove downtown to one of the largest bookstores in Brighton. They went straight to the history section and started looking through all the books. "Okay, okay, here we are," Gabby said suddenly. "Look, Arielle, this might be our ticket." She picked up a book with the title "Gaulle Sixteenth Century." It was not the same book Arielle had found in St. Jean de Luz, but it was about Sebastian's family.

As they opened to the first page and started reading, thumbing through the pages slowly, Arielle's heart was racing.

> *"The Gaulle family moved to Calais, a port city located on the North Atlantic with an active maritime trade with the English, the Dutch and other French ports. At the beginning of the sixteenth century, Marcus Gaulle was a very successful merchant who had made a fortune. The Gaulle became a noble family with enormous wealth. Marcus Gaulle had two sons, André, and Gustave.*
>
> *It was not acceptable for a nobleman to do much of anything except serving in the military, in the royal service, or in the church. Every prominent family made a point of placing at least one son into a lucrative church position, from which they often wielded a great deal of political influence, or they would offer themselves into military service. Some such positions were essentially considered hereditary to certain families.*
>
> *André became a cardinal. The church was the most powerful institution in France after the monarchy. It owned a third of the property and collected approximately 40% of the revenue.*
>
> *Gustave offered himself to the King in military service. In those times nobility depended on wars to make money, so they created wars around the world. Tax exemption was given to those who served the King in a military position. Gustave offered the family the exemption from taxes, which increased*

their fortune.

Marcus became very successful, cultivating a following of noble clients. He appointed them to different jobs, and they were expected to return his favors in wealth. He studied law and made enough money to buy large amounts of land.

In 1548, André married a wealthy noble and had two daughters, Marianne, and Lavinia. Gustave married a Duchess in 1550 and had three sons, who he named after family ancestors: Anton, Marcus, and Sebastian."

Arielle's heart started to pound furiously in her chest, and her breathing became laborious. Sebastian's name had jumped right off the page, and the sight of it made her jump.

"What's the matter?" Gabrielle asked. "What's wrong with you?"

"Nothing, nothing at all."

She turned her eyes back to the book. She was sure that the Sebastian whose name had just jumped out at her must be one of her Sebastian's great grandfathers. Maybe there would be something about him as well toward the end of the book. She kept skimming quickly through pages and pages, trying to get as much information as she could, moving through the centuries quickly.

She went through the whole book, reading about all the sons who were born and died, their wives and children, the lavish balls and expensive properties. Hungrily, she read about their close associations with kings, queens, dukes, and duchesses, but there was not another Sebastian mentioned in the book, apart from the one who had been born in the sixteenth century.

But how could that be? Sebastian *had* to be the son or grandson of one of these Gaulle's that she was reading about. He was the owner of the estate in St. Jean de Luz, carrying on their glorious and noble name. She was becoming really puzzled when, toward the end of the book, a paragraph caught her eye.

"Toward the end of the sixteenth century, it was rumored that some of the nobles had more than money and power, that they were also hiding something from the rest of the world.

This was something greater than money and fortune; it was the gift of living forever. It was said that the nobles with this gift lived for thousands of years, and that was how they made their fortunes. Sebastian Gaulle, born in 1555, was believed to be one of those nobles. It was said that he had eternal life, a timeless existence.

In 1577 at the age of twenty-two, he married one of the most desirable women of the century: Annabel Draper. The marriage was annulled two years later."

Her body went rigid, and she dropped the book. "What? What?" Gabrielle said. "Let me see! Did you find something juicy?"

Arielle bent down, picked up the book, and handed it to Gabby. "No, nothing," she lied. "I think this is just a waste of time." She smiled, stood up and, leaving the book on the shelf, began to head for the door.

"Arielle!" Gabrielle yelled. "Don't you want to buy it?"

"No, I don't think so. I didn't see anything of importance in it," Arielle replied.

Back in the car, she was quiet. She tried to listen to Gabrielle's chatter, but it was hard to concentrate on anything other than the questions burning in her mind. *Where do I go from here, and what do I do with all this information?* She thought to herself.

What was the relationship between the Sebastian in the sixteenth century and the Sebastian in the twenty-first century? Could this possibly be about immortality? But that was just crazy. She didn't believe that immortals existed, and anyway, how would you find out about something like that? How was immortality achieved? Was it inherited? Was it something that happened to you during your life to change you forever? Then she shook herself. What was she thinking? *It wasn't real! There was no such thing!*

Still, her head was filled with questions that she couldn't answer. She would have loved to ask Sebastian these questions, but she was sure she would never see him again. Even if she did, she wasn't sure that she wanted to hear his explanations. She sighed a deep sigh.

"Thanks for being such a good friend, Gabby," she said as her friend dropped her off at home. "I can't wait to meet Troy, I'm sure he's wonderful."

"I'll call you tomorrow," Gabrielle shouted out the window, blowing a kiss as she drove away.

Arielle went to her room and closed the door. Now that she was alone, she felt that the Gaulle book was coming to life for her and that the new knowledge she had was pressing on her chest, making it hard to breathe.

She wasn't hungry at all; she told her mum that she would just read for a while and go to sleep. Then she actually lay down and tried to watch the telly for a while.

But when she finally tried to sleep she would either dream about Sebastian and wake up crying, or have a nightmare about him, and either way she was awake again. She wanted to forget everything that happened to her in the past month. It was a long time before she really fell asleep, only to be awakened by a man's voice. Startled, she listened warily, not sure if she heard a real voice or if it had come to her in a dream.

"*Arielle...*" It was a man's voice full of torment, asking her to come back. She sat up on her bed and then she heard it again.

"*Arielle, please come back.*"

She was dumbfounded not because she heard someone calling her name but because there was such sadness and pain in the voice.

She got up and opened the window. It was dark outside and the night breeze blew softly on her face. Her room was on the second floor facing the ocean, which she loved. But the water was dark now, and nothing about it brought her pleasure. The curtains moved as the breeze brushed against them and she thought she heard the same voice, now in a whisper. She could see that the rain had stopped, but there was still moisture in the air.

"*I love you, Arielle.*" Her heart sped up, and she held her breath again. She thought she recognized Sebastian's voice this time around, but she couldn't be sure. How wild was that?

She looked around the room, but she was completely alone. She went back to bed and tried to sleep. Eventually, she dozed off, and when she opened her eyes, her room was filled with the sunshine.

She had only a week left until classes started, and here she was, planning to do nothing but lie around and think about Sebastian.

How depressing was that? Why didn't she get up and get going? She was sure this part of her life was over, but she just couldn't accept it.

As she lay quietly, thinking about all that had happened, she realized that there was something very strange about Annabel and the way she had made it clear to Arielle that Sebastian was her husband. What a coincidence it was that Sebastian of the sixteenth century had married an Annabel Draper, and the Sebastian in the twenty-first century was also married to an Annabel Draper. It was all just too strange! She started to think again about what she had read about immortals in the book, but every time she started to think about it, she chased the thoughts away from her mind. It was just too weird to even think about it.

Finally, she got up and dressed for breakfast. She was plenty hungry, and she could smell eggs and bacon cooking. As she came into the kitchen, she smiled at her mum and gave her a kiss. Her dad had already gone to work, so she sat in his place to eat her breakfast.

As she was finishing, the phone rang. "Arielle! It's for you," her mother called.

"Hey, you're home!" Eva cried happily.

"We got back the day before yesterday and Gabby told me that you were coming home today. How is your mum?" Arielle asked.

"Oh, she's great, and I'm so pleased," Eva said with a relieved sigh. "We're just getting ready to get on the plane, and I can't wait to see you! I *need* to talk to you. It's very important," she added.

"Okay, have a good flight," Arielle said. She couldn't wait to see Eva either.

"Call me when you get home," she added.

She hung up smiling, wondering what was so important that Eva needed to talk to her about. "Maybe she met someone too," she thought. "That would be so nice!" Arielle had missed Eva, and she was looking forward to having some time with both of her friends together at their flat. It was wonderful to be with her parents, and they did give her the privacy she needed. But it wasn't the same as being in her flat with Gabrielle and Eva.

The only one she hadn't spoken to since her return was Paul. She waited a couple of days and then gave him a ring. She was trying to keep as busy as she could; she was trying to forget about Sebastian.

Paul answered the phone in his deep voice. "Hello," he said.

"Paul, it's Arielle! I'm back and I thought you might want to go down to the coffee shop with me."

"Arielle!" he said, clearly pleased to hear her voice. "Did you have a good holiday?"

"It was great, but I'm glad to be back."

"I'll come and pick you up in about a half an hour, will that be okay?"

"Yes, that will be great. I'll be waiting for you." She was hoping that Paul's company might cheer her up.

As usual, he showed up right on time. She had forgotten how handsome he was, and she smiled with pleasure thinking how wonderful it was to see him again. He smiled as he pulled her into his arms and his lips met hers in a warm kiss. She could see that he was overwhelmed with excitement.

"Are you ready?" he asked.

"Yes, I'm ready, let's go!"

He opened the door for her, and she slid into the car. He seemed perfectly at ease as he looked at her, and the corner of his mouth curved up into a bright smile.

"You have no idea how much I've missed you," he said.

"I missed you too, Paul," she said. She always felt so comfortable being with him.

The coffee shop was busy, and they took a table in the corner. He wanted to know all about her holiday and what she had done for the past two months. She started to talk without paying much attention to the details. She was mainly thinking about how good it felt to be with him. He watched her with fascination as she told him about her visit with Jane to the Gaulle home. Tears welled up in her eyes as the memory of Sebastian's magical face took over her whole existence. Her own personal miracle was in front of her again, and she was unable to speak anymore.

Paul reached across the table, took her hand gently and held it tight, as though he could look into her head and feel what she saw there. She must have looked so miserable. He stood up, walked quietly toward her and without a word took her in his arms and pressed his lips to hers as he wiped her tears away. She didn't pull away. His kiss was warm and comforting, and she needed to feel wanted.

It seemed to Arielle that Paul understood that something important had happened to her while she was away, but he didn't want to ask. He was perhaps afraid of what she might say.

She was grateful that he didn't ask her for details. Her heart felt like a heavy stone pressing on her chest. She couldn't be in any more pain than she was right then and there.

She looked at Paul and felt sad that she had no control over how she was reacting. She knew now she should never have agreed to see him so soon. But she was there now, and she had to try to repair her mood. She looked at him and with a forced smile she whispered, "I'm so sorry, Paul, please forgive me. I missed you, and I'm happy to be here with you. You always make me feel good. You are a wonderful friend, and I love you so much! Please tell me about your summer. Did you have fun? I know that you went to a fascinating place, but I don't think you told me where that place was."

They took their seats once again, and he started to talk. And as he talked, she finally was taken away from her sad thoughts into another interesting world. He told her how he and his parents had gone to Alexandria, and from there, to Cairo. He spoke with excitement about their journey across the desert and the fascinating people they had met along the way. He talked about Cairo with its picturesque sunrises and the enchanted sunsets. He had visited fortresses and beautiful mosques. He chuckled as he added that while walking through the palaces, he had imagined beautiful, mysterious harem girls emerging through secret doors, just as they did in a movie he saw once, *Arabian Nights.*

"I really didn't see any of those girls," he said, laughing out loud. "But in the early morning hours, standing in front of my hotel window, I did see a mystical city that belonged in a mystery or a romance story."

Paul kept talking, and she kept listening with interest. She was happy he had taken her away from her troubled thoughts. She sat back in her chair and closed her eyes, smiling. There was silence for a short time, and when she opened her eyes, he was staring at her with a beautiful smile on his face.

"You look content," he said.

"Thank you, Paul. I'm so happy to hear about your trip. It just took me away to a magical place, and I loved it."

Three hours had gone by, but it felt as if they had just arrived.

They got ready to go, and she thanked him for a wonderful time. He looked at her with his warm eyes and held her tight in his arms.

"Remember that I will always be here for you," he said, his voice soft and comforting.

When they got to Arielle's home, she leaned over and gave him a kiss. "I love you, Paul. Thank you so much for everything."

"We'll talk soon," he said, smiling. She stood and watched him drive away.

A couple of days later, late in the afternoon, she was sitting in the garden reading *Pride and Prejudice* all over again. She was wondering why she kept punishing herself by thinking of Sebastian, but she couldn't seem to help herself.

Just then her mother came outside and called, "Arielle! Are you out there?"

"Yes, Mother, I'm out here reading."

"Monica called from St. Jean to let you know that a young man is looking for you."

Arielle's breath stopped in her throat, and her lungs locked. Monica was the housekeeper that took care of their holiday home. She felt numb, unable to move until she heard her mother's voice again.

"Arielle, did you hear me?"

"Yes, Mother, I did. Did she say what he wanted?"

"She said that he lost the number for your mobile. He wanted her to call you to get the number."

"Thank you, Mummy, I'll call her back shortly," she said. She took a deep breath, another deep breath, and picked up the phone, her hand trembling.

Monica picked up on the second ring.

"Hello, Monica, it's Arielle. Is he still there?"

"No, he left, but he said he would be back tomorrow to see if I had been in touch with you."

"Did he tell you his name?"

She wasn't sure why she even asked that. She just wanted to act as if Sebastian was of no importance to her.

"Yes, he said his name was Sebastian Gaulle."

Instantly her heart began beating at a very fast rate, her face flushed, and that same breathless excitement took over her whole body.

She gave Monica her phone number and thanked her for calling. Then she hung up the phone and sank back on the bench, staring at the trees.

A million questions filled her mind. What would she say if she had the chance to talk with him again? How could she address the Annabel issue without letting him know that she had been intruding in his family affairs? Why would he even want to talk to her? She was sure Annabel had told him that she had been at the house. How would he ever be able to explain Annabel to her? And what about all the things he'd told her in the magical days they had shared at the beach?

Once again she felt like she was going out of her mind. One thing she knew for sure, the next day she would be waiting, all day for his call.

That night she lay awake in her bed, rehearsing the way she would handle the call. She was desperately in love with him, and she couldn't do anything about that. At five o'clock in the morning, her eyes were still open, but her body was tired, and she felt exhausted.

Suddenly her phone rang, and the sound made her jump. She had fallen asleep, and she was completely disoriented. In trying to get to the phone, she fell out of bed. She finally picked up on the fifth ring, totally out of breath and whimpering a bit from the pain of her fall. "Hello," she said sleepily into the phone.

"Arielle?" It was that musical, beautiful, velvety voice on the other end.

Her body went into panic mode, her face felt like it was burning, and her heart was pounding so hard, she thought it might burst.

"Yes?" was all she could manage to say.

"It's Sebastian. You do remember me, right?" he asked, chuckling softly. That he could laugh after all, he had put her through made her mad. She decided to play it cool.

"Yes, I remember you. What can I do for you? " Her voice, though, didn't actually sound very cool; it sounded pretty upset.

"You sound angry. Are you?"

"Should I be?" She was still trying to achieve that cool, jaded tone, but was failing miserably.

"Yes, I think you should. I'm sorry about missing your party," he said. "I'll have to make up for that."

"Is that all you think I'm upset about?"

"Well, I can't think of anything else I have done that would upset you," he said. He sounded truly puzzled, but she was convinced it was just more phoniness from a heartless imposter.

Now she was really angry. She couldn't keep her voice down, and she couldn't stay calm. She swallowed hard before she went on.

"Sebastian!" she exclaimed.

"Yes?" His voice was maddeningly unruffled.

"Maybe you can tell me if your wife is okay with you calling me."

There was silence on the other end for such a long time that she was about to hang up. She thought he was already gone. Then she heard his voice again, hard and steady.

"What did you say?" he finally asked. There seemed to be space between each of the words he spoke, as if what she had said was somehow incomprehensible.

"I was just wondering," she repeated. "I was wondering if your wife, Annabel, is okay with your calling me this morning."

A quiet oath escaped Sebastian's lips. Then she heard him mumble something under his breath in an angry voice. She could hear his voice clearly enough, but she couldn't make out exactly what he was saying. It sounded like cursing, but she wasn't sure. He started rambling and then stopped mid-sentence. "I'm going to have to call you back," he muttered, and then he was gone before she could say another thing.

But he didn't call back, and she was sure that was the last time she would ever hear from him. She felt completely at a loss. Why had she created a fight? Now he was *really* gone.

She hated herself. She burst into tears, sobbing all over again. She couldn't even call him back – his number hadn't registered on her phone – and so she had no way of ever getting in touch with him again.

"Oh my God, I will never get over this!" she sobbed. "I will be a lonely, unhappy soul that walks this earth with no purpose and no hope. I had my dream, and I threw it away!" she said, breaking into sobs all over again.

Somehow she made it through the rest of the day alone. She didn't want to see anyone or be with anyone. She spent all day in her room, reading and listening to music. But nothing would make her feel better, nothing could distract from the greatest pain she had ever felt. She was crying not only about losing the man of her dreams, but about the fact that she had actually chased him away by not giving him a chance to explain. What might he have said if only she had listened to him instead of blurting out her hasty, angry words?

It is so strange to feel that you have the whole world in your hands, only to lose it again in four short days.

 *Chapter 14*

IT WAS SUNDAY MORNING, and the girls were moving into their flat, trying to get settled. Classes would start the next day.

"Arielle, can we talk?" Eva said. She could see something in Arielle's eyes that frightened her, and she was pressing her lips together in the way she did when she was nervous.

"Well? What is it?" Arielle asked again, impatiently.

Eva exhaled a couple of times and then gave Arielle such a piercing look that her heart beat ten times faster.

"Arielle, I don't want to frighten you, but I've been seeing something quite unpleasant coming your way shortly," Eva said. "I can't clearly project who this person is, but I see you, and your eyes are horrified at the sight. Please be careful."

She flinched a bit as silence fell between them.

"What do you mean, Eva? You're scaring me," Arielle said.

"I see danger coming your way," Eva repeated quietly.

Arielle's body went numb and she felt a cold chill down her spine.

A stony silence fell in the room, and they were both startled by Gabrielle's cheerful voice asking for help. She looked at Eva with bewilderment and then shook her head, pretty upset.

"Maybe I shouldn't have brought this up right now," Eva murmured, looking first at Arielle, then at Gabby.

"No, I'm glad you did," Arielle said. "Can you tell if it's a man or a woman?"

"I have had the vision several times, and it's a woman, but she has no face. It's just a shadow."

"Well at least I know what to look for," Arielle said with a rueful laugh. "A shadowy woman…"

They both moved to help Gabrielle carry the telly into the flat. Arielle's mind was unwilling to accept Eva's dire prediction, but in her heart, she felt pretty gloomy. What was Eva seeing? She was kind of scared, but how could she do anything about such a vague premonition?

She went to her room and started to put her clothes away. Eva walked into the room behind her and put her arms around her. "Don't worry, Arielle, I will be watching out for you. I have the power to do that. I know it sounds crazy, but please trust me."

"I do trust you, Eva, but I don't mind telling you that I'm scared to death."

"Well, it's just a vision. But I want to make sure that you guard yourself against any unexpected circumstances."

"Thanks, and don't worry, Eva, I'll do that."

As for Eva, her premonition was embedded in her head, but she had to let go of it to function in a normal way.

The week moved sluggishly along and everything seemed to be the same old thing. Nothing had changed except for Arielle. She felt like she wasn't interested in anyone or anything, and she was slipping into deeper and deeper misery as the days went by.

On Friday morning, Gabrielle asked her to ride with her to class. Arielle declined, knowing that she needed to take her own car. She had to run a few errands after class, and she had also promised her parents that she would have dinner with them that evening.

"See you at school," Gabby said happily, and she went out the door.

Eva met Gabby in the parking lot, and they waited for Arielle to get there. They both wanted to know why Arielle had been so quiet lately. So she told them about the phone call from Sebastian. She also told them that she didn't want to talk about it anymore. They understood, and nothing was brought up for the rest of the day. However, Arielle seemed to be in a fog that she couldn't snap out of.

After her last class of the day, she went outside and took a deep breath of fresh air. She climbed into her car and started to back up carefully out of her parking space.

A knock at the passenger window made her jump. She looked over, and Paul was standing there, motioning for her to open her window. He leaned in.

"Hey, we are all going to the cinema tonight. Do you want to come?"

"Oh, Hi Paul, no thanks, I promised my parents that I would stop by for dinner. Maybe another time. Thanks again!" She smiled at him and revved the engine to let him know she needed to go.

He waved goodbye with a disappointed look on his face. But she knew she didn't want to be with anyone tonight. She pushed on the gas and went into town to do some shopping.

She drove home feeling pretty unhappy. Sebastian's face was as a permanent feature in her mind. She knew that another night would be spent full of thoughts about him. He had hung up on her without saying anything.

But what was there to say, anyhow? Tears filled her eyes again and made it hard for her to see the road. It was a cool afternoon, and the roads were not very busy. It was also cloudy and rainy, and that made her mood even worse.

As she turned into her parents' street, she noticed a beautiful blue Porsche parked across the street from their house. She didn't think she had ever seen this car in their neighborhood before, but she wasn't in a mood to care about anything except her own misery. She pulled into the garage and went into the house through the kitchen door. She grabbed a bottle of water from the fridge and ran up the stairs toward her room. She was looking for a couple of CDs she wanted to take back to the flat with her.

"Arielle!" she heard her mother's voice calling. She had come out of the living room and was standing at the bottom of the stairs. "There is a boy here to see you!"

"Me?"

"Yes, can you please come down?"

She threw her backpack on the top of the landing and walked slowly down the stairs.

"Who is it?" she asked.

"I don't know. He says he is a friend of yours."

"Okay, thanks, mum."

As soon as she stepped into the living room, she was jolted by an overwhelming shock. It was like electricity was infusing her skin and making her whole body tingle. She paused, struggling to gain control of herself. The fullness in her throat came back, and she couldn't breathe. Her face turned bright red as she stood there wide-eyed and stared at him.

Sebastian was sitting in a chair across the room. Once again he was undeniably the most beautiful person she had ever seen. He stood up and met her gaze. His gorgeous green eyes were just as she had remembered them, and his lips were ripe and inviting. He was dressed in tight black jeans and a beautiful black silk shirt that completed his perfection and had her completely transfixed.

"Hello, there," he said, his voice soft and warm. His eyes were dazzling, and he looked faintly amused. "Have you missed me?"

She pressed her lips together, trying to collect her thoughts, wondering how it was possible that he was standing there. "Why have you come?" she murmured. She felt really uneasy. What was going on?

"Arielle, we need to talk," he said. "I can't explain over the phone all the things that I have to tell you."

"There is nothing to talk about," she said turning away from him. She knew that if she kept looking at him, she would be lost.

"Please, let's talk," he said. "Can you please just trust me this one time and give me a chance to explain?"

She tried to avoid looking into his eyes, knowing the reaction she had every time she did that. So she stared at the floor, wanting to believe him, wishing that she could forget all that she knew already.

When she looked up, he was standing right next to her. She never saw him move, but somehow he was right there. His lips were moist, inviting, and his eyes were startlingly beautiful. He touched her face and ran his thumb along her bottom lip. Heat cascaded across her muscles, and she hauled in a deep breath.

"Please, let's go somewhere and talk, Arielle," he whispered pleadingly.

"Sebastian, how can I trust you, after al, the things that I now know about you?" she said. Finally, she had the courage to look him in the eyes, but she wasn't dazzled. What she saw was deep hurt, and her determination to not be swayed by him began to falter.

"You. Don't. Know. Anything," he said. His voice was almost sharp as he annunciated each word.

With tears in her eyes and her voice quivering with emotion, she attempted one more time to graciously decline his invitation, but he wouldn't hear of it.

"Did your wife tell you that I visited your home in St. Jean de Luz?" she asked. She looked at him with defiance.

"Arielle, I'm not married. Annabel isn't my wife. I don't give a damn about her. She's nothing but pure frustration for me, but it's hard to make her go away. We must talk about many things before you can understand the situation I'm in and Annabel's presence in my house. Please don't come to any conclusions before you know the truth." His jaw was tense, and his voice was hard. "It's a big mess, that's for sure," he continued. "But I don't want you to think that she means anything to me. I want us to talk alone, I promise to explain everything. There is no one in my life but you. I've waited for you for so long, and I'm not ready to give you up. I'm in love with you."

Arielle turned away, worried that she was just falling for another lie. But he was so hard to resist! "I'm not sure that I'm up for all this," she said. "I'm not sure I can believe anything you have to say." Her voice was trembling, and she started to sob. He reached over to comfort her, but she pulled away, trying to avoid his touch. Lifting her hand, she wiped away her tears. She didn't want him to make her lose her train of thought again.

Then she pressed her lips together, holding back more tears and fighting to keep her voice calm. "It's not only the fact that you didn't show up at the party as you promised. But you didn't even try to see me in the days following the party. Sebastian, you broke my heart," she said despondently and started sobbing again quietly.

His eyes were full of sadness, his voice low and upset.

"Do you hate me, Arielle?" he asked in a voice not much higher than a whisper.

"No, Sebastian, I don't hate you. I'm just having a very hard time trusting you."

"Do you love me, Arielle?" *Of course, he could clearly see that she was totally in love with him, but he wanted to hear it from her lips.*

She couldn't answer, even though she knew that she loved him more than life itself. He was the man of her dreams, her own miracle. But she couldn't trust him! He cupped her face with both hands and ran his thumbs softly on her cheeks, wiping the tears away as he whispered, "I love you, Arielle."

She tried to pull away from him, but his eyes were piercing hers, releasing dazzling immortal power, making her feel totally incoherent. She tried to pull away again as he wrapped his arms around her waist and pulled her against him tightly. His lips brushed her ear gently. His whisper was overflowing with passion and desire that pulsed through his body and mind. "You have to stop being mad at me. Please give me a chance to explain. Will you do that for me?" He put his hand gently underneath her chin and lifted her face until their eyes locked. This time, she allowed it.

"Okay," she said, breaking away from him. "I'll listen to what you have to say." She sighed, wondering if she was making a big mistake, but it felt right.

The tension lifted from his shoulders and, pressing his lips to her forehead, he walked out the door. "I'll be back to pick you up around seven-thirty," he said. His seductive smile succeeded in increasing her pulse and sent a thrill through every nerve in her body. She blinked, and before her next thought he was gone.

She stood there, unable to move for a long time after the door closed behind him. She was not sure why she had agreed to go out with him. She knew that there was another woman in his life, in his home, claiming to be his wife. She didn't feel very hopeful anymore, but she was curious about what he was going to say.

She turned, walked slowly up to her room, and shut the door. Her feelings were all mixed up again. She was happy to see his beautiful face because she was in love with him, but she was not yet ready to accept his story about Annabel. Looking at the clock, she realized she had a couple of hours before he would be back. She got into the shower and then she heard a knock at the door.

"Can I come in?" her mother called out.

"Yes, Mother, I'm in the shower!"

"Who was that?" she asked.

"He's a guy I met at the beach. He's in London on business, so he came to see me and take me out to dinner."

"He is extremely handsome," she said.

Mmm, yes I know he is, she thought to herself. But to her mother, she said, "I'm going out with him tonight. He's picking me up at seven-thirty. I won't be eating dinner at home as I had promised. I'm sorry, Mummy, but I'll come another night and spend time just with you."

"It's all right, dear. I understand."

"Thanks, Mum."

She chose a simple blue silk blouse that was a little darker than the color of her eyes to go with the new pair of jeans she had just purchased. She took a look in the mirror, smiled a quick, fake smile at herself. She thought of how much she would have liked to have a nice tan, but that was just not meant to be. Then she went downstairs.

She could see her father sitting in the kitchen reading the paper while her mother was preparing dinner. It was a little early, so she walked into the sitting room and sat down at the piano. She would be able to see him arrive from the huge picture window.

For Arielle, playing the piano was a remedy that warmed her heart and always gave her pleasure. Soon lovely music filled the room, and she was completely lost in the melody when the doorbell startled her. There was Sebastian, leaning on the doorframe, his beautiful lips curved up into an amazing smile. His eyes moved from her to the piano, and back to her again.

"I didn't know you could play," he said, the smile never leaving his beautiful lips.

"There are a lot of things you don't know about me," she said.

She invited him in to meet her parents and after a few short words, they were ready to leave.

"Have fun," both her parents said simultaneously.

"I'll be back to pick up my car," Arielle told them.

"I'll take good care of her," Sebastian assured them. To Arielle's amazement, they both nodded with great approval. It was as if he had taken supreme control over their emotions already.

He smiled softly as they left the house. When they got to his car, he held the door open for her. She watched him walk around to the driver's side, and she couldn't help thinking of how seamlessly he moved and how beautiful he was.

"Where are we going?" she asked.

"I thought we might go back to my hotel, where we can talk with no interruptions," he said. "We can order dinner in if you like. Would you like to do that?"

Being anywhere with him was fine with her. Tonight she just needed to have the answers to her questions. She needed to know the truth because she was desperately and hopelessly in love with him.

"Yes, that'll be fine," she said. She felt a bit nervous without knowing exactly why.

He drove quickly through the streets, making her wonder how he was so familiar with the area.

"Have you been here before?" she asked.

"Do you mean Brighton?" he asked and looked at her with a soft smile. She nodded.

"Yes, many times," he said.

"Oh. Was that on business?"

"Yes."

She stayed quiet the rest of the way. She knew he was glancing at her frequently, but she didn't look back at him. She wanted so much to believe him; she wanted so much to fall into his arms and tell him how much she loved him.

When they arrived at the hotel, he let the valet take the car as he took her hand and they walked through the lobby towards the elevator. When he hit the button to the penthouse, she looked at him in wonder.

"The penthouse?"

"Why not?" He smiled.

"It must be pretty pricey!"

"Not really," he said with a soft smile.

The room was incredibly huge and gorgeous. He took her coat, and as she looked around, he came and stood in front of her.

He put his finger under her chin and lifted her face until their eyes met and she stopped breathing. She lost her balance and his right arm wrapped around her waist, holding her steady. She saw a faint smile of satisfaction on his face.

She stared into his gorgeous green eyes and his perfect face, trying to take in every inch of him. She focused on fighting to keep her breath slow and steady even though her heart was hammering wildly in her chest and her hands were sweating from anxiety.

Sebastian made sure she was steady on her feet before he let her go as he pulled her toward the sofa.

"Alright," he said with a smile when they sat down. "This is the moment of truth. Go ahead and ask away."

"Who is Annabel?" Her question came out in a shaky voice as Annabel's face filled her mind and she felt the same sickening feeling in the pit of her stomach as she had stood in the foyer of his house back in St. Jean de Luz. She took a couple of deep breaths.

"Who is she?" she pressed on. "And why did she tell me that you are her husband?"

Sebastian took her hands, gazed deep into her eyes, and said regretfully. "Annabel is my horrible nightmare, the evilest existence on this planet." He paused and stroked her hand. "We used to be married, a very long time ago. It was an arranged marriage that was annulled two years later. And she doesn't want to let go."

The word "annulled" seemed to reach such a sensitive part in her thoughts that it gave her body a strange jolt.

"It's pretty complicated," he continued. "I have no control over when she leaves and when she shows up. I don't care about her, I don't love her, and I have never loved her. The two years that we spent together, I was mostly away, and there was no interaction or relationship as man and wife. In fact, we never actually consummated our marriage."

"When were you married?" she asked.

"Arielle, there is something you need to know before I can answer this specific question. It's going to be hard to accept, but it's the truth, and you must know that truth if you are going to be with me. Do you want to be with me?"

What a strange thing to say, she thought to herself. *There is nothing he could say that would keep me away from him.* She couldn't imagine a future without him.

"Yes, I want to be with you," she said. "I love you."

"Well I'm glad to hear that," he said. "Because what I have to say will be extremely difficult for you to hear."

What was he talking about? She looked at him, and he was looking very distressed.

"What is it?" she asked.

Anxiety had spread across his beautiful face, and his eyes were full of shadows.

He shook his head in despair and squeezed her hands in his. She could hear him sucking in a deep breath before he continued.

"I'm not who you think I am," he said.

"Sebastian, what are you trying to say?"

He took a minute before answering, trying to find the right words. When he spoke, his words came out slowly, deliberately. "I have been on this earth…for a very long time."

"What do you mean by a very long time?"

"I mean centuries…I mean long, excruciating centuries. I've remained twenty-seven years old for as long as I can remember. I never get any older."

It took a second to register the meaning of what he was saying. Suddenly she went still. She was completely horrified. Her mind moved back to the bookstore, back to the pages of the family book, back to the Sebastian born in the sixteenth century. No! Could it be?

But that was utterly insane. Nothing was making any sense at all. She closed her eyes, and she felt a cold chill run down her spine. Terror filled her whole body as if the book was coming to life. She was shaking, and sweat was dripping down her back. She had lost all capability of movement, and she felt faint.

"Arielle! Arielle!" She could hear his voice faintly as if it were coming from a great distance.

When she opened her eyes, she was lying in bed, feeling disoriented. She couldn't remember how she had gotten there. Her eyes rested on his amazing face, his expression apprehensive.

"What happened?" she whispered.

"You fainted, sweetheart," he said. He was sitting next to her, his eyes searching her face as if he were trying to read her soul.

She squeezed her eyes closed and bit her lower lip, trying to shake away the last words she had heard. She didn't want to look at him, she didn't want to accept any of this. She lay there for a long time in complete silence.

When she finally opened her eyes, he hadn't moved an inch. He was still sitting next to her, his eyes fixed on her face, and she could see despair written all over him.

As she stared at him, she felt total panic taking over her. He reached out to touch her, and she jerked away, vaulting out of the bed. He didn't try to follow her or to say a word. She walked over to the window. Her legs were shaking as she stared outside without seeing anything at all. A million questions were swirling in her head, but she was too terrified to utter a single word, frightened of what she might hear next.

This couldn't be happening to her!

It was exactly what she had feared. Sebastian was just a dream, a figment of her imagination. She must have wanted someone like him for so long that she had created him in her mind, and now the dream was ready to end. She had fallen in love with the most beautiful man in the world, who was turning out to be anything but a normal human being. She felt herself drowning in sadness.

"Arielle, please!" she heard his soft, velvety voice begging her. But begging her to do what? She gathered every piece of strength her body possessed and turned slowly to face him.

"I need to know the truth, Sebastian. Are you the same Sebastian I read about in your family book?"

"What book is that?" he asked, puzzled.

"The Gaulle estate sixteenth century book?"

She was afraid to hear the answer. She held her eyes closed tight, and pressed her lips together, waiting for his reply. What if he said yes? Would that change the way she felt about him? Would she love him any less? Would she want just to run away?

Her mind was full of questions, questions with no reasonable answers.

His reply was firm, but his voice was weak and worried. "Yes, I am," he said.

Her eyes snapped open, and she stared straight ahead, pretending that she hadn't heard what he just said. She closed them again and stared into the darkness, knowing that this was a very important moment in her life. It was a very dark and scary moment of enormous significance.

"Arielle, do you hear me? I am the same person you read about in my family book."

Her mind was completely frantic, and her body was cold. She didn't want to accept what he was saying. She was thinking of the things she had read in the book; the parts about immortality kept flashing before her like a movie being run over and over again in her mind.

I have to find out who he really is, and what he really wants with me, she thought. She opened her eyes, a cold expression painted on her pale face.

"So...you never get old?" she asked, her voice shaking.

"No, not at all," he said, a smile brightening his beautiful face. "We stop aging after we become immortal," he added.

She wasn't sure she could process this type of information right away. She was pretty frightened.

"Arielle, I would never hurt you," he added gently.

"So, what are you then? Are you a vampire?" She looked at him fearfully.

He looked back at her trying to hold back laughter. "No, my love, I'm not a vampire, I'm an immortal," he said.

"Well, what's immortal? And how can I believe you?"

"Vampires are made up," Sebastian explained slowly, carefully. "They are scary characters in stories used to entertain mortals. Immortals are real. We have lived on this earth always, even before the beginning of civilization. We are immune to sickness, and we can live forever. We have lived among people for centuries, and we don't need to hurt mortals to survive."

She listened to him, trying to breathe normally, but she was still very scared. Was this real? Was it a dream or a nightmare? Could this possibly be happening?

Sebastian stood up, crossed the room, and tried to put his arms around her. But she pulled away, not sure if she wanted to be there or if she needed to run for her life. Seeing her hesitation, he stood an arm's length away, letting her absorb all he was telling her.

"Okay, you are not a vampire," she said. "But what is so special about being immortal? How are you different from humans?"

"Well, I have a heart if you can call it that, but it doesn't beat anymore," he said. "It stopped beating when I became immortal." His voice was heartrending as he continued. "I'm extremely strong, beyond any human comprehension. I can move faster than the human eye can follow. I can sense people's presence from quite a distance. And if I get hurt I have the ability to heal very quickly. I can't cry. and I can't dream," he added, pain in his voice.

"Unbelievable," she whispered. "Is there anything else I need to know about you?"

His eyes fixed helplessly on her face, worried about the next statement, and his voice dropped to a barely audible tone. "I can read everyone's mind, with no exceptions," he said. He was now looking right at her, waiting for her reaction.

"You know everything I'm thinking?" she exclaimed. Her head started spinning out of control, and she felt the floor giving way under her feet. She grabbed a chair to stop her from falling and closed her eyes to get control of herself. Oh my God, all this time he knew how she felt. Embarrassment consumed her as she welled up with anger. She didn't dare to breathe, afraid she might say something she would regret.

"Yes, I know what you are thinking," he said. His eyes were staring at her with utter awareness.

"If you can read my mind, why did you ask me all those questions at the beach? Why do you keep asking me if I love you and if I want to be with you?" she asked. She was furious. He looked completely unfazed by the anger in her voice.

"I wanted to get the answers from your lips, not from inside your head," he said simply.

"What about using my love of *Pride and Prejudice?*" she asked, in sheer frustration. "You knew my feelings about that book and you used them to deceive me." She turned away from him, seething. She was furious and deeply embarrassed.

"I knew all of that," he said. "But I didn't try to deceive you. The book *is* my favorite too, and I *have* felt like Darcy ever since I met you. There is one more thing that you need to know about me," he said. "Immortals can't lie." His voice was firm and steady.

"Well, how did you become immortal? How did this happen?"

"I have been told that you become immortal when you are dying, and you are in the stage between earthbound and crossing to the other side. Someone is there to give you the gift – if you want to call it that – of immortality. I think I know who did this for me, but I'm not sure. And I'm not ready to tell you that right now." He paused before going on. "I realized that I was immortal as time went by and I remained young and unchanged as others got older. I don't understand the purpose of my existence as an immortal on this earth, and there is no one to enlighten me. I would love to know who the first immortal was and where he or she came from, but I have never been able to get an answer to my question. Nobody seems to know."

He was shaking his head. He looked so worried and sad.

"I know the next question will sound a little silly," she said. "But what do you eat?"

"I can eat everything you eat, but I prefer a particular drink that has been passed down through the centuries to the immortals to give our bodies strength and provide the energy we require to survive."

"What is it?"

"It is called Salve," he said.

"Where do you get it?"

"I'm not ready to discuss this right now either."

"Why not?" she asked.

"Arielle, Immortals belong to a secret society that is bound by a code called The Rule," he explained. He paused for a short moment as if he was trying to decide if he should go on. Finally, he continued. "The details of the salve and its source are a secret that is provided to each immortal, and it's to remain a secret. I hope you can accept that."

She was not sure she was ready to accept any of this, but she went on asking questions. Maybe she was trying to reach a point at which something would start making sense to her.

"So you live forever? And nobody can ever harm you?"

"I do have eternal life," he said. "And it's very hard to hurt me, but it's not impossible."

"What do you mean?"

"There are a couple of ways I can be hurt, but I'd rather not talk about something so morbid right now."

"How have you been able to keep busy all these years? Or should I say centuries?"

"I have been very involved in the family business. I'm the only heir to what my father created. I have attended practically every university around the world and have studied every possible course ever offered. I hold multiple degrees, and I have lived in most parts of the world. I have learned many languages, I have read myriad books, and I have listened to thousands of recordings. I love sports, and I am a passionate horseback rider. I still get bored and try to find new things to do." He chuckled under his breath, and his voice changed to a soft whisper as he added, "Immortality is something that was very hard to accept, Arielle. It is very difficult to live with. I had to move from place to place as people around me started to get older and they started to notice that I wasn't changing."

She was beginning to feel sad for him, and she reached out to take his hand. "Have you ever made friends with mortals?" she asked. "Have you ever dated a mortal?"

"I stopped making mortal friends or getting close to them. It was hard to see them get sick or die. I didn't like the constant pain of losing someone I cared about. It was hard moving away all the time. As the years went by, it all became routine, but it never stopped making me sad. You are the only mortal I have ever wanted to be with. And actually, you are the only woman I have ever loved."

"Are there many like you?" she asked.

"Yes, there are many. One of them is Annabel. This is why I'm trying to tell you that it's not easy to get rid of her; she can show up any time and any place she likes. She isn't ready to give me up even though we have been apart for more than five hundred years."

Arielle wasn't sure what to do with all this information. She felt overwhelmed, but she still loved Sebastian just as much as she had before she knew any of this.

"Sebastian, you can read my mind, so I'm sure you know that I'm completely and utterly in love with you. But I'm also very worried about this relationship. The fact that you can see my thoughts also makes me very uncomfortable," she added.

She looked out the window again and wrapped her hands around her body as she felt a cold wave of fear sweep over her. His voice was low as he responded to her. She could feel him standing behind her but not touching her.

"I think you know just about everything there is to know about me now," he said. "Now you can decide if you want to be with me or if you want to walk away." His voice was full of sadness. He paused and then added, "I love you, Arielle. And I know that I've been looking for you all my long life. I'll never hurt you or let anyone else hurt you. I hope you'll try to understand and accept who I am, and what I am, and that you will not leave me."

His voice was breaking as he continued, "I know that I can't live without you, but if you decide to walk away because you can't accept me, I'll not stop you. I love you, and I think I had loved you all my life – even before I knew you."

Arielle's heart was pounding in her chest and she was trying to breathe normally. She walked out onto the balcony and felt the wind brush her face. It was twilight, and in the distance the daylight was giving way to the night-lights of the city.

 *Chapter 15*

AS ARIELLE STOOD on the balcony, grappling with the meaning of all she had just heard, she was sure he was standing in the same place unmoved, watching her, giving her time to take in and understand all she was dealing with.

There is a lot to understand here, but one thing I know is that I can't walk away, no matter how bad this whole thing seems to be right now, she thought. *God, I love him!*

She turned around and looked back at him, looked into his beautiful green eyes, and once again she lost her train of thought. He was now releasing on her all the power he held in his gorgeous eyes.

She gasped for breath, something she now understood to be a normal reaction from looking into his eyes. Then she felt herself falling. She never saw him move, but his strong arms wrapped around her, holding her steady in a muscular embrace, stopping her from hitting the floor.

Her eyes were full of tears, and she finally realized that she was crying. She was actually crying because she couldn't fathom all that she now knew about him. How could this ever work? He had eternal life, and she didn't. She would get old while he stayed young and beautiful forever. He had lived for almost five centuries on this earth. He'd had a long time to learn to live with whatever this was, or whoever he was, but she'd had only a few minutes to try to understand what had been literally impossible just months ago.

She pulled away from him as soon as the dazzling wore off, and she saw the disappointment on his face. But there was a lot for her to take in. She thought that the best thing would be for her to go home. She was sure he knew what she was thinking, and that was even more difficult to accept. She didn't seem to want to get away from him. She was waiting for him to make the next move, and then he did.

He encircled her with his arms and pulled her tightly against his chest. He put his finger under her chin and tipped her face up. Her lips were pressed together from the stress and anguish over Sebastian's revelations. He bent down and covered her mouth with his, his tongue parting her lips, thirsty for a loving response. His mouth was moist and hot, and she couldn't help but give into the most amazing feeling, the hottest passion she had ever felt, which hit her body like an overwhelming wave of emotion that seized her very soul. Pulling back he slid his hand along her back and pulled her even closer. She stopped breathing as the heat of his gaze, and the feel of his perfect body against hers made her tremble with anticipation.

"Sebastian, you can read my mind, so I don't need to tell you that I love you with all my body and soul," she whispered breathlessly against his lips.

How can I ever live without him? There is no human being that can ever make me feel the way he does, she thought. She wrapped her arms around his neck, and they stayed there, just holding each other for a long time, and she knew this was where she wanted to be forever.

"Arielle, I can't bear the thought of losing you," she heard his magical voice whisper in her ear. "I want you here in my arms, where you belong for all eternity. Am I forgiven for all the things you thought I might have done this last month?"

She pressed her lips together, put her hands on his chest and pushed him away softly. He immediately moved.

"Am I forgiven?" he asked again.

"Yes, you are forgiven," she said. "But it will take time for me to understand and accept everything you have just told me."

He lifted her face to his again. "I know this is a lot for you to absorb, Arielle," he said. "But I know how to wait. I have been looking for you for more than five centuries, and I'm willing to do whatever it takes to keep you right here in my arms." A beautiful smile curved his perfect lips, and his gaze was soft. "If you really want to leave right now I'll take you home," he said, "but I hope you will stay here with me."

She leaned in and kissed him softly, showing him that she wasn't going anywhere. She closed her eyes and tried to fill her lungs with some fresh air as she heard him whisper, "I don't think I can be without you any longer. I'm not sure what is happening to me, but I have to see you be able to breathe."

Now the feeling that she was living a dream grew even stronger. She was afraid to close her eyes, thinking that when she opened them all of this would be gone, including her beautiful dream, Sebastian.

His next question took her by surprise. "So, how did you like the house in St. Jean de Luz?" he asked. She stared at him, instantly remembering her last visit. Her delight was palpable.

"Oh! I think it was the most amazing place I have ever seen," she said. "I would love to go back there someday. But not with Annabel there, of course." She chuckled softly as she added the last thought.

"Is this really something you would like to do?" he asked.

"Yes. I would like to find out everything behind such a beautiful place. I want to know about all those people in the paintings. It must be amazing to be able to trace your family back for centuries. I can't go any further back than my grandmother," she laughed. "And I want to know about the ladies of that house. There must be legends attached to such a great house. Was Annabel the lady of the house at one point in time?"

"No! She was never the lady of the Gaulle estate. She was out of my life centuries before I moved to St. Jean de Luz. I'm telling you, Arielle, she is the most dreadful nightmare. A nightmare that will not go away."

The thought of Annabel made her shiver.

"I'd love to take you there," he said. "But we need to talk more about Annabel. We can do it tonight or this weekend. I'll be here through the weekend, and I want to be with you. Is this is something you'd like to do?"

"Yes," she said softly.

"Arielle, I want to be close to you so I can see you every day."

Her heart was overwhelmed with happiness but she didn't say anything.

"Do you want me to be close to you?" he murmured.

She reached out and wrapped her arms around his neck. She gazed up into his emerald eyes and, setting her mouth to his, she tasted his passion in that intoxicating immortal scent. He succumbed to her burning desire and moaned blissfully.

"I never want you to go away," she said. "And I know you can read my mind, so you know it's true."

He ran his finger along the side of her neck, up to her jaw and around her lips, leaving a hot, burning sensation trailing on her skin.

"I am so glad to hear that," he whispered.

His eyes were warm and inviting, and she stopped breathing as he set his mouth on hers once again. His arms tightened around her waist, and the kiss deepened to a more passionate, more desperate, more scorching level. He led her to the sofa, and she shivered in his arms. They stayed in each other's arms for a long while without saying anything more about immortality, or about Annabel.

It was close to midnight when she decided to leave. She would have loved to spend the night with him, but she didn't think that was the right thing to do. He drove her home slowly, holding her hand. She knew he was happy, and she also knew that she would love him for eternity. The enormity of that word – especially now, given what she had learned about Sebastian – made her chuckle.

Back at her parents' house, Sebastian held the car door open for her, and she stepped out. He pulled her up and into his arms, and took her mouth in a hungry kiss. His lips move against hers, and his tongue found hers in a devouring kiss. A low moan escaped her, and Sebastian felt it deep in his bones.

"I love you, Arielle," he half-moaned. "I'll call you tomorrow."

"I love you, too," she whispered. "I'll be waiting for your call."

Then he walked her to her car and took her in his arms once more. She shuddered in his embrace and this time his kiss sparked a fire in her body. Would she ever stop feeling this way each time she found herself in his arms? She was hoping the answer would be no, never!

She drove back to her flat overwhelmed. She paused at the door for a short moment and, taking a deep breath, she walked inside. She looked around the living room and the kitchen area, and listened for any sounds coming from the bedrooms, but there was complete silence. She let out a breath of relief; Eva and Gabrielle were not home yet. She really didn't feel much like talking, she just wanted to go into her room and close the door. She needed to sort out her thoughts in complete seclusion. She took a quick shower, and, taking her journal from the desk drawer, she climbed into bed. She pushed the pillows against the headboard to support her back and settled down, eager to pour her thoughts onto the vacant pages.

September 3

I am sure that I have found the man that fits the image etched in my very soul. I have fallen profoundly and irrevocably in love with Sebastian, and nothing will deter me from being with him. His revelation was unquestionably frightening, but my need for him is truly beyond my control. I can't lie: I'm terrified of his immortal world, and I've no idea how dangerous of a journey this will be. But I'm intensely curious to see it through. I'm ready to embark on this new path of my life, to hold his hand and walk next to him no matter what. I've discovered to my dismay that nothing matters to me but being in his arms. I'm somewhat relieved that I know the truth about his true identity, and now I'm filled with anticipation of the next step in our relationship. I'm sure that my love for him demands that I embrace every aspect of his life, even eternity. This was a significant day for me, and I can't imagine what tomorrow might bring. It's hard to believe that Sebastian died centuries ago. He is warm, loving and more alive than any other living human being I know. His timeless existence is what I have now embraced, and I'm anxious to find out where we go from here. I love him deeply, and I pray that our lives remain interwoven – for eternity.

Arielle put the journal away, and sliding under the covers, she closed her eyes in sheer bliss. *Eternity!* She thought to herself and chuckled. *What an amazing word!* His face was permanently etched in her mind. She smiled wide, remembering the feel of his body against hers and tensing as heat rippled through her again. She hugged her pillow tight and, drawing in a deep breath, she let sleep claim her.

Sebastian drove away with a heavy heart. He didn't want to go to the hotel alone. He didn't want to be away from her. He wanted to be able to touch her and hold her. He felt the world melting around him whenever she was close, as if everything inside of him was being shaken loose. He felt like nothing could ever keep them apart. The heat he felt every time their bodies touched was like nothing he had ever felt before. Every time he kissed her he wanted to devour her mouth and suck all the sweetness out of it. Her body seemed to fit perfectly against his, and the sugariness of her lips seemed to unravel new feelings in him and challenge the control he thought he had over himself.

His feelings were making him dizzy, and the pleasure he felt was incredible. He wanted to be with her and protect her from anything that might make her sad. He wanted to make her happy, to make her want no other man but him, forever. He knew he couldn't live without her anymore.

He arrived at the hotel, and after taking a shower, he got into bed. He wished he had the ability to dream. He knew that if only he could dream, he would have spent the whole night dreaming of her. He could hardly wait for tomorrow to look into her beautiful blue eyes, those eyes that had mesmerized him from the very first moment.

Tomorrow they had to talk about Annabel. He knew it would not be long before Annabel was following him again. How he hated her! The very thought of her made him furious.

He stared into space, Arielle on his mind and in his heart, and shortly after that he fell into a deep sleep.

The next morning, the sun rose slowly over the small hills, and the leaves on the trees rustled gently in the light breeze. Sebastian opened his eyes and felt completely happy. He was going to be with her again. How could one person make him feel so incredibly amazing? She had bewitched him, and he was happy to yield to that feeling.

He took some salve out of his suitcase and made himself a full glass. He drank it slowly as he gazed out the balcony door facing the park and beyond to the wonderful blue ocean.

He thought of her again. Her eyes were the exact color of the ocean he was looking at. She was graceful, and her hair looked like soft silk under the sunlight. He would love to run down to the beach holding her hand, feeling the damp grass beneath his feet until they reached the warm sand.

He sat back on the bed, picked up his mobile phone, and pressed her number.

Her phone rang before she was even awake.

"Hello?"

"Hello, Arielle! Did I wake you up?"

"No," she lied.

"What were you doing?" he asked softly and eagerly.

"I was lying here just thinking of you," she said with a chuckle.

"I was doing the same thing, so I thought I should call you."

"I'm so happy to hear your voice first thing in the morning."

"How would you like to spend the day with the man who loves you more than you could ever dream of?"

"I would like that very much, but he hasn't called yet. I'm waiting for his call," she said and burst out laughing. He joined in, and they laughed together happily.

"What time do you want me to pick you up?"

"How about in a couple of hours? I need to take a shower, have some breakfast, and get ready. How about around eleven? Is that good?"

"I am not sure I can wait that long, but I guess I will just have to make it until then," he said.

Before he hung up he whispered, "Miss me."

 *Chapter 16*

SHE WAS HALFWAY into the shower when the phone in the flat rang, and she ran to pick it up. It was Gabrielle.

"Hello," she said.

"Hey, I just wanted to let you know that I'm with Troy, and I won't be back until tomorrow night."

"Does Eva have plans for the whole weekend too?" Arielle asked, trying not to sound too concerned about the response. But she was really hoping the answer would be yes.

"Yes, she is spending the weekend with her mum, and she has a date for tonight. I don't know the details. I'm sure we'll find out soon enough," Gabrielle said, giggling.

"A date? Eva? Are you sure?"

"Well, like I said, I've no details. But that's what she said."

"Now that I think about it, she called me and told me she needed to talk to me about something, but we never got around to it," Arielle said. "Do you think she found a new guy?"

"I don't know, but I'm sure we'll find out," Gabby said.

"All right, Gabby, I'll see you later." Arielle hung up the phone and smiled, thinking of Eva's refrain every time she and Gabby talked about guys. She always had such a serious look on her face, and she always repeated the same words over and over again: *"I don't have a love life. There's nobody here for me. I will die an old maid."*

Arielle laughed out loud thinking about her friend as she tried to pick out a nice outfit for her date with Sebastian. She wanted to look really special. After all, this would be their first official date. She smiled to herself, feeling utterly pleased. She took a warm shower, and she was getting ready to dry her hair when she heard the doorbell and ran to open the door. There he stood, more beautiful than ever. His magnificent lips were curved up into that amazing smile that drove her right out of her mind. He was devastatingly handsome, and for a moment once again she was speechless.

"Good morning! Am I too early?" he asked.

Her eyes were full of excitement, and without hesitation she reached toward him and pulled him inside. "No, not at all, I'm almost rea..."

But before she could finish her sentence she was in his arms. His body felt warm, and all she wanted to do was stay right where they were and let him kiss her for hours. She could never get tired of his soft, exciting lips. She had dreamed about them, she had dreamed about every part of him. And now it was real. "Do you know how hard it is for me to be away from you?" he whispered, his lips still touching hers. She swallowed hard and kissed him back.

"Your hair is dripping wet, and you look so beautiful," he said, reaching up and pushing her hair away from her face. "Are your roommates here?"

"Not right now. They are both away for the weekend," she said. She invited him to follow her and wait in her room while she was getting ready.

"Are you sure?" he asked.

"Yes, I'm very sure," she said, tugging on his shirt, amused by his hesitation. He followed her to her room. She proceeded to blow-dry her hair and brush her teeth as he looked around the room.

"It's lovely," he said as he moved to the window and gazed out.

"Not a great view!" she said with a laugh. Her window looked into a courtyard surrounded by flats.

"It's not that bad. It's a college atmosphere, you shouldn't expect too much," he said. "Have you moved all your stuff?"

"I've moved most of my music, clothes, and books. I still have a lot at home, but I'm not sure if I'll bring everything here. I do spend quite a lot of time at home as well. The flat is very close to the house, so if I need something, I can always just get it."

She finished brushing her hair, and as she came out of the bathroom, she saw him bending over and picking up the book that was still lying open on the bed. He looked up at her, a wide grin on his face.

"*Pride and Prejudice?* It would seem to me that you must know this book by heart by now."

"I do, but I still love it. I like to read it now and then."

"So, have you found your Darcy?" he asked her, glancing at her with a sweet, shy smile.

She walked over to him, wrapped her arms around his neck, and looked straight into his eyes even though she knew the reaction that would create for her. Her heart stopped as she pressed her mouth on the curve of his lips. She wanted to breathe in his scent, taste him as deeply as she could. The heat was radiating off of him, and her heart picked up speed. He leaned closer, brushing his lips against her ear, and she found herself struggling to breathe. She flinched as she felt her body nearly overriding her mind, and she pulled back. "You don't have to ask me anymore," she said. "I know you can read my mind, so you know that I have."

"Arielle, I need to hear it from your lips."

"I missed you," she murmured.

"Show me," he whispered.

All the emotions that she had tried to keep in check up until that moment burst out of her as she pulled him closer, pressing her lips against his sensuous lips down the side of his neck, back up to his gorgeous mouth until she couldn't breathe anymore. Sebastian ached with desire for her, and it took all of his strength to resist the urge to tear her clothes off.

"Mmmm," he moaned. His kiss became more and more passionate until suddenly he pulled away.

"I think we'd better be going," he said, "before I lose control of myself."

They went outside, and he held the car door open for her. She got in, thrilled with the thought of spending the whole day with this beautiful man.

He drove to Hove Park, where he parked close to the beach. "I thought we could take a walk," he said. He reached over and gently pushed a wisp of hair away from her eyes.

"Yes, I love the beach," she said.

They walked quietly along the beach holding hands. Their feet dug into the warm sand, and they felt perfectly content. The sun was bright, and a light breeze touched their faces. The waves rolled softly, folded, and broke with a light murmur, kissing the warm sand. The beach was extended for a few long miles down the road, and they couldn't see the end of it.

After a little while, they found a spot on the beach that looked private, and they sat down. He put his arm around her shoulders and pulled her close.

"Arielle," he said, "we must talk about Annabel. And we have to do it today because I am leaving tomorrow. I need to talk to you about her, and then there will be no more secrets."

"Well, I can't say that this is my favorite subject," she said. "But I do need to know what she's doing in your life and why you can't make her go away."

Sebastian sighed a deep sigh. Then he took her hands in his, sighing again.

"The reason I missed your parents' party is that I needed to be in London," he said. "I wanted to meet with the woman who has been my mother since I lost my own parents centuries ago. Her name is Olivia Dillon, and she is a very powerful woman. She has the answers to my problems almost all the time. She is helping me now to find a way to get rid of Annabel forever."

"Your mother lives in London?" she exclaimed.

"No, she lives in Canterbury, not far from Brighton."

"That is incredible! How come you never told me about her before?"

"It never came up before now," he said. Then he looked at her seriously, adding, "The situation with Annabel is very dangerous, Arielle. She will try to hurt you if she finds out about us, and she will find out sooner or later."

"What do you mean, hurt me?" Arielle asked nervously. She felt a sudden rush of fear course though her body. Immediately Eva's warning came back to her, and her face grew tense. She could hear Eva's words again clearly as if she were standing right next to her. *"You are in grave danger,"* she had said. Oh, my God, she was right! Maybe

Annabel was the woman that Eva had been seeing in her visions.

How was she going to deal with this? How was she going to fight an immortal? She was just a mere mortal with no special powers, no ability to protect herself from someone like Annabel.

As he continued to speak, Sebastian's words only compounded her fear.

"She is willing to hurt seriously anyone who becomes part of my life," he said. "She vowed to do that when our annulment went through."

"Sebastian, you're scaring me," she said. Her voice was calm, but her head was full of anxious thoughts.

"You need to take this seriously," he replied. "I have always been aware of Annabel's fury and her promise to hurt any person that I fall in love with. But I have never felt true love for any woman until I met you. Now I'm very worried, and I have to do all I can to keep you safe. Olivia suggested a solution that seems to be the best idea for now," he added.

"Oh? And what is that?"

"She is the owner of a very special necklace – it has extraordinary powers – and she is giving it to you," he said. "You will have to wear it at all times."

As he spoke, he handed her a small black pouch, which she took with a wondering mind. The necklace inside was the most beautiful piece of jewelry she had ever seen. The blue stone was magnificent, and the chain shimmered like sparkling sunlight. She smiled with pleasure and asked him to put it around her neck.

"Is this really going to protect me?" she asked. "How exactly does it work?"

"The stone is very powerful," Sebastian replied. "It belonged to an Egyptian pharaoh centuries ago. It was known to keep evil spells away from the owner of the necklace, and now that is you. Everything you need to know is in this little black book," he said, handing her the book. "You'll need to keep it in a safe place. This is not something you can play around with."

Arielle nodded solemnly as he spoke. Of course, she was completely aware of spell books and their powers because of Eva's interest in the occult.

"Please make sure you never take this necklace off while you are away from me," Sebastian said. "When you wear it Annabel is weak, and she can't touch you."

She was silent for a long moment as he watched her anxiously, waiting for her reaction. She ran her fingers over the necklace and assured him that it would stay on her neck for as long as he wanted her to wear it. Then, without a word, he pulled her into his arms again and kissed her tenderly.

"I love you, Arielle," he whispered. "I'm not sure how I will be able to live without you for the next few months. I'll call you, and I'll try to visit as often as I can. And next year, I'll move here."

"Move here?"

He laughed out loud, thinking how crazy it was for him to attend college yet again, just to be near her, but he didn't say anything. He just pushed her softly down onto the sand and laid his head on top of her chest.

With his beautiful body next to hers she closed her eyes, feeling his warmth, his love, and his sizzling touch. She ran her fingers through his beautiful hair, and as she did, she felt as though they were becoming one body and one soul. They stayed on the beach for hours like that, just holding each other, not wanting to move. But finally, it was time to break the silence.

"What time are you leaving tomorrow?" she asked.

"At two o'clock."

"I want to come with you," she said. "I'll drive you to the airport."

"If that's what you want, then that is what we will do," he murmured, nestling even closer to her.

It was late when they finally decided to stand up. The feel of his body against hers made her tremble. Waves of heat shot through her; she wrapped her arms around his neck, and their lips met with fervor. She was afraid that if she closed her eyes, he might just disappear. She didn't want him to leave the next day; she was so afraid something might happen, that he would never come back.

Reading her thoughts, he pulled her even closer, wanting to reassure her that everything was going to be all right.

"What are you thinking, Arielle?" he asked with a low chuckle.

"Sebastian, why do you keep asking?"

"Tell me what you're thinking. I want to hear you say it."

So she told him about her fears. He smiled wide. "There is nothing on this earth that will keep me away from you, Arielle. Not now, not ever. All I want is to be with you. But we both have to sort through several things before we can be together, don't you agree?"

She nodded, and they walked to the car.

"Can I take you to dinner?" he asked.

"But you don't really eat!" she said.

"Well, I'm sure *you* are hungry, and I will be happy to sit with you and watch you eat something," he replied.

"No, thank you," she said. "I'm not really hungry."

He drove her to the flat. "I wish you could stay with me all night," he said as he kissed her goodbye. He knew that she wanted to do the same thing, but she pushed herself away reluctantly, smiled, and waved as he drove away. She stood there, watching his car move away into the distance until she couldn't see it anymore.

She wasn't sure why she hadn't gone with him to the hotel. She was sure there was nothing that she wanted more in this world than to spend the night with him, but she had made a vow to herself that she would remain abstinent until she was married. She was determined to keep that commitment as she pondered the potential consequences. She just wasn't ready to take that step yet.

She sighed and went to bed, but it took her a long time to fall asleep that night. She was too excited, and she had so much to think about. She was sad that he was leaving the next day but happy that they'd had two days together and that he had cleared up all the questions she had to her satisfaction.

She didn't know how it was going to work out between them, him being immortal and she being a human, but at this point, she didn't care. All she knew was that she loved this man beyond any doubt and that "forever" was the only word she could think of when she thought about how long she wanted to be with him. Finally, she fell asleep, completely exhausted.

The next morning her phone woke her up, and Sebastian's voice sent a warm sensation coursing through her body.

"Good morning! Do you still want to take me to the airport?" he asked.

"Yes, of course, I do!" she said.

"I'll have the hotel take my car to storage and wait for you to pick me up. Will that work for you?"

"I'll be there within the hour. I'm getting up right now."

"Great! We will have a little time here before I have to leave. Did you miss me last night?"

"Missing you is all I seem to do lately," she said, smiling.

"And that is all I want you to do every time we're apart," he chuckled. "Miss me!" she heard him whisper, and the phone went dead.

She got up and put on a plain white silk blouse and a pair of jeans. Her hair spread over her shoulders, and her face was blazing with desire for him.

Getting to the hotel seemed to take a century, she was so eager. When he opened the door to his room, she gasped. He was so stunningly beautiful that she couldn't utter a single word. He was standing there like Adonis, naked from the waist up, showing his amazing bare chest, his lips curved in that beautiful smile of his. Once again she had to ask herself if he was even real. He reached out, pulled her into the room, and closed the door behind them.

"What am I going to do with you?" he said, pressing his lips to hers and kissing her passionately. "Do you have any idea what you do to me every time you are near?"

She threw her arms around his neck and pulled herself close to that amazing body, smiling and letting him know that she was crazy about him. He could read her thoughts, so she knew there was no need for her to say a word.

"Sebastian, I don't want you to go," she said. She hesitated for a moment and then sighed. He bent down and pressed his lips on hers again, his arms tightened around her waist. "I don't want to go either, but I have to."

He took her hand and pulled her over to the bed. He leaned toward her and his lips traced each part of her face, neck, and shoulders. She was burning with desire, and when his lips found hers, she stopped breathing. His kiss was filled with longing. She was trying to keep her mind straight, but she almost lost it when she felt him push her softly back onto the pillows and roll over her. His body pressed softly on hers, and she flinched.

He pulled away immediately. "I am sorry, Arielle, I got carried away," he murmured. "It's hard not to lose control when I'm so close to you. Don't worry, I know how to wait."

They talked for a while longer, and then it was time for him to go.

The drive to the airport was quiet. He held her hand and squeezed it softly several times. She leaned in and pressed her lips to his cheek, and he assured her that he would be back very soon.

At the airport she wrapped her arms around his neck and their lips met passionately. She let go of him with a heavy heart, but he tightened his grip on her again and pulled her hard against him as his mouth landed on hers with unmistakable hunger. He didn't want to let her go, and she was elated. His beautiful eyes were gazing into hers as if he was trying to imprint the image of her face in his mind. She didn't need to do that – his beautiful face had been permanently imprinted in her mind since the very first time she saw him. He pulled her closer to him one more time and kissed the tip of her nose. They stayed in each other's arms, and he finally let go as he turned and walked towards the security gate.

"I'll call you tomorrow. I love you, baby," he murmured. "Miss me, Arielle!"

He asked her to miss him every time they parted. *He knows that I miss him even when he's standing here, right next to me,* she thought.

He waved, and then he was gone. She pressed her face against the huge terminal window and watched the plane taxi down the runway. She watched it lift into the air and kept watching until it finally disappeared into the sky. She drove back to the flat, sad that he was gone, but happy about what they had accomplished and what was still to come.

Sebastian sat on the plane looking out the window, watching the city disappear as they climbed above the clouds. His thoughts were full of Arielle and her beautiful face. He knew how she felt about abstinence and remaining a virgin until she was married, and he didn't want to do anything to make that difficult for her. He was going to marry her, and he knew how to wait.

But he was trying to understand what had happened on the beach when he had put Olivia's necklace on Arielle. He had been taken aback. As soon as he had closed the clasp and the necklace had touched her skin, there was complete silence coming from Arielle's mind. She kept telling him that he knew what she was thinking, but the truth was that after that moment he couldn't hear her thoughts anymore. He hadn't said anything about it, but he didn't like that at all. He wanted to know what she was thinking at all times. *Well, at least I know that the necklace is protecting her from everything, including my ability to read her mind, apparently,* he thought ruefully.

Her face had haunted him every day since the day he laid eyes on her on that beach, and her voice tore through his soul every time she spoke. Being able to read her thoughts had filled him with such pleasure, and the strange silence that had occurred once he put the necklace on her was puzzling and unsettling. He would have to find out why it was blocking her thoughts from him.

 *Chapter 17*

IT WAS SIX O'CLOCK when Arielle arrived back at the flat, and both Gabrielle and Eva were there. They decided to go out and get something to eat and didn't get back until quite late. They knew they had classes the next morning, but they wanted to tell each other all about their romantic adventures, so they decided to open a bottle of wine. They sat on the floor, eager to hear about each other's new guys.

"I fell in love with Sebastian from the very first moment I saw him standing on that beach, just a couple of feet away from me." Arielle's voice came out softly as the memory of his touch fueled her passion and sheer bliss spread across her face. "He explained to me why he missed our party, and we've worked things out. I get the most extraordinary feeling just by standing next to him, just holding his hand," she said and closed her eyes. Pleasure surged through her body, and she quivered.

She was startled to hear Eva's voice saying, "Arielle, snap out of it!" She opened her eyes and smiled wide.

"Oh, I'm just thinking about him," she said. "I hate being away from him," she muttered, frowning. "But he did say that there is a possibility that he will move here next year. For now, it'll be a long distance relationship, and I must say I hate it. He did say that he would try to visit as much as possible. I just can't believe this is really happening," she added. "I just can't believe it!"

She didn't mention anything about Sebastian's true nature to her friends. But how could she explain something like that? She exhaled, feeling his absence almost as a physical ache, longing for his arms.

She did tell them that there was a crazy woman who was infatuated with Sebastian and that she was stalking him. This woman could become a problem for her down the road, and that was something she was a bit worried about. Eva's body seemed to tighten and her gaze pierced through Arielle's. Arielle knew just what she was thinking, and she tried to look unruffled, but in fact, she too was a little shaken up just remembering Eva's prophetic words.

When Eva spoke, her voice was soft but determined. "I promise you, Arielle, if she ever tries to harm you, we will stop her," she said. As she spoke, the softness in her voice gave way to resolve and even anger. Gabrielle looked startled, and Arielle laughed, trying to make light of the situation. She knew that Eva was serious, but deep down inside she also knew that the problem of Annabel was not so easy to dismiss.

"Anyway," she said rapidly, wanting to change the subject, "tell us about Troy, Gabby."

Gabrielle's eyes lit up, and she placed her hand over her heart.

"I'm totally in love," she said. "Completely captivated by his mere existence! He is extremely clever and indescribably beautiful." She stayed silent for a few moments while she took on a faraway look. A wide smile spread across her face, and they knew that she was thinking of him, remembering some sweet moment she hadn't yet shared with them. They let her just enjoy the moment. Finally, Arielle coughed loudly enough to bring her back to what she was saying.

"Oh, I'm so sorry! I guess I got carried away for a moment," she giggled.

Eva and Arielle laughed, knowing exactly how she felt.

"I'll be spending a lot of time with him," she said. "I hope you don't mind."

"Gabby, we don't care what you do as long as you're happy," Arielle said, trying to hold back her laughter. Gabrielle looked away again, and the same dreamy smile appeared on her face while they listened to her barely audible voice.

"He is such a great kisser. I could spend the rest of my life doing nothing else but kissing him!"

At this they couldn't help themselves, they laughed out loud again. Gabby looked startled.

"What?" she said.

"You were thinking out loud. Was that something you really wanted us to know?"

Gabrielle giggled happily. "Oh, I don't mind," she said, blushing just a little. "I want to introduce you to him tomorrow, after class."

Now it was Eva's turn, and they were all ready to hear her same old sob story, but this time they were in for a surprise. Eva had met a guy a few nights before, the same night Arielle was out with Paul.

"Is he a student here?" Arielle asked.

"He is a new student this year," she said. "He transferred here from Manchester University. His name is Ian, and he has swept me off my feet," she said excitedly. "We have been together practically every night, and he is just wonderful! He takes me to dinner, to the cinema, and we take long walks together. We can talk about everything and anything. He brings me flowers, and we watched the sunset together. I want to spend every waking moment with him. I want him to love me forever! He is very handsome, he is warm, graceful, and, by the way, he too is an excellent kisser," she concluded, giggling with delight.

Listening to Eva and looking at her shining face, Arielle could see that she was absolutely crazy about Ian. *Now Ian can become her focal point and she won't be spending her time thinking about spell books, or her special powers, or the cemetery, or summoning someone back from the dead,* she thought. She smiled, pleased and relieved, and moved closer to Eva to give her a hug.

"He has asked over and over again to meet you two, but you haven't been around," she said. "When can you meet him?"

"Anytime, Eva," Gabrielle said, hugging her too. "He sounds wonderful. I can't wait to meet him! What is he studying?"

"He is studying to be a doctor," she said.

"Ohhhhhh! A doctor! So maybe it's true that great things happen to those who wait?" Arielle chuckled.

"It seems to be true," Eva murmured, laughing happily. "Anyway, I can't wait for you to meet him."

It was late, time to retire. So they finished their wine and headed for bed. Before Arielle climbed into bed, she sat down at the computer and sent Sebastian a short e-mail.

"I am getting ready to go to bed, and I was thinking of you. I do so wish you were here. I miss you terribly. I love you!"

She read the words over and then hit send.

She had brushed her teeth and was almost ready to get into bed when she heard the e-mail ping. Her heart skipped a beat; she smiled gleefully and ran back to the computer. Yes! It was a return message.

"I was sitting here thinking of you when I received your e-mail. Thank you for loving me and for making me happy. I love you more than life, and I need you to the point that it hurts. I want you to miss me when I'm not there. I want to be your first thought in the morning and your last thought before you go to bed. I want you to dream about me and only me. You have bewitched me, Miss Elizabeth, and I'll love you for eternity."

The image of his beautiful face surged through her head, and she longed for him. She could see the stunning curve of his lips and could almost taste his immortal sweetness. She closed her eyes as his absence filled her with emptiness. Her fingers moved once again on the keyboard.

"Good night, Darcy. I'm going to bed right now, and I pray that I dream of you because I'm so lonely that I want to cry…I need you here with me."

His next e-mail was short, but it filled her with an aching tenderness.

"I love you, baby. Miss me!!"

She shut the computer down and closed her eyes, trying to see his beautiful face.

They had agreed to e-mail each other, but also to call. She knew she needed to hear his voice. He had also promised to come and visit a couple of times before the semester was over. With that happy thought, she drifted off to sleep.

The next morning she didn't have class until ten o'clock. She got up, made some coffee, and took a cup with her back to her bedroom. Eva had already gone to an early class, and Gabrielle was in the shower. She sat in front of her computer and, switching the power on, she decided to send a short e-mail to Sebastian. She typed a few words in and was getting ready to hit "send" when she saw a new e-mail pop up on her screen. It was from Sebastian.

> *"I woke up missing you, and I wanted to tell you that I love you before you left for class. Please miss me!!! I'll call you soon."*

Complete happiness took over her body, and her fingers moved quickly on the keyboard again.

> *"I just finished typing a note to you and was just getting ready to hit send when I got your e-mail. I'm so happy that you are thinking of me. I'm missing you terribly. I don't think I can stand being away from you this long. I'm glad you still love me because your love is what sustains me right now. Okay, I'm heading to class."*

She hit "send" and ran to take a quick shower. She pulled on jeans and a T-shirt and grabbed her books. She heard the computer ping again just as she started to walk out the door. She whirled, filled with excitement, and ran back to open her e-mail.

> *"I love you more than you could ever love me. Miss me!!"*

How could a few words so change her whole outlook on the day? All she could do was smile as she walked to the door.

"I can't wait to meet your guy," she heard Gabrielle's voice calling from the kitchen as she prepared to leave the flat.

"And I can't wait to meet Troy! Did you say he is coming over today?"

"Yes, he should be here later this evening," Gabrielle said as Arielle walked out the door with a spring in her step.

Paul was waiting outside their chemistry classroom with a concerned look on his face. "Are you all right?" he asked

"Yes, I feel much better than I did last week. Thanks for being there for me," she murmured, and they walked in together.

The day passed quickly, and soon they were all back at the flat, engaged in their studies when a soft knock sent Eva running to the door. It was Ian, and Arielle liked him from first sight. He was a little taller than Eva, well built, and extremely good-looking with brown hair and brown eyes. He pulled Eva into his arms and gave her a warm kiss. She looked so happy, and that made Arielle smile. Then Ian walked over to Arielle and gave her a warm hug as if they had known each other for a long time.

"You must be Arielle," he said. "Eva has told me all about you, and I've been looking forward to meeting you." He had a wonderfully friendly smile, and she immediately knew that he belonged to that special group of people in her head. She could see that he was genuine in everything he said.

"I'm delighted to meet you too, Ian," she said, hugging him back. Then Gabby came out of her room, and her meeting with Ian was equally warm and friendly. They chatted happily for a few minutes, and then Ian followed Eva into the kitchen to get a beer.

Gabrielle and Arielle just looked at each other and smiled joyfully. They were both thinking the same thing – that Ian and Eva made a beautiful couple. When they came back into the room, they were talking about Ian's family. He was a great guy with some very interesting stories to tell, and a fascinating way of telling them, which they all enjoyed while sipping wine.

Around eight o'clock Troy arrived, and Arielle nearly dropped. He was incredibly good-looking, almost as attractive as Sebastian. He took Gabrielle in his arms and their lips locked in a soft kiss. Gabrielle introduced him to them, and he moved across the room to give Eva a warm hug and shake Ian's hand.

While Troy's smile was remarkable, as he turned in her direction and crossed the room toward her, Arielle was sorry to discover that he didn't belong to that special group of people in her head. But as he approached her she sensed something very familiar about his seamless walk. She was still trying to process that thought when he leaned over to give her a hug. As he did, her body suddenly went rigid. The scent was unmistakable. She was stunned since she had never smelled that particular scent until she met Sebastian. She looked at him expecting to be dazzled, but nothing unusual happened. She was very confused, but also very sure about the scent that went along with his amazing looks and his seamless walk.

She was still staring at him, her mind miles away when she heard his voice, soft as velvet.

"Are you all right, Arielle?" He was watching her carefully with a puzzled look on his face.

"Yes...yes... I'm sorry. I was just thinking of something... something else. Forgive me. It's so nice to meet you; I've heard so much about you from Gabrielle." Arielle said, smiling a bit nervously as she saw him walking towards Gabrielle, gazing back at her with a curious look. But he remained quiet.

Oh my, God, she thought to herself, *can he be another immortal? And how or why did he show up here?* Now her mind was going wild. She was sure that he was wondering what she was thinking, and she was wondering if he could read her mind like Sebastian could. But if he could, he gave no indication of it.

As Troy told them about his travels around the world with his parents, Arielle couldn't help noticing that his features, like Sebastian's, were flawless. He told them that his mother was French, his father Scottish. He was dressed exceptionally well and there was a natural elegance about him. He was very attentive to Gabrielle, and she could see that he had eyes only for her. His voice was very appealing, and all this was fuel to the fire that was already in her head. She couldn't read his mind, and the story about his parents didn't seem to fit what she knew about the pattern of an immortal. She was perplexed.

She was so happy for Gabrielle. She loved her dearly and she knew that she was incredibly happy, but there was something strange and unsettling about Troy. She wanted to talk to Sebastian about this, but she knew it would have to wait until he was here again. Could Troy really be another immortal? How strange would that be? What was happening in her life?

Despite her dreadful gift, Arielle really was just a normal girl. Her recent experiences with Eva's special powers; the unknown world of immortal men she seemed to be entering; and the fact that she was the object of the fury of an immortal woman who wanted to kill her was all a bit overwhelming. She wasn't sure she could comprehend the meaning of all that was happening, but she seemed to be right in the middle of it.

She glanced over at the rest of the group, letting her gaze linger over the four of them. They were laughing and enjoying each other's company. She finally managed to shake off her anxious thoughts and join in the fun.

Arielle and Sebastian exchanged e-mails almost daily, and he called her a couple of times a week. She missed him so much! Every night she went to bed feeling lonely and depressed. She wanted so much to feel his body next to hers. Her life went on pretty much routinely for the next couple of months: school, studying and partying on the weekends.

Meanwhile, Gabrielle and Troy, Eva and Ian were getting closer and closer. Arielle was the only one missing her beautiful dream. She couldn't stop thinking of him no matter where she was or what she was doing.

It was midweek, and she had just walked in the door when he called. It was so exciting just to hear his voice.

"Hello! Did you miss me?" he asked. As always his musical voice on the other end of the line enchanted her.

"Yes, I miss you," she said quietly. She was feeling pretty lonely.

"What's wrong, baby? You sound so sad."

"I am sad," she said. "I don't like being without you. Are you ever coming to see me?"

"Well, what are you doing next weekend?" he asked.

She stopped breathing as she processed his question. "You're not joking with me, are you?"

"I never joke when it comes to you, Arielle."

She couldn't keep her excitement from spilling over the phone. "I'll be right here, waiting for you," she said. Her heart raced, and that familiar rush of desire shot through her.

"I'll e-mail you my flight details," he said.

"I'll pick you up," she said eagerly, happily, barely able to contain herself, adding, "I think I'll burst before you get here."

"Don't do that," he joked. "I need you just as you are." He chuckled and before he hung up said, "Miss me!"

When he was gone, she fell onto the sofa, overwhelmed. She was going to see him again soon. That short phone call made her a changed person.

Gabby noticed it first and then Eva. Of course, both wanted details. She told them that Sebastian was coming to see her and that she was going to plan a great weekend for the two of them.

"Will we get to meet him?"

"I can't promise, but I'll try," she laughed.

They both understood how she felt and laughed along with her. Then Gabrielle went to take a shower, and Eva took the chance to drop another bomb while Gabby was out of the room. "Arielle, there's something I want to talk about with you," she said. She paused for a moment and then added, tentatively, "There is something very different about Troy. It's in a good way, but I'm not sure exactly what it is. I'm not getting a clear picture of him."

Arielle's body became tense. She didn't want Eva to know anything about immortality, not just yet. She was hoping that Eva's visions would stay murky for the moment.

"I think he is wonderful, Eva," she said. "I didn't see anything unusual about him except that he was extremely good looking, just like Ian."

Eva smiled, and to Arielle's relief she dropped the subject.

 *Chapter 18*

FINALLY, THE WEEKEND ARRIVED. Her heart was leaping with anticipation, and her expectations were welling up. Sebastian would be there again! There were simply no words to describe the sensation that was sweeping through her, intoxicating her very soul.

A light mist hit the windshield as she drove to the airport. As she pulled close to the baggage claim exit, the sight of him strutting toward her took her breath away. It would take every bit of strength she possessed to control the deep desire and the strong temptation that was burning in every fiber, every nerve, and every vein in her body.

No sculptor could create such a beautiful statue. He was simply perfect. His striking lips were curved up into that familiar smile, making his face look even more gorgeous than it already was – as if that could be possible. She noticed that many people were turning to look at him as he strode toward the door. He truly looked more like a painting than a real person.

He stopped when he saw her, and she flew out of the car and into his open arms. He pulled her against his body and bending down, he crushed her lips beneath his with an incredible hunger. As she pressed close to him, she could feel heat cascading throughout her body.

Sebastian smiled and breathed in her perfume, closing his eyes in sheer bliss. He pulled back and opened the passenger door for her. She got in, feeling heavenly. He pushed on the gas pedal as he drew in a huge breath. Taking her hand, he pulled her to him and pressed a soft kiss on her lips.

"I missed you," he murmured as he broke away from the kiss, his eyes filled with want and desire. She stopped breathing. The longing she felt for him had been building in her for two whole months. She pressed her lips together as she felt the stress of battling the desire she felt for him against the vow of chastity she had made to herself. He pressed her hand softly, and his lips curved up into that sensuous smile that filled her body with a hunger for him. She couldn't resist leaning in and pressing a passionate kiss on the side of his mouth with all the longing she possessed. The urgency she felt was astonishing and more than a little frightening.

He pulled away so he could look at her. "Have you missed me?" he asked, the smile never leaving his face, but his eyes alert.

She shook her head in a hopeless attempt to avoid the distraction his amazing existence created for her once again. She smiled and looked down shyly, trying to keep her voice steady.

"I missed you more than you will ever know," she murmured.

"What are you thinking?" he asked, reaching over and taking her hand again.

"You can read my thoughts," she reminded him. "I am sure you already know what I'm thinking."

"First, let me explain something to you about being able to read your thoughts," he said. "Ever since the day I placed that necklace on you, I actually *can't* read your thoughts anymore, so you'll have to let me know what you're thinking. I need to know what you're thinking. Promise me that you'll do that." He was clearly anxious, and she looked at him in astonishment.

"Sebastian, I'm not trying to hide anything from you," she said. "I just thought that you already knew."

He smiled and pulled her close to him as he brushed her ear with his lips, and she knew he could feel her shiver.

"Arielle, I may not be able to read your mind any longer, but I'm completely aware of the commitment you made to yourself, and I know how to wait. There are plenty of ways we can enjoy each other without breaking your vow." He chuckled and looked at her gently, knowing that with her limited romantic experience she had absolutely no idea what he was talking about.

Strangely enough, she felt relief that he couldn't see all that she was thinking. "I can make it easier for you by going home," she said, her voice now barely a whisper.

"I don't want you to go anywhere," he said. "I want you to stay here with me. I've been away from you long enough."

"My head is so consumed by... you know... you," she said, motioning with her hand towards him. "I always seem to be waging a battle with my emotions because I'm so in love with you," she added.

"I don't think that's so bad. Do you?"

"No, it's not bad, but it makes it hard for me."

When they pulled up at the hotel, the bellhop greeted Sebastian politely and warmly. Sebastian took Arielle's hand as they walked toward the elevator. His eyes locked on hers as the doors closed, and he released all the dazzling power he possessed. She grabbed the railing as she felt herself becoming completely disoriented, and started to fall. His arms closed around her, and he locked her in a passionate embrace. His lips encircled hers, his tongue parted her lips and searched her mouth as the kiss deepened and he softly groaned. She pulled back, gasping for air as the doors opened to the penthouse.

He supported her down the hallway, locking the doors behind them as he turned. Reaching around her, he drew her face up toward his as their lips locked in a hot kiss again. She bowed towards him as he ran his fingers underneath her shirt, leaving a burning sensation on her bare skin. He moaned, and she sighed through the kiss.

"Arielle, you are going to be the death of me," he chuckled.

She kept her arms around his neck and intertwined her fingers in his beautiful, sandy hair, keeping him locked to her lips, refusing to let him go. His hands moved slowly, caressing her body and moving down to her hips, making her shiver as the kiss became voracious and they both moaned with excitement. She couldn't take her eyes away from his beautiful face, and he seemed to have the same reaction to hers.

She simply couldn't believe that such a beautiful creature could love her and want her. His tongue was circling her lips again, before landing in her mouth. His scent was amazing, and she could feel the fire burning her very soul; the feeling was unbelievable. Finally, he released her, reluctantly. He cleared his throat, shook his head as if awaking from a dream, and walked over to the balcony. He stepped outside and she followed him.

They settled into a very easy conversation about the details and the excitement of her school life, her friends, and all the small and unimportant events they had experienced since they had last seen each other. He wanted to know the people she was spending time with.

"I'm not so sure about this Paul guy," he said. "Should I be worried about him?"

"Jealous, are you?" she asked, smiling at him just a bit teasingly.

"Extremely jealous when it comes to you," he said. "I want to be the only guy in your life."

"You are the only guy, Sebastian," she answered him. "Any other guys are just friends, nothing more." She couldn't help laughing as she realized once again how incredible this whole thing was. How could someone like Sebastian be jealous over someone like her?

She was doing most of the talking while Sebastian just sat and listened to her laughing now and then at the funny little things she told him. Finally, she decided to talk to him about Troy.

"I have something pretty big to tell you," she said.

"Oh, what is it?"

"I have a strong feeling that Troy is immortal," she said.

He looked startled. "Are you serious? No, you're kidding, right?"

"Why not? You're immortal. Why couldn't someone else come along just as you did?"

"I must admit that I'm intrigued," he said. "However, it's hard to believe that there would be immortal in a town like this."

"Why? Why not in this town?"

"Well, it's just not a typical hangout for immortals. However, I could be wrong," he allowed.

"Sebastian, his looks are similar to yours, he walks as you do, his voice sounds like yours, and the most important thing of all is his scent, which is just like yours."

"Well, I'm looking forward to meeting him," he said. He still sounded doubtful, but interested in learning more. "Are you hungry?" he asked.

"No, I seem to lose my appetite when I'm with you," she chuckled.

They talked some more and then fell into a restful silence. She started falling asleep on the chair and the next thing she knew she was in his arms, being carried to bed. His face was but a couple of centimeters away from hers, and he locked their lips into another blistering kiss. She felt that a million butterflies were fluttering in her stomach from the anticipation of this moment, and she was happy just to be with him in complete bliss. She changed into a little camisole as he watched her, with eyes full of excitement. She lay in bed and waited, breathless, as she felt him climb into bed next to her. His body heat made her shiver with excitement. His arms encircled her, and she sank closer to him, pressing her body against his. She could feel his excitement hard against her abdomen.

"You look very sexy," he whispered. His lips moved against hers as he pushed her softly onto her back and rolled over her. She thought she would shatter. He pulled back, gasping as he remembered how she felt about abstinence before marriage.

"Sorry, baby," he said, completely out of breath, rolling onto his side.

She wanted to tell him how much she loved the feel of his body on top of hers, but she didn't. He gathered her in his warm embrace, and she sank blissfully against his body as she drifted off to sleep, feeling safe and breathing quietly. She wasn't sure how long she was asleep, but when she opened her eyes, she could feel his arms pulling her even closer. She peered at the clock on the nightstand and was astonished to see that it was four o'clock in the morning.

"What's wrong?" she murmured, still half asleep.

"I love you," he breathed softly into her ear. He didn't want to tell her about the impossible battle he had fought for the past two hours, against his own desires. The sensation of her warm body resting against his had painfully aroused him. All he wanted to do was to take Arielle down the path of pleasure and show her ways to enjoy being together without breaking her commitment to abstinence. However, he needed to put a stop to his wild thoughts and try not to scare her away.

His fingers traced her jaw line slowly, seductively, sending a prickling sensation down to her toes. He leaned closer and set his mouth on hers. His lips moved against hers, pulling her deeper into a whirlwind of passion and sheer longing.

Arielle stopped breathing. She could taste his incredible immortal scent and heat spread across every inch of her body. His lips were moving slowly as they brushed the side of her face, down her neck, across her collarbone and stopped, lightly pressing the hollow of her throat, intoxicating her to a new level of excitement. A soft moan escaped her lips, and he felt it in the core of his bones. His warm palms moved gently down to her waist, over her stomach, and stopped at the beautiful curves of her hips, making her writhe in his arms. He shifted slowly, pulling her flat against his body, and she lost track of time. The tectonic plates of her mind shifted dangerously, and she couldn't breathe, she couldn't think. She was lost in a sea of wild emotions. He paused for a long moment, trying again to restrain his desire. He was learning, touching, and enjoying the feel of her silky skin against his fingers. She held on to him, growing hotter, utterly captivated. She moved into him, and he moaned as he felt her trembling with eagerness. His chest was pounding. "I want you," he gasped, "I've never wanted another woman like I want you; I'm crazy about you!"

His breath was scorching her skin and Arielle's mind was lost in a sheer fog of pleasure. Then suddenly, reality slammed into her mind like a massive iceberg, reminding her of where she was and what she was about to do. And she remembered that she wasn't ready to take that step. She poured every ounce of strength she possessed and, putting her hands flat on his chest, pushed him softly away. "Sebastian, no," she whispered, anxiously. She felt his hands ease immediately, and he pulled back.

"I'm not going to make you break your vow, Arielle. There are a lot of ways to enjoy each other," he said.

"How?"

"Trust me, and let me show you." His voice was warm, loving, filled with emotion.

Arielle remained unmoved for what it seemed like a century. Then, slowly her muscles eased and relief spread across her body. *What am I doing?* She thought. *I trust him implicitly, I trust him with my life.* She was sure that Sebastian would never hurt her, that he would never make her do anything that would be as damaging to her as breaking her vow.

"Will you trust me?" he asked patiently. She didn't answer his question. She just moved into him, searching for his lips, and drew him into an intoxicating kiss. She had decided that she wanted to explore the pleasures that he spoke of – right here, right now – with *him* as her guide.

Sebastian had waited patiently, and now he was delighted to pull her once again into his warm embrace and hold her tight. Her hands twined around his neck, pressing him even closer as their lips locked in a ferocious kiss. His hands were moving over her again, caressing every inch of her body. She was burning up with desire, and he knew it. He lifted his head and gazed down at her. He smiled gently and, bending down, pressed his lips on the hollow of her throat. His hands roamed her body tenderly, and he touched her in ways that made her sob with delight as heat ignited and spread wildfire through her veins. Arielle was lost in the heat of passion as an unfamiliar surge of sensation coursed through her muscles, sheared them, scorched them, and her body shuddered uncontrollably. A loud moan escaped her lips, and the sound resonated through his body. His mouth covered hers, and absorbed her sounds of pleasure, cherishing the moment.

"You will be mine for eternity," he moaned, completely out of breath as his lips met hers one more time.

She was completely exhausted. He pulled her into his arms, and she rested her head against his chest. They savored their absolute bliss and fell asleep in the early morning hours.

Arielle was shocked by the amazing sensations she experienced under his skillful touch. He had been right when he said that there were many ways to enjoy each other without her breaking her promise to herself, and he showed her all those ways, making her want him even more.

It was almost noon when they finally left the room. They went downstairs to get something to eat while she talked nonstop. She was so excited to be with him, and he laughed along with her, enjoying her stories and her enthusiasm. Later they drove to the beach and took a long walk. She was filled with such pleasure, just walking next to him and holding his hand.

But then she began to fret. She was thinking about earlier that morning, feeling very anxious and worrying that she hadn't pleased him.

"I love you, Sebastian, and I want you so much, but I can't... "

But he didn't even let her finish her sentence. His mouth found hers, he kissed her, and she stopped breathing. He held her even tighter against his body and whispered in her ear, "I don't care about this morning. Making love to you is something I think about all the time, but it's not going to be an issue for us right now. I don't want you to do anything you're not ready for," he said, and repeated, "I don't." He bent down and kissed the tip of her nose.

"Can we talk about you and your family today?" she asked. "You know everything about me, but I don't know anything about you, your family, your friends, what you do with your free time."

"What is it that you want to know?" he asked, touching her face gently.

"Tell me about your family."

They sat down on the soft sand, and he started to talk.

"I had a wonderful family," he said. "My mother was very beautiful, and my father was very powerful. My brothers were my best friends, and we grew up in a very warm and loving home. But I lost them all during the influenza epidemic that hit practically every country back in the sixteenth century. It was the most painful experience I had ever been through. I had a very hard time moving on with my life. I loved them all and missed them so very much." He sighed and paused for a moment, lost in thought. Then he continued. "I became the sole heir of the family fortune at a young age and found myself involved in a very complicated business. It took a lot of time to become familiar with everything required to run the business as well as my father had done. It took a long time, but I was successful in accomplishing my goal." Here he paused again. "Then, when I turned twenty-seven, something changed my life forever. I never got a day older, I never got sick, and I didn't know why. I was desperate for answers to what was happening to me.

"One day while I was in Germany – I was trying to get away from Annabel – I met a young lady named Loren. She was the daughter of the Dillon family, a very powerful family in that part of the world. I already told you about Olivia Dillon, who gave you the necklace you're wearing. She took me under her wing and told me all about immortality. We both think it was Annabel who gave me immortality so that she could torture me for all eternity rather than just for a short segment of my mortal life." Sebastian laughed ruefully. "Olivia has been like my own mother for centuries now," he said. "And Loren is my one and only sister, and I adore her." He paused again, seemingly lost in thought. "I do remember that early on, during the change in my life, I was in utter shock. But I had to get used to my new self and move on."

She turned toward him so that he was facing her and put her hands on either side of his face. She pulled him down toward her, searching for his lips. He encircled her in his arms and crushed her lips beneath his with a wild hunger.

"Sebastian, I love you no matter what. You are my own personal and private miracle," she murmured, without taking her lips away from his.

"Thank you," he whispered.

There was a pause as they both just gazed at the ocean, watching the waves break on the shore.

"Who are your friends?" she asked. "Who do you spend time with when you're not with me?"

"I have three very close friends. One lives in Paris, and two are in Germany. We see each other often, and we talk on the phone, sometimes daily. We have been friends for centuries," he laughed.

"What are their names?"

"Jon Lacroix and Pier de Zorzi live in Germany. Jacques Louvser lives in Paris. All three work in my company from different locations. Nathan is another very close friend," he added. "He is in the London office."

"What do you do with your free time?"

"I mostly think about you," he said, smiling as he bent down and kissed her.

"No, really, Sebastian, what do you do for fun?"

"I love horseback riding," he said. "That's my passion. I also like to ski. And I love to read and listen to music."

"Gabrielle loves to ride horses," she said. "I'm not one for riding horses at all. I do like to water ski. And I love to read and listen to music, too."

"We have a lot in common," he said softly. "I do want you to learn to ride because that is one of my favorite sports. And I want to have you with me all the time. Will you give it a try?"

"We'll see," she said. "I don't want to make any promises I may not be able to keep. Unlike you," she teased, smiling to let him know that her barb was all in fun. He smiled back, good sport that he was.

Back in the hotel, Sebastian announced that he had something to tell her, and she was stunned to hear his next words.

"I've decided that it has been a long time since I've attended college. So I thought it would be a good idea for me to attend the University of Brighton this coming year. It's one school I've never attended before." He laughed and she joined him, thinking he was kidding, but then his face turned serious.

"Really?" she asked.

"I never joke when it comes to you, Arielle."

"Are you bored?"

"No, I'm not bored, but I'm tired of being away from you."

"Have you applied?"

"I sent my papers in, and I have willed them to accept me. That is another gift of mine: being able to make people do what I want or need."

For several minutes, she was stunned and didn't know what to say.

"Why do you feel you have to do this?" she finally managed to ask.

"Well, I think that this is the only way I can keep you close to me until you get out of school."

She was at a loss for words. Of course, she was extremely happy and excited knowing that he would be with her, but she was also completely overwhelmed with this new information.

"What is it?" he asked. "Don't you want to be with me?"

"Oh, there is nothing that would make me happier than having you near me," she answered. And just to make sure he understood just how happy she felt, she leaned in for another long passionate kiss.

"Well, I guess it's time for me to go home," she said, as the sun began to fall. "I haven't been out of the same outfit since yesterday morning."

"Please don't go," Sebastian pleaded. "Stay with me and I will try to control my crazy desire of wanting to touch you every time you're near me."

"But I really need to change my clothes," she objected. "I've been wearing the same jeans and top since yesterday morning."

"I don't think you need any clothes at all," he teased.

"I need fresh clothes," she repeated.

"I don't think you need anything," he insisted again with a soft laugh. "But if you must, then go ahead." He kissed her on the forehead, moved away from her, and went to lie on the bed as if he wanted to show her that she had her freedom.

She smiled back at him and, hard as it was for her to leave him on that bed looking the way he did, she knew that she had to go at least to the flat and pick up some fresh clothing if she was going to stay the night.

"I won't be but a few minutes," she promised.

"I'm not going anywhere," he said. "I'll keep your spot warm until you get back."

When she got to the flat, she was happy to see that no one was there. She really didn't want to share Sebastian with anyone – not yet, not even for a moment. And she didn't want to waste a moment in getting back to him either. This weekend was for *them*. He was there for her, and she was there for him alone. A strange feeling had taken over her. She felt like a whole, complete person, not just a girl in love. It was an incredible feeling and one she had never before experienced.

She chose a couple of outfits and drove back to the hotel. To her surprise, Sebastian hadn't moved from the bed. He was watching the telly, looking better than any actor on the screen, and she smiled with absolute delight to find him there, just waiting for her. They never left the room for dinner. They were very content just talking and holding each other. He ordered room service for her, but she wasn't very hungry. When she was with him, she was never hungry for food.

They had another amazing night; she was sure that he had mastered the art of love through the centuries. Their lips remained fused as he swept her away until passion and desire made both of them surrender to the swirling exhilaration. She wanted to learn from Sebastian and share the pleasure he was giving her without breaking her vow, and he was a wonderful teacher. It was late when they both drifted off to sleep in each other's arms.

Sunday came all too quickly, and he had to prepare to leave again. Tears blinded her eyes, and her heart was full of sadness. He folded her in his arms and held her closer as their lips locked in a passionate kiss.

"I don't want to say goodbye to you again. I am getting tired of the same routine," she said as they kissed. "It breaks my heart every time you get on that plane."

"The more time I spend with you, the more difficult it becomes to leave you," Sebastian agreed. "But I'll be back soon. I wish you could understand how hard it is to be without you; you are my life now, and we are going to be together."

On the way to the airport she told Sebastian about the party, her parents were planning for her twenty-first birthday. "It's the week after next," she said. "It's very sweet of them, but nothing will be good enough without you. I'll think of you and miss you every moment of every day until I see you again."

"I'll call you often, and I'll see you sooner than you think. I want to look into your beautiful blue eyes and see the love you hold for me, not the tears," he said. He pulled her back into his arms, pressing his lips against hers, leaving her gasping in pure exhilaration. Then with another intense kiss, he was gone.

As she drove back to their flat, she noticed that the weather was exactly as she felt inside: dark and unexciting. When she got back to the flat, she went straight to bed. She had never believed that any of this could ever happen to her. She had never had feelings like these for any man, and she couldn't stand the idea that she had to be without him for any length of time. She felt lonely and sad, and she couldn't think of a single thing that could make her feel good at this point. That was the last thought she had before falling into a deep sleep.

Sebastian kept staring out the window until the plane was above the clouds and he couldn't see the city any longer. He could not stop thinking of Arielle and the two days they had spent together. He could still feel the passion aroused in him when their bodies touched, and the feeling of incredible excitement that he had never known before.

Just listening to the rhythm of her heartbeat and feeling her breathing by his side overwhelmed him with contentment. She was the woman he had been looking for throughout the centuries. He was overtaken by a desire that made him wake her up at four o'clock in the morning just to hear her voice and kiss her lips.

For the next hour, he kept thinking about her response to him and the passion that had enfolded them. He remembered how his voice was shaking as he had spoken to her, and he now wondered if she had heard that change. If she had, she hadn't said anything about it. He thought of how they had walked along the beach together holding hands, and his arms ached with emptiness. He needed her there with him to make him feel complete.

Sebastian loved Arielle deeply, and he was planning a huge surprise for her twenty-first birthday. He was going to come back. He shivered with excitement and smiled with pleasure at the thought. He smiled, even more, thinking about their first dance. Then he groaned at the memory of the utter passion her touch had unleashed into his very soul, and anticipation of the next time they would be together. He closed his eyes, and his lips curved. There was no question in his mind, he would have to ask her to marry him soon. He wanted to be wherever she was; he wanted to be able to hold her, love her, and protect her. Being away from her was sheer torture.

Suddenly the thought of going home made him sick. He would have a firm talk with Annabel. She was to stay away from him, and he would make sure she had absolutely no access to the house ever again.

He remembered looking at Arielle, standing alone at the airport, watching him walk away and how he had wanted to run back, take her in his arms and kiss her sensuous lips one more time. She made him so happy just to be alive. He was stunned to realize how much he missed her. Every minute away from her was now painful. How was he ever going to make it through the rest of this year without her by his side?

He arrived home late in the evening and drove through the streets of St. Jean de Luz, so peaceful and so beautiful. He did love the little town, and he didn't really want to leave it. *I can bring her here next summer*, he thought, and the thought made him smile.

The house was quiet when he arrived, and he went straight to bed, thinking only of Arielle. He wished she was there with him, but he would have to live with just thoughts of her for the time being.

The next two weeks flew by. Arielle told Gabrielle and Eva most of the details about her weekend with Sebastian. She also told them that she didn't want to share him with anyone just yet, and they understood.

As it turned out, they had all similar weekends, and none of them had worried about what the others were doing. They laughed, thinking of the way their lives had changed. They didn't try to figure out when or how that had happened. They just knew that they were completely happy.

 *Chapter 19*

IT WAS HER TWENTY-FIRST BIRTHDAY, and to be with Sebastian was Arielle's only wish. She was looking forward to her party, but she knew that all she *really* wanted was to share her special day with him. She got into the shower, feeling the hot water run on her back as she closed her eyes and let the memory of his beautiful face take over.

She was completely lost in her thoughts when she was startled by Eva's voice calling from the other room, telling her to hurry up. She smiled, knowing that Gabby and Eva were waiting in the sitting room to give her their birthday present. She knew she would love the earrings they had gotten her, but she would have to act surprised. She finished up her shower quickly, threw on a bathrobe, wrapped a towel around her head and walked into the other room.

They were waiting, huge smiles across their faces. "Happy birthday!" they called out in unison, and Gabby handed her a small box, beautifully wrapped. She hugged them both warmly and opened the box enthusiastically.

"They're beautiful!" she cried. "You two are the best friends a girl could ever want." She put the earrings on and they were very beautiful – silver, with a striking blue stone in the center that matched the color of Arielle's eyes. "I love them!" she cried, and her friends both beamed.

As she poured milk over her cereal, they discussed the incredible changes in their lives and the men that were now sharing their lives with them.

"What are you going to do this morning?" Eva asked.

"I need to stop by the house and see if my mother needs help with anything before tonight," Arielle chuckled.

She was almost ready to leave the flat when they heard the doorbell ring. Eva answered, and there stood a deliveryman with a huge bouquet of flowers.

"Delivery for Miss Arielle Lloyd," he said, and her heart skipped a beat from sheer joy. She saw the freesia and knew it was from the most wonderful man in the world. She ran to the door and signed for the delivery as her eyes welled up with tears. She took a deep breath and inhaled the unbelievably beautiful aroma of the flowers. She pulled the card out of the envelope and pleasure filled her heart as she read.

"I'll love you for eternity."

The card wasn't signed, but she knew who had sent them, and she was in a state of bliss. She was putting the flowers in water when her phone rang, and she saw Sebastian's name pop up on the screen. She melted hearing his velvety voice.

"Happy birthday, baby!"

"Sebastian, thank you so much for the beautiful flowers. They are gorgeous! You've made my day."

"Well, that's the least I can do from here," he laughed. "Remember that I love you, and I need you more than anything in this world."

"I feel the same way."

"Have a happy day – and miss me!"

She smiled hearing the last part. That was the way he always said goodbye to her.

"I'll miss you more than you'll ever know," she promised.

She heard him chuckle, and the phone went dead.

When she arrived at her parents' house, everything looked more beautiful than she had seen it look in the last few years. "Wow!" she exclaimed. The chandeliers were sparkling, the floors were polished, and flowers filled the rooms. A small stage had been arranged in the ballroom, and the band was unloading equipment and setting up. She was in shock; she had never expected anything so fine.

Her mum was looking at her, smiling, waiting for her to say something. "Mummy! I couldn't have dreamed anything this beautiful. You really shouldn't have gone to all this trouble."

"This is a very important birthday, Arielle. We have to make it more special than any of the others," she said.

"So what do you think?" It was her dad's voice behind her. She turned around and wrapped her arms around him warmly.

"I love you, Daddy, you are my number one man," she said. He squeezed her and whispered, "I know you're getting older, but you're still my little girl and don't you ever forget that."

Arielle assured him that she never would forget it and that she would love him forever. Then she began helping her mother by running a couple of errands for her and doing a few odds and ends. Soon it was time for her to get ready. She scaled the stairs two at a time and went to her room.

The dress she had chosen for the occasion was a little black cocktail dress that made her look a bit older than she was and shoes with stiletto heels. She decided to take off the necklace Sebastian had given her; it seemed a little too much with a dress that had all that glitter. She put it in her jewelry box, thinking, after all, what could she possibly be afraid of in her own home? Her little diamond studs were the only jewels she wore. When she looked in the mirror she almost didn't recognize herself – she looked so grown up!

As she came down the staircase, some of the guests were arriving, some already had drinks in their hands, and others were just mingling. As she entered the room she saw Tristan watching her. He seemed nervous. As she started to walk towards him, she saw him put his hands into his pockets and lean against the wall, smiling and trying to look natural. He looked anything but natural. She smiled, trying to make him feel comfortable.

"Hello, Tristan," she said, a wide smile on her face. She really was happy to see him. He was just so cute.

"Hello, Arielle," he said. His voice sounded a little strained as if it were an effort to make it sound natural.

Tristan was not sure why he was acting like this, except for the fact that he had not been able to get Arielle out of his mind since last summer in St. Jean de Luz.

She's so beautiful, and her voice soothes my soul, he thought as she walked towards him. It was as though everyone at the party had vanished for a moment but her. When she reached out and hugged him, he felt as though his insides had melted, and he had to remind himself that he needed to cool off.

"How's school?" he asked. He sounded just a bit uneasy, and she wondered why.

"I'm almost finished with my last semester this year," she said.

"So, you are twenty-one now?"

"Yes, twenty-one is the magic number," she laughed. And after pressing his hands softly, she walked off to talk with some of her friends. She was so happy to see everyone.

As usual, her mother had done a great job arranging the party to perfection. The music was blasting, and almost everyone was dancing, drinking, and enjoying the music and the surroundings.

The next song was a slow one, and Tristan invited her to dance. He pulled her to the dance floor, and as they moved to the music, he gazed at her with a warm look in his eyes that she didn't really understand. He started to say something but then he suddenly stopped as if he had thought better of it.

"What is it, Tristan?" she asked. "Is there something you want to tell me?"

"I came to wish you a happy birthday before I leave for Africa," he said.

"Africa!" she exclaimed. "What are you going to do in Africa?"

"I've joined a group of doctors called Doctors Without Borders. I'll be leaving on Tuesday."

"Oh!" she said. "I didn't know that." She paused, absorbing the surprise. "It sounds like a great adventure," she added. "I've read and heard great things about what those doctors do for poor people in those countries. You must be so proud! I'm certainly very proud of you, too." She stood on her toes and kissed him, and he let out a tremulous breath.

There was a hint of sadness in his voice, and for a moment, she felt a pang in her heart. She wasn't sure why, but she held him tighter. Looking into his eyes, she repeated her admiration for what he was about to do. This was going to be a tremendous opportunity for him professionally – and what a great thing to do, to share his medical knowledge and skill with those in such need of it.

Tristan looked at Arielle's beautiful hair and her gorgeous shoulders, wanting to hold her like that forever. He liked the feel of her skin under his hands and noticed her perfume as they were dancing close. *Maybe I shouldn't have come,* he thought. It would have been easier not to see her again.

"I would love to take you with me," she heard him whisper wistfully.

"Oh, but Tristan, I'm not a doctor or a nurse. I'd be useless there," she said, laughing softly.

The song was over but his arms stayed firmly fixed around her waist, and they stayed on the dance floor through the next song. She gazed at his beautiful face and smiled. His touch was warm; it made her feel safe and content, but his eyes looked troubled. She was sure that if Sebastian had not come into her life, Tristan would have been a significant someone for her. She shook her head and chuckled at the thought. When the song was over, he bent down and softly pressed his lips to hers.

"Thank you, Arielle," he murmured. "I'll never forget this night. Or you!"

"I won't forget you either, Tristan," she said. "And I'll be waiting to hear about your adventures." She squeezed his hand, smiled at him, and then said, "Well, I'd best talk to my other guests…"

"Of course, Arielle," he agreed, and he let go of her hand.

A strange but pleasurable heat ran across her body, shaking her to the point that she felt a little dizzy. As she walked away, she wasn't sure what had just happened, but she felt that it was a turning point in her life.

On the other side of the room, Eva and Ian were talking with some of their friends. She walked up to them to get her birthday hugs. Ian handed her a small gift-wrapped box and told her that Eva had helped him choose his present for her. She could hear him thinking that the gift was a beautiful, custom-made necklace, and she smiled with pleasure. She opened the box and acted completely surprised, making him smile with delight.

"May I have this dance?" he asked her.

"Why yes, I'd be delighted," she agreed. They waltzed around the floor together, and then returned to Eva, who was standing right where they had left her, with a concerned look on her face. She was looking intensely somewhere past her.

"What's the matter, Eva, what do you see?" Arielle whispered in Eva's ear, as Ian released her hand and gave her a sweet smile. Eva shrugged her shoulders, and for a moment, it seemed as though she would say nothing. Then hesitantly she said, "Well, Arielle...I see extreme happiness and extreme danger both at the same time."

"Tonight?"

As she nodded, Arielle pressed her lips and looked around as if she might see something materializing in front of her. Her hands instinctively moved up to her neck, and she got a chill remembering that she had taken off the protective necklace Sebastian had given her. Then she shook her head and reminded herself that she was inside her house, protected from anyone who might want to hurt her. However, the very thought that she might be in danger still made her shiver. Eva reached over and grabbed her hand, and then she glanced at the distance between her and the front door.

"Is someone coming? Who?"

"I don't know. I don't see a face."

"Oh, Eva, these visions of yours are making me crazy. Can we just forget them for tonight? It's my birthday, and we're all together. I don't think anything bad can happen."

"All right," Eva agreed, and she smiled a worried smile, pressing Arielle's hand in hers.

Arielle hugged her and whispered, "Don't worry." Then she started moving about the room, talking to the other guests.

Jane came in with her parents and ran to Arielle with open arms. "Happy birthday, Sis! You look fabulous!" she said, hugging her. Arielle hugged her back and gave her a big kiss.

Next, Gabrielle and Troy arrived carrying a huge bouquet of flowers, and Arielle was so happy to see them. But when Troy leaned down to kiss her, there it was again, she could smell the sweet scent of his breath that she had never smelled until Sebastian. Once again this unsettled her, but she was able to find the strength to smile at them and thank them for the flowers as Gabrielle hugged her, her face filled with joy.

"Happy birthday, Arielle," she said. "I love you."

"I love you too, Gabby."

Next, Paul arrived with a group of their friends. He looked fabulous! She had never seen him dressed so well. He came up and planted a big kiss on her lips, held her tight, and wished her a happy birthday. He didn't seem to want to let go, so they lingered in their embrace. Then he handed her his present, which was wrapped in a huge box. "Thank you, Paul!" she said, and placed it in the pile with the others. Then he pulled her onto the dance floor.

"I love you, Arielle!" he said as they glided around to the music.

"I love you too, Paul. You are my best friend," she said.

In reply he squeezed her tighter, making her giggle.

"Tonight you'll be my dance partner," he said.

She closed her eyes as they moved around the dance floor and his beautiful face appeared before her, making her smile with pleasure. The song ended, and she walked over to talk to her mother. Tristan and his father, André Roux, were standing there talking with her.

"Hi, Arielle, you look so grown up tonight," Mr. Roux said with a smile. She thanked him and made some polite small talk as she took Tristan to the dance floor again. He held her tight, and she let herself move to the music with her eyes closed. She was lost in her thoughts when a musical voice behind her made her breath halt in her throat, and her body shivered.

"May I cut in?"

She spun around and there he stood – her beautiful dream, the love of her life.

"But-but-but – how? When?" she stuttered, unable to complete a sentence.

"Did you really think that I would miss your birthday?" He smiled.

She was so surprised that at first she almost couldn't move. But then she flew into his arms and buried her face in his chest, crying from sheer joy. He held her tight against his chest, and then with a sudden move, he pulled her even closer to him and she stopped breathing. He was the best gift she could ever wish for.

He pushed her away from him softly and looked her up and down.

"You look absolutely fabulous," he said. "That dress makes you look very sophisticated, and with the high heels, your face is closer to mine. How about that? I don't have to bend down to kiss you tonight," he added, smiling at her tenderly. He looked so pleased, and she could hear the satisfaction in his voice.

Then he pulled her back into his arms, bent down, and pressed his lips to hers in a long, hot kiss.

"Happy birthday, baby," he murmured without moving his lips from hers. Suddenly she noticed that Tristan was looking from her to Sebastian and back again, apparently wondering what was going on and who this guy was.

"Oh Tristan, I'm so sorry. This is Sebastian, my boyfriend. Sebastian, this is Tristan, one of my dearest friends."

They shook hands and smiled a bit awkwardly at each other. Then Tristan excused himself and walked off, looking a bit shaken. But she couldn't spend much time worrying about Tristan. All she could think of was the fact that her own personal miracle was there.

She fell back into his arms, and as he held her, they started to move to the music.

"Dancing with you has been a dream of mine ever since the first day I laid eyes on you," he said. "And now here we are. Dreams do come true!" He held her at arm's length and gazed at her again with complete satisfaction. "You seem to become more beautiful each time I see you, Arielle," he said. "How do you do that? You are going to drive me mad, you do know that, don't you?" he added, smiling.

"I wish I could believe you," she said. "But as it turns out, you are the beautiful one, and I'm... well, I'm just me."

"Just in case you haven't noticed," he said, "there are a lot of guys here that would like to be in my place. If you don't see that, then you must be blind."

"Sebastian, that's not true," she protested.

"Remember, I can read everyone's mind," he said, and suddenly he went very still as an unsettling realization seeped into his bones and shook him. His eyes dropped down to her neckline, and he frowned.

"What?" she asked anxiously.

"I can read your thoughts..." he said, his words trailing off. "Where is your necklace, Arielle?" he asked, his voice tense.

"Sebastian, nothing is going to happen to me inside my own home," she insisted. "And furthermore, how lucky can I be? You're here! So stop worrying about me."

"Arielle, I'm not joking. Why don't you have it on?"

"Whatever for? I'm not going outside," she said stubbornly. But glancing up at his worried face, she added gently, "It didn't go with the dress, and I felt safe enough inside my house."

"Well, I don't like it," he said. He cradled her chin in his hand, and lifting her face to his, peered into her eyes. "But I'll let it go this time since it's your birthday," he murmured and took her mouth in a passionate kiss. He pulled her back into his arms and held her tightly. After a long pause, he sucked in a deep breath and added, more seriously, "What about Tristan? Do I have to compete with him?"

"Tristan is just a friend," she answered.

"That's not what he thinks," Sebastian said. "He is in love with you, Arielle. And so is the guy that is standing over at the bar looking at us."

"Paul? He's my best friend at school besides Eva and Gabrielle. He's in my chemistry class."

"What about Tristan? I've never heard you talk about him."

"Tristan is the son of my parents' best friends, the Rouxes. He's a surgeon, and he lives in Paris. He's leaving for Africa on Tuesday with a group called Doctors Without Borders. They help poor people in other countries. I've read about them, have you? Tristan is a very nice guy," she added.

"I am very familiar with that group of doctors. That makes it even harder to compete," Sebastian said a bit sulkily.

"Please, Sebastian! You know how I feel about you." She closed her eyes, blissful just to be with him, and moved to the music, feeling the warmth of his beautiful body, not quite believing yet that he was really there. But then suddenly Eva's words from earlier in the evening made her body go stiff. Sebastian felt her tension and, pushing her softly, he held her at arm's length. She smiled, trying to hide her fearful thoughts from him, but she knew there was no point since he knew exactly what she was thinking. So she fell back into his arms, and he tightened his grip on her.

"I can see that Eva has warned you about someone. What exactly did she say?"

"She said that someone was coming, but nothing specific," she murmured.

"Well, she was right about that," he grinned, and looking down at her, let his gaze rest on her beautiful face.

"What do you mean?"

He chuckled and pulled her even closer. He ran his fingers along her spine, spreading a blistering shiver through her muscles. "I'm someone… and I'm here," he purred, brushing his lips across her ear.

"Yes, you are," she replied. "And nothing could be more wonderful," she sighed, tightening her arms around his neck.

"Why then do you keep thinking about danger?" he asked, lifting her face again to his until their lips met.

"Well, she did say there would be a danger," she whispered. Suddenly Annabel Draper's sickening face filled her thoughts, and her heartbeat sped up. She hoped that Sebastian couldn't feel it, but he did. His lips pressed into hers.

"What is it?" he asked without moving his lips away from hers.

"Annabel. I thought of Annabel, and I got scared," she admitted.

"Why would you ever think of her on a night like this?" Sebastian asked.

"I'm not sure, I can't explain it," she replied, looking up to meet his eyes.

"Please don't worry about Annabel," he said with a teasing smile. "This is the best night of your life. You are officially a woman, and you are all mine." There was an amazing smile on his sensuous lips as he spoke.

When the music stopped, he took her by the hand and pulled her out onto the balcony. "I love you, baby. Happy birthday," he said and drew her into a scorching kiss. Arielle smiled in complete ecstasy. She loved him so much. What an amazing man! He was so beautiful. And he was all hers. That had to be the best birthday gift ever.

Pulling away from his arms, she took his hand and led him toward the doors to the ballroom. "You are about to meet my friends, and maybe I'm crazy, but I do want you to talk to Troy. I told you my theory about him, but I may be wrong."

"Wrong about what, baby?"

"Sebastian, he's an immortal. I'm almost sure that I'm right about that. However, he doesn't dazzle me like you do when I look into his eyes." She paused for a short moment and went on. "I can see by the look in your eyes that you don't believe me, but please do this for me. Talk to him."

"Arielle, I choose to dazzle you because I enjoy looking at your face when you become disoriented. Every immortal has the same power, and they can use it by choice. If he's immortal, he probably just chose not to dazzle you."

"Can you please talk with him?"

"Sure," he said, "I'm just as curious as you are."

At this point, Sebastian didn't know how much Annabel knew about his relationship with Arielle. He had been sure that she would find out eventually, but he didn't think it would be this soon. However, Annabel did know that Sebastian's love for Arielle was the real thing and that he was planning to marry this "horrible human." And so she was determined to hurt both him and Arielle, and her plans were already in the works.

Annabel had met with Savanna and Julia, two other women who detested Sebastian just as much as she did. They were willing to put into place all the powers they possessed to exact revenge on Sebastian by hurting Arielle. Annabel had been watching Arielle, and she had decided that her birthday party was the perfect place for her to strike. She arranged with Savanna, who had been waiting for centuries to take revenge on Sebastian, to show up at the party with the sole purpose of killing Arielle, and Savanna was elated at being given the chance to destroy someone that Sebastian truly loved. Like Annabel, Savanna was pure evil, and like Annabel, she had only one thought. Retaliation.

Arielle and Sebastian moved over to where Gabrielle and Eva were standing. She had given Sebastian permission to dazzle them, and she could hardly wait to see their reaction.

"Gabrielle! Eva! This is Sebastian," she said.

They both turned toward him at the same time, and as soon as they met his eyes, they both went numb. They could hardly talk; they looked dazed, unable to move. Arielle could hardly control her laughter.

"Sebastian, these are my best friends since fourth grade," she said, giggling. He smiled at them with his amazing smile, and as he took their hands, they both seemed to forget where they were and what they were doing. They both tried to say something, but neither was able to utter a single word. Arielle took Sebastian's hand, and they walked away, leaving Eva and Gabrielle flustered and confused. "We'll be back soon, don't worry," Arielle promised her friends, knowing that they needed a break to recover.

As she and Sebastian walked away, they both broke into laughter, knowing what had just happened. It was just too funny to watch.

Arielle continued to lead Sebastian around the room, introducing him to everyone. He seemed to create an astonishing reaction in the women, and she knew that his good looks were the reason for that. She had seen the same thing happen when Troy had come into the room.

Finally, they made their way to her parents, and Sebastian instantly fell into an easy and very pleasant conversation with them. Arielle's parents too had fallen in love with Sebastian, just as she had thought they would. Her father made a point of coming over to her and telling her that she had made a great choice.

"Well done, Arielle," he said. "He is charming, and I feel we can trust him to take good care of you. You can't know yet what a great relief that is to a father." He smiled and kissed her gently on the cheek. She was so happy to hear him speak these words! She respected her father immensely and his opinion mattered a lot to her. She was sure that nothing would ever change her mind about Sebastian, but all the same, it was great to have her parents' approval. At that moment, Arielle felt as if her life couldn't get any better.

Next, they moved over to where Paul, Ian, and Troy were standing, and she introduced them all to Sebastian. They all shook hands and made polite conversation. Ian was always animated, happy and laughing. Troy was a bit more reserved. Sebastian took the time to stay and talk with them, and by the end of the evening, she noticed him talking with Troy alone on the balcony. They seemed to be in deep conversation for a long time, and she could hardly wait to hear what they had been talking about. But she stayed close to Gabrielle and Eva chatting about this and that. All the while she kept looking in Sebastian's direction. Finally, the men all shook hands and smiled at each other. As they walked back toward her and her friends, Arielle saw Troy look directly at her, a warm smile on his face. She smiled back, took Sebastian's hand, and moved back onto the dance floor with him.

"Well, was I right?" she asked as soon as they were out of earshot.

"Yes, you were," he said, with a smile. "I think he is a bit shocked to find out that I'm an immortal also and that you recognized his scent. He's a very nice guy. I'm really happy to know that he will be near you when I'm not here."

"Sebastian, this is huge!" she said. "How in the world did he end up here?"

"Let's talk about that when we're alone," he said, smiling over her shoulder at someone who was dancing near them.

"All right, I'll wait. I can't say that it will be easy, but I'll wait."

Sebastian laughed out loud, squeezing her tight and twirling her around the floor. She rested her head on his beautiful chest. He was her best birthday present, and she wanted to enjoy him. She was daydreaming of bliss to come when she felt a light tap on her shoulder. Startled, she looked over and saw her father asking to take Sebastian away for a few minutes to meet some of his friends. She let go of him reluctantly. He gave her an adoring look and one more squeeze as he leaned in and whispered, "Miss me." Then he walked away with her father.

Arielle was so happy about him being there that she could hardly contain her emotions. As she walked dreamily back towards Ian and Paul, she caught a glimpse of Eva in the corner of the living room, looking extremely worried, and motioning anxiously for her to come over. As she got closer, Arielle could see that Eva was having difficulty breathing. She reached over and held Eva's hand.

"What is it, Eva?" she asked, staring at her face. She looked as if she were in a trance.

Eva leaned close to her ear and whispered, "Danger. I can see danger approaching the house!"

Terrified, Arielle's body went rigid. She stared towards the ballroom entrance, but saw nothing unusual. Her mind began to race as conflicting feelings overwhelmed her. Eva's visions had always been accurate before. Who was coming? Could it be Annabel? She looked around in a complete panic. Her breath was coming in uneven gasps. She was trying to decide if she should run and find Sebastian. She looked back at Eva, whose expression gave her warning only a second before panic did. She pressed her eyes closed and gulped mouthfuls of air, trying to calm herself down. She felt she was totally irrational. She was in her own house, among her family and friends. What could go wrong?

Then, before anyone could move, they heard the doorbell ring. Arielle froze in place as she saw her mother move toward the door. Soon she walked back to where Arielle was standing, followed by a beautiful young woman with dark hair and a seamless walk. Their eyes met. Arielle had never seen her before. But Eva's look didn't escape her; her eyes were filled with horror. She looked back at the woman who was approaching, and she heard her mother's voice. "This is Savanna," she said. "She says she is a friend of Sebastian's."

Arielle understood the look on Eva's face. Savanna's perfect features, her seamless walk, and her incredible beauty all suggested that she wasn't human. Still, Arielle had no idea who she was. Instinctively she reached up to touch her necklace and was horrified as she remembered that she had left it in her jewelry box. She turned to look at Troy with a desperate look, and he seemed to understand that something was not quite right. Eva was still standing next to her, unable to move, and Troy was moving closer, never taking his eyes off of Arielle.

Arielle's mother smiled politely and walked away, completely unaware of the danger Arielle might be in. Arielle turned toward Savanna and said, her voice a bit shaky, "Oh, can I help you?"

"I'm an old friend of Sebastian's," Savanna said. Her voice was soft as velvet and her smile was absolutely beautiful. "I was told he was here, and I came to see him," she lied.

Somehow her smile seemed just a bit too friendly, but it never touched her eyes. "How do you know Sebastian?" Arielle asked, her voice barely a whisper.

"He was my boyfriend for a very long time. The last time we saw each other was in Spain at the Garniere ball with the Dillons," she said. Her smile remained as if pasted on her face, and she never took her eyes off of Arielle. Arielle was extremely uncomfortable. "We had a wonderful night together, and he asked me to look for him if I ever found myself bored and somewhere close to him. I found out he was here, so here I am," she lied again, chuckling softly. Her laughter was full of insinuation.

"Who told you where to find him?" Arielle asked, her heart hammering in her chest. Here was yet another woman from his past, looking for Sebastian, wanting to claim him. Arielle shifted her gaze slowly from Savanna's face to Troy's. Savanna followed her gaze and turned to look at Troy, but, oblivious to the fact that she was looking at another immortal, seemed totally unruffled by his presence. Then Arielle turned back to Savanna, who was looking intently into her eyes.

"So, you must be Arielle?" she asked, her voice completely composed.

Arielle took a couple of deep breaths, then answered in a low and shaky voice, "Yes, I'm Arielle. And you are in my house." Savanna looked completely unmoved by her words. Arielle, not wanting to create a spectacle in front of her guests, decided to walk to the dining room without thinking about her safety. Savanna followed her with Troy and Eva keeping a sharp eye on both of them.

"What exactly do you want?" Arielle asked Savanna, in a near whisper. She was still trying to prevent a scene.

"I want to see Sebastian, of course," Savanna said, her lips curling in an ugly, insincere smile. "I've been thinking about him, and I thought that we could maybe just pick up where we left off. I hope you have no objections." Her low chuckle drove a dagger into Arielle's heart. She couldn't believe this was happening. Savanna was now laughing openly, looking at her with a smirk, knowing the anguish she was creating for her.

"Well, how about that?" Savanna said, chuckling again with a satisfied look on her face. "You thought he was perfect, did you not?" Then, not waiting for an answer, she added, "But how wrong you are! He is not your white and shiny knight; he is the dark prince that leaves broken dreams on the way to his kingdom." As she spoke these chilling words, she was looking directly into Arielle's astonished eyes.

Finally, something snapped in Arielle, and she became angry. She stepped toward Savanna and said to her in a very low voice, "Please leave this house immediately. And leave Sebastian alone!"

"You miserable, breakable human, you have no idea who you are dealing with. Annabel was right, you are no match for me!" She practically spat the words at Arielle, and before Arielle could blink, she had grabbed her arm and squeezed it tight, making her gasp from pain. Arielle tried to pull away from Savanna, but her grip was like a vise. Then she made a fist with her other hand, and Arielle felt a crushing weight, like a rock, land on her chest. She stopped breathing and gasped desperately for air. She would have been on the floor writhing in pain, but Savanna yanked her back up like a rag doll. She was still squeezing her arm extremely tight, and Arielle could feel her nails sinking into her flesh like sharp blades. She gritted her teeth in agony and let out a low wail as she watched Savanna raise her arm one more time. She shut her eyes, waiting for the impact that she was sure would incapacitate her.

She waited for a few seconds, anticipating another blow, but nothing happened. When she opened her eyes, she saw that Troy was standing between her and Savanna, his left hand holding Savanna's hand in the air as it was about to come down, ready to strike Arielle; his right hand gripped Savanna's throat with enormous power. Arielle heard a noise like crushing bones, and she saw Savanna's arm fall to her side; she knew instantly that it was broken. She saw Savanna's face register complete shock and agony as she tried to shake loose from Troy's grip, her eyes wild with anxiety.

Arielle collapsed and fell to the floor as Savanna's other hand let go of her arm, and Eva rushed to her side.

"Jesus, Eva, help her to her room," Troy said, taking advantage of Savanna's confusion, pushing her out the room at such a fast pace that Arielle was sure no human eye could follow them.

Arielle was in extreme pain. Eva helped her stand up as she looked anxiously toward the door. Nobody seemed to be aware of what had just taken place in the dining room. But Arielle's arm was bleeding, and her eyes welled up from the sharp throbbing in her chest.

"Oh my God, Arielle you look absolutely awful. I knew something bad was going to happen," Eva murmured, distressed.

"Eva, I'm sure Troy needs help. Can you please go and find Sebastian as quickly as you can, and tell him that Troy needs him to go outside *right now*. Don't tell him anything about my being hurt; just have him go outside first. I don't want anyone to see me the way I look right now," she lied. "I'll go to my room the back way and change. My dress is ripped, and I need to clean my arm."

"Don't you want me to help you?" Eva said. "Don't you want me to get your mum?"

"No!" she said sharply, and then added more softly, "I'll be fine, just get Sebastian now!" Eva looked back at Arielle once more in concern, and then she was gone.

Arielle took another look around, making sure that she hadn't drawn anyone's attention. Then she walked slowly up the stairs to her room and shut the door.

In her bedroom, she looked in the mirror. There were four small cuts on her upper arm that looked red and a little inflamed. She ran cold water over the wounds and washed the blood off. She put a large Band-Aid over the cuts and took her dress off. At the center of her chest was a large red spot, but there was no bruising at the moment. She was hoping that she had no broken ribs, as the pain was sharp and she was having a hard time breathing. She lay down for a few minutes to pull her thoughts together before she changed her dress and rejoined the party. She didn't want anyone to notice she'd been gone.

She closed her eyes and reflected on how happy she was that no one had noticed her distress. She quivered at the thought of what might have happened had a mortal guest tried to protect her from Savanna. She knew that the significance of the injuries to a human being confronting an immortal could be devastating. Her hands were clenched into tight fists just thinking about what could have happened to her if Troy hadn't been there. She lay there, not quite believing what she had just been through.

Her eyes remained closed for a few more minutes as she wondered what was happening outside, what Troy was doing with that woman. She was sure he had heard her use Annabel's name, and she felt sure that he and Sebastian would get to the bottom of this. She felt herself calming down as the pain in her chest eased. The pain of the cuts didn't bother her. Yet.

 *Chapter 20*

TROY, USING HIS IMMORTAL SPEED, had moved quickly and taken Savanna outside through a side door, where he tightened his grip on her throat.

"What do you want with Sebastian? Who sent you?" Troy asked. His voice was dripping venom, and the hardness in it would drive chills down any human's back. Savanna didn't reply. She kept her lips closed tight, and glared at him with total disgust as he continued squeezing her throat tighter.

"There is no Garniere family in Spain, you made all that up. What do you want with Sebastian, and what are you doing here?"

"Who are you?" she asked as she tried to pull away from his grip.

"Don't worry about who I am. Tell me who sent you before I kill you."

Sebastian joined Troy and looked at Savanna in complete shock. He recognized her face and couldn't understand how she had ever found him.

"Sebastian, do you know this woman?" Troy's voice was sharp.

"Yes, I dated her a couple of centuries ago for a short time," Sebastian said, staring at her, still puzzled. "How did you find me?" he asked her with a firm, cold voice.

Savanna remained silent and didn't look at either one of them.

"What happened, Troy?"

"She tried to hurt Arielle," Troy said.

Sebastian's body went rigid, his eyes filled with anger. "Did she touch her?"

"Yes, she did, but I'm sure she'll be all right. I don't think it's that bad, but I was in a hurry to get her out of there. Eva is with her."

"Did Annabel send you?" Sebastian hissed at Savanna.

She glared at him while gasping for air.

"I heard her mention Annabel's name to Arielle," Troy said.

"Can you take care of this so I can check on Arielle?" Sebastian asked.

"Yes, no problem at all. I just wanted to know if you had ever seen her before. I'll make sure she never comes back or bothers anyone at all." His grip was now so tight that the girl's body had gone limp, and her eyes were rolled back in her head.

Troy lugged Savanna's body off to finish her off in a remote area. Sebastian hurried to go and check on Arielle, so worried that he could hardly hold back his anger. He passed Eva on his way inside and stopped to question her for a few moments. Eva pointed to Arielle's room, and he ran up through the back stairs. He opened the door to her room and rushed in.

Arielle was lying on the bed undressed, her eyes closed. His jaw dropped as he saw the huge red spot in the middle of her chest. He noticed the large Band-Aid on her arm, and he started to quaver.

She opened her eyes and saw Sebastian standing there, reaching for her hand. "Arielle!" he murmured tenderly. "Baby, how are you? What happened?"

When she tried to take a deep breath, the pain felt like a sharp knife going through her heart. Sheer distress spread across her face, and her grimace didn't escape Sebastian's notice. She took a small, painful breath, then, looking at his beautiful face, she smiled softly.

"I'll be okay," she said. "I just need to pull myself together. I'll go down in a few minutes. I need to change my dress, she ripped it," she said in a tone of wonderment. She truly couldn't believe what had just happened. Then she smiled at Sebastian softly and gritted her teeth to keep from crying. His eyes locked on her face and anguish shattered his gaze as his lips pulled back in sheer fury. He pulled the Band-Aid away, looked at the mess of cuts and let out a low growl, as he looked again completely dumbfounded. His eyes took on a wild look before he stormed out the door, his movement so fast that she couldn't follow him. Where was he going?

With a great deal of effort, she got up and put another Band-Aid on the cuts. Then she changed into another cocktail dress, one that would cover the red mark on her chest. It was quite painful to move her arms, but she knew she had to pretend that she was fine and get back to the party. She went down the stairs slowly and ran into Gabby at the bottom of the stairs.

"Where are the guys?" Gabrielle asked in an anxious voice.

"I'm not sure. They said they had to run an errand, and they would be right back," Arielle lied. "Where's Eva?"

Gabby led her in the right direction. Eva searched her face as Arielle walked up to her and asked if she was all right. Eva put her arm around Arielle's shoulders and smiled softly at her friend. "What a birthday!" she said. "I'm sure that crazy woman must have sent her here to get you all upset."

"I'm sure she did too," Arielle replied, not wanting to go into any details with Eva. She knew Eva had been right about the danger she had predicted. If she only knew how close she had come to really being hurt. If not for Troy, Savanna might have killed her. Arielle shuddered at the thought.

"Arielle, why did you change your dress?" asked Gabby.

"Oh, I spilled some food on it, and it was ruined," Arielle said. She gave Eva a meaningful look, and Eva understood that Arielle didn't want her to say anything about what had really happened.

Just then Paul came up and asked Arielle to dance. "Oh, I'm sorry, Paul," she said. "I'm afraid that I'm a bit tired. Maybe a little later on?"

"Wow, what happened to your arm?" he asked.

"I scraped it on the corner of my dresser, no big deal," she lied.

"Where's Sebastian?"

"He's with my father somewhere." She smiled.

"He seems like a very nice guy," Paul said.

"He is. And I'm very much in love with him."

"I know. I can see that, and I'm happy for you," he said. "A bit jealous, too, I must admit," he added with a crooked smile.

She smiled too, then turned away and moved toward the bar to get a glass of wine. She felt like she really needed a drink.

It seemed like hours had passed when suddenly she heard Sebastian's voice, soft and velvety, behind her.

"Hey, baby, how would you like to dance with me?" She turned around slowly and let him encircle her in his warm embrace.

"I'm so sorry," he murmured as he leaned down and pressed his lips to hers. His arms pulled her closer, and she winced, feeling the pain in her chest.

"Does your chest hurt that bad?" he asked. He looked so worried.

"Yes, please don't hold me so tight," she said.

"Why did you take the necklace off?" Sebastian chided. "I told you, you must keep it on you at all times. You must!"

"I never thought something like this could happen to me in my own home."

His lips found her mouth, and he stopped her from protesting any further.

"Please put it back on," he said, his voice sweet but firm. "You will be the death of me one way or another, I'm sure of that now," he said. "What would have happened if Troy had not been here?"

"I don't know," she said. "But he was, and now it's over. What happened outside, anyway?" she asked. "Can you tell me?"

"Not now, later," he said. The song was over, and he moved her over to where Troy was standing. Leaning closer to Troy she gave him a kiss and whispered how thankful she was for his help. He smiled softly.

"Is your arm okay?" he asked in a low voice.

"It'll be all right. But I'm afraid that I'm going to have a huge bruise on my chest. It feels like she broke my ribs."

"Are you serious?" Troy looked at her, concerned.

"What is it?" she heard Sebastian's voice ask her.

"Nothing, nothing," she said, trying to keep him calm.

"I see that it is something, and I need to know what," he insisted.

"We'll talk about it later," she said. She looked at him firmly and to her surprise, he backed off.

Suddenly Annabel's image flashed in front of Arielle's eyes, and she reached for Sebastian's hand. He immediately put his arm around her waist, pulling her close.

Finally, the party was winding down, and everyone was getting ready to go home. Arielle left with Sebastian after the last guest had left, but not before retrieving her necklace from her jewelry box. She couldn't wait to get to bed. She was still in terrible pain.

"So what did you and Troy talk about?" she asked when they were in the car.

"He's in a very difficult situation right now, trying to find a way to tell Gabrielle who he is, and what he is. She is his Lizzy, Arielle, and he has found in her what I found in you. I know how he feels, and my heart – if I had one – would be breaking for him."

He was clearly trying to avoid talking about the incident with Savanna, but Arielle pressed on.

"What happened with Savanna?" she asked.

"She won't bother anyone anymore."

"What are you saying?"

"I would prefer that we drop this conversation," he said.

"And Annabel is behind the whole thing?" she asked.

"Yes, she is," he said. "But Savanna is gone, and won't be bothering anyone else ever again."

A cold chill ran down her spine as he spoke those words, and for a moment there was an awkward silence.

"How in the world did Troy end up here?" she finally said, changing the subject.

"This is the interesting part," he said. "Troy is from Italy. He saw Gabrielle from a distance in San Marco where his estate is located. And he watched her for a couple of summers. He fell in love with her. He didn't have the courage to approach her there, so he followed her here. And now he's going to school again so that he can be with her."

"Oh. My. Gosh!" she said.

"What is it?" he asked, smiling at her look of excited incredulity.

"She told us about a mysterious rider that was following her and her friends every day. But he never got close to them, and she never saw his face. He has remained a wonderful mystery for her, and she couldn't wait for her next holiday. If her mystery rider is Troy, that will be wild! Don't you agree?"

"Yes," Sebastian smiled. "That will be a wonderful story."

"How old is he?" she asked.

"Oh he's a little older than me," he chuckled.

"Good Lord! What in bloody hell!" she exclaimed, giggling.

"Now, now, Arielle, you should know by now what true love can do."

"I know," she said. "But, I just can't get over this."

"Well it's true, and now he knows that you know who he is, too. He's happy that you know, and that you approve. He feels he has a friend in you."

"Is there anything I can do to help him?"

"Just be there to support them both. I told him how afraid I was to talk to you about who I am, and he feels the same way about talking to Gabrielle. Please try to help them if you can. You'll know when and how."

"Wow!" she said as she absorbed this latest news. "Life certainly is full of surprises." Then she fell silent as he reached over and took her hand.

"Do you love me?" he asked, his voice soft as velvet.

"Why do you feel that you have to ask, Sebastian?" she smiled.

"I want to hear you say it!" he insisted.

"I love you, and you are the best birthday present I could ever get."

They were at the entrance of the hotel, and he was helping her out of the car.

"Good evening, Mr. Gaulle," the hotel manager greeted Sebastian.

"Good evening," he replied.

They went up to his room, holding hands as they always did. When the door closed behind them, he turned around, and she could see the longing in his eyes.

"I don't think I can do this anymore, Arielle," he said, his voice husky with emotion. "I can't be away from you. I have been tormented for a week and a half, just waiting for this moment. I think I'll go out of my mind."

He pulled her into his arms softly, and she let out a small gasp of pain. "Sorry, I just want to devour you completely!" he chuckled.

"I think she hit my chest pretty hard," she said.

"I saw the red spot on your chest," he said, shaking his head again angrily.

"Where did you go when you left my room?" she asked.

"I went and found Troy. I was angry, and I had to do something."

"I'm sorry you got so angry," she said.

"You've nothing to be sorry about. I'm the one who needs to be sorry for bringing all this misery into your life."

He reached around her, unzipped her dress, and let it fall to the floor. Then he pulled back and she heard him gasp as his eyes narrowed in anger.

"Oh, *mon Dieu*, Arielle! Why did you not tell me how badly you were hurt?"

"What do you mean?" she asked. Instinctively she moved her hands to cover the red mark on her chest, but he took her hand gently, firmly and looked at it carefully.

"Do I need to take you to the hospital?" he asked. "How bad does it hurt?"

"I don't think anything is broken," she lied. "But it does hurt."

She walked in front of the large mirror and gulped in horror. Right in the center of her chest there was a huge bruise. It looked horrible and extended a little way on either side of her breasts. As she looked at herself, sickened, he came behind her and wrapped his arms around her, his soft lips touching the back of her neck.

"I'm so sorry, baby. I love you so much, and I'm really worried about you." His eyes looked so troubled. She lay down on the bed and asked him to lie down next her. He lay to her right, trying to avoid touching her left arm. He lifted himself onto one elbow and gazed down at her. He ran his fingers across her cheek, down the side of her face, and back up again, sending a hot sensation throughout her whole body. His eyes were locked on hers as he bent down and crushed her lips beneath his with wild hunger.

She was overwhelmed with desire, and she could feel his passion too as he whispered over and over how much he loved her, his lips pressing on hers with an urgency greater than ever before. She forgot all about her pain and her worries as she was totally consumed in his touch and the heat of her incredible desire for him. Then he broke away from the kiss and pulled back, a worried look on his face.

"Sebastian, please hold me," she said.

"Baby, I'm afraid I might hurt you."

"I'm in some pain, but I need you close to me," she murmured.

"I'm here, but I'm worried about you," he said. "I think I should be taking you to the hospital."

"Don't be ridiculous," she said. "I'm fine. It's not as bad as it looks." She smiled, trying to convince him she was okay. His eyes were still troubled, so she reached up and put her hand onto the nape of his neck. She pulled herself up and ran her tongue around his lip line. He moaned and reluctantly moved his hands slowly down to her hips and around her stomach, sending her heartbeat into double-time.

"I don't seem to able to breathe right when we're apart," he murmured.

"Your calls and your e-mails are all I look for every day when I get out of bed," she said. "I want you near me, I need to be in your arms to feel safe."

"That's a good thing," he chuckled joyfully as he pressed his lips on hers again.

She ran her fingers over the hard planes of his gorgeous chest and drew her fingers slowly down his stomach, making him quiver with excitement. He lightly caressed her breasts and, bending down, he fastened his mouth around them. He groaned as he took his clothes off with soft movements. His mouth was hot and she could smell his magnificent immortal scent. He put one arm under her neck carefully and with the other arched her body toward him, keeping her against him without pressing on her chest. She could feel his arousal pressed against her side. Her heart surged, full of anticipation and a sweet, aching pleasure. His lips moved slowly down her stomach and with his tongue he softly caressed her skin, filling her with longing. Moving his face back up to her, he groaned loudly and placed his hands on her hips, gently pulled her toward him and held her close. Their lips locked in a deep, sensuous kiss, and it wasn't long before their senses soared and they swirled into a shattering obliviousness of heat and passion. Their breathing was exceedingly elevated as pleasure consumed them. Arielle's heartbeat pulverized her chest before she slowly surrendered to a heavenly profundity of fulfillment.

She looked at his face; his eyes were closed tightly as his expression showed intense satisfaction, and she saw him smile in a way she had never seen him smile before. She held him softly, not believing the deep fulfillment he had given her without forcing her to break her commitment to abstain. His lips were moving against hers again, and his body was moving closer. She was astonished at what had happened and how they felt about each other. She was completely surprised at herself, not knowing where she had learned the things she had done to please him as she gave herself up to his intoxicating heat.

Afterward, they both lay on their backs, staring at the ceiling, smiling with complete and utter satisfaction. She noticed that he seemed to have difficulty finding the strength to move and that his breathing was still uneven. She laughed in sheer bliss, and he looked at her smiling.

"What's so funny?" he asked.

"Are you having trouble moving?" she giggled. "I thought I was the one who was hurting. Is your age catching up with you?" He laughed out loud, and she heard his voice muffled.

"Yes, that's it," he laughed. "And you'll be the death of me for sure." Still laughing, he encircled her in his arms and pressed his lips to hers. They lay together, their bodies scorching in a conquering heat, and continued the absolute enjoyment of touching, exploring, and caressing each other. She had forgotten all about her pain as the feelings she was so enjoying took over completely, filling her with sweetness and a deep contentment.

Finally, the spell was broken and, as he caressed her arm softly, Sebastian's brow once again was furrowed. "I'm worried about you," he said. "I don't like the looks of the bruise on your chest and the swelling on your upper arm. I think you should see a doctor."

"Oh, I'm okay," she said. "It doesn't hurt that much. I'm sure it'll be better by tomorrow." She really didn't want to go anywhere, not even across the room. She just wanted to stay in his arms forever.

Sebastian grimaced, looking at the nasty bruise on her body and the bloody cuts on her arm. "I'm sorry I wasn't there for you when you needed me most," he said. "Let's make sure not to forget the necklace from now on." He put his arms around her and pulled her closer. They fell asleep in each other's arms and didn't get up until late in the afternoon.

Sebastian had a very late flight out of Gatwick, so they got up and got ready slowly.

"Arielle," he whispered when it was almost time for them to go. "I don't want to leave you. Promise me that if you don't feel any better by tomorrow, you will go to the doctor. Please promise me."

"I promise," she said, "but I'm sure I'll be all right."

Before they left the room, he made her sit on the bed, and he handed her a small black velvet box.

"Happy birthday, baby," he whispered, and kissed her softly.

She opened the little box, and she fell speechless. There, staring her in the face, was the most beautiful emerald ring she had ever seen. The emerald was surrounded by a small pear shaped diamonds. She was overwhelmed.

"Sebastian, I can't take this," she said. "It looks very expensive."

"I had it made especially for you. And you will wear it if you love me," he said. He reached down, took the ring, and put it on her right finger. It was a perfect fit.

"The next ring will be for your left hand," he whispered as he brushed his lips against her ear.

She held her hand up and couldn't stop looking at the ring. It made her hand look so beautiful! She smiled with gratitude and wrapped her arms around him.

"Thank you, Sebastian, I love it. It's the most beautiful ring I have ever seen."

"You are perfectly welcome, and you completely deserve it," he said. "Happy birthday, my love."

They drove to the airport without saying a word. He held her hand, and she stared at him, trying to memorize every detail of his beautiful face. He looked at her as his lips curved up into that smile that she loved so much. Then she sighed and said, "Sebastian! I'll never get used to the fact that you love me."

"Why would you ever say that?" His voice was a little surprised.

"Well, look at you, and then look at me!"

"I am looking at you, and all I can see is the most beautiful girl I have ever seen in my life – and that is a very long time." He smiled warmly. "Arielle, you are the only one for me, so you should just get used to that. Our lives are intertwined for eternity."

The drive back to the flat was lonely and empty. Despite the terrifying encounter with Savanna and the pain it had caused Arielle, it had been a great birthday, and Sebastian's presence her most amazing gift. When she arrived back at the flat, it was nearly midnight, and she assumed that Gabby and Eva would be in bed since they had early classes on Monday morning. But they were both up, waiting to talk to her.

"What's up?" she asked, surprised to see them still awake.

"How are you feeling?" Gabrielle asked. "Eva told me what happened. I just can't understand why she can't let go of Sebastian. What's wrong with that woman?"

"I don't know, but I certainly am happy that Troy was there to help me."

"I don't know how I missed all that activity," Gabrielle said. "Troy told me that she was bloody crazy."

"It seems that Annabel sent her, and there is nothing I can do about it." Arielle said. She looked down and shook her head, upset all over again thinking about the incident that had almost ruined her birthday. "Eva, thank you, as well, for being there," she added.

"I love you, Arielle, how could I do anything else?"

"Sebastian is so wonderful!" Gabrielle said, a huge smile lighting her face.

"I think we are all very lucky to have great guys that seem to love us," Arielle said.

Eva and Gabrielle both smiled and agreed with her. But they also made it clear that they had never seen anyone affect them in quite the way Sebastian had. Well, Arielle knew all about that already, but she didn't want to go into any detail, so she just smiled. Then she showed them her new ring, and they were amazed.

"Wow, Arielle, that looks expensive! That must have set him back quite a few pounds," Eva exclaimed.

"I don't know anything about his finances, but I do know that I love him, and that is good enough for me," Arielle said. They chatted a bit longer before going to bed. Eva followed Arielle to her bedroom, seeming like she wanted to talk some more.

"What is it, Eva?" Arielle asked.

"How do you know that Annabel sent her?" Eva asked, then added, "I could see that she was evil. She wanted to hurt you. I'm so glad Troy took care of her."

"She mentioned Annabel just before she hit me," Arielle said. "Anyway, I'm just glad it's over."

"How is your arm?"

"I think it will be fine in a couple of days," she said, rubbing it. She wasn't actually so sure about that, but she didn't want to worry Eva.

"There is something very special about Sebastian and Troy," Eva mused. "I can't put my finger on exactly what it is, but it's something. The vision I had about him is all good, but it's a little strange."

"Well, as long as they are good to us, I'm happy," Arielle said. "I think Ian is amazing too, and he is going to make you very happy. Your gifts will be a big plus in your life; keep using them wisely," she said and chuckled.

"I hear you, Arielle. I will try not to summon anyone tonight," Eva replied, grinning.

They both giggled and hugged each other as Eva wished Arielle a happy birthday one more time, and then they went to bed. Arielle wanted to write in her journal, but she didn't feel well enough. As she lay down and closed her eyes, she knew this would be a birthday she would always remember.

She had embarked into a very strange world, and she had found the man of her dreams. As she drifted off to sleep, she could hear both the warmth of Sebastian's voice and the coldness in Savanna's – an astonishing contrast, almost as if to demonstrate the balance of good and evil forces in the universe. She couldn't believe how his presence made her dizzy with excitement. She smiled, thinking about all that had taken place over the last two days as sleep claimed her.

 *Chapter 21*

THE NEXT MORNING the sound of Eva's voice woke her up. She had a class at ten o'clock but no desire to get up and move. She missed Sebastian terribly, and the emptiness inside her was palpable. As she tried to move, she felt a sharp pain on the left side of her chest. She walked to the shower gingerly, finding that every small movement caused pain. Washing her hair was an ordeal. Lifting her arm brought tears to her eyes as she let the hot water run over her body, hoping it would make the pain a little more tolerable. As she reached for a towel, her eyes fell on the beautiful emerald ring sparkling on her finger. Bliss stretched across her face and once again the vision of Sebastian completely engulfed her mind.

She heard her e-mail ping just as she stepped out of the shower, but when she glanced at the bathroom mirror her jaw dropped. The spot in the center of her chest was now black and her whole left side, including her breast, was bruised. The upper part of her left arm was swollen, and as she looked closer, she could see that pus was oozing out of the four cuts from Savanna's nails. Her throat was burning, her lips were dry, and she felt a sharp pain each time she took a breath.

She couldn't seem to focus on anything but the pain. Her whole body was clammy, and sweat was dripping down her forehead. She suddenly felt weak and no matter how hard she tried to stand, her legs gave out, and she found herself on the floor.

She knew something was terribly wrong, and she called for help, desperation in her voice. Eva and Gabrielle came rushing in, and she heard them gasp as they entered the bathroom and found her on the floor. They helped her to her bed, and she could barely hear Eva's voice as she called for an ambulance. She became extremely nauseous and could hardly keep her eyes open. She had no clue what was happening to her. She was desperately trying to understand; that was the last thing she remembered.

She tried to open her eyes a few times but soon gave up. She had no idea how long she was asleep. She could hear people and voices all around her, but she was unable to understand what was being said, or to communicate herself. She felt numb and very drowsy. Her throat was dry, and she was extremely thirsty. She didn't seem to have the strength to talk, and she couldn't move her arms. What was happening to her? Where was she? Why couldn't she open her eyes?

She felt like she was trapped in a terrible isolation and there was nothing that she could do about it. Tears rolled down the side of her face, and she moaned, trying to understand where she was.

Then she felt someone's soft hands cup her face, their thumbs wiping her tears away. A low voice was telling her to relax and be quiet. When she was finally able to open her eyes, she saw her mother's worried face.

"Hello, my darling!"

"Mummy, where am I?"

"You are in the hospital, Arielle. You need to try to stay quiet, dear."

"What happened?"

"You had some poison in your body. You have some broken ribs, and you have been in a deep sleep. Don't worry, dear, I'll take care of you."

"How bad is it?"

"Your fever is down, but not by much. However, it is better than it was yesterday. You are improving every day, but you'll still need to be in bed for the next few days.

"What day is it?"

"Friday."

"Oh my God, have I been sleeping for five days?"

"Not quite five, but pretty close to that. You have been trying to wake up, but you kept falling back asleep. There's a lot of medication in your body," she explained.

Arielle was trying – trying hard – to think, to remember. Something was bothering her, but she couldn't think clearly, and she couldn't express what she was thinking about. She felt exhausted, and all she wanted to do was sleep.

"Your friends have been coming by to check on you," her mum said. "Eva and Ian, Paul, Gabrielle and Troy…"

Troy's name jolted her mind alert, and suddenly she saw his face in her head. *Oh my gosh! What about Sebastian?* She thought. *He must have been trying to call me, and he must be worried.*

"Mother have you seen my mobile phone?" she asked anxiously.

"No, dear. But I have your purse right here. Let me check."

She came back with the phone, but the battery was dead.

"Oh, Mummy, can you please call Gabby and ask her if she can bring me my charger? I need to call Sebastian, and I only have his number on my phone. He'll be so worried. I haven't been able to talk with him, and we usually talk every day."

"Sebastian is here, dear," she said, smiling, and added, "When your phone kept going to voice mail for three days, he flew back in to check on you. He was really worried."

"Where is he?"

"He was here for three days straight, day and night, while you were running a high fever. When you started to get a little bit better, he began to go back to the hotel to take a shower and change his clothes. He'll be back shortly."

Arielle smiled at this piece of news. "Oh, Mummy, please help me clean up a little. I don't want him to see me this way."

"Arielle, he sat on this very chair right next to your bed all those hours. He was worried about *you*, not about the way you look. You have been sick, and he understands that."

Arielle didn't have the strength to argue. She felt very tired, and she drifted away into a deep sleep.

The next time she opened her eyes she saw Sebastian's beautiful face before her.

"Arielle! How are you, baby?" His soft voice was more familiar to her than the air she was breathing.

She tried hard to smile, wanting to show him how ecstatic she was to see him, but she didn't quite succeed.

She reached over to take his hand and grimaced as she felt a pinch from the IV setup that was holding her arm in place.

"What is it?" he asked, his voice full of anxiety.

"Nothing, just a little pain when I tried to move my arm."

He held her hand, and his lips curved into that smile that she now felt she needed to breathe, the smile that filled her heart with joy.

"I'm sorry you had to come back so soon," she said. "But I'm glad you are here. I must look terrible. I don't feel all that good," she murmured with a weak smile.

He leaned down and pressed his lips softly to hers. She could taste the sweetness of his scent, and she was elated.

"You are the most beautiful girl I know, Arielle. You are my life and the reason I get up every morning." His velvety voice made her heart skip with joy.

"Don't kiss me," she protested. "You might get sick."

"Oh, but didn't I tell you? That's one of my gifts," he whispered. "I never get sick." he chuckled.

All she could do was smile.

It was late in the afternoon when the doctor walked into the room with her father, his face showing extreme concern.

"Arielle, how do you feel?" the doctor asked.

"A little better."

"I need to ask you a couple of questions that nobody would have the answers to but you," he continued. She looked at him, worried about what he was going to ask and how she should answer.

"Where did you get those cuts on your arm?"

She felt anxious as Sebastian's hand pressed on hers. She sucked in a couple of deep breaths and her voice came out hesitantly. "I scraped myself against something, but I don't remember what," she lied. "Why do you ask?"

"Try to remember," the doctor said. "These cuts were full of a rare and deadly poison. You could have died within two days if you hadn't gotten here in time. It's a very slow working, fatal poison that subjects its victim to excruciating pain." Fear consumed her as she heard his words, and her heart was hammering in her chest. The pain was still strong, and her face grew distorted as she tried to keep her breathing normal. She felt Sebastian's hand pressing hers softly, and when she looked at him, distress was etched across his beautiful face.

"I have one more question," the doctor continued. "Where did you get that huge bruise on your chest? Do you know that you have three broken ribs? How could you stand it? Didn't you feel any pain?"

"I did have some pain, but I didn't think anything was broken," she said. "I was driving the day before my party, and I didn't have my seat belt on. I had to make a sudden stop, and I hit the steering wheel with my chest. It didn't bother me that much and I didn't even notice the bruise."

"Unbelievable," the doctor muttered and shook his head. Then he added, "You'll need to take better care of yourself, young lady if you want to live the rest of your life unscathed."

"Unbelievable," he murmured again as he walked out of the room shaking his head. Her parents were also puzzled, wondering what was happening to their daughter. They were relieved that she was okay, but still worried about what had happened.

"Arielle, are you trying to kill your old man? Please do me a favor and be more careful," her father said. He was pretty upset.

"I'm so sorry, Daddy, I had no idea about the poison. And the bruise was not that bad, honest!"

She smiled as he shook his head in disbelief. Then they both kissed her on the forehead and walked out of the room, smiling and waving goodbye.

Stony silence fell in the room as Sebastian and Arielle stared at each other, thinking over what the doctor had said.

"A rare poison? Is that what she used to try to kill me? How am I ever going to protect myself from her?" she wondered frantically.

His face was only a centimeter away from hers as she placed her right hand on the nape of his neck and held him close so she could breathe his sweet scent.

"She almost succeeded in killing you," he growled. "Don't *ever* take that necklace off again." His eyes were filled with horror, and his expression frightened her. "If you'd had that necklace on she would never have been able to get close to you."

"I'm okay, Sebastian, please calm down. You're scaring me," she whispered.

"You are not okay," he said. "You would be in incredible pain if not for the medication you're on. You have three broken ribs, and you went through a very painful procedure to take all that poison out of you. Whatever do you mean by saying you are okay?" His voice was tense and angry, but she knew that his anger was because he loved her so much. So she just smiled and pulled his head closer to steal another kiss.

"What am I going to do with you?" he said. "Nothing scares you. And you tolerate pain as if it were nothing at all." She tried to smile, but again she felt a wave of fatigue.

"You need to rest," he said. "When the fever is gone you can get up and spend some time with me. I'm going to leave now so you can get some rest."

"Oh Sebastian, please don't go," she whispered as she closed her eyes.

She felt his lips on hers; she smelled that wonderful scent of his and heard his voice murmur close to her ear. "Sleep, my sweet angel! I'll be right here when you wake up."

The next morning she woke feeling rejuvenated. The medicines and the sedative that the doctor had prescribed had made her fall into a deep, deep sleep. When she opened her eyes, she knew instantly that she felt much better. Sebastian was standing by the window talking with her dad. Her mum was standing over her bed, smiling. She bent down and gave Arielle a hug. "Your fever is gone!" she whispered ecstatically. "I'm so glad you seem to have turned the corner."

Both Sebastian and her dad turned toward her, and she heard her dad's voice. "Well, little girl, you certainly gave your old man a bad scare. You can't be doing this. I worry about you, I want you to be happy and healthy."

"Thanks, Daddy, I'll try to do that since this doesn't seem to work for you," she said, chuckling softly, then wincing from the pain. Her dad and Sebastian laughed, too.

Her dad smiled again and kissed her on the cheek. Then he and her mum walked out of the room.

She looked into Sebastian's beautiful eyes, and she felt so happy to be alive. "I'm delighted that you're alive as well," he said softly.

He must have been reading her thoughts again. She immediately groped around her neck and was horrified to realize that her necklace was missing.

"My necklace!" she cried out.

"Don't worry, baby, your mum has it," he said calmly. "They removed your jewelry when they brought you into the hospital. I must admit I love being able to read your thoughts again. Seeing that you love me as much as you do makes me extremely happy."

He sat on the side of the bed, wrapped his arms around her waist, and pulled her close to his body gently. His lips pressed hers.

"Are you hungry?" he asked.

"Yes, I'm famished. But I also want to go home. When am I going home?"

"I think the doctor is coming to see you in a little while. We'll make sure to ask him that."

"When do you have to go back?" she asked.

"I'll stay with you until you are home, and you feel one hundred percent better. I'll get someone to bring you something to eat."

"Only if you can do that with your mind," she said, "because I don't want to let you go."

He chuckled and as he pressed her a little tighter against him she giggled with pleasure.

"You must be one of the prescribed medications I need," she said. "Your touch makes me feel so much better."

He laughed, pleased that she was joking again, and she laughed too.

"Well, you are the perfect medicine for me, so I'm glad to know that I'm the perfect medicine for you as well," he murmured.

"I am sorry you had to fly right back here again," she said.

"Nothing is more important to me than you. I would come to the ends of the earth to be with you."

"I love you, Sebastian," she murmured.

"Thank you for that. I need you to love me," he said.

She was sure that plenty of girls would love to love him and that there were plenty more who did love him. She was still quite amazed that of all the girls in the world, he had chosen her.

Early that afternoon the doctor came and examined her carefully.

"Well, Arielle," he said. "You are a very lucky girl. I think you are doing just fine. You can go home this afternoon if you want to."

"Yes, I would love to go home. Thank you, Doctor!" She smiled.

The plan was for her to stay with her parents for a few days until she was completely well. Before leaving the hospital, she made sure the necklace was back on her neck, and the first day at home she just kept to her bed. She was still quite weak, and now that she was home, she had to either take care of herself or let her parents help her.

Her friends came over to visit, and she was happy to see all of them. When she saw Sebastian talking with Troy, she could see Troy's face changing to a look of shock. She was sure Sebastian must be telling him about the poison. While the guys were sitting in the living room talking, Eva and Gabrielle stayed with Arielle in her room. When she told them about the poison, Gabby gasped, but Eva just gave her a knowing look.

"I saw it coming. I just didn't know exactly how it was going to happen," she said.

"I know, Eva, and I do believe in your visions. Every one of them has come true. This woman is crazy, trying to get me out of the way." She shook her head in disbelief.

"There are a lot of things we can do to protect you. And I promise you, Arielle, I will be working on that," Eva said.

"Oh, Eva, please," she said. "I don't want you to go back into all those dark spells. Don't summon any spirits. Just be happy with Ian and spend time with him. I'll be fine," she assured her.

"I can do both," Eva said emphatically, a very serious look on her face.

"Okay then. I'll let you protect me," Arielle said, laughing quietly. And as they looked into each other's eyes they laughed again, appreciating the sincerity and depth of their friendship.

Late in the afternoon her friends left, and she and Sebastian took a walk in the garden.

"It was so good of you to come, Sebastian," she said. "But you need to go back. I'm okay now," she whispered.

"Don't you want me here?"

"I want you to stay forever, but I know you have your work. And I'm okay now. Besides, you've already been here for nearly another week."

"You are the reason I get up in the morning, Arielle."

"Well, I know that you can't read my mind anymore," she said, touching her necklace, "but by now you should have no doubts about how I feel." She smiled at him and squeezed his hand. He just smiled and nodded.

His phone rang and, pulling it out of his pocket, he looked at the screen. Giving her a loving squeeze and a soft kiss on her lips, he walked away to answer it. She heard him talking to someone in French. He was very animated and seemed a little upset. Suddenly he closed the phone with an angry gesture, a tense look darkening his handsome face.

"Is something wrong?" she asked when he returned.

"Nothing that should interfere with the time I have with you. Just business," he said. But there was a nervous edge to his voice, not at all the usual loveliness. "I think I'll go back to the hotel to make my flight arrangements for tomorrow. You get into bed, and I'll come back later," he said.

"I am a little tired," she whispered as he leaned in and kissed her passionately. As the kiss ended, he gazed deep into her eyes and smiled softly.

Trying to catch her breath, she watched him walk away. Every move he made was so seamless. And as she watched him leave, she missed him already.

Back in her room she lay back down and closed her eyes. When she awoke, it was dark and the clock on the nightstand showed one-fifteen a.m. She had slept right through dinner and whatever else had happened since five o'clock in the afternoon.

She sat up in the dark and wondered what had happened to Sebastian. He hadn't come back. Did it have something to do with the phone call he had received earlier that afternoon? Suddenly she felt a jolt in her spine and a sick feeling that Annabel might have had something to do with that call. Fear took over her body, and she couldn't seem to be able to stop herself from panicking. Her fingers moved quickly to touch the necklace that was to keep her safe, making sure it was still there. She tried to lie back down and stay under the covers, but she couldn't relax.

Noises outside her window seemed ominous, so she got up, still holding her pillow and walked quietly over to the balcony doors, peering out carefully from behind the closed curtains. It was nothing, nothing at all – just the wind making the limbs of trees brush against the side of the house. She told herself to stop her imagination from going wild. She got back into bed and eventually went back to sleep.

The next morning she woke to the smell of coffee. She got up slowly and walked down to the kitchen where her parents were having breakfast.

"Good morning, darling, how do you feel?" her mother asked.

"I feel great," she said. "I can't believe I've gone through a whole week of feeling miserable."

"Well that is good news," her father said, never looking up from the newspaper.

"Sit down and have some breakfast. That will make you feel even better," her mother urged. She couldn't argue with that because she was starving.

"Mum, I have a few more things that I would like to take over to the flat," she said. "Can you take me there later?"

"Sure, darling, any time you're ready. Would you like to have lunch with us first?"

"Yes, that'll be fine."

"What ever happened to Sebastian?" her father asked.

"I don't know," she said. "He received a call yesterday afternoon and had to go. He said he would come back here, but he never did."

"Oh well, sometimes things like that happen when you are involved in business," her father said.

"Do you know what business he is in?" she asked curiously.

"Yes, we talked about it yesterday while you were sleeping. He's the owner of one of the largest corporations in Europe. He's involved with important landowners who are running businesses throughout the world. That is a very big burden for someone as young as he is. He's a fascinating young man, and extremely smart. I sure would love to have someone like him running my business, but from what I can tell he's quite wealthy. He would never be interested in my world," he added, chuckling.

Just then her phone buzzed, and she saw Sebastian's name pop up on the screen. "Hello!" she said. "What happened to you?"

"Something very important came up, Arielle, I'm sorry. I can't talk about it over the phone. I'm coming over." Then the phone went dead.

Her thoughts instantly jumped to Annabel, and again a cold shiver ran down her spine. His voice sounded low and troubled; she was extremely anxious. This was the first time he had ever ended a call without saying, "Miss me."

She sat back down and kept quiet, waiting and wondering, full of concern.

"Is there something wrong?" both of her parents asked at once.

"I'm not sure what is going on," she said. "He's on his way here."

A few minutes later she heard the front door bell ring. He was standing in the doorway, his face as beautiful as ever, but his eyes troubled and dark.

"What is it?" she asked, worried. She took his hand, and they walked into the living room. Then he put his arms around her and pulled her close.

"Arielle, I need to leave tonight for Australia and from there to New Zealand," he said.

"Australia? New Zealand? What happened? How long will you be gone?"

"I have a long trip ahead of me. I have to fly from Paris through Singapore for refueling, and from there to Sydney. It's about twenty-three hours altogether. It'll be exhausting, but I have to do it. I can't say much more about it right now, but we have a very serious situation at our headquarters here in London. I met with some of the board members as well as a couple of Interpol agents, and we tried to work out a plan of action during the night." He sighed and shook his head.

"Why is Interpol involved? What happened? Please tell me, Sebastian. I'm going out of my mind."

He pulled her to the sofa and asked her to sit down. "I can't discuss the details, but we have had a major break-in at the London office. Very valuable secret documents and product designs that we are developing in Australia and New Zealand were stolen. The designs can be used to create weapons of a catastrophic magnitude."

"Why do you have to go there?" she asked. "Can't you have the authorities work on it?"

"Arielle, Nathan and I are the perfect people to handle this.

Remember, you are the only one who knows about our immortality. We're stronger and faster than humans. I can read people's minds, and Nathan can see ahead into the future. We have powers that no one in our business world is aware of."

"Is Nathan going too?"

"Yes, he's going too. We have been working together for centuries. He's one of my closest business associates."

"Why don't you ever talk about him?"

"Well, his personal interests are different than mine, but when it comes to business, we are perfect for each other. Our gifts as immortals are a little bit different, and they complement each other, making us a great team. We have some information from people who were on duty when this happened, and that is where we will start the hunt." Seeing that she was still worried he added, "You don't need to worry about me, I'll be perfectly fine. We have to get those documents back, and we'll be able to get them back faster than Interpol or any other agency out there. These documents are very dangerous in the wrong hands and very important to the success of all the companies we hold and the people who work for us."

"Oh, it's dreadful!" she said. "Sebastian, I'll be worried about you no matter what you say." She took his face in her hands and tenderly gazed into his beautiful eyes. "I can understand that your special gifts will be a great advantage for you, but I still don't like it. How long are you going to be gone?" Her face fell into a frown.

He laced his fingers through hers and said softly, "Right now I'm not sure about anything. I'll keep you informed as well as I can. I love you, and I'll have the details of your beautiful face imprinted in my mind. You'll be with me for as long as we are apart."

"I don't like the sound of that either," she said.

He pressed his lips to hers with a strange hunger and held her tight. "Don't take that necklace off as long as I am gone," he said, his voice suddenly stern. "I've already talked to Troy; he'll be watching out for you. He has my mobile number, and I'll be in contact with him."

Her frown had deepened, and Sebastian looked at her with great concern. He put his finger under her chin and lifted her face to him so he could look into her eyes.

"What is it, baby?" he asked, and her gaze became more intent. "Well?" he persisted, inquisitively. She searched his eyes and, leaning closer she locked her lips with his in a hot kiss. He moaned and held her tighter.

When she finally pulled away, she said, "Why don't you and Nathan use your immortal speed and get there tonight instead of enduring such a long flight? The sooner you get there the sooner you'll come back to me."

Sebastian blinked, a bit shocked for a moment by the question, and then he chuckled softly, shaking his head. His lips found hers again, and the kiss sent a heat wave through her body.

Then he broke away and explained. "Baby, there are other people – humans – involved with this issue, and they are flying with us to Melbourne. Nathan and I also just finished talking with our contacts in Melbourne, and they will be picking us up at the airport. Do you understand now why I need to do things the human way?" He chuckled again and gathered her in his arms one more time.

"I have to go, Arielle. Let's say a word to your parents."

He walked into the kitchen and told them that he had to leave due to an urgent business matter, and thanked them for their hospitality. "Have a safe trip," Arielle's father said, and her mother added, "Arielle will miss you, but don't worry, we'll take good care of her."

Then, taking his hand, Arielle walked Sebastian to the door. His strong arms wrapped around her waist and suddenly his eyes met hers. Her heart skipped a beat, and she thought she was going to lose consciousness. Her breath halted in her throat and her knees buckled. His lips trailed from her ear down to her mouth, and he kissed her softly. His mouth was hot and inviting, and his warm breath and wonderful scent made her body quiver with desire. He held her tight until the dazzling sensation wore off as he held a smile of complete satisfaction on his face.

"I'm not sure I'll make it without you. Please come home soon," she whispered, her eyes full of tears as they kissed goodbye.

"Miss me," he whispered, and his lips curved up into her favorite smile as he walked out the door. She stood there, watching him walk to his car, and before long he was gone. As she walked back to the kitchen, her heart felt empty and sad.

"Is he gone?" her father asked.

"Yes."

"Well, honey, that's normal. I've been away from your mother many times and have had to be gone for a week or more as business required."

"That doesn't mean I liked it," her Mum said with an understanding smile. She came over and gave Arielle a big hug.

"You really like this guy don't you?" she said.

"I love him, Mum. He is the man I want to be with for the rest of my life."

Her dad looked at her, and with a smile on his face, he said, "Well, that's a good thing, because he's clearly in love with you, too. I'm sure he'll be back as soon as he can."

"He told you that he loves me?" she asked.

"He did indeed," he said.

"What else did he tell you?"

"Nothing more," he said. He laughed and got up from the table to walk out to the garden.

Arielle headed upstairs, her heart full and empty at the same time.

Chapter 22

AS SOON AS SEBASTIAN had seen Nathan's name on the screen of his mobile phone, he knew it had to be urgent since he had specifically asked not to be disturbed. "What's up?" he asked, feigning a casual attitude, not wanting to alarm Arielle.

"Sebastian, we have a very serious situation on our hands," Nathan said. "You need to come down here as soon as possible."

"What's the problem?" he asked, walking away from Arielle.

"We've had a break-in the main vault here in London and all the product designs are missing. The certificates are still here, and so is the money. I have a terrible feeling that this was not just a simple robbery."

Nathan paused for just a moment to let the news sink in, then added, "I've also received calls from the North Island and Auckland that groups of men simultaneously attacked both of our laboratories and abducted Dr. Swanson and Dr. Walker. We don't know if they are being held for ransom or if they've been killed. Some of our best security officers were taken by surprise and were either hurt or killed trying to stop them." He paused again. "These attacks were extremely well organized. There must be moles in our buildings. I don't have any more details as of yet, but you need to come down straightaway. I called Interpol, and I spoke with Dylan Jamison, the head of British intelligence. He is sending two of his agents to meet with us here at headquarters. I've been trying to call you, but your phone was shut off."

"Yes, I'm sorry, Nathan. Remember, I told you I was going to be with Arielle. She was very sick, and I didn't want to disturb her, but she's doing better now. I'll be there shortly. As a matter of fact, I'll leave right now."

He had tried to cover up his level of concern as he had said his goodbyes and "miss me," but once he had left Arielle, he was filled with a feeling of profound wretchedness. The situation sounded pretty bad. Sebastian had said the design documents that were missing would generate a disaster for companies around the world, and that millions of dollars would be lost if they fell into the wrong hands. Worse yet, they could even be used to create weapons with disastrous, destructive powers. Obviously, he couldn't permit this to occur.

As he jumped into his car and drove off, he took a last fond look at Arielle, who was standing at the door with tears in her eyes. He had thought his heart would break. But how could that be possible when his heart had been dead for centuries now? It was as if his love for her was bringing him back into a fuller state of existence.

An hour later, Sebastian arrived at headquarters in downtown London. Everyone was there, including the two Interpol agents, Mark Salvador and Tony Westbrook, who would be taking charge of the operation. The agents started to ask questions, but there were very few details to be provided. There were no fingerprints found at the London office, and there were no witnesses who could provide any useful information.

Sebastian and Nathan's special intuitive gifts were telling them that they were dealing with a very dangerous group of spies who must have somehow infiltrated various company locations. They were both aware of just how deadly the results of such espionage could be. After all, in the past this type of espionage had shaped governments, even changed the course of wars.

This operation had been perfectly organized to hit all the company locations at the same time, creating mass confusion. It was unsettling, to say the least. Following a detailed briefing of what Nathan already knew, Sebastian, Nathan, and the two Interpol agents agreed to be on an eight o'clock flight to Australia that night.

It was a long flight, approximately twenty-one hours. It felt even longer to Sebastian since he was worried about the situation in New Zealand on one hand and the necessity of leaving Arielle behind on the other. He slept fitfully, and in between bits of sleep he was tormented by violent visions.

When they landed at Sydney airport, the head of operations at North Island headquarters met them and took them immediately to the lab. There they were informed of the bloody details. Two of the three guards at the gate had been shot dead. So had a young engineer in his early twenties, Theodore Samson, whose body had been found next to the main laboratory. The third guard was in the hospital in critical condition.

This too was a clean job; there were no fingerprints anywhere near the bodies. It seemed as if Dr. Swanson had vanished into thin air. The only witness was Michael Swanson, Dr. Swanson's son, also an engineer at the lab. He told them he had left the laboratory for a short time to get dinner for his father, and when he returned his father was gone.

"Did you see anyone on your way out of the building?" Officer Salvador asked. "Did you see any cars driving towards the building?"

Michael thought for a while, and then he said he did remember seeing a dark van with a white stripe along the side, but he wasn't sure if the van was blue or black. It was too dark, and he hadn't seen the color very well. He had seen two men in the front of the van when his headlights momentarily illuminated their car. "The driver wore glasses, that's all I remember," he said apologetically.

As Michael spoke, Sebastian was able to conjure up the faces of the two men whose memory was in Michael's mind. He looked at Nathan, and his lips moved, but no human ear could hear, and no human eye could perceive the immortal ability he was using at that moment. He would discuss the details of those two men with Nathan when they were alone.

Sebastian could see that Michael didn't have any more information, and he smiled at him, gently assuring him that he would do his best to find his father and bring him back safe. The officers asked Michael a few more questions, writing down all the little details of his answers. Unfortunately, there was very little to aid them in their investigation.

The next morning Sebastian and Nathan flew to Auckland, where they heard a similar story. Dr. Walker had vanished from the Auckland lab in much the same way Dr. Swanson had disappeared in Sydney without a trace left behind. As in Sydney, both guards at the gate had been killed. However, in Auckland, the four engineers who were present at the lab were bound with duct tape around their mouths, ankles, and wrists, and left alive, locked in a closet.

"Why would they have left witnesses alive in this location?" Officer Salvador wondered aloud. He proceeded to question each of the victims individually about what they had witnessed. They all stated that they had heard shots, and then three men had burst into the lab, making them lie on the floor facedown as they bound them and locked them in the closet.

Unfortunately, the men had worn masks and heavy gear, so their faces were concealed; however, the victims remembered that they had spoken with Russian accents.

One of the four engineers, Khalhemah, was very quiet, and Sebastian could clearly read his thoughts. And because he could read his thoughts, he knew that this man was a conspirator who had helped the assassins succeed in the abduction. *So that's why they were spared,* he realized.

The other three men were completely truthful in everything they said and had had absolutely no part in the assault. When Officer Salvador had gathered all the information he could, they went back to the hotel. "I don't know what to think," he said, shaking his head. "Let's try to put it all together and start fresh in the morning."

After the officers had retired for the evening, Sebastian and Nathan met in Sebastian's room and discussed what Sebastian had seen in Khalhemah's head, as well as what Nathan had been able to foresee using his special powers. Then they left the hotel.

Another immortal gift they possessed was an exceptional ability to trace people by their scents, and they wanted to see if they could discover anything by just wandering around. Following their scents, they ended up in a small residential neighborhood, in front of an old, beat-up apartment building. They stopped in front of a door and tapped softly. Khalheman opened the door without taking the chain off the lock and saw Sebastian and Nathan glaring at him.

Later he could only remember trying to close the door, but he couldn't for the life of him comprehend how Sebastian and Nathan had ended up standing in the middle of the room. He tried to reach for his gun and was amazed to find that suddenly Sebastian had him in a headlock, and his gun was in Nathan's hands. He watched in complete shock and dismay as Nathan squeezed the gun between his fingers, turning it into pure dust before his astonished eyes. He was petrified with fear as he realized that he was dealing with something beyond his ability to understand.

"Don't make me hurt you," Sebastian growled, and the anger in his voice stunned Khalhemah.

"What do you want from me?" he asked, his voice shaking with fear.

"We know you are a liar and that you are party to extortion and theft. Don't try to tell us any more lies because we can see into your mind. You have no idea what we can do."

Khalhemah looked at them warily, wondering whether to believe what he was hearing, but he didn't move.

"We want to know who broke into the London office and where we can find them," Sebastian continued. "You are also going to provide us with the names of the people who abducted our scientists." Sebastian could clearly read his mind, but he wanted to make sure that nothing was hidden in one of the murky corners of his head.

"I can't tell you anything, they'll kill me!" he said.

"*I'm* going to kill you if you don't start talking right now," Nathan said. His voice froze the blood in Khalhemah's veins as he felt Sebastian's hands tighten around his neck. He started to lose consciousness, barely able to breathe.

"We will shatter each one of your bones slowly and then we will bury you alive. Start talking now!" Sebastian hissed. His voice struck terror through Khalhemah's bones, and Nathan's eyes pierced through his soul, making him shiver with fear. Khalhemah knew that these two men were not joking. He could feel the strength of Sebastian's arms and remembered watching what had once been his gun turning to dust between Nathan's fingers. He looked at each of them and when his eyes met theirs, he felt the cold chill of death run through his spine.

"All right, all right..." he gave in. "But I only know the name of the guy who broke into the London office. His name is Alexie Miroslav and he has the documents. He is the person in charge of all the groups engaged in extortion, and murder. They are located in every country outside Russia. But we don't know any other names, or who is the head of the organization. I know there will be two meetings in Nigeria. The first meeting will take place at the Ald Gausha restaurant in Abuja Sunday night, at ten o'clock." He paused as if considering whether to say more, but one glance at the two men continuing to glare at him convinced him to tell everything he knew. "All the people involved will gather their documentation and hand it over to Alexie at that time," he said. "The second meeting will take place at the African Institute of Science in Abuja on Monday at two o'clock in the afternoon. That is where Alexie will hand over the documents to the higher-ups from Russia."

"Where exactly are they going with those documents?" Nathan asked.

"I don't know the exact location, but they will be flying to St. Petersburg to deliver the documents and your scientists. I don't know the names of the people in Russia, and I don't know the names of the people he is to meet with at the museum, and that is the truth." Sebastian, who had not loosened his grip on the man, now let go, and Khalhemah collapsed, holding his head in his hands.

Sebastian knew he had all that he needed now. The man was telling the truth, and he didn't know anything more. Before they left, Nathan used another of their immortal gifts to make sure that Kahlhemah would remember nothing about them or their conversation by erasing his memory of recent events.

They returned to the hotel around three o'clock in the morning, satisfied with the progress they had made and went to bed.

Early the next morning, Sebastian's phone rang. It was Officer Westbrook wanting to know if Sebastian and Nathan would like to have breakfast. Sebastian politely declined and asked if they could meet in a couple of hours in the lobby. Then he called Nathan to give him the meeting time and headed to the shower. He took his time dressing and then called Arielle. Her phone rang several times and then went to voice mail. "Miss me!" he whispered and hung up.

He met Nathan outside his room, and they walked down to the lobby. There, the officers were waiting for them.

"Good morning, officers," Sebastian said, reaching out his hand.

"You can call me Mark," Officer Salvador said.

"And me, Tony," Officer Westbrook added.

"Very well, Mark and Tony," Sebastian said. "We received information this morning from a company informant who advised us that there will be a meeting of the people we are after in Abuja, Nigeria at two o'clock in the afternoon on Monday." He refrained from telling them about the other meeting because he and Nathan were planning to handle that meeting themselves.

"I've already arranged for us to fly to Nigeria, arriving Sunday afternoon," he said. "We can spend some time getting familiar with the museum, the rooms where the exits and entrances are, and so on, in case there is an unexpected turn of events. I think this will give us the upper hand on Monday."

"Now, now, Sebastian," Mark said, smiling. "I appreciate you coming along and helping, but you need to let us do our job."

"Of course, that is our intention," Sebastian agreed. "The only thing we're here for is to get our documents and our scientists. You can handle everything else; we promise we won't be in the way," Sebastian said, casting Nathan a meaningful look.

Next, they went to their rooms to pack and got ready for their flight. As he packed, Sebastian's thoughts turned to the kinds of problems they would face if those documents ever fell into the wrong hands. The new owners of the documents would be able to locate ample Polonium, a very rare radioactive metallic element that Sebastian's company used to make various products – some significant, and some more common.

Sebastian and Nathan were very familiar with Russia's thirst for power and its corrupt government. They knew that Russian spies were less interested in ideological fights for geographic spheres of influence and more interested in prying into secrets hidden in boardrooms and laboratories. These were Russian spies who had most likely spent their whole careers in the old KGB and were now in the FSB. They had been instructed to abduct the scientists and steal or photograph important documents – documents that could provide the information they needed to create dangerous nuclear weapons that would help them maintain political control.

So the task before them was pretty daunting. Simply put, Nathan and Sebastian had to return the stolen documents and the abducted scientists to their rightful places. And quickly, too.

Sebastian was sure that there must be more than one spy who had infiltrated his company. But that was a problem, which would have to be resolved when they returned from Nigeria.

The flight was long and tiring. When they arrived in Nigeria late Sunday afternoon they went directly to the museum, where they walked around, slowly making themselves familiar with all the rooms in the building. They located all the entrances and exits, and then returned to the hotel to get some sleep. They agreed to meet Mark and Tony the next morning in the hotel lobby and went to their rooms.

Once again Nathan and Sebastian met later that night. This time, they flagged a taxi outside the hotel and headed over to the restaurant where the meeting would be held. Arriving about nine-thirty, they took a poorly lit corner table where they would be less conspicuous, and that would give them a better view of the central open area of the restaurant. They knew exactly what Alexie looked like from the picture in Khalhemah's mind, so they ordered some drinks, waited, and watched.

Several groups of customers were dining throughout the restaurant. Sebastian focused on the tables with more than two people and set his mind to work reading people's thoughts. It was not long before he stopped at a table with five men and two women. They were sitting very close to each other and seemed to be involved in an intense conversation. They didn't look Nigerian, they looked European, and their voices were very soft to most listeners. However, Nathan and Sebastian were able to clearly understand what they were saying, and their minds were completely open to Sebastian.

They were too absorbed in their conversation to worry about possible eavesdroppers. Now that the job had been completed according to schedule, they believed that nothing could conceivably go wrong. Or so they thought.

"This assignment was a piece of cake," the first man said, and they all shared a good chuckle.

"Surely you can see that the guys we had inside did an excellent job," the second man said, smiling wide. His gaze flitted from face to face around the table and he saw all of them nodding in agreement.

The man who seemed to be the leader of the group took a sip of his drink. Leaning forward, he said, "Jonathan, we only succeeded because their security team was so pathetic," the corners of his mouth lifting arrogantly. Jonathan blinked at the man's comment. He knew that what the man had said wasn't exactly a lie, but nevertheless, he didn't like what he heard.

"Scott, what is it that you are suggesting?" he asked, obviously offended. When there was no response to his question, he continued an irritable tone in his voice. "Are you saying we only succeeded because they were weak?"

"Calm down, Jonathan," Scott replied calmly. "That's not what I said. But the fact that they were weak made it a lot easier for us."

Jonathan opened his mouth to say something but closed it again, feeling Scott's sharp gaze on him.

"Now that we have all the documents here and the two scientists in a secure place, all we have to do is hand all of it to Alexie, and we're done," Scott stated firmly. They all nodded quietly in agreement, but somewhat tentatively. They knew that they weren't in the clear until all the documents were out of their hands.

Sebastian and Nathan were wondering if the two women in the group were among the assailants or if they had some other role. The next statement convinced them that they were, in fact, co-conspirators.

"This will be one of the nicest paydays we've ever had," one of the women said, clearly delighted. There was a short pause and the next piece of conversation sparked Sebastian and Nathan's interest.

The fourth guy in the group had been quiet throughout the exchange between the thugs. He seemed to be looking over his shoulder most of the time, impatiently. Finally, he looked like he was ready to say something, but he was interrupted by one of the women.

"Scotty, where did they take the two scientists?" she asked.

"I'm sure they took them to the same place we are staying tonight. We have security to make sure they remain in our custody until Alexie picks them up in the morning." Scott replied. "Then Alexie will deliver the two scientists, along with the documents, to his contacts from St. Petersburg sometime tomorrow morning."

"What is it, Miles?" Scott asked, staring pointedly at the fourth man, who still seemed to be quite nervous. "What's wrong? You seem jumpy."

Miles took a deep breath and, looking around one more time, he leaned close and whispered, "I have this strange feeling that we're being watched." Immediately they all tensed up and took a good look around. Everyone in the place seemed to be engaged in private conversations, and nothing seemed to be out of place. Sebastian and Nathan were sitting quite far from their table, so they didn't even notice them. After a long, careful survey of the restaurant's patrons had reassured them that everything was okay, they turned to face each other.

"You've just got the jitters, old man, nothing to worry about," Scott said confidently. Miles smiled with relief, but he still didn't seem completely convinced.

Sebastian and Nathan now knew that they had to follow the assailants after the meeting and get the scientists freed. The next day they would be at the museum along with the Interpol agents for Alexie's meeting with the Russians. A low cough from Nathan snapped Sebastian out of his thoughts, and he returned to listening again.

"Fortunately, we didn't get interrupted during the invasion. This was a quick and clean job," noted a fifth man, who seemed to be just as quiet as Miles.

"I'm sure that Alexie will be extremely pleased with the outcome," Scott said.

Soon after, their conversation shifted to other topics. Then, just before ten o'clock, a stocky man with slick blond hair walked into the restaurant. His face was stern, his lips were pressed together anxiously, and he was carrying a briefcase. He stopped for a short moment at the entrance while his eyes intently scanned the room, stopping at the table with the group of assailants. He crossed the room with a few large strides. There were handshakes, soft smiles, and low talk, but none of it escaped Sebastian and Nathan's notice. Envelopes, which

Sebastian was sure contained the stolen documents and files, were handed to the man, and he placed them in his briefcase.

"Your guests are secure," the man called Scott assured him with an obnoxious smile, adding, "They're all ready for their trip to St. Petersburg."

As soon as they began discussing the prisoners, Sebastian could see clearly in their minds the details about the abduction of the two scientists, as well as their flights to Nigeria. He could see in their minds that on arrival in Nigeria, the scientists had been turned over to a group of armed men who had put them into a van and moved them to a large building. They now knew it was the same location where the assailants would be staying tonight.

Alexie nodded, looking pleased. After a brief discussion, he stood up, took a few small envelopes from his coat pocket and handed them to each of the five men and the two women. Then he walked out of the room, taking all the documentation with him. Sebastian and Nathan let him go. They knew that he would be meeting his contacts at the museum the next day and handing the stolen documents over to them. Their priority, for now, was to free the scientists.

The assailants ordered several more rounds of drinks, celebrating their success. Around midnight, they stood up and walked out the door noisily, clearly quite drunk. Sebastian and Nathan followed them out to the parking lot and watched them get into a van, which they followed from a distance using their immortal gift of speed.

A few kilometers away they arrived at an old two-story building with an armed guard at the entrance. They watched the assailants stagger to the entrance and stopped to make senseless conversation with the guard. He laughed at their jokes as he opened the door and followed them inside. He was gone for a short minute, but it was long enough for Sebastian and Nathan to take their places on either side of the entrance and wait for him. As soon as he stepped outside, they disarmed him, knocked him out, tied him up, and pulled his body out of sight. Then they went inside.

The first room they came to was full of guards drinking and joking. Sebastian and Nathan moved faster than the human eye could follow and before long they had disarmed all the guards, bound them, and locked them in the room, making it impossible for them to contact anyone outside the building.

All of the other rooms on the first floor were abandoned and destroyed, in a state of complete ruin. Sebastian and Nathan hurried through the long hallway and proceeded to the second floor. They were using their immortal speed and strength to make sure that the job was done both quickly and efficiently. Moving like a hurricane they had no problem disabling, binding, and locking up the five drunken assailants along with the two women and the last four guards, who were occupying rooms upstairs. Then they pushed the last door open, where they were delighted to find Dr. Swanson and Dr. Walker alive, bound to the wall with chains.

The scientists looked exhausted. Their eyes were red, puffy, full of fear and distress, but brilliant joyful smiles broke out the minute they saw Sebastian and Nathan enter the room. Their relief was evident, and their eyes welled up with tears of pure elation.

"We are so glad to see you!" Dr. Walker said softly, his voice fragile but very happy. Sebastian and Nathan removed the chains and helped the scientists walk outside the building. Then Nathan called the British embassy at Abuja and requested to speak to the chief of intelligence, while the scientists massaged their wrists, getting the feeling back into their hands. Nathan waited for the chief to come on the line. Then, in a few words, he explained the situation and requested assistance in moving the guards and the assailants to a secret location so that they wouldn't be able to notify their contacts and compromise the rendezvous planned for the next day.

"Interpol is helping us," he said. "We're working with Mark Salvador and Tony Westbrook."

Within twenty minutes several British police cars had surrounded the location, and the guards and the assailants were taken away. As they were being cuffed and put into the cars, the head of British intelligence in Abuja strode over to Nathan and Sebastian and held out his hand.

"I really can't thank you enough," he said. "We've been after the members of this group for a very long time. I'm extremely pleased to have at least these seven in custody. I'd love to be involved in the meeting tomorrow," he added. "I'll contact Mark for the details. Can I give you both a lift back to the hotel?" he asked.

"Yes, that would be most welcome," Sebastian said, glad that it hadn't occurred to the head of intelligence to wonder how he and Nathan had gotten to that location, and specifically to that building.

Back in the hotel, Sebastian secured two rooms near his room for the scientists, handed each of them a room key, and said with a smile, "Nathan and I have one more thing we need to handle tomorrow with Interpol, and then we will be on our way back home. Sleep well, relax, and try to regain some of your strength. Our meeting is tomorrow afternoon. If you need anything, call Nathan or I and we will be happy to assist you in any way we can. Call your families and let them know that you are safe and that you will be home on Tuesday evening."

The scientists both thanked Sebastian and Nathan profusely, then headed to their rooms. Sebastian, pleased with the outcome of the first part of the plan, thanked Nathan for his help and went to bed, but not before trying to call Arielle one more time. This time, a man's voice answered her phone.

"Hello!"

"Can I speak to Arielle, please?"

"Is this Sebastian?"

"Yes, who is this?"

"Hi Sebastian, this is Paul. We all went to see a film the other night, and she must have dropped her phone in my car. I just found it."

"Hello, Paul, could you please let her know that I've been trying to call?"

"Certainly," Paul replied. "Talk to you later,"

"Later," Sebastian echoed. He hung up with a frown on his face. Why was Arielle spending so much time with Paul? He could neither understand nor explain the strange feeling that made him ache, needing to hear her voice. She was his life, and he couldn't stand the idea of another man spending any time with her. His face was stressed. He wanted to see her, to talk to her, to make sure she still loved him. He tried to close his eyes and conjure the image of her face, but that only made him ache worse. He had never experienced this feeling before. It was new to him, and he didn't like it.

He exhaled deeply and tried to pull himself together. He knew he couldn't afford to have these feelings when he was dealing with a matter of life and death. He tried to use his immortal powers to suppress his personal feelings, only to find out that he didn't possess the power to do that. He was stunned to realize that the feeling taking him over was jealousy. He couldn't stand the idea of Arielle being away from him, especially with another man. He got into bed and lay there with his eyes wide open. He could see the image of her face in front of his eyes, and it made the ache even stronger.

If he could cry, he would, but instead. he pinched the tip of his nose and clenched his fists into two hard balls. If he had touched anything at that moment, it would have been crushed, so intense was his frustration. For a long time, he remained like that, tense and wide awake, filled with emotional pain. Finally, he felt into an uneasy, fitful state of sleep.

The next morning, Mark called for Sebastian and Nathan to meet him in the lobby. "I need to talk to you before this afternoon's meeting," he explained.

Sebastian called Nathan. "Mark sounds eager to meet with us this morning," he said. They arrived at the lobby at ten-thirty, where they found Mark pacing back and forth, looking anxious. Tony was standing nearby, staring out the lobby door.

"Good morning," they both said simultaneously as Sebastian and Nathan approached. Mark could hardly wait to speak, and he went right to the point.

"I received a strange call early this morning from my boss Dylan Jamison. Ryan Mansfield, the head of British intelligence here in Abuja, contacted him to discuss some excitement that took place last night on the south side of town. Dylan called me early this morning and told me that the two of you were involved," Mark said. He stopped and gave them a quizzical look.

"Yes, quite right, I gave your name as well as Dylan's name to the British intelligence agent," Sebastian said. "I had left my phone in the hotel, so I was unable to call you."

"What happened?" Mark asked looking a bit confused.

"Nathan and I decided to go out for a drink last night. We got into an argument over some girls with five guys who were completely inebriated," Sebastian explained. "We got into a fist fight, and they lost. The women helped them to their car and were yelling at them about how angry Alexie was going to be, and that they needed to get back to the prisoners. We had a feeling that they were talking about the person we're meeting today at the museum so we followed them and they led us to a location that seemed to be heavily guarded."

"Amazing!" Tony said.

"There was a public phone to call for help, but we couldn't remember your number. So we called the Embassy, and they were there within a few minutes. We explained why we were there. We told them we thought our scientists might be trapped as prisoners inside, and that we needed their help to get them out safely. We were advised that they had been after this group for a very long time. Within a few minutes, they had rescued Dr. Swanson and Dr. Walker. They are upstairs in their rooms safe and sound," Sebastian said.

"I just can't believe this!" Mark said. He looked dazed.

"Well, I asked him to call you and ask you about today's operation, since this is your investigation," Sebastian added.

Mark seemed pleased with his last statement and smiled. "I'm glad your men are safe," he said. "And I told Ryan, the head of intelligence, to meet us at the museum at one-thirty."

"Perfect!" Sebastian said.

"I hope we can get the documents back," Nathan added, suppressing a grin.

Sebastian and Nathan returned to their rooms, relieved that this awkward hurdle had been overcome. As soon as he was in his room, Sebastian sat on the bed and called Troy, who picked up on the second ring.

"Hello, old man, how is everything going?"

"Hello, Sebastian. Fine here, is everything okay with you?"

"Yes, everything is working out just fine," Sebastian said. "I'll tell you all about it when we see each other. But I haven't been able to reach Arielle for several days. Is she all right?"

"Yes, she's fine, I just saw her about an hour ago at the pub. She said something about losing her phone."

"Yes, I found out this morning that Paul has it. She dropped it in his car when you all went out," Sebastian said.

"Oh! Good to know. I'm sure Paul will let her know. Don't worry; I'm keeping an eye on her. She is missing you terribly. I just wish she would stop talking about you every time we are all together."

Sebastian smiled with pleasure to hear these words, and he could feel his spirits lifting. "You don't know how good that makes me feel," he said. "I was getting pretty anxious, not being able to talk to her."

"She's fine! I'll let her know you called. Be safe and let me know how it goes."

"Thanks, Troy. I'll see you soon." Sebastian put the phone down. He was relieved and happy to know that Arielle was thinking of him and that she was having fun with her friends, too.

Next, he called Nathan, and they both went downstairs to wait for Mark and Tony to arrive. Around one o'clock they all flagged a taxi and left the hotel, headed for the museum. There they met Ryan Mansfield and two agents who were with him at the entrance. Mark and Ryan spoke in low voices for a few minutes as Sebastian and Nathan walked around, blending in with the visitors that were buzzing around the various rooms. Though they pretended to be following Mark and Tony's lead, they were using all of their immortal powers, keen to any information they might glean in the minds of the visitors that might prove useful to them.

As the hour drew closer, Tony became visibly more anxious and began rubbing his hands together incessantly. Meanwhile, Sebastian and Nathan's eyes were taking in and analyzing every person's moves while they pretended to be carefully studying the artifacts. At 1:53 p.m. the tension in the room was almost unbearable. Just then Sebastian noticed two very well-dressed men with light brown hair and very light complexions standing in a corner, looking at a museum map. But he noticed that their eyes kept checking the entrance every few seconds.

One man had a briefcase in his hand and a newspaper under his arm.

The second man was holding a map. He had a camera strap draped around his neck like a tourist.

Sebastian exchanged looks with Nathan and their lips moved in such a way that no one could hear what they were saying. Then Nathan walked to the left of the men and Sebastian stood on the right. Before long they saw the same stocky man they had seen at the restaurant the night before standing at the entrance to the room, holding the briefcase. He stopped, just as he had the night before, took a careful look around, and when his gaze fell on the two men in the corner, he moved towards them. There were handshakes and low conversation between them. No one but Sebastian and Nathan would be able to understand what was being said, but to them, it was perfectly clear. Mark, Tony and Ryan were also watching the men carefully. Mark leaned over and whispered something to Tony. Sebastian and Nathan exchanged a look, and both smiled, having heard Mark's words. "Make sure those two don't get hurt," was what he had muttered, referring to Nathan and Sebastian.

Suddenly the two men swapped briefcases and exchanged a few words in an awkward, coded language. But both Sebastian and Nathan clearly understood that Alexie was not the key man in the operation. The man with the fake briefcase was the key man. He was now giving Alexie instructions about their next move, which was to get the prisoners to the airport in time for the flight the next morning. They shook hands and Alexie walked out the door carrying the fake briefcase, followed by Ryan and the other two British policemen. Their plan was to arrest him outside, inconspicuously, avoiding harm to any innocent people. The two other men remained in the museum, pretending to look at and discuss the art objects while carrying the real documents and files from one room to another. Sebastian and Nathan waited by the exit along with Mark and Tony while keeping a sharp eye on the men.

After a few minutes, Ryan walked back inside and leaned over to Mark. "He has been arrested without incident," he said. "He's on his way now to join the others."

Twenty more minutes passed. Then finally, the two men in possession of the briefcase made their way toward the exit. As soon as they stepped outside, the briefcase was in Sebastian's hands. Nathan was holding both men by the throat, and they were unable to move. Ryan's agents were shocked, but they hurriedly slapped handcuffs on the two men, who were utterly astonished by the outcome.

Nobody in the museum had observed the arrest. It had taken place so quickly and so quietly that no one saw anything at all. Ryan ordered his officers to put the prisoners in the car and take them away, and then he turned to Sebastian.

"Sebastian, that was some move," he said. "In fact, I don't think I ever even saw you or Nathan move. How'd you get those guys?"

"Oh, you know... adrenaline," Sebastian laughed, and added, "you didn't do yourself badly." They all laughed, Mark still shaking his head in amazement. He intuited that there was something different, something special about Nathan and Sebastian, but he couldn't figure out what it was. He was just happy that they were on the same side.

What a great relief. This was exactly the outcome Sebastian had fervently hoped for. The documents were back in his possession, and the scientists were safe.

"Thanks, guys, for all the help," said Ryan.

"Thank *you* for helping us get our scientists back to the hotel safely," said Sebastian with a smile.

 *Chapter 23*

WITH NATHAN'S ASSISTANCE, Sebastian had managed to accomplish a major part of the task before him. However, there were still a few important items that needed to be taken care of. He needed to visit each of the company buildings worldwide and hold interviews with each employee individually. His purpose was to locate and eliminate all the enemy moles within the company. He didn't want anything like this ever to happen again. He was determined to rid the company of impostors.

However, his thoughts were now a bit freer to turn to Arielle. How he wished he could return to England right now. He was extremely upset that this next step would keep him from getting home earlier, but he knew it was essential to the wellbeing of his company and the safety of his employees.

They left Nigeria the next morning and arrived in Auckland a day later. There they met with Jonathan Locklear, the head of operations.

"Jonathan," Sebastian said, "Nathan and I need to walk through the building with you tomorrow and meet all the folks that work here. It is of the utmost importance that we talk with each one of them individually. We'll be back to meet with you first thing in the morning." They shook hands and Sebastian, and Nathan went to get a hotel room.

Once settled, Sebastian took a shower and got ready for bed. Then he pressed Arielle's number on his phone, and this time, she answered on the second ring.

"Sebastian!" she cried, her voice full of excitement.

"I've been trying to call you, Arielle, but you never answer your phone. Paul answered it yesterday for you. I guess you haven't missed me too much," he said, his voice a bit forced.

"Oh, I know, Sebastian! I'm sorry, I dropped my phone in his car the other night when we all went out."

"I don't like you spending time with other guys," Sebastian said tightly.

"Jealous, are you?" she chuckled.

"Yes, I'm jealous. You're mine, and I don't want to share you with anyone else. Is that so wrong?"

"No, it's not wrong, but you aren't here most of the time, and I need to spend time with my friends. But I love you, Sebastian, and nobody else. Why are you so worried?"

"Arielle, I'm planning to spend eternity with you, so anything that has to do with you is a major concern for me."

"When are you coming home?" she said impatiently, wanting to change the subject.

"I know what you're trying to do."

"Oh, please, don't be mad at me. I can't wait to see you. When are you coming back?" she asked again, pleadingly.

"Oh, it'll still be a while," he said, dreading her reaction when he had to tell her that he was not going to be back for another month. How could he break such terrible news to her? "The situation has turned out to be quite serious for our company," he said. "We could be losing millions of dollars even as we speak. I'm meeting with some of our executives tomorrow, and then we have to do some quick work throughout all our international locations. It's going to take more time than I thought it would, baby," he said, almost wincing as he anticipated her next question.

"How long will it be?" she asked.

"Well…probably about a month," he said.

There was dead silence for a long time.

"But that will be December!" she finally said. "That's crazy! I'll die without you for that long. Sebastian, I just can't wait that long," she said. "Can't you come back here first?"

"That's not how it works," he said in a very low voice. Again silence fell for another long moment.

"Arielle, are you there?" he asked, finally.

"Yes, I am here, but I'm not happy."

"Arielle, I'm doing the very best I can with this situation. Please try to understand," he said.

"I'm trying," she said. "But I don't think you know how hard it is for me to be away from you."

"I feel the same way, baby," he said, a huskiness in his voice. "How is school going?" he asked, trying to change the conversation.

"Oh, it's fine, nothing exciting. A few tests and we'll be getting ready for exams pretty soon."

"How are your parents?"

"They're fine, and they keep asking about you. They fell in love with you, too. But you know that," she snorted.

Sebastian smiled at her remark and felt relieved that she seemed to be finding her way out of a snit. All he wanted to do was finish his work and get back to her. He loved her so much!

"Are you being safe?" she asked fretfully.

"Yes, all is well," he said. "I should be able to wrap everything up and come home by the first week in December. I'm really sorry about this, Arielle. I didn't know things were going to turn out this way. I ache for you, and when I think about you being sad, it makes me feel even worse."

"I love you, Sebastian, I've missed you so much, and December seems so far away."

"I know, but this is what I have to do. Miss me!" he whispered. Then he ended the call.

Early the next morning Sebastian and Nathan went to the laboratory to meet with Jonathan. The next few days were very busy. They met with each and every one of the employees and used their immortal powers to determine who had been involved in the conspiracy. In all, five people who worked at different stations in the same building had been conspiring against the company. Their names were put on a list to be arrested by the end of the day for conspiracy. For now, this location was clean, and anyone who was hired from then on would be checked thoroughly by the London office. Jonathan was a very good and trustworthy employee, and Sebastian knew that his orders would be followed to the last detail. They got back to the hotel late and went right to sleep. The next day they flew to Sydney to do the same thing.

In Sydney, they only found two spies, but Sebastian could see in their minds that there were other connections in other countries, and Nathan could see that they were planning more extortions and break-ins in the future. Clearly their work was not over.

"We have more than one spy in our labs, and we need to find out who they are and get rid of them," Sebastian said as they sat discussing next steps in their hotel after a long day's work. "We'll have to do the same thing in all the other locations in every single country," he said, sighing. "And I think it needs to be done now before they have time to reorganize. I think we'd better get to Germany and start interviewing everyone there. I'll call Jon and Pier to meet us there and help with the interviews."

"When?" Nathan asked, rubbing his forehead wearily.

"I think we should start right now and finish all the locations as quickly as we can," Sebastian said. "It will probably take until the first week in December. Is that okay with you?" He looked at his friend, thinking how lucky he was to have such an uncomplaining companion.

"Sure, no problem at all," Nathan said.

Before going to bed, Sebastian decided to check in on Arielle. She picked up on the first ring and sounded excited.

"Have you changed your mind? Are you coming home?" she cried when she saw that it was Sebastian calling.

"No, baby, please, don't make me feel bad. You know I'm going to Berlin first. I'll be calling you all the time. I'm getting pretty anxious being away from you this long."

"Text me," Arielle said. "It will be easier for me to leave my phone on vibrate. Then I can see your messages and reply even if I'm in class. I'll make sure my phone is in my pocket at all times," she said. "I miss you so!"

"Okay," he agreed. "But I need to hear your voice, too. So I'll try to call when I know you're not in class. I love you, baby!"

"I love you too, Sebastian. Please be safe, and come home soon."

"I'll see you as soon as I can," he promised.

"Wait... wait... Why are you ready to hang up?" she said. "I want to talk to you."

"Is there something wrong?" he asked.

"No! There's nothing wrong, but I've missed your voice. I just want to talk to you. Are you alone? Is someone there with you?"

"Now you are being ridiculous. There is no one here but me," he said.

"Tell me, then, that you love only me."

"Arielle, you're my life, and I love no one but you," he said patiently. He smiled, satisfied with her questions. Sebastian knew that Auckland was eleven hours later than Brighton and that it was four o'clock in the morning for Arielle.

"I know it's very early in the morning there," he added. "You should go back to sleep."

"Okay, I'll let you go," she answered. "I'm going out tomorrow evening to see a new film, with Gabrielle, Ian, Eva, Troy, and Paul. I'll shut my phone off while we're in there. Just in case you decide to call."

"Arielle, I feel like you are spending way too much time with Paul," Sebastian said. Even though he knew Arielle's love was true, the situation still made him uncomfortable.

"He's just a friend, Sebastian. Really."

"Well, we'll talk about that later."

"Sebastian! Don't hang up," she said quickly again.

"What is it baby?"

"I have something very important to talk to you about when you get home," she murmured thoughtfully.

"Oh, can't you tell me now?"

"No, you have to be here."

"Oh...now I am really intrigued. You sound eager," he murmured.

"I am, I think it's one of the most important decisions I've ever made. It makes me nervous," she said without taking a breath.

"Arielle, it sounds serious. Are you sure we can't talk about it over the phone?"

"No...no, you have to be here with me," she purred and felt her nerves scorching.

"Ohh!" he said, intrigued. "All right baby, I am anxious to hear it. I love you desperately, please miss me!" And the phone went dead.

He walked out of his room, totally preoccupied with Arielle's last statement. It sounded pretty cryptic to him. He went down to the hotel lobby where he found Nathan. As usual, their exceptionally handsome looks attracted a good deal of attention, so they were not surprised to see heads turning wherever they went. They found a corner table in the garden and sat there to enjoy the quiet. Before long they were deep into their conversation when they heard female voices calling out to them.

"Sebastian! Nathan! What are you doing here?"

They looked up, startled, and turned toward the voices in shock. They knew both of the women very well, but they pretended not to remember them.

"Sebastian, it's me Julia, Julia Venhousen. We dated for a very long time, you can't tell me that you forgot me."

As Sebastian was thinking about how to reply, the other girl spoke.

"Nathan, it's me Paola, Paola Gordioni. Remember?" Nathan looked at her in confusion, as if he didn't recall her.

"Julia, what are you doing here?" Sebastian finally managed to say.

"I live here, or I should say we both live here," she said waving her arm between her and Paula. "We've lived here for the past seventy years. I still look great don't I?"

"Yes, you still look beautiful," Sebastian allowed.

"Sebastian, I've missed you. What happened to you? You disappeared without a word."

"Well, we never had anything serious going," Sebastian said. "I didn't think there was a need for goodbyes."

"I sure would like to start something serious right now," she said, fluttering her eyelashes and smiling a coy smile. "You look just as delicious as you always did." She looked at him as if he were a tasty meal she would love to consume. She turned to look at Paola, a crude grin on her face.

"I must say he is," Paola agreed, "but so is Nathan. I remember how great he was in bed!" she said, snorting. They both laughed, making Sebastian and Nathan feel pretty uncomfortable.

"Come on, Sebastian, let's go out and have some fun tonight," Julia said. "I remember very well what a great dancer you were, among other things," she added, laughing suggestively.

"I'm sorry, Julia. We have an early flight in the morning. Besides, I'm not available any longer."

"Ohhhh! There is a lucky girl out there? I envy her," she said with an exaggerated pout. "We were good together," she added.

"That was centuries ago, Julia," Sebastian said, standing up. "It was nice seeing you again, but we do have to go. It was nice seeing you too, Paola. *Ciao!*"

"What about you, Nathan? Are you involved with someone else right now?" Paola asked.

"Yes, I am, and we do have to go. It was nice to see you again, though. And nice meeting you, Julia."

They turned and waved as they walked away.

"We will find you again someday," Julia called after them. "And we will talk again."

"That was unfortunate," Sebastian said as they got into the elevator. "Julia was one of my more steady girls. It wasn't serious, but it was a long relationship. I would hate for her to show up around Arielle."

"I feel the same way about Paola," Nathan said. "I've been dating someone for a long time, and I'm ready to propose. She's human, and I'm completely in love with her," he said, heaving a deep sigh.

"I totally understand, Nathan. Arielle is human as well, and I'm getting ready to propose also. Isn't life peculiar? We roam the earth for centuries before we finally find true love. And then it is with humans, not our kind." They laughed at the irony, but both knew how happy they were with their choices.

"Well, goodnight, Nathan," Sebastian said as they got out of the elevator.

"Goodnight, mate," Nathan replied, slipping into the local style. "See you in the morning."

Inside his room, Sebastian watched the news, had a tall drink of salve and went to bed. But an hour later, he heard a knock and went to the door reluctantly. Julia was standing there, alone, with a sexy smile on her face. "Mmm-mm!" she said, staring at his gorgeous bare chest.

"What do you want, Julia?" Sebastian said, more patiently than he felt.

"But you are what I want, darling…of course! What else would I want? I want you to make love to me one more time. I fall apart just thinking about how wonderful you were in bed. I know you liked me a lot, you told me so many times."

"Things have changed, Julia. I'm not the same man you knew before. I'm in love with one girl, and I'm going to be faithful to her for eternity."

"Sebastian, please!" she pleaded. "She will never know, and I'll never tell her."

"No, Julia, I need you to leave. I'm serious about this. There's not going to be anything else between us – tonight or any other night."

"We'll see about that," she said angrily. "You know I don't give up that easily." She tossed her head, turned angrily, and strode back down the hallway, hips swaying.

Sebastian shut the door. *She hasn't been the first one to say that*, he thought. She might as well get in line, right behind Annabel. Then he chuckled ruefully as he got into bed. He knew he didn't have much time for Julia and her issues. He had put all that behind him centuries ago. As he closed his eyes, the thought of Arielle's beautiful eyes made him feel warm and excited. He smiled and drifted off to sleep.

The next morning the plane to Berlin took off right on time. The flight attendants made sure that Sebastian and Nathan had everything they asked for, trying very hard to get their attention, but they weren't interested.

They knew that their looks made people treat them a little differently than everyone else. They read their books, watched a couple of films, talked about their girls, and slept. The plane landed twenty minutes ahead of schedule. There was a lot to be done, and they headed to their hotel.

In his room, Sebastian was still wondering about Arielle's cryptic statement over the phone. Her voice had sounded eager, and her excitement was palpable.

She had made the most important decision in her life, she had said. He began pacing, trying to discern the meaning of the unspoken words that were embedded in that statement.

Suddenly, abruptly, his thoughts came to a screeching halt, sending a scorch of wakefulness deep into his bones. He stood in the middle of the room unmoving, in deep thought. His excitement was tangible. Could what he was thinking – hoping – be her decision? But, why would she ever change her mind about such an important commitment right now?

"Holy cow…" he thought. A burning desire washed over him as the thought delved deep into his soul. He needed to get home soon. The thought made him grin widely, his emotions leaping into an astounding level, and his desire to see Arielle again intensified, turning into pure passion.

The End

*Enjoy a sneak peek of **Arielle Immortal Seduction***

 *Chapter 1*

SEBASTIAN HAD BEEN in New Zealand for almost two weeks and Arielle hadn't spoken to him once. She hadn't been able to call him because his number was on her mobile phone, and she couldn't find the phone anywhere. She was sure that it would turn up sooner or later. She spent her days in class, shopping with Gabby and Eva, and studying for exams. She managed to keep her mind on the books, but she ached for Sebastian's touch every moment of every day.

She went out with Paul a few times, sometimes to nightclubs for drinks. He was an attentive friend, but she could feel that something was different between them now. She didn't want to ask him about it, though, and encourage any heart-to-heart conversations about their friendship. At times, the temptation to clear the air was dangerously strong, but her instinct to leave it alone was stronger.

Paul called her house to tell her that he had found her phone under the back seat of his car and that Sebastian had been trying to reach her. There was an undercurrent of jealousy in the tone of his voice.

Arielle frowned and stifled an oath. *How stupid of me,* she thought to herself as a flare of guilt spread across her mind. She had promised Sebastian she would have her phone with her at all times. Anxiety spread through her, partly because of Paul's jealous tone but mostly because she knew that Sebastian would be furious with her about Paul answering her phone.

"Please bring the phone to school tomorrow," she said.

"I will," Paul, replied, his voice short.

What's wrong with him? Arielle thought, but she chose not to ask. "Thank you, Paul, I'll see you tomorrow in class," she said quickly and ended the call.

When she got the phone back, the battery was dead, and it wasn't until later that afternoon that she retrieved nine missed calls, four voice messages, and several text messages, all with the same question, "Where are you? I've been trying to contact you." His voice on the first message was warm and eager, but by the third and fourth voice message, his voice was clipped, filled with frustration.

Arielle scowled at the tone of his voice, but she understood why he was disappointed with her. She wasn't very happy with herself either. She regretted missing a bunch of his calls, but there was nothing she could do about that now. When they finally spoke, she tried to explain to him what had happened; she emphasized how much she had missed him, but Sebastian was not happy about the amount of time she was spending with Paul. She felt vaguely dissatisfied with the way their conversation had ended.

The third Friday Sebastian was gone, Arielle and her friends decided to go out. They were at their regular pub, laughing and talking, having a lot of fun. The conversation was stimulating and before long it was after midnight. Arielle was tired, her eyes were watering, and her throat ached. She began to feel like she might be coming down with a cold.

She was busy talking to Frances, a new girl, and was engaged in their conversation when she heard someone making a lot of ruckus sitting in the seat next to her. She looked over and noticed a tall, blond, and extremely good-looking guy gazing at her and Frances. There was an arrogance about him; he had that kind of expression that proclaims, "There is no female on earth that would reject me."

Arielle turned away from him and continued her conversation with Frances, but he leaned closer and rudely interrupted,

"Hi. I'm Matt, and you are?"

"My name is Frances," her friend said excitedly.

Arielle glanced at her, surprised that anyone would fall for that kind of guy.

"Are you here with anyone in particular?" he continued, looking directly at Arielle.

"No," Frances replied. She was either clueless or determined to take advantage of what she thought was an opportunity.

Arielle was a little uneasy and slightly startled. She couldn't tell what this man was thinking; he didn't belong to that special group of people in her head. He was looking at her like he was getting ready to start some superficial game playing. She was sure that he was directing his questions at her, but she got up and let Frances pick up the game since she was clearly interested.

She walked over to the bar to tell Eva and Ian that she was leaving.

"Is something wrong?" Eva asked.

"No, I'm just tired. It's almost one, and I'd like to get to bed. I think I may be getting a cold." They both hugged her, and she started to walk toward the bar exit.

"Where are you going?" It was that rude man again, his voice right next to her ear. Arielle turned and looked at him startled, but she didn't stop walking and didn't answer.

"I think you're very beautiful, and I'd love to get to know you better," he said as she increased her pace.

"I'm not interested," she said.

"Aren't you interested to know anything about me?"

"No, not at all."

"You don't look to me like you're not interested," he said with an insidious grin on his face.

His words took her by surprise. She was close to the exit now. She stopped and turned to face him, an annoyed look on her face. She hesitated for only a short second, "What would ever give you that impression?" she snapped.

He closed the distance quickly and pulled her close forcefully. He leaned forward and kissed her on the lips.

Shocked, she drew back and slapped him. He put his hand on his cheek and just smiled.

"I can't understand why you're so mad," he said. "I just want to be friends and have some fun together."

"I have plenty of friends," Arielle said. "I don't need your friendship, and I'm not interested in anything you have to say, so please go away."

She started to walk towards the door again, but he grabbed her wrist and pulled her back. Arielle's jaw nearly dropped. She whirled around to face him and tried to snatch her hand back, nearly losing her balance.

"Let me go, you idiot," she hissed.

He kept smiling, totally unaffected by her outburst. "Don't go," he said. His voice was hard. His eyes conveyed that he had drank too much. "I think you like me, but you don't want to say it," he said. His voice had taken on a luring overtone.

"I think you see things that aren't there. You need to let go of me because if you don't, I'll scream." Arielle's heart raced, but her voice was surprisingly composed.

"I find you very exciting, and if you have a drink with me, I promise I'll behave."

"I'm involved with someone, and I don't want to give you the wrong impression. Please let go of my hand. I hate to make a scene, but I will if I have to."

He finally let go of her arm but said, "I don't see any ring on your finger, so I know you are neither engaged nor married. I'm not giving up."

"You can do whatever you want to do, but I'm telling you one more time I'm not interested. I have a serious boyfriend. You're wasting your time."

"Oh, but you don't know me," he said, chuckling in a distasteful way. "I never waste my time on anything I don't think I can have."

Arielle suspected that his attitude was related to his drinking, but she wasn't interested in analyzing him. She wanted to get home and go to bed.

"Hey, Arielle, are you leaving?"

She turned and saw Paul walking in. Her face lit with pleasure and she grinned wide. A delightful feeling of relief overwhelmed her. He came close to her, wrapped his arms around her, and gave her a kiss on the cheek. He was warm and cheery. There was no hint of the jealous disposition she had detected in him during their last awkward conversation about Sebastian.

"Did you just get here?" she asked.

"Yes, I had to go back home to get my wallet. Nothing is free," he laughed, and Arielle joined in. She was so relieved to see him and grateful that he had gotten her out of a difficult situation.

"Are you okay? You look a bit pale."

"Oh, I think I'm getting a cold, and I'm tired," she said, and looked down at her shoes, trying to hide her anxiety. Something in her voice made him look at her quizzically. Reaching out, he hugged her again, and she returned his hug affectionately. Paul was one of her best friends. She liked spending time with him and hoped that Sebastian would get over his jealousy. She got distracted when out of the corner of her eye she saw Matt watching them intently. His gaze was creepier than his appearance. At least he wasn't coming closer. Arielle relived the distress she felt when he had grabbed her wrist. She quivered and pressed her eyes shut for a long moment. She shoved the weird feeling out of her mind, and when she opened her eyes, she found Paul watching her carefully.

"What is it?" he asked. Looking past her, his gaze fell on Matt. "Is there a problem?" he asked again, without taking his eyes off Matt.

"No, I just don't feel very well," she replied quietly.

Paul sensed her uneasiness and arched an eyebrow. "It doesn't seem like nothing to me," he said and rolled his eyes. "Are you all right?"

She hesitated to speak but then chose to remain silent. She glanced quickly toward Matt. He was still there staring at them.

"Do you want me to take you home?" Paul interrupted her thoughts. "It's no trouble at all."

"Oh, please, that'd be great," Arielle said, trying not to be overly enthusiastic, but she didn't want another encounter with Matt. She felt much safer going home with an escort.

Paul put his arm around Arielle, and they walked out. As they drove home, a tense silence filled the car.

"What happened back there?" Paul finally broke the quiet.

"Oh, there was a guy trying to pick me up. He was drunk, and he made me nervous," she muttered.

"You should've told me," he said protectively. "I would have taken care of the creep right then and there."

"I didn't want to create any problems for you," she said.

"That wouldn't have created a problem for me, sweetheart," Paul snorted. "But it would have created a huge a problem for the creep," he added, laughing quietly.

Arielle chuckled at the smug tone in Paul's voice and pressed his hand gratefully with her own. A long silence followed as they both fell deep into thought. Arielle got the feeling that something else was bothering Paul. She didn't want to ask but felt a caring urge rise inside of her from wanting to be there for him.

When Paul pulled up to the flat, Arielle cleared her throat and decided to ask the unspoken question that had been lingering between them. "Paul, I've noticed that there is something strange about you lately. What's going on? Can you tell me?" Arielle asked, gently.

"Do you mean what's wrong with me besides that fact that I'm in love with you and you are in love with someone else?" A dash of sadness was in Paul's voice.

Arielle turned to face him, stunned. She closed her eyes for a long moment and took a deep breath. "For the love of God, Paul, I thought we had cleared the air about that a while back."

He shrugged, and a smile brushed his lips but swiftly disappeared. "Please forgive me, I didn't mean to say that," he said apologetically.

She watched him carefully and remained quiet, giving him time to say what was on his mind.

He drew in a deep breath and seemed lost in thought. She smiled dimly and snapped him out of his trance. "Paul, what else is wrong? Please talk to me."

He shifted slightly and gave a nervous laugh. "I think there is something going on between my parents. They're hardly talking to each other, they are arguing a lot. And they're not sharing the same bedroom any longer."

She looked stunned. "Have you tried to talk to them about it?"

Paul's face paled. "No, they seem to quiet down whenever I go home, and they never say a word. But I know things are not right. I have a feeling that my father may be cheating on my mum."

"I'm so sorry, Paul," Arielle said. "They are in a very challenging business and around a lot of beautiful people. I'm sure they have to deal with enormous temptations."

"I understand all that. But he doesn't have to be submissive to every shallow bimbo he encounters just because she's beautiful."

Arielle was quiet. She knew that she didn't have any good solution for Paul's problem. Nothing anyone could say would make him feel better about a situation like this.

"I'm so sorry, Paul," she said again. "I hate to see you hurting." She reached over and gave him a kiss on the cheek. He smiled and gave her a grateful look.

"Thanks, Arielle," he said. "I feel better just being next to you."

"Well then stay *next* to me," she said. "Because I like to see you happy. I've been worried about you the last couple of weeks. I wish you had said something to me about this. I thought maybe you were mad at me."

"I love you, Arielle," Paul said, shaking his head. "Even though I know how you feel about Sebastian, and I do respect your decision, I can't stop loving you. Anyway, I hope you can forgive me."

"I feel privileged to know that you love me," Arielle said. "I'm just sorry that I can't return your love in the same way. But I'll love you as my friend forever. I'll be here for you anytime you need me. You can count on me for that."

He leaned over and kissed her softly on the lips, and she didn't pull back. He needed her; she could see the tears in his eyes. His kiss felt like a call for love and understanding, not a sexual thing, and she was glad to kiss him back, as a friend.

"Are you all right?" she asked gently after he pulled away.

"Yes, I'll be okay, don't worry about me," he said as he stepped out of the car. He walked around and helped her out. After a warm hug, Paul made sure she got in the door safely, and she waved as he drove away. She went to bed and fell asleep immediately.

The next day, Sebastian called to tell Arielle that he was going to be away for a much longer time. "I just can't wait that long..." she said, sighing deeply. She could hear him chuckle with pleasure at her longing for him.

"Do you miss me?" he said.

"Just a little," she lied.

"Well, then, I may have to stay away a little longer, to make sure you miss me a lot," he teased.

"I miss you more than life itself," she replied. "Will that make you come back tomorrow?"

"I miss you too, baby, but I need to finish up here. Don't worry, I'll be home as soon as I possibly can." He was now laughing quietly.

"I'm glad you are amused while I'm dying here."

"Arielle, your face is in my mind constantly. I'm having difficulty getting my thoughts together. All I seem to be able to do is to think about you. You are in for big trouble when I get home," he said, laughing again.

"I can't wait to see you!"

"Arielle, just one more thing. Please don't worry if there are lapses of time between my calls. I'm facing some serious issues. However, I'll try to text you every chance I get."

Arielle groaned. "What do you mean by 'lapses of time,'" she asked glumly, unease sweeping through her.

"It may be a couple of days between calls, and maybe sometimes even longer. I don't want you to worry, it just means that I can't break away to talk. But like I said before, I'll text you." A long, awkward silence followed.

"Arielle, are you there?" he prompted.

"Yes, I'm here," Arielle mumbled.

"What's wrong?" he asked anxiously.

What kind of a ridiculous question was that? She thought. "I hate being away from you," she whimpered.

"I love you more than life," he reassured her, but she remained deliberately silent. "Arielle, did you hear me? I love you," he whispered, his voice filled with emotion.

"I love you, too." She spoke lightly, her voice overwhelmed with disappointment.

"Arielle!"

"What?"

"What's wrong, baby?"

"Oh, for God's sake, Sebastian, I miss you. I want you to come home, I want you here with me!"

Sebastian smiled, his heart filled with joy knowing that she wanted him home. "I love you," he murmured. "Try to understand, I'm doing this for both of us. This is all about the security of our company. Yours and mine."

Arielle knew that he was right. "Okay," she replied. "Anyway, it's not like I have a choice."

"I'm sorry," he said and chuckled again. Arielle was a constant heavenly thought in his head, and one he couldn't simply set aside, even if the issues he was facing were quite complicated.

"Don't feel sorry for me, I'll survive," she said petulantly.

She heard his soft chuckle. "I'll call you soon, I promise. Miss me!" And he was gone.

Note to Readers

Thank you to my fans. It is the most rewarding and surreal experience to receive your wonderful feedback after reading my book. To the future readers, thank you for loving books and making my book your choice. This is the first book in my "Immortal Rapture Series" I hope you will enjoy it.

Contact Information
My website: lilianroberts.com
My Twitter: @lilian3roberts
My Blog: lilianroberts.blogspot.com

www.ingramcontent.com/pod-product-compliance
Lightning Source LLC
Chambersburg PA
CBHW021519240626
47154CB00002B/704